continued . . .

"A sizzling story . . . fun and fresh reading."
—Romance Junkies

"Fresh, witty, sexy, and sure to please fans."
—The Romance Readers Connection

"The dialogue is smart and sassy."
—Romance Reviews Today

Praise for Maureen Child's Other Novels

"Sassy repartee . . . humor and warmth . . . a frothy delight." —*Publishers Weekly*

"Maureen Child infuses her writing with the perfect blend of laughter, tears, and romance . . . well-crafted characters. . . . Her novels [are] a treat to be savored."
—Jill Marie Landis, *New York Times* bestselling author of *Homecoming*

"Absolutely wonderful . . . a delightful blend of humor and emotion. . . . This sexy love story will definitely keep readers turning the pages."
—Kristin Hannah, *New York Times* bestselling author of *Firefly Lane*

"Maureen Child always writes a guaranteed winner . . . sexy and impossible to put down."
—Susan Mallery, *New York Times* bestselling author of *Sweet Trouble*

Beguiled

A QUEEN OF THE OTHERWORLD NOVEL

MAUREEN
CHILD

A SIGNET ECLIPSE BOOK

SIGNET ECLIPSE
Published by New American Library, a division of
Penguin Group (USA) Inc., 375 Hudson Street,
New York, New York 10014, USA
Penguin Group (Canada), 90 Eglinton Avenue East, Suite 700, Toronto,
Ontario M4P 2Y3, Canada (a division of Pearson Penguin Canada Inc.)
Penguin Books Ltd., 80 Strand, London WC2R 0RL, England
Penguin Ireland, 25 St. Stephen's Green, Dublin 2,
Ireland (a division of Penguin Books Ltd.)
Penguin Group (Australia), 250 Camberwell Road, Camberwell, Victoria 3124,
Australia (a division of Pearson Australia Group Pty. Ltd.)
Penguin Books India Pvt. Ltd., 11 Community Centre, Panchsheel Park,
New Delhi - 110 017, India
Penguin Group (NZ), 67 Apollo Drive, Rosedale, North Shore 0632,
New Zealand (a division of Pearson New Zealand Ltd.)
Penguin Books (South Africa) (Pty.) Ltd., 24 Sturdee Avenue,
Rosebank, Johannesburg 2196, South Africa

Penguin Books Ltd., Registered Offices:
80 Strand, London WC2R 0RL, England

First published by Signet Eclipse, an imprint of New American Library,
a division of Penguin Group (USA) Inc.

First Printing, August 2009
10 9 8 7 6 5 4 3 2 1

For my mother-in-law, Mary Child

She's never been a big fan of paranormals, but she's always been a big fan of my writing! Thanks, Mom, for too many things to list here. I love you.

Chapter One

Being a queen wasn't the thrill ride Maggie had expected.

Where were the jewels? The crown, for God's sake? Where were the adoring crowds, simpering minions and life o' luxury?

Where was the fun? Shouldn't she at least have had a mall named after her?

So far, being the newly crowned Queen of the Fae had been a royal pain in the ass.

Sure, it had been only a couple of weeks since Maggie had tossed Mab, the former queen, out a window. But come on. No way was Maggie going to spend every freaking day of—oh, let's see—*eternity* listening to a bunch of whiny Faeries.

Which was why she was back in her own world doing something important.

"I need more snow, Maggie. It has to look really Christmassy, you know? And don't forget the wrapped presents under the tree. Oh, and the rocking horse—remember the rocking horse."

"I know, Barb," Maggie said, forcing a smile at the older woman, who owned Barb's House of Beauty. Every year, she paid Maggie to paint Christmas scenes on the front window of her beauty shop. And every year, Barb wanted to outdo Sam's Hardware. Which was no small feat.

Sam's windows had been painted for two weeks already, so Barb had had plenty of time to study what Maggie had given him and think up ideas for one-upmanship. Always a good time in Castle Bay, California.

A tourist stop on Pacific Coast Highway, Maggie's hometown was small, familiar and just the antidote she needed for the *bizarreness* that had become her life. The town was slow, except in the summer when tourists clogged the streets and made cash registers ring. During the winter, it was no more than a rest stop on the road, as tourists hit the bigger towns farther north, such as Monterey and Carmel. And that was fine with Maggie.

She liked Castle Bay just the way it was. Here, she was just Maggie Donovan, artist and glass painter. Here, Maggie was Nora's sister and Eileen's aunt. She was a tiny part of the community, not some mythic queen expected to ride herd on the weird inhabitants of Otherworld.

Barb went back inside. Maggie picked up a white paint–laden brush, leaned out from her ladder, touched the glass and shrieked like an idiot when Culhane, Fae Warrior, would-be lover and current pain in her ass, popped into existence beside her.

"Damn it," Maggie shouted, glancing through the window into the shop to make sure Barb hadn't noticed the tall, dark, gorgeous hunk-of-hormone-happiness appearing out of nowhere. She hadn't.

Leaning against her ladder, Maggie looked down at him and instantly knew she shouldn't have. Seriously, the man was just eye candy. Six feet five inches of completely amazing male. He had sharp features, a strong jaw and green eyes so pale they looked like windows into another world. His shoulder-length black hair gave him the look of a pirate, and the white shirt, dark green pants and knee-high brown leather boots he wore completed the picture nicely.

Also he had a great mouth, a nasty disposition and the ability to make Maggie nuts in a heartbeat.

"I cannot believe you have come back here to paint pictures on glass." He set both fists on his hips, widened his stance and gave her a look that said he was ready to do battle. "You are expected at the castle. Maggie, you must return to Otherworld," he said, as if issuing a damn command.

That's what being the head Fae Warrior for two hundred years will do to you. Make you an immortal arrogant bastard.

Culhane had been ordering her around since he'd pushed his way into her life nearly a month ago. Claiming that Maggie's destiny was to defeat Mab and take over Otherworld in her place, he'd pretty much orchestrated everything to make sure his "prophecy" came true.

Plus, the whole time, he'd been making Maggie crazed with lip-sizzling kisses, and the promise of a Fae-driven orgasm had her strung so tight, the wrong word might snap her in two. He was probably doing it on purpose, too, she thought. Keeping her all stirred up and achy just so she'd go along with whatever the hell he wanted her to do. So far, it had been working. If this was her eternity, there was just no way she was going to make it.

She'd be damned if she was going to be done in by her own horniness. So she was going to cling with both hands to however much "ordinary" she could get. An ocean breeze slid past her, ruffling her shoulder-length auburn hair and carrying the scent of the sea, which was just two blocks away. At the skate park across the street, kids were riding the cement slopes on their boards and shoppers were competing for parking spaces.

All blissfully normal. All quiet. All ordinary. Except for the fact that she had a damn Faery practically snarling at her.

"I can't go to Otherworld right now," she told him. "Busy here. See? Actual *work*."

He snorted. "You are a queen, Maggie. You do not ve to work."

"Hah!" She turned to the window and laid a brush full of white paint down into the first of several snowdrifts. "Seriously? Being Queen is a boatload of work. Listening to all of you guys whine about what needs changing and what shouldn't be changed and how I should do it and how I'd better not do it. How'm I supposed to know who to listen to?"

She paused for breath, added more snow to the window and then kept talking. "I've been Queen for like two weeks, okay? I don't know anything about Otherworld—"

"I can teach you."

"And I don't want to know," she added, giving him a quick glare over her shoulder. "I didn't ask to be Queen, you know. You guys came to *me*."

"You were the one who killed the demon and claimed the Fae power."

True. She had accidentally killed what had turned out to be a demon, and then for her trouble Maggie had been imbued with the Faery dust of the five slain Fae the demon had been carrying around. All of that power was still sizzling inside Maggie, causing changes she hadn't even begun to deal with yet. Not to mention, when she had thrown Queen Mab out a window, Maggie had also been given Mab's power. Maggie was now a raging tornado of Faery strength with not the slightest clue what that might mean for her in the future.

"That demon was eating my ex-boyfriend, remember? And then tried to chow down on *me*." Just the memory of that day gave her chills. "And I didn't mean to kill her, anyway, and believe me, if I knew then what I know now . . ."

"What?" He laughed shortly. "You would do something different? You would allow the demon to kill you instead?"

Well, he had her there. Damn it.

"Okay, no. I still would have done what I did, but the I would have given the power to Mab. She was suc bitch, she deserved to have to be Queen." Remembering how she'd tossed Mab out the window, Maggie sort of regretted it now. Of course, if Mab were still around, then she'd be trying to kill Maggie, which would just be a whole *different* sort of problem, so what the hell? Guess it was better to be Queen than dead.

But that didn't mean she didn't have to paint windows, pay bills, buy groceries and you know ... be a person.

Culhane blew out a frustrated breath. This, Maggie was used to. She got it a lot from Culhane and the nasty-ass pixie Bezel, who was still living in the oak tree in her backyard.

When did her life turn into a paranormal soap opera?

"It is your destiny."

"Right. Well, destiny can get in line," Maggie snapped, stepping down off the ladder and walking to the array of paints she had lined up neatly against the building. Culhane was always pulling out the destiny card. "I've got sixteen more windows to do before Christmas, and in case you didn't know, Thanksgiving was last week." Maggie sighed in fond memory of the gluttonous feast she'd enjoyed, Faery guests and all. Well, Bezel hadn't been much fun, but then he was a two-thousand-year-old pixie and lived in a tree, so what could you expect? "I'm barely over that. Plus, Christmas is getting closer all the time and I'm gonna have to do most of that, too, because Nora's got some kind of weird flu, which I think your stupid Fae Warrior Quinn gave her."

One more thing to think about, she told herself as she mixed red and blue tempera together to get a rich violet color. She added just enough water to thin the mixture and idly stirred while she considered how her family had been dragged into Maggie's new adventures. Of course, Nora hadn't been dragged so much as she had *leaped* into this strange new world. But then, Nora had always been drawn to the supernatural. Unlike Maggie, who preferred more "natural" and less "super."

"The Fae do not get sick," Culhane said, breaking her concentration.

"They're just carriers?" Maggie frowned, picked up another brush, swirled it into the violet paint and stood up again, still frowning as purple tempera slid off the brush and down to her hand.

Her sister, Nora, had been sick for days and refused to go to a doctor—which was probably just as well, because she was having so much Faery sex lately that Quinn's powers had started to affect her, and Nora kept floating at odd moments. How would they explain *that* to the doctor?

Add that to the list of worries, she thought. With Nora sick, her daughter, Eileen, had been spending more time with Maggie at the main house, because if Nora had some weird Faery plague, they didn't want Eileen to get it. Which meant that Maggie was getting to listen to play-by-play descriptions of life in middle school and which boy was the cutest and which girl had it in for Eileen.

God, even thinking about what was going on in her life made her tired. "I sooo don't have time to be Queen."

"Time or not, you are the Queen, Maggie, and nothing can change that. You must come with me."

Culhane grabbed her arm. The minute his hand touched her, Maggie felt a blast of heat that shot straight through her system and down to her core. Energized with expectation, her hormones did the little clog dance of happiness and started to make her ache with a need that she knew wasn't going to get answered anytime soon.

Fabulous. Because what she really needed to make this day complete was to be so horny it hurt.

Carefully, she used her paint-smeared hand to pry his

fingers off her arm. "God, Culhane, please do me a huge favor and go bug somebody else. I'm busy here."

He ignored that. Big surprise. Glancing down at the violet paint on his fingers, he frowned, waved his other hand over them and the paint disappeared. Instantly. Maggie frowned and looked at her own hands. She'd be scrubbing for hours to get all the dried paint off her skin. She wasn't completely Fae yet, though the change was definitely happening. Culhane had told her it was going to take some time for her to come into her full range of powers. But maybe she should take some time now to have him teach her a few more things.

The moment she considered it, she dismissed it. Normal. That's what she wanted. A scrub brush and a hot shower were good enough for her. Scowling, she laid her brush against the glass and quickly painted a Christmas present into the snow scene; then, moving farther down the window, she painted another just beneath the Christmas tree she'd already sketched in.

"You must listen," Culhane told her. "The banshee contingent is insisting on speaking with you."

She sighed, set the violet paint down and dumped the brush into a can of rinse water; then she picked up the jar of red paint she'd already mixed and reached for a clean brush. Quickly, she layered in ribbons winding through the branches of the Christmas tree. Glancing at him, she asked, "Banshee have contingents? I thought they just went around screaming when people died."

He smiled, and damn, that quick grin had a way of making her knees wobble. Good thing he didn't do it very often.

"They do," he told her. "The banshee are demanding a wider territory now. They've been in Ireland for millennia. They want to move to the New World."

"The New World?" Maggie laughed and turned back to the glass, where she painted a frothy red ribbon at the base of a Christmas wreath. "Who're you? Columbus? It's not the New World, Culhane."

"It is to us," he muttered, throwing a quick glance up and down the street.

"Fine," she said, grabbing the yellow paint and a fine-line brush to lay in candle flames. "Let 'em leave Ireland. What do I care?"

He reached out as if to grab her again, then noted the wet paint dotting her skin and rethought it. "Maggie, this is what I have been warning you about. You cannot make decisions so blithely. You must learn. The banshee cannot leave Ireland for here. If they do, it will create a war with the Cree-An."

"The *who*?"

Grumbling under his breath, Culhane shook his hair back from his face and said, "The Cree-An have been haunting this ground for centuries. If the banshee invade, the war will spill into the world of human dreams, and the nightmares they cause will follow mortals into the waking."

"Freaking nightmare faeries now?" Maggie groaned, and looked up and down the suddenly deserted street as if looking for an escape. She didn't find one. Though for the first time, she wondered where everyone had gone. She didn't even hear the low rumble of skateboard wheels on cement anymore. Weird.

"You just made my point about all of this, Culhane. I don't know Otherworld. Don't have a clue about the Fae." And that was the bottom line, Maggie told herself. Why she couldn't bring herself to be a queen. How could she be?

"I am willing to teach you," he ground out in a tight, low tone.

"And that will take how long?" Maggie looked down into the red paint and stirred it so that it wouldn't develop a dried-out skin across its surface. "You want me to sit on a throne and make decisions that affect not only *your* world, but mine, too. I can't do it."

"Maggie . . ."

She lifted her gaze to his, and staring into those pale green eyes, she finally managed to say, "What if I screw it up? What if what I do causes a war?" Hearing the words spoken aloud made her shake her head. "No way. I can't risk it. And *you* shouldn't want me to."

Culhane moved closer and Maggie breathed in the clean, almost foresty scent of him. Did he *have* to smell so damn good? Wasn't it enough that just looking at him could make the most stalwart feminist throw all of her ideals out the window and *beg* him to take her? Culhane was a walking, talking orgasm-in-waiting and being this close to him made Maggie's hormones jangle so loud, her brain practically shut down.

"You are the destined Queen, Maggie," he reminded her for the twelve thousandth time. "Your reign was foretold."

She choked out a half laugh. She knew what he said was true. She felt drawn to Otherworld now. But that didn't mean she was comfortable with her role. How could she be? Maggie hadn't been raised to believe in the Fae. She'd always assumed her grandmother's stories were just that. Stories. And even if she had believed, knowing about the Fae would not have prepared her to be their Queen.

Despite the gleam of confidence in Culhane's eyes when he looked at her, Maggie was afraid she just wasn't up to the challenge of what he expected her to be. Yes, she was a strong, independent woman. A woman of the twenty-first century, master of her fate, captain of her soul, owner of her own business. But that didn't make her queen material, now, did it?

"I don't suppose that prophecy of yours said how my 'reign' would turn out," she said.

"No. Only that you would be Queen. The rest of your fate is up to you. You must write your future, as we all must."

"Fabulous."

He smiled, apparently guessing where her muddled thoughts were taking her. "We make our futures what we will, Maggie. Fate twists our paths and some things are immutable." Culhane shrugged his wide shoulders. "Your destiny was to become Queen. It is up to you what you make of it."

"But no pressure."

"You will be a great queen, Maggie. You've the heart for it. The strength for it." He lifted one hand to tuck a strand of dark auburn hair behind her slightly pointy ear. "We make our own destinies. We forge the future, one decision at a time."

"That's what I'm afraid of," she admitted.

"I am here with you, Maggie. We will work together."

Yes, she thought, but he'd spent two hundred years at Queen Mab's side, too. And what had that gotten the former queen? Deposed and thrown out a window into the void between dimensions, that's what.

"Together? For how long?"

One corner of his amazing mouth tipped up and something inside her fisted. "For as long as we will it. The Fae are immortal, Maggie. And you are quickly becoming completely Fae. Soon your mortality will drop away."

"Along with my humanity, huh?" She wrapped her arms around herself and scraped her paint-spattered hands up and down her arms to battle a sudden chill. "What if I don't want to stop being human?"

"In that, you've no choice at all," he told her, lifting his chin and looking down at her with the fierce, proud expression she'd come to know so well. "You will be Fae. You must accept it and your new duties."

Maggie had already known that she had no way out. No way to backtrack and undo any of this. The only path open to her was the one that led straight ahead. Into unknown territory.

"Being Queen requires the art of compromise," he told her briskly. "Start with this. I suggest you give the banshee England. The Cree-An do not like the British. They think them unimaginative and old-world."

Maggie laughed shortly. "Faery prejudice?"

"I know this is a lot to take in," Culhane said, moving in even closer to her, crowding Maggie enough that she could feel heat pouring off his body and reaching for hers.

"You say that," she told him, taking a step back to put a little distance between herself and the delicious scent of Culhane. "But you really don't get it. You can't possibly. You've been alive for thousands of years, Culhane. I'm thirty. You've always been Fae. I'm human."

"Not anymore."

"Stop saying that."

"You will learn, Maggie. You will be the queen destiny has named you."

"What if I don't want to be?" she countered. She held her breath and risked looking directly into his eyes again. Oh *God*, how could she be expected to think when he looked as he did? When his eyes locked with hers? When his scent surrounded her so she couldn't think straight? Shaking her head, she muttered, "What if all I want is to be me, Maggie Donovan, failed artist and glass painter extraordinaire?"

His hands moved to cup her face, and Maggie felt that touch right down to the soles of her feet. Heat simmered and slid throughout her body like flames dancing on the surface of spilled gasoline. Oh, that wasn't a good sign, she thought. Why did it have to be Culhane who could turn her into a puddle of needy goo? Why couldn't she have fallen for a nice plumber? Why did it have to be a Fae Warrior who made her want to toss her panties into the air?

"You are so much more than *just* Maggie Donovan. It is in your blood, your heart, your very soul." He bent his head and his breath brushed her cheek. "You are the one, Maggie. The only one—"

The one. The one for him? Or the one for Otherworld?

Which did he mean? And how would she ever know for sure?

At that moment, one corner of her mind whispered, did it matter? He was here. Right in front of her. Torturing her with his nearness, making her want things she knew she shouldn't want. But maybe he was right, she thought as he drew nearer. Maybe she could do this. Maybe it was all meant to be. Otherworld. Him. Her. *Them.*

Maybe . . . She leaned into him. Her eyes closed, her breath caught, her insides went into a flash burn and Maggie felt herself wanting to believe. Wanting to let herself . . .

"We've got a problem," a woman announced, shattering the spell weaving itself between them.

"Damn it!" Maggie hissed out a curse aimed at fate or whatever else was interrupting her when she'd finally decided to take that long, luscious leap into Culhane's arms; then she looked past her warrior to see her sister, Nora, looking pretty pukey, leaning up against her Fae lover. Worry eclipsed whatever had been building inside her, so Maggie pushed away from Culhane and took a few steps toward her sister.

"Nora? What's wrong? What's going on?" She looked up and down the empty street again and demanded, "And where did the rest of the world go?"

"They did not go anywhere," Culhane grumbled, glaring at the other Fae male even as he fisted his hand around the silver-bladed knife tucked into his belt. "Quinn has enchanted all of us, which he should not have done. Using magic in this world is always dangerous. You call attention where none should be drawn."

"Better than having people watch me float," Nora muttered, and swallowed hard, lifting one hand to her mouth. "Oh God, my moons are *soooo* out of phase."

Maggie rolled her eyes and fought for patience. Nora had always been the one in the family to depend on fortune-tellers, horoscopes, spiritual advisers and the cleansing of her auras. Since discovering that she was part-Fae, her fascination with all things mystical had only gotten worse. But at the moment, Nora just looked awful.

"God, Nora, you look crappy."

Nora gave her a tight grimace.

"What kind of disease did you pick up in Otherworld, anyway? It's been nearly a week and you're still no better. What is going on here?" Maggie looked from Nora to Culhane to Quinn. Impatience simmered and battled with the fear that she was the only one who didn't know what was happening. "If I'm the damn Queen, somebody *talk* to me."

"Get off me, Your Freaking *Majesty*," Nora snapped. "I'm feeling pukey and pregnant right now, so just back off."

"Pregnant?" Maggie shook her head and blinked at her sister. "You're *pregnant*?"

"I am proud," Quinn announced.

"I'm sick," Nora moaned.

"I'm speechless," Culhane added.

"Well, I'm not," Maggie yelled, turning on him. "If Faery sperm is that fast acting, you can just keep your sexy Fae body far, far away from me!"

Chapter Two

A month ago, Maggie's life had been falling into a rut. She even remembered resenting that fact. Now, in retrospect, that rut looked damn inviting. She had her house in a small town on the California coast. She had a sister, a niece and a dog devoted to sleeping its life away. She had a good business, painting signs and holiday decorations on storefront windows and enough time to paint the landscapes and portraits that fed her soul. Mostly, what she'd had in her life was all *normal*.

Now, not so much.

And as an extra, added bonus, it seemed she was going to have a Fae niece or nephew, on top of everything else.

The knots in her stomach twisted even tighter. "This is so not what I needed to hear today."

"How do you think I feel?" Nora said, leaning against her lover, Quinn Terhune. The tall, blond Fae Warrior, who looked like an ancient Viking, draped one arm around her shoulder and bent nearly in half to press a kiss to the top of her head.

"Did you know about this?" Maggie asked, turning on Culhane.

"No, I did not." His gaze was fixed on his fellow warrior, but Quinn was too wrapped up in Nora to notice.

Maggie's head was spinning. She didn't know what to

make of this latest situation, what to think, what to do. Nora had leaped into the whole Fae heritage thing with both feet the minute she'd heard about it. She had been thrilled to discover that their grandmother's stories about the Fae lover who had impregnated her were all true. Nora had been eager to explore her roots and had fallen hard for Quinn, the warrior Culhane had once assigned to watch over her.

Apparently though, she'd moved from concentrating on her roots to sprouting a whole new branch.

Nora's daughter, Eileen, was even more into this stuff. She spent half her time on the Internet, researching the Fae, and the rest of her time was spent campaigning for Maggie to use her powers as Queen to make Eileen a full-Fae. Maggie didn't even know if that was possible and wouldn't do it even if it were.

Eileen and Nora looked at the new things in their lives and saw only the magic. Maggie, on the other hand, had been faced with some of the less-pleasant aspects of dealing with the Fae.

Heck, she was barely healed from her fight with Mab. And Mab wasn't really dead. She wasn't even actually *gone*. She was just . . . away. And one of these days, Maggie knew the tiny blond queen with the mad eyes would come back. And Maggie and her family would be on the top of Mab's hit list.

Yet no one else seemed to be worried.

Oh, no. She was the only Donovan woman who was fighting the whole Fae invasion thing tooth and nail. To everybody else, magic looked like a good time and Otherworld was just a great vacation spot. Amazing, Maggie thought, that *she* had become the voice of reason in the family. How was she supposed to protect her family when they kept getting pulled deeper and deeper into Otherworld?

"Maggie!" Nora's voice was sharp and loud. "Hello? I'm having a problem here."

"Yeah, I get it." Maggie shot Culhane a dirty look because she was sure he'd known all about this pregnancy. He knew everything else that went on, didn't he? But the warrior wasn't important at the moment—she'd deal with him later. For now, she looked at her sister. "Are you okay with this?"

Nora's milk white complexion paled even further, but her mouth curved into a half smile. "I really am, Mags," she said, then swallowed hard. "You know I love being pregnant. But this one's a little different—"

"I'll say," Maggie muttered.

Nora continued as if she hadn't spoken. "So Quinn's taking me to see someone because I just feel so . . ."

Well, *that* got Maggie's attention.

"Nora, you can't go to a doctor. They'll do a blood test, and God knows what they'll find," Maggie said, her mind building an image of Nora on the front page of a grocery store tabloid with a headline that read WOMAN PREGNANT WITH FAIRY—complete with sketches of a baby with wings. Oh God, would it have wings? Female Fae could fly, but she'd never seen wings on Mab, and—*so* not important at the moment.

Determinedly, she shook that disturbing little vision away. "And even if your blood test isn't all wonky, what happens if you float in front of the doctor?"

"Not a mortal doctor." Quinn looked horrified at the idea. Think you I would allow one of your medieval torturers to put his hands on my woman?"

Medieval? Well, to the millennia-old Fae, that's probably just what human doctors looked like, Maggie guessed; then she realized what else he'd said. *His* woman. Not a huge surprise, Maggie thought, since Quinn and Nora had practically been joined at the hip for the last few weeks—not to mention the *months* they'd spent together in Otherworld. But still, seeing Quinn's obvious protectiveness toward Nora made Maggie feel just a little bit . . . jealous. And she couldn't help sliding a sideways glance at Culhane. But he wasn't looking at her; he was still glaring at his fellow warrior with a fierceness that would have made Maggie's knees quiver if it had been aimed at her.

Quinn spoke again, his deep voice rolling out around them like thunder. "I'm taking Nora to Otherworld." He stared hard, first at Maggie, then at Culhane, as if daring either of them to challenge him. When they didn't, he continued. "The Fae women can tell her much about carrying a Fae child."

Sounded like a good idea to Maggie. Still, she had to ask. "Why don't you take her to a Fae doctor or something?"

"There are no Fae doctors," Culhane muttered. "We do not become ill."

"Oh. Well, how nice for you." Imagine that. Never getting sick. Not to mention not aging. She already knew Culhane was thousands of years old and didn't look a day over thirty-five. That thought had given her a few sleepless nights, planning Botox injections and maybe a facelift in a few years, but now that she was turning Fae, she probably wouldn't need to worry about that, would she? Oh God. Now she'd worry about that.

Who needed to live forever?

Back burner, she told herself. Stay in the now. And at the moment, she wasn't real thrilled with the idea of her sister spending even more time in the Faery dimension. After all, a few weeks in Otherworld had gotten Nora into this mess in the first place. What choice did they have, though?

"I need you to pick Eileen up from school," Nora was saying.

"What? Oh. Right. Of course. Don't worry about it."

"It's early day. She's out of class at two," Nora said.

Maggie glanced at her wristwatch. Eleven o'clock now; she might be able to squeeze in her other two windows before picking Eileen up. "I'll take care of it. But you're coming back, right? No long vacation this time?"

"I'll be back tonight," Nora said, then turned her face into Quinn's chest. The warrior wrapped his arms around her and nodded to Maggie and Culhane. Their outlines blurred, shimmered briefly and they were gone.

"I need to learn how to do that," Maggie muttered. But then there were lots of things she had to learn. *Damn it.*

With Quinn's enchantment gone, suddenly the sounds of the street rose up around them again, the noise level horrific after the hushed silence Quinn's spell had provided. Maggie winced as the growl of skateboard wheels reached her, a car horn blared repeatedly and from somewhere nearby, a radio blasted out a classic Rolling Stones tune.

"Maggie—"

He was still beside her. The Fae Warrior she spent far too much time thinking about. But Maggie was in no mood at the moment to pick up where they'd left off. In fact, she was starting to think that Nora's interrupting what might have been a toe-curling kiss had been a very good thing. She had to stay focused. Not just on her life here, in Castle Bay, but on her new duties as Queen, and keeping her family safe as Otherworld interfered with their normal lives. And if that meant locking her knees together whenever Culhane was around, well then, she'd just have to find a way to live with that.

"Don't start with me, Culhane," she snapped. Her head was pounding, her stomach was a little jumpy and now she not only had to paint two more windows, but she had to be at the school by two to pick up her niece.

"Nora's pregnancy changes things," Culhane told her, taking her upper arm in a firm grip.

Heat poured from his hand through her skin to slide along her veins. Her blood was sizzling, as if she'd been slapped by a sudden, inexplicable fever. Her skin felt raw and sensitive, her nipples went hard and somewhere low inside her, need awoke with an urgency that left her almost breathless.

For weeks, she'd been lusting after Culhane. His teasing smiles, his pale, nearly magic eyes, his tendency to snap out orders and expect them to be followed. He'd helped her, tormented her, irritated her and somehow had become an integral part of her life. She barely remembered a time when he hadn't been there. Worse, she didn't *want* to.

He'd confessed once that he'd been watching over her throughout her life. He had even awakened long-buried memories for her so that she could recall the stormy night he'd saved her from drowning, the shining day in Ireland when he'd given Maggie her first kiss. And she wondered whether there were more buried memories. Times when she and Culhane had touched or spoken or loved. And would he show them to her one day? Would he dole them out to her like treats to a well-behaved child?

There was so much between them, most of which remained unspoken. Culhane had slipped into her heart and everything in her wanted to embrace that. But Maggie couldn't quite bring herself to trust him. Hence, the locked-knee thing.

"You think? Nora's *pregnant* with a Fae baby! Of course, this changes everything!" Deliberately, she looked away from him to let her gaze slide across the Christmas scene she'd nearly completed on Barb's windows. "I just don't know what they're changing *into*." Even while her stomach twisted into a knot of worry over her sister and what could possibly happen next, a different corner of her mind clung to the everyday facts of life. To the fact that she had to finish up here and get over to the real estate office and then the art boutique to decorate their windows before getting Eileen at school. Thank God, her last job for the day was a small shop with one window.

"When news of Nora's pregnancy spreads through Otherworld, some won't be happy about it."

"What does that mean?"

He scrubbed one hand across his jaw. "There is talk about removing the half-Fae from the throne."

"Me?" Maggie swallowed hard and forced a deep breath into suddenly straining lungs. It was one thing for her to be a little ambiguous about this queen thing. It was something else to realize that maybe there were a few Fae planning on staging a coup.

"Yes." His eyes were fixed on her and his features were grim. "There are some who believe a human has no business being in Otherworld at all, let alone sitting on the throne."

Couldn't really blame any of them for that, since she'd considered the same thought once or twice herself. But one thing she didn't understand. "What's Nora being pregnant got to do with people not liking me?"

Culhane's scowl looked even fiercer than usual. "It is because of you that Quinn met and fell in love with Nora. They blame you for the warrior's fall from grace."

"Fall from—"

"Without you, Quinn would not have taken Nora to his bed, and now a child . . . There are some who believe it's muddying Fae blood to mix with humans."

"Muddying?" she repeated, less worried now and more insulted, both on her own behalf and for Nora. "Quinn's lucky to *have* Nora and you know it."

"I do—"

She kept talking, cutting Culhane off before he could sputter another word. "And *muddying*? Nora was a quarter-Fae before she and Quinn got together, and now their baby is going to be even *more* Fae than we were. So excuse me, but there was some other Faery *muddying* things up with my grandmother a long time ago. And he's the one who set all of this into motion."

"Yes, he—"

Maggie grabbed a fine-line paintbrush, loaded it with yellow paint and, even while she was raging, kept a steady hand to fill in the flames of several candles on the glass. "I don't see anybody going after *that* guy."

"You're wrong," Culhane spoke up quickly. "The Fae who seduced your grandmother has been ... unpopular in Otherworld lately."

"Lately?" Maggie grabbed that one word out of the sentence and pulled the brush away from the glass. "You mean our grandFae-father is still alive?"

"Of course." He shrugged. "Fae are long-lived. You knew this."

"Yeah, but I never thought—" Of course, things had been a little crazy in the last couple of weeks. Hardly surprising that she hadn't had a chance to consider that their mysterious grandFae was still alive and out there somewhere. But now that she knew, she had to wonder why no one had said anything to her before this. Why hadn't Culhane mentioned it? Why hadn't Quinn said something to Nora?

Or had he? No, she told herself just as quickly. If Nora had known about this, no way would she have been able to keep quiet about it. So she didn't know, either.

"Why didn't you say something?" she asked, her voice quiet, careful. "Didn't you want me to know? Or was it that good old grandFae is one of the ones who doesn't want me on the throne? Is that it?"

"Maggie ..."

She shook her head and fought down a surprising swell of disappointment. Why should she care what a grandparent she'd never met—and had believed until recently was just a figment of Gran's imagination— thought of her? Still, it stung to think he didn't approve of her as Queen. "Too bad for him," she whispered. "I am the Queen and he'll just have to deal with it like everybody else. After all, he's the one who started the whole Fae line in the Donovan family."

Culhane moved in closer and carefully eased her paintbrush from her fingers. "He is not one of those against your reign. I told you, he is having trouble in Otherworld because of his relationship to you."

She bit her bottom lip and thought about that. Until a few minutes ago, she hadn't even known about him. Now there was a thread of worry for him running through her system. "You should have told me about him, Culhane."

"There wasn't much time before Maggie. And I confess, I do not know your grandsire. I am a warrior. He is not."

She almost argued with that reasoning, but then figured it must be like saying to someone here, *Oh, you live in Los Angeles. You must know my cousin, Wanda.* Big city. And Otherworld was even bigger. Hell, it was a *world* all by itself, with cities, countries, continents. . . . Of course Culhane wouldn't know everyone there.

But imagine. The Donovan girls weren't as alone in the world as they'd thought they were. They still had a relative. A Faery grandfather. Who hadn't bothered to call and say hi or anything in like forever. Okay, that colored things a little, Maggie admitted silently and took her paintbrush back from Culhane.

Deliberately, she set thoughts of her mysterious grandfather aside for the moment. She'd have time later to think about him and decide what she was going to do about him. She'd have to meet him. Nora would want to meet him, too. But that meant being in Otherworld and right now, she had to be *here.*

"You are pulling away from me again," Culhane whispered.

When had he dipped his head so close to hers? And why did her insides immediately start jumping up and down in excitement the minute he did?

"I'm not," she said, even as she did just that, stepping

to one side, keeping a small, but necessary distance between them. She felt at a loss. He knew so much more than she did. About her life. Her family. Her new duties and her place in Otherworld. She felt as if she were standing over a chasm in the earth. One foot in Faeryland, one foot in the real world, and the tiniest wrong step would send her tumbling down into the gap between both worlds.

Forever falling, just like Mab.

She shivered and this time it had nothing to do with Culhane's nearness. There was just too much going on in her world for Maggie to be thinking about Culhane and, God help her, Faery sex. Especially now that she knew Faery sperm were hearty enough to get through the birth control pills she *knew* Nora was on.

Though she wanted him more than she had ever thought it possible to want anyone, how could Maggie possibly stop long enough to enjoy sex when there were so many other things cluttering up her life and her thoughts? No, it looked like she was going to die a vestal virgin.

All right.

Not exactly a virgin.

But close. She'd been celibate—not by choice—for several weeks now. And the shower massage she'd installed a few nights ago? Not really the same.

Culhane blew out a breath. "You're angry."

"I'm . . . something. But, maybe angry's mixed up in there somewhere."

"Ah." He nodded sagely, then shook his head as if he were disappointed. "I see. Somehow you blame *me* for Nora's announcement?"

Actually, she was blaming him for pretty much everything lately. But then, why not? Wasn't *he* the one who had started all of this you're-the-destined-Queen thing? Whom else could she blame?

"You should have warned me," she said flatly.

"I didn't know about your sister's pregnancy."

She glanced at him and couldn't read his expression at all. That's what happened when you lived for thousands of years, she guessed. You had plenty of time to develop an excellent poker face. Culhane was on top of everything, though. Nothing surprised him. And he was damn good at keeping secrets. "Wish I could believe that."

"You may."

Maggie almost laughed. Now he wore that fierce, of-course-you-must-believe-me-I'm-a-Fae-Warrior-who-was-not-informed-of-all-I-should-have-been look on his face. Okay, maybe he hadn't known after all. Even Culhane couldn't possibly pretend to be *that* insulted.

"I would not have kept it from you had I known, but Quinn," he added with a snarl, "did not tell *me*."

She studied him for a long moment or two, then finally nodded, at least partially convinced. "Somehow that makes me feel better. At least I'm not the only one out of the loop."

"Maggie," he said, with a very human-sounding sigh, "as Queen, you *are* the 'loop,' as you call it."

Wouldn't that be nice? But . . . "Clearly not."

He scowled again, folded his massive arms across his broad chest and planted both feet wide apart. Maggie's breath hitched unsteadily. He looked so damn good. Like a pirate on the cover of a steamy romance novel. His black hair lifted in the cold sea breeze and his pale green eyes narrowed on her. Strange, that even when he was crabby and pissy, Maggie still felt sparks dazzling through her system.

Seriously, Culhane was enough to tempt the saints right out of heaven.

"I will speak with Quinn," he promised, and from his tone, Maggie almost felt sorry for the other warrior. "But there is more to think about than the coming child."

"I know, I know." Maggie forgot about her paint-stained fingers and shoved one hand through her hair, giving it a yank so that the tiny jerk of pain would make her focus on something else besides the urge to throw herself at Culhane and forget all about everything but how he could make her feel.

Didn't really work.

"I'm the Queen; I've got to pay attention. I have to be in Otherworld, trying to fix what's wrong; like that won't take a couple of decades. . . . Oh, and a shiny new—old—grandfather to think about, not to mention that there are Fae who don't like me, not that they even *know* me." She looked up at him and blew out a breath. "But Otherworld isn't the only thing I've got to think about and you don't seem to get that. This is still my world, Culhane, and here, I've got to eat and I've also got to pay bills—"

"You could live in the palace and never pay another bill," he whispered.

That sly hush of sound probably was just what the snake in the Garden of Eden had sounded like. Tempting. Alluring. Making her envision a life of pampered luxury. She'd been in the palace a few times and it was pretty damn impressive. Huge and beautiful, its white marble and crystal walls shimmered with an inner light. Windows that overlooked gardens so breathtaking you could hardly force yourself to stop looking at them. Breezes that tickled and teased your skin, carrying with them the tangled scents of those flowers, the far-off seas and foreign spices.

For one brief shining moment, Maggie let herself think what it might be like to surrender her version of normalcy to live forever in that world so far away from her own. Imagine having no electric bill, no phone company getting snippy because the check was late. No insurance bills, car payments, ooh, and no taxes. She sighed. "Wouldn't that be something. . . ."

For the first time, she didn't consider all of the palace intrigue, the pixies against the Fae, the women against the men, the rogue Fae threatening to break loose of the icy world they'd been imprisoned in, to wreak havoc in *her* world. Nope. All she thought about was the incredible notion of having no responsibilities beyond, you know—ruling.

Then she caught herself, frowned at the Fae Warrior watching her with a knowing gleam in his eyes and said, "You're evil, Culhane."

He smiled and her stomach did a quick spin.

"I know what you're trying to do," Maggie said, shaking her head and holding up both hands, forming a cross with her fingers, as if she were trying to hold off a vampire. "You're trying to seduce me onto the throne. Well, it won't work. I told you. I'll be Queen. On my terms. I have a life, Culhane, and I'm not ready to give it up."

Muttering something under his breath in a language she didn't understand, he practically snarled at her; then he moved so fast she didn't see the motion, him sweeping in close, grabbing her upper arms and dragging her up against him. He held her so tightly pinned against his body, she felt the hard, solid length of him pressing into her belly and lower.

She blinked, her head tipped back and he loomed over her, staring directly into her eyes. "Your life is not your own anymore, Maggie. Do you not see that? Do you not see that this"—he lifted his gaze to sweep the town of Castle Bay with a dismissive glance—"is no longer where you belong?"

"No." She said it firmly. Loudly. Convincing him? Or herself? Didn't matter. Both of them needed to hear it. "I won't give it all up, Culhane. I can't. This is who I am and hey, it should not be a big surprise, Mr. Great Fenian Warrior." She yanked herself free of his grip. "You're the one who's been peeking into my life for years. Not like knowing who I am is a big shocker. So dial down the caveman attitude, okay?"

"You try my patience, Maggie Donovan."

She clucked her tongue at him. "Is that any way to talk to your Queen?"

He gritted his teeth so hard, Maggie was pretty sure she actually *heard* his teeth dissolving into powder; then his eyes blazed a pale green fire at her and his image shifted, blurred and disappeared.

Alone again, Maggie shot a look into the beauty shop, hoping to hell no one had seen Culhane doing the vanish thing. But everyone inside was busy combing out hair, sitting under dryers reading magazines and slurping down coffee while gossiping—none of them had a single clue that a Fae Warrior had just been outside their cozy little shop. They would never dream that a place like Otherworld existed.

Lucky bastards.

Chapter Three

Culhane embraced the change, letting his body dissipate, molecules disbanding, as he shifted dimensions, moving through time, space and the magic doorways that separated his world from Maggie's. He appeared a brief moment later in his home at the Warriors' Conclave—his body hard and tight, his temper tightly leashed but straining to be free. And the familiarity of his rooms did nothing to ease the tension clawing at him.

"Damn woman will not listen," he muttered, sweeping one hand through his hair impatiently. "Will not do as I say. Can she not see that without my help she's no hope of surviving what comes next?"

Could she not see that his hunger for her was making him half crazed with want? Since the moment when she'd awakened to her new power—no, *Ifreann* take him—since long before that, Maggie Donovan had been nothing but a temptation to him. His mind tormented him daily with thoughts of what he wanted to do to her. With her. He wanted his hands on her breasts. He wanted to explore each curve and valley her body possessed. He wanted to taste her, delve deep with his tongue until she screamed his name and begged for the release only he could give her.

And damn if he could manage any of it.

But then, mayhap she *did* know what she was doing

to him and was enjoying it as well. She was no shy virgin. He could sense that there had been other men in her life before him. Men who hadn't deserved her. Men unworthy of her, he told himself with a shake of his head. But since she was no innocent, why then did she keep him at arm's length?

Why had they shared no more than a few kisses? He'd had only the one lingering touch of her heat—the night Mab had slapped him into prison before she'd gone on to be defeated by Maggie.

Why was she being so bloody *coy*? She felt the rush of passion between them. He saw it in her eyes when they were together. Her destiny—*with him*—was there before her and she clung to her past. To the mortal world when she had no reason to. Was her life so perfect that she could not bring herself to turn her back on it? Was what he offered her worth so little in her mind that she refused to reach out and take it?

She felt the fire between them. The hunger. Yet she fought her own nature and held instead to the idiotic notion of celibacy, when raw, wild sex would have freed them both.

What kind of woman was she?

In his long life, thousands of mortal years, Culhane had never known any woman to resist him. Fae females were as free with their bodies as the males, and sex was something to be shared and gloried in. There was no wasted time or effort. If they wanted, they took.

Mortal women were different, of course. Entranced by the power surrounding a Fae male, they were attracted almost instantly and just as easily seduced. Culhane had seen other Fae males indulge with mortal females, though he'd never bothered himself. For Culhane, they seemed to be far more trouble than they were worth. As powerful and ancient as he was, human women—Maggie in particular—could reduce him to wanting to tear his own hair out in frustration.

Most mortal women wanted to talk about their *feelings*. They wanted to be courted, romanced, and at the same time, they wanted to be treated as equals when any fool knew that could never be so.

It was a male's duty to care for and protect his woman, whether she wanted him to or not.

Human males, though, to ease the pain in their groins, had been reduced to placating their women, to giving in to their silly demands and notions. The males pretended to feel equality when what they were thinking was, *Lie back and let me have you.* They played word games, hiding their true natures in order to provide their women with the illusions they craved.

By the gods, he would be damned if he would play according to their rules. He was Culhane. Immortal Fae. A Fenian warrior of such repute, the mere mention of his name was enough to send chills down the cowardly spines of his enemies. And he'd curse his own name before he'd surrender his pride for the sake of any woman.

Even Maggie.

"Blasted woman wants me, too. Does she think I don't feel the strength of her desire pushing at me?" He saw it in the way she walked, how her breath quickened when he was near. He watched her lick her full lower lip and it took all of his legendary strength to keep from licking it for her.

But he had his pride. And when Maggie came to his bed, it would be because she *asked* for it.

"Though she'd damn well better ask soon." His patience was wearing thin.

Only that morning, while he watched her as she perched on her silly ladder and reached out to paint her ridiculous pictures on glass, her shirt had pulled up from the waist of her jeans and he'd been mesmerized by the exposed inch or two of her taut, firm belly. He'd noted the way her soft T-shirt had molded to her breasts, how her jeans molded lovingly in all the right places to her long, shapely legs. And his mouth had watered.

The woman was killing him inch by slow inch.

He stalked across the room, stared out the window at the training grounds far below him and idly watched as his warriors staged mock battles with swords and knives. The clang of steel on silver rang out. A sharp wind slid through the open window and lifted his long hair from his shoulders, cooling his skin but doing nothing to cool the fires burning within.

Maggie's face rose up in his mind and everything in Culhane tightened even further. How was it, he wondered, that a mortal woman could make the mighty Culhane nothing more than a slavering beast?

And now, thanks to Quinn getting her sister with child, Maggie was bent even further on distancing herself from him! By the gods, his cock would rot and fall off if he didn't use it soon.

"Damn woman will be the end of me."

"Our Queen remains unmoved by the great Culhane, then?"

He spun into a crouch, his hand slapping at the handle of the silver blade he kept at his waist. But an instant later, Culhane cursed, straightened, and said, "You've no call to be here, McCulloch."

The warrior only smirked at him. He'd noticed to his own irritation that since Maggie had taken the throne, even his own men were want to chuckle at his frustrations. Only the bravest—or the most foolhardy—dared *show* him their amusement, though.

Keiran McCulloch shook his head and smoothed one hand across the neatly trimmed, dark red goatee he was inordinately proud of. "It's rumored that our Queen has no need for you, Culhane."

"She has need," he muttered darkly, remembering the flash of hunger in her eyes only that morning. A cheering thought, he told himself, wondering if she lay in her empty bed aching for his touch. Perhaps it was time to pay a night visit to induce her into dreams of him.

Then, shaking his head at his own desperation, he walked across the wide room to the crystal bottle of nectar he kept on a shelf. To ease the ache in his body, he poured himself a glass of the Fae liquor, richer and sweeter than any mortal wine. He relished the taste for a moment, then studied the honey-colored liquid in the crystal he held. Without looking behind him, he said, "She's stubborn, is all."

"Aye, and getting no less so as time goes on."

Culhane whipped his head around then to stare at the warrior across from him. "Mind your tongue. Maggie Donovan is your Queen."

The other warrior inclined his head but didn't bother to hide his smile.

"And your witch?" Culhane asked slyly, knowing the warrior had been spending far more time at Maggie's home than necessary. All because of Maggie's friend Claire, a seer and a witch.

McCulloch snapped him a hard look, then reluctantly smiled. "We both must deal with stubborn mortal females, I suppose."

"True enough, gods help us both." Culhane blew out a breath. "Was there a reason you've come? Or are you here merely to annoy me like a common pixie?"

McCulloch lifted one dark red eyebrow into a high arch. "Would a common pixie know that the Dullahan are riding again?"

Everything in Culhane went cold and still. His gaze fixed on McCulloch, he watched the other warrior stride toward him, his features hard, implacable. "How do you know this?"

"There's more. The palace guards are planning an assault on Casia to stop them."

Casia, the frozen continent where the worst of the rogue Fae were imprisoned. The Dullahan were a vicious, bloodthirsty race, sentenced to Casia eons ago for their crimes against the mortal world. Even Mab had known that there were lines not meant to be crossed.

"You know this for a fact?" If the palace guards went after the Fae on Casia themselves, they would be killed and gods knew how many of the rogues would be set loose. For centuries those jailed on that miserable block of ice had been trying to escape. To once more ride free on the human world, bringing destruction and fury to a race of people who didn't even know they existed. If the Dullahan somehow managed to find a way into Maggie's world, the humans there would be helpless against them.

"Aye." McCulloch plucked a glass off a shelf and filled it with nectar. Downing it in one long gulp, he continued. "One of their number told O'Donnel."

Culhane's eyes narrowed. "Why would she do that?"

McCulloch shrugged. "O'Donnel was bedding her at the time."

Disgusted, Culhane thought briefly that everyone but *he* was enjoying sex.

Studying the empty glass in his hand, McCulloch said, "After speaking to O'Donnel, I went to Audra, the guard commander. Told her that the Warriors would deal with this threat. She insists that her guard be given the chance to fight. Since Mab's defeat, the guards have grown restless. The damn females believe themselves to be warriors."

"They're not," Culhane muttered darkly, his mind drawing up an image of the Fae who had been, for centuries, the only security force Mab had allowed at the palace.

The palace guard, all female, had been Mab's personal protection. After a millennia or two of power, the former queen had become distrustful of all males, even her warriors, so she'd trained females to safeguard both her and the palace. A slap in the face to the Warrior clan, but to Mab's way of thinking, a way to keep the males in line while stripping them of any ideas of gaining future power.

But with Mab gone, her guards were restive. They wanted more duties than Maggie had given them. Blast the gods, they wanted to fight.

True, they had stood sentinel over the palace and the Queen for centuries. But they weren't warriors and had no business in a real battle. They'd never fought an enemy like the Dullahan. For too long, they'd thought themselves impregnable. Undefeatable. This false sense of importance had clearly gone to their heads, since everyone knew that only males were true fighters.

Yet, as that thought raced through his mind, he remembered Maggie defeating a Fae queen, and he knew that she'd been as brave as any Fenian warrior. She'd gone into a battle untested, untried, and had managed to snatch victory from the hands of a queen far more experienced than she. Nodding, he admitted that Maggie, at least, was a formidable female.

But the palace harpies were the least of his troubles at the moment. If the Dullahan were truly readying a strike against the walls of Otherworld in an attempt to breach them, then there was much to do.

"Have you seen evidence yourself?" he asked, his gaze narrowing on the tall warrior opposite him.

"No," McCulloch admitted with a nod. "I thought first to warn you of Mab's guards and their plans."

Culhane set his now-empty glass on the sideboard, folded his arms across his chest and said, "As you should. I'll deal with them. You take Riley and go to Casia. Find out if the Dullahan are actually planning something or not. We have to know the truth before we act."

"It's done." McCulloch inclined his head again, in acknowledgment of the order, and an instant later, shifted out of Culhane's apartments.

"Maggie Donovan, the palace guard and the Dullahan," Culhane muttered. It seemed as though the gods were bent on testing his new Queen. But he wouldn't face Maggie with this news just yet. First he would gather information to make a plan; then, and only then, would he go to Maggie. And he would make her see that giving him leave to act in her stead was the wisest course to take.

&

Maggie was late.

She hated being late.

Especially when she was picking up Eileen. Somehow, knowing that five *million* other kids had all been taken home at the appropriate time and only Eileen was left behind made the guilt worse.

But the stupid window at the stupid art boutique had taken her twice as long as she'd planned. With only one small window fronting the main street, it should have been a half-hour job, tops. But naturally, the new owner had wanted a whole damn Currier and Ives scene painted in, complete with carolers and horse and carriage and, of course, that upped her fee, but had taken twice as long as it otherwise would have. Maggie blew out a frustrated breath, deliberately rolled her shoulders to ease the tension and then turned off the engine of her PT Cruiser.

Opening the door, she stepped out onto the worn blacktop of the school driveway and let her gaze slide over the familiar territory. Castle Bay wasn't very big, especially considering that the community's one elementary school, one middle school and one high school were easily able to accommodate Castle Bay's students as well as those from the surrounding area. And if you'd lived in town all your life, as Maggie had, you knew each school like the back of your hand.

The weathered brick facade had faded over the years until it was now a pale rose color and the outside of the principal's office window was dotted with flyers announcing everything from "Just Say No" campaigns to the coming Christmas party. Although these days it was called the "Holiday Celebration." Politically correct could get really sad and ugly sometimes.

"So where are you?" she murmured, looking around and seeing only long, empty outdoor hallways and a custodian pushing a cart loaded with brooms and mops. The rattle of its one bad wheel echoed in the stillness. Eileen should have been waiting right here. In front of the principal's office. Inside Maggie, guilt blended with a sudden sense of unease. What if some random Fae had shown up? What if an ordinary human bad guy had shown up? "I'm a rotten human being. A lousy aunt—and if anything happens to Eileen, I'm going to have to throw myself under a train."

But what could happen?

Oh, only a few weeks ago, she would have been telling herself that Eileen was fine. That the chances of her niece being kidnapped or worse were pretty damn slim. Castle Bay was small, insulated, and everyone in town knew everybody else and a kidnapper would have been hard put to get away with snatching a kid without being surrounded by furious citizens.

But that was back when Maggie had been just a little smug about the safety of the town she called home.

These days, though, she knew the truth. That there were more than just human predators wandering around. There were demons and pixies and rogue Fae and God knew what else that could pop in, grab a cutie like Eileen and pop back out again before anyone even realized what was happening.

"Shut up, brain," she whispered as worry skittered up and down her spine like thousands of stings from tiny needles. "Eileen's fine. She's probably just making me pay for making her wait."

Good. That was good. And very Donovan of her, to

exact a little payback. Maggie wouldn't even be mad. Just grateful. As soon as she found her.

Someone laughed and Maggie's head whipped around, her gaze darting in the direction of that familiar sound. Eileen strolled out from between two of the buildings, a tall, thin girl with dark red hair and milk white skin who wasn't alone. A *boy* walked beside her.

"Oh God. This is all your fault, you know," Maggie told herself in a muttered whisper. "You were late, so she had time to get friendly with a boy. Nora's so going to kill you."

She reached into the car, tapped on her car horn and when Eileen glanced up, Maggie waved. "Let's go, kiddo!"

Her Donovan blue eyes rolled skyward as an expression of complete humiliation crossed Eileen's face. Maggie recognized that look. She'd worn it often enough when she was a kid. Was there anything more mortifying than having other people find out you actually had a *family*?

The blond boy walking with Eileen took one look at Maggie before ducking back between the buildings. Maggie frowned a little at his secretive move. Who was this kid, anyway? Could this be the fabulous Grant Carter Eileen had been mooning over a couple of weeks ago? If it was, she told herself, the kid looked a lot older than thirteen.

"At least fifteen," Maggie said softly, watching Eileen smile and give the hidden boy a finger wave good-bye.

Then the girl turned and hurried toward Maggie's car with a mutinous expression on her normally pretty face. When she was close enough, she hissed, "Did you have to embarrass me like that?"

"By saying hello?" Maggie countered.

"I knew you wouldn't understand." Eileen opened the car door, climbed inside and dumped her backpack on the floor at her feet.

Maggie got in, too, but not before she looked again at the spot where the boy had vanished. He hadn't shown himself again, which just made Maggie that much more curious. She fired up the engine, buckled her seat belt and made sure Eileen had done the same before she drove out of the school parking lot.

"Sorry I was late, kiddo."

"No problem," Eileen muttered, staring through the windshield, apparently not having forgiven her aunt for existing just yet.

"Your mom's in Otherworld, but she'll be back by tonight."

"Okay."

"Was that Grant Carter I saw you with?" An age-old technique for interrogating kids. Get them relaxed, then slide in the real questions.

Eileen turned and faced her then. "No, his name's Devon."

Devon. Hadn't heard about him before, Maggie thought and quickly braced herself for coming worry. "Who is he?"

Apparently, the opportunity to talk about the great Devon was too good to miss. Even if it meant speaking to an adult you were trying to ignore.

"He is so cool, Maggie. He's new in town and he's totally cute and all of the girls like him, but he likes me and he's really smart and funny and—"

"New?" Maggie stopped at a red light and slid a glance at her niece. The girl's eyes were sparkling and her cheeks were flushed. Oh God, she was in love. "How new?"

"He moved here last week and Amber told me today that he told her that he kinda liked me and then when you were late picking me up, he showed up and kept me company and he was totally nice and he likes the same music as I do and the same TV shows and"—she paused for breath, but first had to give a little sigh of female satisfaction—"he is sooo cute."

Maggie took from that that Eileen's best friend, Amber, was the go-between until Maggie herself had given new boy an opening to talk to Eileen himself. Should she be glad the kid had arrived to keep Eileen company? Maybe. And maybe she should just worry about this a while longer.

"Does he go to your school?"

"What? Oh. I don't think so. I only see him after school sometimes."

Didn't go to school there. And he was new in town?

Was he human new? Or demon new? Was he really a teenage boy with rampaging hormones? Or was he some kind of bizarre creature with different plans entirely? God, she didn't know which of those two bad ideas to hope for. And how would she ever know for sure?

Only one way. She'd have to get this Devon alone at some point and blow Faery dust on him. If he exploded, then she'd know he was a demon and she'd apologize to Eileen later. If he *didn't*, then he'd just think Maggie was weird and she'd apologize to Eileen later.

Seriously? When had her life gotten so peculiar?

"I went on the Internet again at the library," Eileen was saying, and Maggie pushed her own thoughts away to listen up. Apparently, they were finished with Devon for the moment, which was okay by Maggie.

"The librarian is so a control freak." Reaching down for her backpack, Eileen unzipped it, pulled out a sheaf of folded papers and straightened again. "She like hovers over us when we're online like we're going to be attacked by some cyber monster or something, even though they've got so many child locks on the computers, we can barely sign on."

"It's her job," Maggie said, stepping on the gas, then signaling to pass a car moving so slowly it was practically going backward. But, she thought, this is how it would be for the next few weeks at least.

With Thanksgiving over, the hard-core shoppers

would be cluttering up Main Street every day between now and Christmas. There would be traffic jams, too many tourists looking to buy something from one of the gift shops and not enough parking spots for the locals.

But all the storekeepers in town would be happily ringing up their cash registers, hoping to make enough to tide them over during the slower times until their *next* big season, summer.

"Did you get your driver's license in a pet store?" Maggie shouted at the woman who had stopped dead in the middle of the street to make an illegal U-turn.

While Maggie tapped her fingers impatiently against the steering wheel, Eileen said, "Someone should tell the librarian that seventy-two percent of all children thwarted in their attempts to use computers become cyber-hackers in retaliation."

Maggie snorted and glanced at her niece. "*Thwarted*? What're you, thirty?"

Eileen grinned and just like that, she was back to being her old self again, irritations—and budding romance—forgotten. "It's a good word, huh? I saw it on-line and had to use it."

To support one of the statistics she was forever quoting. Maggie wasn't sure where she picked up all of these obscure facts, but she was pretty sure Eileen made up most of them. Still, they were always impressive in an argument.

"Finally!" Maggie crowed as the driver in front of her finished tying up traffic. She stepped on the gas again, but she didn't get far. Two pedestrians leaped off the curb to cross the street and Maggie slammed on the brakes to avoid running them down.

"Anyway," Eileen said, unfolding the papers, "I was reading about Otherworld again and you know how Culhane says the humans have gotten everything wrong about the Fae? Well, I think he's right."

"He'll love hearing that," Maggie muttered as she

stuck out her tongue at the jaywalkers, who had slowed her down enough that she got caught at another red light. The car beside her shuddered from the power of its stereo blasting out on a frequency that caused what felt like small earthquakes. The bass boomed and the pounding of the drums seemed to echo in Maggie's mind. She turned her head to scowl at the guy responsible for the hideous sound machine and shrieked a little.

"Holy crap!"

It wasn't a *guy*; it was a demon. Green skin, black eyes and two mouths, it was using both of them to sneer at her as it lifted a middle finger in a silent salute.

Eileen looked past her. "Whoa."

In an instant, the demon's human disguise glamour was back in place and he looked like nothing more than a twenty-year-old weirdo with spiky hair and several piercings jutting through his eyebrows and nose. Tough call on which of his images was the yuckier.

"Demon?" Eileen asked.

"Oh yeah," Maggie told her as the light changed to green. She just sat there, watching the demon in the beat-up car peel out. Well, until the driver behind her started honking.

Grumbling about the traffic, she stepped on the gas and headed for home.

*

"In six of your months," Leanna said with a smile, "you will have a Fae child."

"Only six?" Nora smiled past the wave of nausea and laid the flat of her hand against her abdomen. Was she imagining it, or was the baby moving already? So very different. When she was pregnant with Eileen, it was forever before she felt the baby stirring. But clearly, this pregnancy was going to be nothing like her first one.

"That's great," she said, though she felt a quick thrill of—not fear exactly, but maybe . . . okay, fear. She was having a Fae baby. Who knew what that would mean? Of course, that's why Quinn had brought her to Otherworld. So she could get some answers to her questions. "Three months shorter than I was expecting."

"Fae children develop much more quickly," Leanna told her with just a touch of smugness; then the lovely Fae female sat down on a pale lavender chair that seemed to enfold itself around her.

Nora managed to stifle a shiver. It was bad enough sitting on this silver couch that continually shifted and moved beneath her like something alive. Sure, it was comfy, but she preferred her furniture to be inanimate.

The place was beautiful, but then, everything in Otherworld was pretty. Mostly. It was the differences that kept Nora off balance. Like the quivering couch and the way her hostess waved one hand in the air and produced a tray filled with fragile-looking glasses shaped like delicate tulips and a bottle of some honey-colored liquid.

Not the kind of thing she was used to, even if she did try, unlike her sister, Maggie, to keep an open mind to the supernatural.

"Are you all right?" Quinn's deep voice rumbled from close by and he reached over to slide his big hand up and down her spine. Nora leaned into his touch. This was worth it. He made it all worth it.

"I'm fine," she said, straightening up a little and moving closer to the edge of that couch. She was half convinced it would try to swallow her soon. "Really, sweetie, I'm good. I'm just . . ."

Feeling out of place? Couldn't really say that since Leanna was a friend of Quinn's. But Nora didn't think she'd ever be able to relax in such a completely elegant house. A suite of rooms in a shimmering crystal tower in the middle of the great city, the walls of Leanna's home sparkled and shone iridescently in the afternoon sunshine. The walls were curved, the windows were wide and afforded a view of the far-off sea. A floral scent perfumed the air and soft music that sounded like harps and flutes drifted through the room like a caress.

It was fabulous and beautiful and the woman who lived here had been nothing but welcoming, but Nora really wanted to be back in her quirky but completely cozy little house. At least there, when she felt hurly, she knew where to go.

Leanna shifted in her chair, drawing Nora's attention. Really, was *every* Fae woman gorgeous? Leanna was tall, mostly leg, with waist-length, pale yellow hair that fell in froths of curls around her shoulders. Her wide, silvery eyes shone in the light of the two suns slanting through the windows. She had a figure that most women would kill for and knowing that she had given birth twice only made Nora more jealous. But she was being helpful and right about now, Nora needed all the help she could get.

"Is the child female?" Leanna asked, sliding a glance to Quinn.

"Why're you asking him?" Nora wondered aloud, shooting her lover a quick, quizzical glance.

Leanna answered. "Because the males of our race decide the gender of the child."

"Oh." Nora let her breath slide out. "It's that way for us, too."

"Really?" Leanna leaned forward, curiosity stamped on her features. "Human men can *choose* the gender of their children?"

"Choose?" Nora looked at Quinn again. "No, they don't *choose*, they just . . . you mean," she narrowed her eyes on the huge male beside her, "Fae males can *actually* decide on a boy or girl?"

"Of course," Leanna said. "So I ask again, which is your child?"

Quinn shifted uncomfortably, but said, "Male. He will be a warrior."

"Of course," Leanna said with a sigh that sounded bell-like. "The warrior class do prefer their own sort."

"A boy?" Nora wasn't listening right then. Instead, she was focused on the child within. A boy. She was having a little boy. She smiled to herself. If Quinn had bothered to ask her, she thought, she too would have chosen to have a son. After all, she had a daughter. What fun it would be to have one of each. To experience all of the different things a little boy would find fascinating and—

"A *warrior*?"

Quinn nodded, laid one huge hand on her shoulder and gave it a squeeze. "He will be proud and strong and will one day take his place at the Conclave."

"He's not even born yet and you're handing him a sword?"

Nora squirmed and shoved and finally managed to push herself out of the woman-eating couch. When she was standing on her own two feet, she turned her back on Leanna, glared at Quinn and said, "I sooo don't think so."

Chapter Four

&

"So anyway," Eileen said a half hour later as she slid into a seat at the pedestal table in the kitchen, "all of the old myths and legends about Faeries are so far-off what Culhane and Quinn talk about, it's funny."

"Big surprise," Bezel quipped from his post on a stool at the counter. He shifted position on his wide feet, then waved his long, skeletal fingers, producing a white china platter with magic. "Humans getting something wrong. Wow. Alert the media."

Why she'd been so eager to get home, Maggie couldn't remember. Used to be, she'd walk into the house where she and Nora were raised and instantly feel soothed, comforted. Especially this room. The only room in the house where her grandfather hadn't been allowed to "tinker" with anything.

Grandpa had been a man who liked to keep busy, so he'd whiled away his retirement by turning the Donovan family home into a mini–Winchester Mystery House. There were doors that opened onto nothing. And a front door that had been paneled over on the inside. A set of stairs—more than thirty steps with risers no more than an inch high—designed in a zigzag fashion to rise two feet from the floor. And there were hidden passages linking the rooms together in a rabbitlike warren behind the walls.

But here in the kitchen, Gran had put her foot down. The walls were sunshine yellow, the cabinets were painted a gleaming white and the worn counters looked cozy instead of shabby. It was as if the walls themselves were imprinted with the warmth of family.

Here, in this house, everything she touched or saw reminded her of her grandparents. The scent of fresh cookies always brought back images of Gran, and glancing out the back window, she could see the guesthouse Grandpa had built himself so that he could leave home whenever he wanted and never be far away.

Now, Nora and Eileen—and Quinn, too—lived in that guesthouse and Maggie had the main house mostly to herself. Except for those times when Culhane was popping in and out or when Bezel the pixie came down from his tree house to raid Maggie's stores of chocolate.

Though the place was a lot less soothing these days, what with everything crazy going on, she was at least at home. Where there were no demons masquerading as goth punk rockers. She hoped.

Eileen ignored Bezel, reached for a Double Stuf Oreo from the open package in front of her and took a bite, talking around the cookie. "It says here that the Fae kidnap humans all the time, but Bezel says that's stupid—"

"*Why* would we want to clutter up Otherworld with you people?" he demanded.

"And according to Wikipedia," Eileen went on as if the pixie hadn't spoken, "a human who's half-Fae is welcome in Otherworld, but Bezel says nobody likes a half-breed."

Maggie slid a hard look at the pixie, who was now whistling and pretending to be invisible. "Nice. Thanks."

Sheba, Maggie's golden retriever, wandered in from the living room and lay down beneath Bezel's stool, hoping the pixie would drop something edible. Instantly though, the dog started snoring.

"Am I a half-breed, too?" Eileen asked.

"No, you're a quarter-breed," Maggie said, "or maybe an eighth-breed. I hate math." Which made her think back to Culhane's talking about the Fae grandfather she'd never known.

When she and Nora were kids, their grandmother had always told them stories about the time when she was young and visiting Ireland and how she'd met a handsome man who'd whisked her off to Faeryland. She claimed to have lived there for several weeks, but when she'd come home, she'd actually been gone only overnight.

She'd also been pregnant. Of course, no one had believed her wild tales about a Faery lover. But she'd met Grandpa a few months later and married him. He adopted Nora and Maggie's mom, and no one really thought about the past anymore—well, except for Gran. She'd never really gotten over that magical lover she'd known so briefly. So when Nora and Maggie were old enough, she'd told them everything she remembered about Otherworld and the Fae who lived there.

Nora had believed.

Maggie hadn't.

She did now, though. She only wished she could have five minutes with Gran so she could apologize about ever doubting her.

"So the baby will be a quarter-breed, too?" Eileen asked.

"No," Maggie said without really thinking about it, "since Quinn's the father, it'll be mostly Fae and . . . *what*?"

"Don't expect me to be a babysitter," Bezel grumbled.

"God forbid," Maggie said solemnly as she stared at the hideously ugly pixie whipping up dinner in her kitchen. Bezel stood three feet tall, had wispy silver hair and an even wispier silver beard. His blue eyes blazed in a face so wrinkled he looked like a shar-pei puppy, and the green velvet suit he wore had been made by the wife he never stopped talking about, Fontana.

The very same wife who had tossed his ugly pixie ass out of Otherworld for spending "too much time with humans," therefore ensuring that he would spend even *more* time with them. Now he was living in a magically built tree house in the oak out back and quite literally *whipping* up dinner nearly every night.

He wasn't much of a cook—traditionally speaking, with a stove and, say, pans—but the little pain in her ass could really magic up some great meals.

"I'm just saying," he continued, as if Maggie hadn't spoken at all, "I don't mind helping out around here— mostly because if you keep cooking, I'll *die*. And watching over the kid once in a while is okay, 'cause she doesn't bug too bad. But no babies."

"How'd you find out about Nora's baby?" Maggie demanded.

"I told him," Eileen said. "Mom explained this morning before I went to school."

"She told you about the baby already?" Had Maggie been the last one to know? Even Bezel knew before she did? How was that fair? Well, just went to prove, being Queen didn't bring many perks.

"Well, *duh*." Eileen grabbed another cookie from the open bag on the table. "Thirty-five percent of parents try to hide the coming of a sibling," she pronounced. "It never ends well."

Bezel lifted both silver eyebrows, then shook his head and went back to muttering some incantation over the white china platter on the counter in front of him.

Leaving him out of this for the moment, which she tried to do as often as possible, Maggie studied her niece. Twelve years old, Eileen had the Donovan blue eyes, dark red hair that hung just past her shoulders and pale skin softly dotted with freckles. Maggie couldn't have loved her more. "So are you okay about the baby?"

Eileen thought about it for a second or two, then shrugged and smiled. "Sure. It's good for Mom to have a baby, since I'm practically grown."

"You're twelve," Maggie reminded her, making another grab for the cookie bag herself.

"I'll be thirteen in nine months. That's practically tomorrow."

God, it really was. As fast as time was moving lately, Eileen could be a grandmother by next week. Maggie's head hurt and the cookies weren't helping.

"After dinner, can somebody come over?"

"On a school night?" Maggie countered, already shaking her head. "Your mom would kill me."

"She's in Otherworld, remember?"

Maggie narrowed her gaze on Eileen. God, was the sneaky maneuvering—trademarks of teenager-hood— starting already? "Somebody *who*?" she asked, remembering the boy who'd been so intent on hiding from her.

Eileen smiled and got a dreamy look to her eyes that she usually reserved for her favorite actor on *Supernatural*, Jensen Ackles. Oh boy.

"Is this about Devon?"

Eileen didn't answer, instead concentrating on licking the thick white icing between the two chocolate cookies.

That more than anything spiked Maggie's internal radar. Donovan women were *rarely* quiet. Which meant that either Devon was getting her to be quiet or Eileen had already reached the hormonal stage where she wanted to shut her family out of her life. Oh, please not that.

"If I told you it was Amber who wanted to come over, that would be okay?" she asked, clearly unable to keep quiet for long.

"Still a school night, and besides, it's not Amber, is it?"

She smiled. "Not so much."

"Then who?"

"Devon, okay? It's Devon," Eileen grumbled to herself as she finished off her cookie and grabbed another one. "But it's not like I was trying to sneak out to see him. I wanted him to come over here where you could interrogate him and humiliate me. See the trust I have in you?"

"Touching. Truly." And it went without saying that she *would* be interrogating good ol' Devon at the first opportunity.

Eileen sighed and pouted. At the same time. "You're my aunt. You're supposed to be the fun one who spoils me."

"Uh-huh," Maggie said, folding up the cookie bag before she could eat another one herself. Yes, since she'd gotten all the Fae power dumped into her system, her metabolism had been excellent. But why push the envelope?

"You know I love you, sweetie," Maggie said. "But when it comes to boys and you? Nobody's the 'fun' one."

"My life sucks," Eileen complained.

"I hear that," Bezel seconded.

"What's for dinner?" Maggie demanded.

Bezel sniffed. "Torkian beast."

Maggie frowned. "What?"

"Think roast beef but better."

He always said that. Like everything in Otherworld was superior to Earth. He even insisted their version of hell, *Ifreann*, was scarier. But Maggie had her doubts. She'd been to weekend religious classes when she was a kid. She'd been taught by nuns, and nobody did hell better than Catholics.

"Is it endangered?" Eileen asked.

Bezel laughed and the sound was like a dry paper towel against cloth. Raspy and irritating.

"*Ifreann* take me," he admitted. "For humans, you're pretty entertaining."

"Aunt Maggie's not all human anymore," Eileen reminded him. "And she's Queen."

Bezel's gaze moved over her paint-stained jeans, green-streaked hair and spattered hands. "Yeah. I'm getting that royal vibe."

"And, I'm not *all* human, either," Eileen reminded him proudly. "I'm part-Fae, too."

Which brought Maggie back once more to thoughts of the grandfather she'd just found out was alive and well and living in Otherworld. When she told Nora about him, her sister was going to want to search for GrandFae and Maggie wasn't sure that was a good idea. After all, they might not have guessed that he was still around, but she was betting he had known about *them*. Which made her wonder just why the hell he'd never come around.

"It's ready!" Bezel announced, and jumped off his stool, carrying his platter of, Maggie had to admit, great-smelling roast Torkian. So she put off thoughts of her grandfather in favor of a hot meal she hadn't had to cook herself.

God knew, there'd be plenty of time later to worry.

❧

A few hours later, Culhane shifted into Maggie's bedroom and went perfectly still. Moonlight speared through the window and lay across his sleeping Queen in a silvery caress. Her hair spilled around her head like a dark red halo. Her lashes made soft half circles on her pale cheeks. Her mouth was curved as if she were enjoying her dream, and that made Culhane smile as well.

Her dreams would soon bring her more enjoyment than she would have thought possible. Three long strides took him to the side of her bed. He sat down gingerly on the edge of the mattress, then reached out with one hand to gently brush a lock of hair from her forehead. She stirred, shifting position, pulling the sheet down from her shoulders. Culhane's gaze locked on her breasts—full, ripe and hidden from him by nothing more than the sheer fabric of her nightgown. He wanted to lift it from her, bare her skin to his gaze. But that would wake her and he wanted her to sleep deeply. Tipping his head to one side, he quietly studied her and felt a powerful surge of desire grip him. Years he'd waited for her.

At first, she'd been nothing more than a random prophecy he'd found in an ancient scroll. But he had believed and held on to the promise of her in his darker hours. Then she was a girl. A part-Fae girl who touched his heart when he'd thought it long dead. Finally, she was Maggie, his Queen. She'd defeated Mab, come into the power that had been foretold and now she was, for him, the One.

The one woman, mortal or Fae, who could bring the mighty Culhane to his knees.

She sighed in her sleep and he leaned over her, his face just inches from hers. She still had no idea just what she was. How much she was becoming. The moonlight was soft and a breath of wind slipped beneath the partially opened window. It was cold and carried the scent of coming rain. Maggie, unaware of his presence, slept on, lost in her dreams.

All around him, the house was silent, as if the building itself had taken a breath and held it. She was alone in the house, he knew. He sensed it. Her friend Claire—the woman McCulloch spent too much time lusting after—wasn't there, though in the last few weeks, she had been spending more time here than not. Maggie's family was in the house at the back of the yard and even Bezel was tucked away in his tree.

This moment was *theirs*. His and Maggie's. Even if she didn't realize it. If she wouldn't allow his touch when she was awake, he would stir her soul, her mind, her body, in her sleep.

Should he have been ashamed of intruding on her dreams? He wasn't. He would do what he must to bring her to him. To show her what it would be like when they came together. As it was meant. "You will feel me, Maggie," he whispered. "Your dream will become reality."

Then he laid his hand to the side of her head, closed his eyes, focused, and built her dreams.

Maggie knew she was dreaming, but still she sighed as Culhane's hand cupped her breast; then that sigh became a groan when his skillful fingers tugged and pulled gently at her hardened nipple. Her center went hot and wet and needy and she whispered his name, turning into his touch.

"Culhane . . ."

"I'm here, Maggie. With you. Always with you." He bent his head and took first one hard, sensitive nipple into his mouth, and then the other.

She whimpered, arching into him, in need, needing so much. His hands slid over her skin and in the moonlight, his green eyes glittered silver as he lifted his head to meet her gaze. There was want stamped on his features. A hunger deeper than any she'd seen on his face before. A need so deep, so rich, she quivered at the thought of fulfilling it.

But this is what she wanted, too. She wanted him inside her. Wanted to forget what had brought them together. What threatened to tear them apart. She wanted only the touch of him. The slide of his skin on hers. The silken glide of his long, black hair against her heated body. The taste of his mouth. The thick, hot length of him, buried deep within her.

She wanted it all.

Now.

"Take me," she whispered, cupping his face in her palms. "Please, Culhane, take me."

"I want nothing more," he vowed, and slid down along her body, hands exploring, mouth trailing hot, damp kisses on her skin.

She called out his name again and lifted her hips from the bed, demanding fulfillment, but he ignored that maneuver and instead, tortured her slowly. With more kisses. Each caress was a testament to his strength and her hunger. Her skin flamed, her blood boiled and still she hungered. Still she needed.

His mouth moved lower, down, over her abdomen, across her thighs, and then to the very heart of her. Maggie felt his breath on her most sensitive flesh and held her own breath while she waited, praying, hoping that he would end the torment and give her what she so desperately needed.

Then he took her, his mouth closing over her center.

She jolted, moaned his name aloud and moved into him, lifting herself for him, fisting her hands in the sheets beneath her so that she wouldn't slide off the edge of the world.

His lips and tongue worked her, moving over her, in her, tasting, seducing, licking. His breath brushed her skin, his hands cupped her behind, lifting her higher, holding her off the bed, his fingers kneading her flesh even as his mouth took her places she'd never been. Never thought to be.

Maggie felt as if her whole body were alight, sparkling somehow with an inner brilliance that was spilling through her system, engulfing her, claiming her.

Then he pulled back, drawing away from her, leaving her body pulsing, humming, screaming for the release that was so close, that even in her dream, Maggie could sense it.

"No, don't stop, Culhane. Don't leave me like this. . . ."

"Come to me, Maggie," he whispered, his mouth beside her ear now, his breath sliding across her cheek. "Come to me and I will make you scream my name. Together, we will share pleasures so rich, so deep, neither of us will be whole without the other ever again."

"Now," she pleaded, and hated the whine in her own

voice. But she ached for him. And he was already gone.
Slipping from her dream as easily as he'd arrived.

Maggie knew the moment he left her, because she
felt a chill and the light within her flickered briefly, then
whiffed out. As if a candle had been snuffed. As if a
freaking power plant had been hit by a rocket and been
completely destroyed.

"Culhane?" Jolting upright in bed, Maggie pushed
her hair out of her eyes and fought for breath. Whipping
her head from side to side, she searched the shadows for
any sign of Culhane. Had it really been a dream? Or had
he actually been in the room, doing those things to her,
and it had only been her own brain making her believe
in the dream?

A dream. That was all it was. Which meant, she
thought, that now her own body was torturing her.

"Just perfect," she muttered, and flopped down again.
Staring up at the moonlit ceiling, Maggie waited for
dawn, sure she wouldn't be sleeping any more that
night.

Outside her window, Culhane watched her. And
smiled.

&

Two days later, Maggie got home late. She'd done five
windows, killed a demon who'd sneaked up on her when
she was painting Tina's Knit and Yarn Shop, and then
had ended her day with a parking ticket. She was covered in streaks of brightly colored tempera paint, her
back ached and she was so hungry she was willing to
fight Sheba for a cupful of kibble.

That's when her day went from bad to crappy in the
blink of an eye.

"Finally!" Nora flung the door open, reached out to
the front porch, grabbed Maggie's arm and dragged her
into the house. Nora let go just as quickly, looked down
at the smudges of white paint on her own palm and said,

"Jeez, do you not wash the paint off you when you finish a job?"

Since Maggie was covered in paint and Nora was boasting a tiny smear, she couldn't work up an apology. "What's going on?"

"You'll never believe it," Nora said. "I even called Madame Star to tell her and she was surprised. She hadn't seen this coming at *all*."

Since Madame Star was Nora's favorite psychic and couldn't "see" her own tush, Maggie wasn't entirely surprised by this revelation.

"See what? What're you talking about and can it wait until I've had a shower at least?" Maggie plucked a strand of hair from the side of her face and shifted her gaze to examine it. "I've got globs of green paint in my hair, thanks to that stupid demon scaring me, and the paint's hardening as we speak."

"No, this can't wait." Nora's eyes were sparkling and a grin kept tugging at one corner of her mouth. "It's too exciting. Now come on; he's in the kitchen."

"He? He who?"

But Maggie didn't get an answer as Nora headed off at a trot, clearly expecting her sister to follow. Which, of course, Maggie did, albeit more slowly and cautiously. As she got closer to the kitchen, she heard voices rising and falling and then Eileen's laughter. She could pick out her niece, and Bezel. But there was a new voice in the mix. Male. And despite the hopeful leap of her heart that it might be Culhane, she knew right away it wasn't. This was a voice she didn't recognize.

So Maggie braced herself, just in case a glamoured-up demon had infiltrated the house.

Following Nora into the familiar room, ready for whatever the strange new life she was living might throw at her, Maggie's gaze swept the scene in an instant. Eileen and then Nora, at the table, laughing as the golden chrysanthemums in the vase on the table swayed and dipped on their own, as if dancing to music only the blossoms could hear. Then there was Bezel, standing off to one side, his long, spidery fingers dug into Sheba's fur, holding the golden retriever in place as the ancient, ugly pixie stared daggers at the stranger sitting at the table with Maggie's family.

The stranger looked about thirty-five. He had dark red hair, shining blue eyes and a wide, laughing mouth. He was waving his fingertips at the flowers, clearly orchestrating their magical dance, but he stopped short when he spotted Maggie. Grinning, he stood up, spread his arms wide as if expecting her to rush into an embrace, which so wasn't happening, and announced, "There's my granddaughter. The Queen. Don't you have a kiss for your grandFae?"

"Can you believe it, Mags?" Nora asked from her spot at the table. She was watching their grandfather with stars in her eyes and even Eileen looked completely taken with the man. "Our grandfather's *alive*."

"And making flowers dance. BFD," Bezel muttered.

The stranger ignored that remark and winked at Maggie. "Of course I'm alive. Immortal, remember?"

"He just showed up," Bezel muttered. "Shifted in out of nowhere."

Maggie nodded, but couldn't look away from the Fae in front of her. She hadn't had a chance yet to tell Nora about their grandfather. Every time she'd tried to in the last couple of days, Nora had been sick to her stomach or had been arguing with Quinn over some damn thing or other, so she'd put it off. Thinking she had time. After all, it wasn't as if good ol' gramps had bothered to check in at all over the years. She hadn't considered the possibility of him showing up *now*.

Although clearly she should have.

Silence stretched out in the kitchen until it was almost a live thing, pulsing out around them. As if everyone in the room were holding their breath, waiting to see Maggie's reaction.

Well, hell. She didn't know what to think.

There he stood. The guy who seduced Gran so long ago in Ireland. This was the Fae who'd started their line, then never once in all these years bothered to stop by to see if they were alive. This was the guy who'd made it possible for her to be the freaking Queen.

Maggie was in no mood to thank him for *that*.

"You knew." Nora's voice suddenly sliced through the quiet. The scrape of her chair legs against the wood floor sounded like a scream. "You knew we still had a grandfather and you didn't tell me."

Maggie kept her gaze fixed on the newcomer, but said, "I meant to."

"Great," Nora snapped. "You *meant* to tell me about Jasic—"

"Jasic?"

He bowed slightly.

"And Quinn *meant* to tell me that he deliberately gave me a boy baby so he could raise him to be a warrior. But nobody *actually* tells me anything."

Finally, Maggie turned a quick look on her sister. "A warrior baby?" she asked, her mind instantly filling with the image of a sword-wielding baby sliding from the womb, then shook her head. Not the time. "I'm sorry, okay? I did mean to tell you. Culhane only told me a few days ago, but—"

"Ah yes, Culhane the Mighty," Jasic whispered.

Maggie's head whipped around and she pinned him with a hard look. "You know him?"

"I know of him," Jasic said, examining his fingernails as if trying to read a foreign language. "We don't mix in the same circles."

Bezel snorted.

Jasic's lip curled at the sound.

"You should have told me, Maggie," Nora said, more quietly now. "He's *family*."

More than temper, there was hurt in Nora's voice and Maggie cringed to hear it.

"I'm sorry, Nor. Really. But"—she looked at her grandFae again— "why are you here?"

"To meet my family, of course," he said, waving both arms expansively. "I would have come sooner, but I didn't want to intrude."

"Sooner," Maggie repeated, and thought to herself, *You've had more than thirty years to drop by. Why now?* And all of a sudden intruding was okay? What had changed? What had motivated this surprise visit? Why was she so suspicious of a Fae she'd never seen before?

"Of course," he told her, moving out from the table to walk across the room toward her. His smile was wide and bright, his eyes shining with sincerity and his arms were open, still inviting an embrace she hadn't given him.

"You're the Queen now, Maggie," he soothed, his voice nearly musical. "I didn't want to be in the way. I thought to wait until you had settled in before ... reacquainting myself with my loved ones."

Loved ones. Maggie shot a look at Bezel and saw the pixie's eyes roll so far back in his head, they practically disappeared. She knew just how he felt. Jasic was smooth and charming and handsome, and Maggie didn't feel a thing toward him.

Should she, though? Weren't feelings for family grown and nurtured? Should you really be able to meet a stranger, think, "Oh, he's my grandfather," and turn on the affection? She didn't think so.

"Isn't that wonderful?" Nora said, sniffling a little as she wiped away a stray tear. "So thoughtful. Putting you first, Mags. He's been so brave. And so lonely."

Jasic's features slid easily into a sorrowful expression as he wrapped Maggie in a hug she didn't feel completely comfortable with.

While he held her, Nora kept talking. "He didn't come back before, because he didn't want to upset Gran and Grandpa's marriage. And then when they were gone, he saw that we were fine, so he didn't want to upset us."

"A real giver," Bezel muttered.

Again, Maggie had to agree, but couldn't really say so, since her face was currently buried in her grandFae's shirtfront. She and Nora hadn't been fine, after all. Nora had been married to a bona fide creep and Maggie had been struggling with her own sense of loneliness. No family nearby until Nora had divorced and moved home. If Jasic had shown up then, she might have welcomed him as he so clearly expected to be now.

But things were different these days. She had more company than she knew what to do with and a grandFae showing up out of nowhere was really more trouble than blessing.

Boy, she wished her best friend, Claire, were around. A psychic and a witch, Claire might have been able to get a vision telling Maggie exactly what Jasic wanted. But was there ever a witch around when you needed one? No. So she'd have to handle this situation on her own.

Jasic patted Maggie's back as she tried to pull free.

"He came now," Nora was saying as she walked to join them, "because he wants to know us. To be part of our family. He's tired of being alone, Maggie."

Jasic lifted one arm to draw Nora close, too. He held them both as Nora finished.

"He thinks Gran would have wanted him to be with us."

Maybe, but they'd never know for sure, would they? Maggie managed to squirm free and then stepped away from the group hug before Nora could start singing "Kum ba yah" or something. Maggie idly wondered whether she would have been this cynical a few weeks ago, then assured herself that yes, she would have been. Why was Jasic tired of being alone *now*?

Could it possibly be because his granddaughter was the Queen? Maybe he had hopes for a nice retirement or whatever in the palace? A quiet, more reasonable voice in her head asked, did it matter? Would it kill her to be nice? To help him out? No, she told herself, it wouldn't. But she couldn't help wondering why Grand-Fae was all of a sudden so lonesome for family.

"Um, Aunt Maggie?" Eileen's voice was quiet, hesitant. "Jasic—he said I could call him that—knows lots of stuff about Great-Gran and Otherworld, and he said he could help Mom and me get used to things over there, since we'll probably be there a lot now that Quinn wants Mom to stay there until she has the baby and all and—"

Maggie took an instinctive breath, as always impressed with just how many thoughts Eileen could cram into one sentence.

"I'm not moving to Otherworld," Nora said, easing away from Jasic to face Maggie. "Quinn can't force me to, can he? I mean, you're his Queen and everything. . . ."

"Force? Quinn? Otherworld?" Maggie felt as though she'd been dropped into a conversation that had been going on for hours. Nothing was making sense.

Jasic chuckled and Maggie scowled. She'd been working all day, had come home to get sideswiped by a grandfather she'd never known and now Quinn wanted to kidnap Nora to Otherworld? *Again?*

Just a couple of weeks ago, Quinn Terhune, Fae Warrior, had swept Nora off to Otherworld—at Culhane's orders—to force Maggie to fight and defeat Queen Mab. Weeks had gone by in Faery time while only a couple of days had passed here, but the point was, Nora had been Quinn's prisoner—though she had come back happy and pregnant—and Maggie wasn't going to allow that to happen again.

"What're you taking about?" she asked, despite the headache currently setting up shop behind her right eye.

Nora jammed her hands at her hips. "Quinn thinks it would be safer for me to be at his place in Faeryland until I have the baby, but I don't want to go."

"So don't," Maggie told her, and idly scratched at the drying paint on her forearm. "He can't make you and if he tries, I'll stop him." She wasn't sure how yet, but being Queen had to have some advantages, right?

"See?" Jasic cooed, giving Nora a comforting pat. "As I told you. The Queen will not allow your warrior to abduct you."

"Good," Nora said. "That's good."

"Great." Maggie moved away from all of them, stepping back into the hall. She really needed some space. Both physical and mental. She wasn't at all sure how she felt about Jasic showing up and she needed some time to think about it. "Now, I'm going to go take a shower and maybe have dinner."

"Fine," Jasic told her, still smiling that wide, I'm-so-wonderful-don't-you-just-love-me smile. "We'll be here."

Maggie sighed. There wouldn't be any relaxing after dinner, then. Shifting a look to Bezel, she asked, "What're we having tonight?"

Bezel snorted and slid a furious glance at Jasic. "Your Fae grandfather wouldn't let me cook."

"Of course not. Pixie food?" Jasic shuddered. "Surely we can do better than that. I'll get something at a local restaurant."

"Not like I *enjoy* cooking for a bunch of humans, you know. I'll be in my tree if you need me." Bezel shifted in place, disappearing in an insulted huff.

And Maggie, as much as Bezel annoyed her, was feeling surprisingly protective of the ugly little guy. "Bezel's a good cook."

"He's a pixie," her grandFae explained. "We don't

really . . . associate with his kind." Then he backpedaled, clearly noting the less-than-pleased expression on Maggie's face. "Of course, there are exceptions," he said smoothly. "I'm sure Bissel has been very helpful."

"Bezel," Eileen pointed out before Maggie could.

"Of course. But for now," Jasic urged, turning Maggie around and giving her a push down the hall, "why don't you clean up and I'll take care of my girls tonight?"

She hadn't taken two steps out of the room before the chatter rose up again. Jasic's laughter. Nora's happy chuckle. Eileen's excited questions.

His girls. Funny, Maggie thought as she headed toward the zigzag stairs. He hadn't cared about *his* girls until one of them turned up wearing a crown. But whatever, Maggie told herself as she headed up the series of tiny steps that led to her bedroom. She'd figure out what to do about Jasic later.

Laughter followed her down the hall, niggling at the back of her brain. It seemed that Nora and Eileen had already decided to accept Jasic at face value. But then, they could. They didn't have to worry about conspiracies and coincidences and rogue Fae and maybe a grand-Fae who wasn't what he claimed to be.

They weren't the Queen.

Chapter Five

Culhane gathered his most trusted warriors for a meeting within the walls of the palace.

He looked at the five, sliding his gaze from one familiar, steely face to the next. McCulloch, Quinn, Riley, Muldoon and O'Hara. These warriors had been with him for eons and had fought at his side in innumerable battles. Though all of the Fae Warriors were his brothers in arms, these few he would trust with his life. With Maggie's life.

And so he was.

"The Dullahan are indeed riding again," he said, remembering the full report McCulloch had delivered only hours ago. His insides fisted, not with fear, but determination. The rogue Fae—even now planning an assault on the walls of their frozen prison, and from there an escape to the mortal world—could not be allowed to succeed.

"And we stand here when we should be fighting?" Muldoon demanded, looking at his fellow warriors, eager to be off.

"We meet here first," Culhane told him shortly. "To decide the best way to proceed."

"What says the Queen?" O'Hara spoke up, bracing his fists at his hips and tossing his long black hair back from his face.

"The Queen doesn't know about this."

Quinn cleared his throat uneasily, but Culhane watched the faces of the other men. Though it didn't matter what they thought of his decision, he would rather have their agreement before they faced the Dullahan. And though he knew Quinn felt that Maggie should be told—probably because he was in love with Maggie's sister and dreaded the drama once this truth was known, he also knew Quinn would support him.

Culhane wasn't going to involve Maggie in this until it was absolutely necessary. She already dreaded the responsibilities of the throne. To throw an uprising at her now would only undermine his efforts to bring her full-time into Otherworld. He had to manage that soon. Since the night he'd joined her in her dreams, he'd been walking the ragged edge of control. He needed her with him. Needed her to decide to become what they both knew she was destined for.

So as her chief warrior, he would stop this insurrection before it could gain strength and take care of the Queen's business. As he'd been doing for centuries for Mab. He knew what he was about—and hadn't this been his plan from the beginning? Get Maggie on the throne and rule at her side? Ease her into ruling by showing her how it was to be done?

Certainly, once she found out about this, she would thank him for his diligence.

"Maggie is in the human world, with worries of her own," he told his men. "There's no need to trouble her with this. The Dullahan are still trapped in Casia and we will remove the threat before they escape. Put it down completely. Then I will inform her of what we've done."

Muldoon shifted uneasily. "You have my allegiance, Culhane, as always. But she is the Queen. We serve at her command."

"Is he not the Chieftain here?" Quinn spoke up, anger flashing in his eyes and vibrating in every inch of his large frame. "Do we sit back and ask the females what we are to do when our duty lies stretched out before us so that even a blind man could choose his path?"

"She is *Queen*," O'Hara countered in a calm, deliberate voice.

"She is not here," Riley pointed out companionably.

"I do this not to strip Maggie of power," Culhane told them all, walking a small, tight circle around them, looking at each of them in turn, "but to show her she has our loyalty. That we stand at her back, ready to defend— even when she cannot be here."

There were mutterings, but then one of them nodded and soon enough, the others joined. Quinn looked ready for a fight; the warrior fairly bristled with impatience. Clearly, he wished to work out his frustrations with his woman on the battlefield. Culhane knew the others would fight as well. They would stand with him, do as he ordered and quell this uprising before it reached the walls of Otherworld and beyond.

The Dullahan would be broken and resigned once again to remain in Casia, their cold, frozen prison. Even if Culhane had to fight each of the damn things himself.

"Now, who fights with me?" He asked the question in a low, controlled voice that rumbled through the crystalline halls of the palace like a challenge.

As one, the five Fae Warriors slapped one hand to the hilts of their swords.

"We do," they said together, and Culhane nodded.

"Then we go now." He shifted, knowing his friends, his brothers, would rematerialize right beside him.

*

The worst thing about your birthday being December 26? Maggie sighed. It wasn't the whole Merry Christmas– Happy Birthday–present thing. It was having to go to the DMV in December.

The Department of Motor Vehicles was a trip into

the seventh level of hell *anytime*. But in December, people were crabbier than usual, less patient, more harried and in no way happy to be there.

"Deck the halls with thoughts of suicide," Maggie sung just under her breath as she shuffled forward another half inch.

It wasn't as if she had all kinds of extra time to devote to this place. And she hadn't arrived in a good mood, either. Since the night before, when Jasic had appeared in their lives, it had seemed as if her life was unraveling even more than usual. She checked her wristwatch. Already she'd been in line for two hours and she felt as if her feet had become rooted to the dirty, scarred linoleum.

Hundreds of people muttered and grumbled in long lines that snaked and wandered through the building until their constant, low-voiced complaints sounded like white noise. Probably for the best, she told herself, since that rumble of sound drowned out the Muzak version of "Rudolph the Red-Nosed Reindeer." One more Christmas carol in this place and Maggie was liable to—well, she couldn't think of anything dire enough—but it would probably be pretty damn impressive.

A baby cried, an old man coughed so hard Maggie was sure he was hacking up a lung and from somewhere behind her, a woman sneezed like a million times in a row. Goodie. If she ever got out of here, she'd probably leave with the plague. She was going to have to take a bath in her antibacterial lotion just to scrub off all the cooties.

Plus, she thought with yet another glance at her watch, she was hungry. Crabby and hungry and her feet hurt. Not a good combination.

She huffed out a breath and let her gaze slide around the building. There were plastic holly garlands hanging from the ceiling and, sitting on a counter, an artificial, three-foot-tall, white Christmas tree with half of its lights burned out. A couple of the clerks wore sad, limp, Santa hats, and the scent of burned coffee and too many people lay over the room like a thick fog.

Maggie was *thrilled* to be standing in line to renew her driver's license, because what better place to spend an afternoon? With such an exciting slice of humanity? Yes, she could have taken care of this by mail if she had remembered to send in the damn paperwork. But between becoming Queen of the Faeries and having to defend herself against demons every time she turned around, paperwork sort of got pushed to the side.

"Crap," the woman behind her muttered as she gave Maggie a solid-enough nudge to send her stumbling into the guy in front of her.

"Sorry, sorry," Maggie said when the big guy glanced at her with a scowl; then she turned around to look at the woman who was really crowding into Maggie's personal bubble. At first glance, the woman was fiftyish with straggly gray hair, hard blue eyes and crumbs on her T-shirt. At second glance, she was some kind of demon. The flash of red in those bored eyes gave it away.

"Big deal," she said with a sniff. "The Queen. You don't look so tough."

"Oh, fabulous," Maggie muttered. Even here? In line at the DMV? "Just what I needed to make this day complete."

"Yeah, I'm not real happy about being this close to you, either," the woman snapped. "I've got a blister and my back hurts and I've been in this damn line so long, I'm about ready to *beg* you to blow some dust on me and finish me off."

All it took for Maggie to kill a demon was concentrating hard enough to focus the Fae dust that was now a part of her into a steady stream to blow at whatever demon was threatening her at the time. A little Fae dust and boom! Demon explodes, dust everywhere. "Hmmm . . ."

The woman's eyes went wide. "Never mind," she blurted just before she sprinted out of line, apparently rethinking that last complaint.

Maggie watched her go and knew that no one else there would see the woman for what she was. People saw exactly what the Fae wanted them to see, which was creepy when you thought about it, because *anything* could be sneaking up on you and you wouldn't have a clue. Why, if the rogue Fae that Culhane was always warning her about actually took it into their heads to invade this world, the humans wouldn't have a clue what was happening. And the enemy wouldn't even have to come in swinging swords. Hell, they could sneakily infiltrate and take over from the inside. Glamour themselves as politicians . . . hmmm.

That thought could explain a lot of what went on in Washington DC.

A sudden draft of cold settled over Maggie, making her shiver and look around for whatever was causing it. There wasn't a draft and the air-conditioning wasn't turned on, so where was the cold air coming from? The temperature continued to drop, though it looked like only she felt it, despite the fact that her upper and lower teeth were clicking against each other so loudly, it sounded as though she had a set of castanets in her mouth.

But the cold was more than just icy. It was desperate. Lonely. Heartbroken. Her body sagged beneath the weight of the onslaught of despair and *that's* when she realized what was going on.

There had to be a Gray Man nearby.

God! Had every demon and Fae in Otherworld waited until she was trapped in this endless line to come and make a try for her?

Maggie's stomach knotted and fear, thick and sludgy, pumped through her veins. She'd seen a lot of creepy things since discovering this whole new world a few weeks ago. But the Gray Man was way up there on the creep factor ladder.

A rogue Fae, the Gray Man was mist. Fog. Long, snaking tendrils of icy sensation that sapped away any hope or joy or happiness a person had, eating away at their souls like acid dripped onto bone. They reveled in the despair they caused and sucked whatever light they could from their victims before leaving them empty husks. Soulless humans who would never again smile or feel or love.

Shivering, Maggie scrubbed her hands up and down her arms and slid her gaze around the milling people. He was watching her and when she spotted him, he smiled.

To anyone else, he looked like an elderly bookworm. A round, bald head, wire-rimmed glasses and an ill-fitting suit with a lopsided bow tie. His glamour reeked of innocence, vulnerability. Which no doubt helped him in trapping prey.

The line inched forward again. Maggie had only five people in front of her now. She should be at the counter by March.

"What're you doing here?" she asked, glaring at the Gray Man in disguise.

"Came to see you," he said, and when he spoke, the temperature dropped again. Damn it.

She couldn't exactly blow Fae dust on him to kill him. He *was* Fae. She could have used the nifty trick of shooting lightning bolts out of her fingertips, but that would probably be noticed here at the Department of Motor Hell. So instead, she glared at him, gave him her best, I-am-Queen-so-back-the-hell-off stare and said, "Go away. Can't you see I'm busy?"

"I know you killed one of us," he said in a whisper of sound.

Yeah, she had. A couple of weeks ago. Down by the lighthouse, and it hadn't been easy. But she'd done it, with those lightning bolts that she really wished she could let loose right about now.

Maggie leaned over and said in a hushed tone, "He came after me and if you don't get lost, I'll give you the same right here."

"We're going to kill you," he said, and finally, the guy in front of Maggie reacted. He jerked a look at the Gray Man, looked like he might bolt, then changed his mind, unwilling to give up his place in line. She so understood.

"You know what," Maggie said with a sigh, suddenly tired of all the nuttiness surrounding her. "If you're gonna kill me, just do it already. Anything's gotta be better than spending the rest of my freaking life in *line*."

"Step away from the Queen." A new voice. Commanding. And completely female.

"What?" Maggie looked to her left. A tall woman in jeans and a black sweater walked up. She had a hard look in her silver eyes and her waist-length brown hair was pulled back in a ponytail from her sharp, elegant face. Fae. Those silver eyes were a dead giveaway, even if the woman hadn't been tall and gorgeous.

"Hey," the Gray Man protested with a glare, "I didn't do anything to her. Though I could. I'm just standing here."

"Stand somewhere else," the woman said, and waited until the bookish looking little Fae backed away and wandered off somewhere.

Poor bastard would now have to go to the end of the meandering line and probably wouldn't get to the counter before summer.

"Thanks," she said to the Fae. "But what're you doing here?"

"Majesty," the woman said, with a bow of her head.

"Cut that out, okay?" Maggie hissed the order, hoping no one else had heard the whole majesty thing.

The Fae female frowned, then glanced around at the

people crowding the old building. "You should not be unprotected. Where is your warrior?"

Apparently, gossip was alive and well in Otherworld as much as it was here. There was no doubt in Maggie's mind that the woman was referring to Culhane. But talking about him as if he were a toy poodle on a leash was so out-there, Maggie almost laughed. If Culhane *were* to be a pet, he'd be more like a Rottweiler.

"I'm just fine on my own, thanks, and besides, Culhane's not *my* warrior and"—Maggie looked at her—"who're you?"

"Forgive me." The elegant brunette dressed like a biker chick inclined her head again. "I am Ailish, secondary commander in your guard."

Guard. The palace guard. The female security force who used to work for Mab and who now worked for Maggie. She didn't really know any of them very well and couldn't remember having seen Ailish before. But then she hadn't actually spent much time with the Fae females, since she spent as little time as possible in Otherworld altogether. And in spite of everything, a small twist of guilt tugged at her insides.

She hated to admit, even to herself, that Culhane was right, but she did have commitments in the Fae world and she should be paying closer attention to them. Especially since every Fae and demon in the world seemed to be seeking her out for a little one-on-one time. Which, at the moment, made Maggie really glad to see one of her personal guards show up. With Ailish at her side, fewer demons and Fae would be willing to bother her.

Still, she had to ask. "What're you doing here?"

The line inched forward. Hallelujah. One less person between Maggie and freedom.

"I came to speak to you on behalf of my sisters," Ailish began, keeping her voice low enough that even the guy in the next line making eyes at her would have had a hard time hearing. "We want you to know that we're happy guarding the palace."

"Oh, that's good." Maggie nodded, pleased to hear that at least *one* faction in Otherworld was happy enough.

"But we want more."

And, here we go, Maggie thought tiredly.

"We want to fight," Ailish whispered.

"You already do, don't you?"

Ailish frowned and waved one hand as if dismissing anything they had done to date. "We do, when our Queen or the palace is in danger. Small skirmishes all, though we have been trained for generations to be worthy of more. We do appreciate that you, Majesty, are much easier to serve than Mab. The former queen could be quite the—"

"Bitch?" Maggie offered.

Ailish smiled and nodded. "As you say."

"Well, thanks for saying I'm better than Mab, anyway." She smiled and moved forward again. Only two more people ahead of her. Barring earthquake, fire or swarms of locusts, she might just make it to the counter and live through the day.

"Oh, you are better," Ailish said. "That is why we come to you with a request." She lifted her chin and waited until Maggie's attention was fully on her again before continuing. "We wish to be warriors. We want to take our rightful place in the Warrior clan. We are good fighters all, and only the females can fly. We could be a help in major battles."

"True," Maggie said thoughtfully. If nothing else, Ailish was helping distract her from the misery of being in line. But she was also making Maggie think. Why wouldn't the males be happy to have some *flying* warriors added into the mix? Seemed like a great idea to her. A little aerial combat could really come in handy in a big fight.

Ailish frowned at a man as he moved in too close to her and he instantly scuttled backward. Looking to Maggie again, she said, "The warriors refuse to have us. But if the declaration came from their Queen, they would have no choice but to accept us as sisters."

Well, Maggie had known going in that there was unrest in Otherworld. Hadn't Culhane told her even before her battle with Mab that the males were treated as second-class citizens—but for the warriors? He'd told her that a war was brewing between the males and females and that it would be her job to prevent a civil war. She'd been avoiding the whole problem by avoiding sitting on her throne too often.

Yes, that made her sound like a big coward and in a way, she was willing to admit that's exactly what she was. Maggie didn't know the first thing about being a queen. About ruling an entire *world*. What if she made the wrong decision? What if something she did only worsened an already bad situation? But if she was going to be Queen—and frankly, she hadn't found a loophole yet, so it looked as though she was stuck with the job— then maybe it was time to start making those tough decisions and just trust her instincts. Do the best she could with what she had.

Isn't that all anyone could do?

"You know what, Ailish?" Maggie said thoughtfully as she prepared to make her first major proclamation as Queen. She knew damn well Culhane wasn't going to be happy about this, but he'd simply have to deal. "You're right. You guys would be a good addition to the Warriors."

The Fae woman's face lit up and a brilliant smile crossed her face. "My Queen, if you allow this, you will earn the eternal loyalty of your palace guard. We will fight to the end of time to protect you," she said, her voice getting louder and more vehement. "Your slightest wish will be seen to. You will have our devotion, our allegiance, our—"

"I get it," Maggie interrupted, with a wary look around her. Ailish was so excited now, she was beginning to draw stares from the crowd. "I'll talk to Culhane about this as soon as—"

Ailish's smile disappeared. "The Chieftain will not approve," she said.

Oh, Maggie knew that better than anyone. And she wasn't really looking forward to the argument she was sure would be coming. Still, if she was going to do this, she was going to have to start somewhere. Might as well be with this decision.

"Yes, but he's not Queen, is he?" Maggie said.

The line moved again and she thought, *A miracle!* Only the one man ahead of her and she could sign her papers and get out of there. Her stomach rumbled and she silently promised it a giant cookie from Carrie Hanover's diner as soon as she was free of this miserable place.

"So you will decree this?" Ailish sounded as if she wanted to believe, but needed convincing. "I may tell my sisters that a change is coming?"

"Yeah," Maggie said, feeling powerful and generous. And it was a logical move as well. Why should they be wasting highly trained fighters? Why shouldn't they go into battle alongside the men if that's what they wanted? Worked for Israel's military.

"Tell them," Maggie said. "I'll get to Otherworld as soon as I can, talk to Culhane and then I'll make it official."

Ailish bowed deeply, then in a blink, shifted out of the DMV, leaving a few startled people shaking their heads and rubbing their eyes. Thankfully, since they were probably close to brain-dead from all the waiting, they would most likely convince themselves that they were simply seeing things. Maggie knew this because a few weeks ago, she would have done the same thing.

But then it was Maggie's turn at the counter and she

was so pleased, she didn't care what anyone else was thinking. She laid her paperwork down, leaned her forearms on the counter and looked into the eyes of a Fae wearing a red headband with a pinecone decoration stuck to the side of it.

"Oh, you've got to be kidding me," Maggie muttered. "Please tell me you actually work here and I don't have to go wait in another line."

"Of course I work here," the Fae snapped irritably. Her glamour was that of a sixty-something woman with frown lines carved deeply into her cheeks. Her silver eyes looked tired and her lipstick was bleeding into the creases on her upper lip. "What? You think I'm just sitting here for my health?"

She picked up Maggie's paperwork, flipped through it, made a couple of notes and said, "Thirty-seven bucks. Cash, credit or check?"

"Cash," Maggie said, and counted out the money. Funny, she'd never really thought about the fact that maybe some Fae had to work for a living. She'd just assumed they all lived in Otherworld and only came over to this dimension for fun and games. She handed the money over. The woman took it with crabbed hands, gave back her change and when Maggie moved to take it, the Fae grabbed her hand and held on.

"Hey!"

"I'm Cree-An," she said, her voice low and fast.

"Cree-An?" Maggie flipped back through her memories and pulled out the nugget of information she needed. Culhane had told her about these guys. "Oh yeah. You guys are death screamers. Like banshee, right?"

The Fae snorted. "The Cree-An are *nothing* like those Irish howlers. But not the point," she said. "And not what I wanted to talk to you about. I just want to warn you that you're in danger."

"*Duh.*" Maggie stared at her for a long moment. "Just since I've been here, I've been bugged by a stray demon and a Gray Man. Not like danger is a big surprise for me right now."

The Fae refused to release Maggie's hand. "I'm not talking about these rogue Fae or the pesky demons. . . ."

Pesky?

"I'm talking about Mab," she said, her grip on Maggie's hand tightening until it felt as if she were crushing the bones to powder.

Just the mention of the former queen's name made Maggie feel a little twitchy.

"Not like Mab's dead, you know. She's not. She's just out of the way. Doesn't mean she's gonna stay that way." The Fae leaned in closer, gave a quick glance around, then whispered, "Word is, some of the rogue Fae are planning on busting her out of that dimension and bringing her back into ours. They pull that off, you're the first one Mab's going after."

A sense of dread dropped into the pit of Maggie's stomach and felt like a couple hundred cold steel balls that rolled around clacking into one another. "Why are you bothering to warn me?"

"You did us a favor. Kept the banshee out of North America." She shuddered and released Maggie's hand. "They give me the solid creeps and that's a fact."

Amazing. One screaming harbinger of death put off by another. Well, it took all kinds.

"All I'm saying is, watch your back." Then she slid Maggie's paperwork toward her and said, "Here's your temporary renewal. You'll get the permanent one in a few weeks."

The Fae looked beyond her and shouted, "Next!" Then she slid one last glance at Maggie. "Oh, and Merry Christmas."

Ho ho ho.

Chapter Six

Casia had its own beauty.

Harsh and barren at first glance, there was also a stark grandeur to the continent at the far reaches of Other-world. Snow and ice ruled here, with vicious winds and churning seas battering at the land mass continuously. White-topped mountains speared into the sky and in the valleys below, the twin suns of the Fae dimension shone brilliantly down on the villages sprawled across the frozen landscape.

The worst of the rogue Fae lived here. Those who had, eons ago, sentenced themselves to an eternity of banishment. These Fae had committed crimes both against Otherworld and the mortal world and Mab herself had ordered their punishment. To be kept separate from the inhabitants of Otherworld by a shield of power. Here they lived out their eternities and for the most part, accepted their fates. Some had even, over eons, earned their way back into Fae society. But there were those who would never leave Casia. Those who were not to be trusted. Ever.

Like the Dullahan. They were the things of nightmares. The source of terrifying legends handed down through generations of humans and told over campfires, the Dullahan were interested only in destruction for the sheer, wild joy they derived from the act. They hunted, they killed and if given the chance, would only rain down misery on any creature in their path.

Culhane wiped blood from the blade of his sword and tossed his windblown hair out of his eyes to stare at Quinn when he materialized beside him. Already, the six Fae Warriors had battled the Dullahan for hours, but the beasts refused to be turned back. Instead, the creatures clung to the hope of escape.

Culhane had known that this would be a hard fight, but took only the five warriors with him because he'd believed that the Dullahan had only begun to foment their rebellion. But the beasts were greater in number than he had anticipated and he and his warriors had been forced to fight like madmen.

The howling, icy wind sliced into him as it pushed past, carrying away the nearly overpowering stench of blood that filled his nostrils. Culhane's blood was still pumping hard and his heart jolting in his chest. Flashes of recent memories staggered through his mind. The beasts swooping down at the warriors from out of the sky. The Dullahan's ability to fly had seriously hampered the warriors' efforts to quell the uprising. But they had evened out the odds by shifting in and out of position, appearing astride the beasts, and then below them.

The other denizens of Casia had kept to their homes, not wanting to be caught in the middle of the battle, which had been a lucky break for the warriors. In this icy prison, one inmate rarely considered risking his own neck for another. And the Dullahan had no friends among the Fae.

Thankfully. If the Dullahan had gotten any support from the others imprisoned here, the battle might have turned out differently.

"McCulloch?" Culhane demanded, needing to know how the other warriors had fared. The last time he'd seen McCulloch, the huge warrior had been hanging from the neck of a Dullahan in midflight, slicing at its throat with his blade.

"Well." Quinn turned his face into the bitter wind. "Mac shifted to safety before the beast fell." Then he glanced down at the fallen Dullahan lying around them. "It was a good fight."

"A hard one, but perhaps it will be enough to quell any burgeoning thoughts of uprisings," Culhane said, following his friend's gaze.

The enemy wasn't dead, he knew. But the beasts were broken. It would take some time for them to gather their strength before another attempt at a revolution.

Broken bodies of the beasts lay around them on the snow, blood staining the pristine white with a nearly obscene splatter. One or two of the wounded beasts screamed in pain and thrashed at the ground as if trying to escape their own broken bodies.

Eyes gritty with the blowing snow, Culhane studied them, mentally trying to find a way to describe them to Maggie. They were a bit like horses, he thought, though they were the size of small cars. Their coats weren't just black, but were the absolute absence of light. A black so deep it was as if midnight had turned in on itself, swallowing the very stars to become a darkness that devoured whatever it touched.

The beasts boasted huge, leathery wings with a span twice the size of their own bodies. When they flew in on an attack, the heavy thump of those wings against the air chilled the blood almost as much as a glimpse of the long, jagged teeth they used to tear the flesh of their prey. Dullahan hooves were sharp as knives and their strength . . . formidable.

Fatigue pulled at him. Culhane felt rivulets of blood trailing down his own body, and knew that the pains and aches shrieking in his bones would ease soon enough. For now, he had to gather his warriors, then make further plans. If the Dullahan revolted, there might be oth-

Beguiled 81

ers just biding their time, waiting for a chance to move on the Queen's forces. He needed to face Maggie with all of this. Make her see that now was the time to pick up her new responsibilities and embrace them.

"Have you seen the others?" Culhane shifted his gaze to the nearby village, where already the Fae who lived there were staggering outside to witness the damage done in the battle.

"Fine, all of them," Quinn said with a shrug of his broad shoulders. "O'Hara was burned when one of the bastards hit him with a stream of fire. But he will recover. Muldoon took a hoof down his back, but repaid the Dullahan in kind." He smiled grimly. "There's one of our enemies that won't be thinking of escape for quite some time."

"Good." The beast at his feet roared and stirred, as if trying to rise for another attack. Culhane leaped into action. Straddling the beast's neck, he grabbed hold of the long, matted mane and yanked its head around until he was staring into its flaming red eyes.

"Hear me," Culhane muttered, his voice deep, nearly lost in the moan of the rising wind, yet even more compelling because he refused to shout. "You've seen what a handful of warriors can do to your herd. Sow more seeds of rebellion against your Queen and I will bring the full force of the Warrior clan down on your heads."

The Dullahan shrieked, lunged, its huge teeth snapping shut mere inches from Culhane's leg. Then it struggled to pull away, refusing to give quarter even though it was grievously wounded. But Culhane held on, his grip tightening, his gaze locked on his prisoner's. "I am Culhane. You know of me?"

The beast's eyes wheeled and it shuddered in his grasp. "Good. Then tell your brothers. This ends here or you will all die. Immortal or not, the Warrior clan will slice your brethren into so many pieces, it will take centuries for the Dullahan to heal. You made your attempt," he added, giving the beast's head a push into the ground. "You failed. Continue on this path at your own peril."

Straightening up, fury still blazing in his eyes, he turned to look at Quinn. Seeing approval in his old friend's gaze, Culhane nodded grimly. "This task is done. Gather the others and let us leave this icy pit."

They shifted together as a group and the cold wind blew across their footprints in the snow, eradicating even the memory of their presence.

❧

"Nonsense, you've nothing to worry about. The Cree-An can't be trusted." Jasic gave his pronouncement as if speaking from the Mount. "Mab is in another dimension."

"Alive and pissed," Maggie pointed out, and Bezel, off to one side of her, nodded sagely.

She hadn't meant to discuss any of this with her grandFae, but he'd overheard Maggie talking to Bezel and had jumped in with his opinions. Actually, she thought, he seemed to be around a lot and spent most of his time listening in on other conversations. Curious? Or was there another reason for his interest? He didn't seem worried by the threat of Mab, but then, why should he be? It wasn't as if he had a target painted onto *his* back.

"Yes, alive," Jasic argued, and slid the pixie a dirty look, "but away."

"For now," Bezel said, facing the other Fae with his long fingers fisted at his sides. "You don't know what Maggie went through defeating the bitch."

Jasic's eyebrows arched before he gave Maggie a proud smile. "The point is she did beat her."

"No, the point is she coulda been squashed like a tree beetle."

"She wasn't, you irritating creature. And how dare you suggest that I would wish my granddaughter harm."

"That's just what you're doing if you're telling her not to worry about Mab."

Bezel was worried—and that made Maggie's spine twitch. If her resident pixie thought she was in trouble, Maggie was willing to bet he was right. She'd come home from the DMV, and found Bezel the only one there, since Nora was at her place napping and Eileen was at school. The pixie had spent the last couple of hours training Maggie.

He'd had her leaping and crouching and shadow-boxing and spinning all over the backyard like a crazy person. He'd made her practice the focusing ability necessary to blow Faery dust at an opponent so intensely that she was light-headed from all the deep breathing. The next hour, he'd had her work at sketching portals in the air. She was getting better at that, but she really wanted to learn how to shift from one place to another. For that, she'd have to learn from a Faery, but she really didn't want to ask her grandFae to be her teacher.

Illogical or not, she just couldn't bring herself to fully trust the grandFae who'd so recently barged into her life. The rest of her family didn't seem to have a problem with him, though. So why did Maggie? She wasn't sure. It was just a really vague sense of . . . *uncomfortableness* around him. Probably not even a word.

Plus, Bezel didn't like him. Of course, Bezel had something nasty to say about almost everyone. Still, Maggie trusted the pixie more than she did the stranger so intent on invading her life. What did that say? she wondered.

She took another sip of ice water, leaned against the kitchen counter and tuned back in to the battle raging in front of her.

"Besides," Bezel was saying, his pointy, bewhiskered chin jutting up at the Fae sneering at him, "even though Maggie won that fight with Mab, who's to say she will again?"

"Oh, thanks very much," Maggie put in.

Bezel waved one hand at her. "Didn't say you couldn't do it, did I?"

"She's the Queen now," Jasic argued. "She has warriors to protect her, a palace to retreat to and she certainly shouldn't be spending time rolling around in the dirt with a pixie, of all things."

Retreat? He meant *hide*. She briefly considered it and felt a sudden yearning for a blanket to pull over her head.

"It's called training, you useless pile of trollshit."

"Just one minute there—"

"Both of you shut up," Maggie shouted, and instantly, both of the males currently bothering her turned furious gazes on *her*. "I really don't need this crapola right now, okay? I've got enough going on in my life without you two going at each other, looking at me to referee."

"Hey"—Bezel held up both hands—"no biggie to me. Train or don't train. You want your ass kicked, that's your problem."

"You're a queen now, Maggie," Jasic explained slowly and quietly as if talking to a not-quite-up-to-specs three-year-old. "There's no need for this pixie to rule your life."

"Oh, please!" Maggie shook her hair back from her face. "Like Bezel's in charge around here? I don't think so. Anyway, I'm done training for the day. I'm going to Otherworld. I need to talk to Finn about all of this. See if there's any way to really keep Mab from escaping from wherever the hell she is."

"First good idea you've had all day," Bezel told her.

"A *wizard*," Jasic sneered.

"Is there *anyone* you like?" Bezel asked, then answered the question himself. "Besides yourself, I mean."

"Bezel—" Maggie headed for the backyard, mainly because she knew Jasic wouldn't follow her. Her grand-Fae had become way too fond of her living room couch and the hidden wine fridge behind the faux fireplace. He'd already gone through three bottles of Chardonnay in the last two days and if he drank her last one, Maggie was going to kick his ass all the way back to Otherworld.

When she was out in the yard, halfway between her house and Nora's, she stopped and turned around to look at Bezel.

"That grandsire of yours is a whole new level of *Ifreann*, if you ask me," he said, giving Maggie a look that dared her to argue with him.

She wanted to. It was pretty much instinctive for her to defend family. Besides, who wouldn't want to discover a grandfather you hadn't known existed? For years now, the entire Donovan family had consisted of just Maggie, Nora and Eileen. They were great together, but she understood why Nora, especially now, what with the baby and everything, wanted to connect with her roots. To have extended family was a gift. Another branch on the family tree. A link to a world that was new and scary and overwhelming at times.

Heck, Maggie wanted him to be a good guy, too. She just couldn't bring herself to believe he was. His fault? Or hers? She didn't even know anymore.

"Just ignore him," Maggie said, and wasn't surprised to hear Bezel muttering something unintelligible. "Okay, yes, he's hard to ignore. But Bezel . . ."

"I know, I know. He's *family*. What am I? Chopped Tarkian?"

Maggie tipped her head to one side and blinked at him. "Why, Bezel. Are you jealous?"

"*Hah!* Me? Jealous? Of *him?*" He kicked at the dirt and a soft cloud of dust rose up, and settled on his green velvet suit. Quickly, he brushed it away, then blew out a breath. "I don't want you getting the wrong idea or anything, but for a part-Fae, you're not all bad. And besides, until Fontana lets me come back home, you're all I've got."

"Wow." Maggie smiled and wiped away an imaginary tear. "That was beautiful."

He sneered at her. "Nobody likes a smart-ass queen, you know."

She sighed. "I know Jasic's bugging you, so while I'm gone, keep an eye on him, okay?"

Instantly, his pointed ears twitched and his eyes narrowed with suspicion. "Don't trust him, do ya?"

"I didn't say that."

"Didn't have to."

Maggie rolled her eyes at the satisfied expression on Bezel's wrinkled face. "Fine. Look. I'm just saying, it's a little . . . coincidental that he shows up now. So why don't you see what you can find out, okay? Watch him. See who he talks to. What he does." God, should she feel guilty for spying on her grandfather? As soon as that thought rose up, she squashed it. There were way too many other things she could do guilt about. "There's probably nothing going on. I just want you to keep your eyes open, okay?"

Bezel slapped his palms together and scrubbed them in anticipation. "I'll watch him, all right. We'll be closer than a Dinci demon and its parasite."

"What?" Maggie held up a hand. "Wait. Stop. Never mind. Don't want to know. Just watch him." She shot a look at the house before adding, "If you notice anything weird, tell me about it."

"I'm all over that," he assured her.

"And I need you to look out for Nora and Eileen, and if Claire comes over . . ."

"Forget it." Bezel shook his head so hard, his silvery hair lifted and twitched like live snakes. "I draw the line at babysitting witches."

Maggie's best friend, Claire MacDonald, had been spending most of her time at Maggie's house in the last few weeks. Well, except for the past few days.

Claire and Maggie were both artists, the only difference being that Claire actually made a living selling her paintings and Maggie had to decorate glass windows to support herself and paint in her spare time. And since Claire was off finishing up a mural for a client, she hadn't been around much in the last few days. Too bad, too, because Maggie was more anxious than ever to get Claire's read on Jasic.

After all, being best friends with a psychic witch had to have some perks, didn't it?

"I thought you and Claire were getting along all right now," she said.

His mouth pursed as if he were tasting something sour. He stroked the wispy beard at his chin and said, "Got nothing against her except she's a witch and witches and pixies are like . . . chocolate and tuna."

"Ew."

"Exactly."

"Anyway . . ." How did he manage to drag her off topic so fast? "Claire's not here, so I just want you to look after Nora and Eileen—"

"Where you going?" a perky young voice asked.

Maggie sighed, turned and smiled at her niece. "I have to go to Sanctuary. Talk to Finn."

"Oh!" Eagerness was stamped on her young face and Maggie felt herself weakening almost immediately. "Can I come?"

Bezel chuckled and Maggie accepted the inevitable. Eileen, the most book-loving kid she'd ever known, had been drooling to visit Sanctuary ever since Maggie had first told her about the place.

It was, in a word, impressive. Like an old-world library, only as big as a state, Sanctuary held all the knowledge of the Fae—not to mention thousands of years' worth of mortal history. The kind that humans didn't have access to. The kinds of things that were destroyed when the Library of Alexandria was burned to the ground. There were answers to the world's questions in that place and it had been only a matter of time before Eileen found a way to indulge her curiosity.

"This isn't a sightseeing mission, Eileen," Maggie warned her. "I've got to talk to Finn and—"

"I'm quiet," Eileen interrupted, then shrugged. "Okay, I'm not. But I could be. If I tried. And I'll try. Come on, Maggie. You said you'd take me sometime. Why not now? Mom's taking a nap and Bezel's crabby—"

"I am not—"

"And anyway, forty-seven percent of promises made to children are broken. You don't want to be a statistic, do you, Aunt Maggie?"

Eileen lowered her head and looked up at her from under her lashes. Her bottom lip poked out just enough to be pitiful and the slump of her shoulders completed the picture. If there was one thing a Donovan knew how to do, it was pout.

"Wow," Maggie said, "you're good."

Eileen's head snapped up and she grinned. "So I can go?"

"Yeah, you can go." Maggie grinned, shook her head and told Bezel, "When Nora gets up, let her know where we are."

"Right. Uh . . ." He paused. "I'll watch out for you know who, too."

Maggie frowned. She didn't need Bezel letting Eileen know she was keeping an eye on Jasic.

"You need some help drawing a portal?"

Now it was Maggie's turn to sneer. "I'm not a complete idiot. I've been practicing." She lifted one hand, focused her mind, concentrated on the spot in Sanctuary where she wanted to be and then drew a circle in the air.

Golden light defined it and the air within shimmered with light and wind and the soft scent of . . .

"What is that?" she asked, wrinkling her nose.

"It ain't Sanctuary," Bezel muttered. Quickly, he dispersed Maggie's portal into the wrong place and drew a new one. This time, the colors were familiar and the faint scent of flowers sighed from its center.

"There you go, Your *Majesty*."

"Yeah, yeah," Maggie said. She grabbed Eileen's hand and stepped into the light.

e

Sanctuary was living up to its name on this visit.

Maggie felt like a refugee from a war zone. There was so much going on at home, just stepping through the portal into Sanctuary's cool, calm atmosphere helped her breathe a little easier. Though she hated to admit it, the Cree-An she'd spoken to at the DMV had made her more nervous than she'd like. She'd also made Maggie think about Mab—*Where was she?* And that led naturally to *Could she get out?*

Could Mab somehow find a way to free herself? Because if she ever did, Mab would come after Maggie in a heartbeat. No sense fooling herself. Maggie knew that the once-mighty Fae Queen would want a little payback and she would for sure want her throne back. Which would mean getting rid of Maggie.

Just one more thing to worry about, she told herself, with a glance at her surroundings. She and Eileen had materialized in the main room where she'd spent so much time on her first visit.

Now, as Maggie looked around at familiar surroundings, Eileen was entranced with the otherworldly.

"This is *amazing*," the girl beside her whispered, awe in her voice.

"It really is, isn't it?" Maggie's gaze slid over the pale, marble walls, where threads of silver in the stone sparkled like secret treasure. The marble should have given a feeling of cold sterility, but instead, warmth radiated from the walls, enveloping the visitor with a sense of well-being.

Gleaming tables held crystal vases filled with a riot of blossoms in every shade of the color spectrum. Their scent and what Maggie thought were probably the lingering effects of lemon polish filled the air with a homey kind of atmosphere. And the miles of bookshelves that studded the walls were stuffed with tomes both ancient and new. Their brightly colored leather bindings made them look like jewels shining in the dark.

The windows in Sanctuary were always open and sheer white panels danced in the constant breeze. Soft, delicate scents wafted in and just as before, Maggie had to wonder from where they came. Sanctuary was literally a castle in the sky.

No ground stood beneath it, no sky hovered over it. Instead, pale blue surrounded the building that was out of time and space and wisps of white clouds sailed past like ships gliding across a glassy ocean.

"It's so . . . big," Eileen said, her head turning first one way then another, as she tried to see everything at once.

"And this is just one room of the place," Maggie told her.

Eileen's gaze shifted to hers. "There's more like this?"

"Oh yeah." Maggie grinned, and relished the sensation. She'd been so worried, so anxious lately, that she hadn't taken the time to really step back and see the magic in what her world had become. Now, looking through Eileen's dazzled eyes, she was seeing this place for what it was.

In a word, *spectacular*.

"Look up, sweetie," she said, and lifted Eileen's chin with the tip of her finger.

"What? *Whoa* . . ." That last word slid from Eileen's throat on a sigh of delight so pure that it made Maggie's smile even broader.

She looked up, too, and just as she had the first time

she'd stepped into this room, Maggie felt a tingle of raw wonder sparkle to life inside her. Fifty feet above their heads, the ceiling put the Sistine Chapel to shame.

Brilliantly colored murals streaked across the broad expanse, depicting life in Otherworld. The trees, the crystal towers, the Queen's castle. There were representations of every kind of Fae she'd ever seen and some she'd yet to meet. There were rivers and oceans and forests so richly detailed, her artist's soul ached to find a paintbrush and canvas and lose herself in creating her own masterpiece. But just as before, she wasn't here as an artist. She'd come for help.

Again.

"Majesty."

She dropped one hand onto Eileen's shoulder and turned around to face Finn, the wizard and scholar in charge of this amazing place. Tall and lean and so gorgeous most women would have toppled over from the force of his smile, Finn had long blond hair, deep blue eyes, the temperament of an angel and the wicked smile of a devil. He wore black slacks, a long-sleeved white shirt that was open at the throat and black shoes that made barely a whisper as he walked on the silver-veined marble floor. He was, like most other Fae males Maggie had met, quite the hunk.

But with Culhane a part of her life, Maggie was pretty much immune to Finn's charms.

"It's just Maggie," she reminded him, and wondered if she would ever get used to the idea of someone referring to her as "Majesty." "I really need to talk to you."

"Of course." He walked closer, held his hand out to Eileen and said, "You are the Queen's niece. I've heard much about you."

"Really?" Eileen grinned. "That's so cool. Maggie said I could come with her and you wouldn't mind."

"Not at all." He escorted the girl to a nearby table, waved one hand and a tray holding milk, cookies and a bowl of apples appeared in front of her. "Please, Eileen. Make yourself comfortable. As the Queen's niece, you are most welcome here. Look around. Explore. Enjoy yourself. That's what Sanctuary is for."

"Excellent," Eileen said. She was already turning to look at the immense bookshelves lining the white marble walls.

Maggie chewed briefly at her bottom lip. Eileen was in her care, so she just had to ask. "You're sure she's safe here on her own?"

"Aunt *Maggie!*" The humiliation in Eileen's voice was complete.

Finn only smiled. "Certainly. You know better than anyone, Maggie, that when a Fae enters Sanctuary, their power is stripped from them, not to be returned until they leave the same way they entered."

"Right." That was, after all, how she'd beaten Mab in their big fight. She'd tricked the Queen into showing up at Sanctuary, knowing that Mab would lose her power and they would be closer to even ground than they would have been anywhere else.

For just a second, she remembered that fight—it had happened here, in this very room. If she closed her eyes, she could see it all again, hear the hissed breathing and the slap and punch of kicks and fists that she and the enraged Faery Queen had shared. And she could see, very clearly, the last image she'd had of Mab, just before Maggie had pushed her out of one of the windows.

The Queen's golden hair flying about her exquisite face, her pale eyes flashing with fury and the smile that had curved her mouth when she'd whispered one last warning . . . "You think you've won—but just so you know, when Culhane whispers in the night—he lies."

She swallowed hard and released that memory, wishing she could simply block it from her mind entirely. Not that she believed Mab or anything, but did she really know Culhane well enough to say that he *wasn't* a liar?

"Maggie?"

"What? Oh. Sorry." She shook her head, forced a smile for Finn and Eileen and then shrugged. "I was just . . . never mind."

"You okay, Aunt Maggie?" Eileen looked worried and instantly Maggie felt guilty. The girl was twelve years old. She didn't need to be worried about her family. She needed to be a kid. To be protected from the big bad world, not bothered by it.

"I'm fine, kiddo. Hey, don't you have like a zillion books to read or something?"

Eileen stared at her for a long second or two, as if trying to decide whether to take Maggie's reassurance at face value or not. But finally, the lure of this amazing library was too much for her. "Yeah, I guess so." Then she looked up at Finn. "I can read anything I want?"

"Anything," he said with a half bow. "As I said, you are the Queen's niece. Sanctuary is always open to you."

"Very cool."

"You just made a friend for life," Maggie told him. Then turning to Eileen, she said, "We won't be long, okay?"

"Take your time. Seriously." Eileen was already wandering off to the closest bookshelf.

Maggie laughed a little as, beside Finn, she walked out of the room, her heels tapping on the marble floor. He led her down a long hallway that was as elegantly appointed as the main room. Paintings dotted the walls, along with brilliantly executed tapestries in colors so vibrant they might have been made yesterday.

❦

Eileen darted back to the table, picked up a couple of cookies and then began to wander through the room. She didn't even know where to start. There were so many books. Her gaze skimmed titles at random. *The*

Demon Threat. The Care and Feeding of Cyrillian Cats. The Human Problem Through the Ages. Warrior Clans and the Fae. The Templar Experiment.

"Ooh, that would be a good one," she murmured, and ran her fingers lightly over the dark blue leather spine of the book. The books didn't seem to be in any particular order. The librarian at school had a cow anytime somebody put a book back on the wrong shelf. But these were all jumbled up together.

"*The Human Problem*?" Eileen read again, and almost reached for the light brown leather book. She pulled her fingers back, though. Maybe there was something even more interesting here. "It'll take me for like . . . *ever* to look through all of these." Suddenly she had a new appreciation for the crabby school librarian. How were you supposed to find anything if everything was all over the place? She didn't see a computer or one of those old-fashioned card shelf thingies that told you where the book you were looking for was.

Frowning now, she turned in a slow circle, wishing she were quintuplets so she could look at everything at once. Who knew when Maggie would bring her back here?

And this was just one room in Sanctuary, she reminded herself. She wondered how many more there were in this place. Just how big was Sanctuary? Could she do some exploring? Would anyone know?

"Probably not," she told herself as she headed for the massive door through which Finn and Maggie had left. She tiptoed, even though her tennis shoes hardly made a sound on the floor. Her stomach twisted a little with nerves, but she ignored it and kept moving. "Finn said the Queen's niece was welcome anytime," she reminded herself in a stern whisper. "He said I should make myself at home. So that means I can look around all I want, right?"

Of course, Maggie might not like it. Eileen almost stopped again. But then, she told herself, Maggie didn't have to know. Eileen would just look around quickly, and be back in the main room before her aunt and Finn got back. No biggie.

She poked her head out first, wanting to make sure the coast was clear. And when she was sure the adults were nowhere around, Eileen smiled to herself, made a sharp right and started walking.

"This is amazing," she murmured, taking mental pictures so when she got home she could tell Devon about this place. Of course, she'd have to tell him at school since she was practically a prisoner in her own house and couldn't have a boy come over at all because Mom and Maggie were so weirded out by the thought of a *boy* actually wanting to come and see her, which was totally normal and everything. Eileen's best friend, Amber, had already *kissed* a boy, that icky Brian Stone, and she said it was gross, so Eileen was in no big hurry to try it herself, although she thought kissing Devon probably wouldn't be gross. But if she told her *mom* that, she'd be locked up in a convent until she was forty.

Eileen stopped to look at a painting of Otherworld and sighed a little at the beauty of it. All those trees. Silver streets and a river so blue, it was like a sky on the ground. It wasn't just the boy stuff bugging her mom and Aunt Maggie, Eileen told herself now. It was the Fae stuff, too.

Her mom was feeling sick and mad at Quinn. Maggie was fighting with Culhane and Bezel and sooo didn't want to be Queen, so she and Mom were just not getting how great all of the Fae stuff really was. They had this cool new world to explore, but instead of being psyched, all they did was worry about everything.

Adults just didn't get it.

Grinning to herself, Eileen crept on, peeked into another room, saw it was pretty much the same as the one she'd just left and continued down the hall. Devon said Mom and Aunt Maggie were just old and that's why they didn't understand how cool all of this was. He was being so completely frosty about everything and she couldn't even bring him home because Mom and Maggie would both start interrogating him. Like Eileen was a little kid or something.

"Oooh." One glance into the next room convinced Eileen this was something she wanted to investigate. No books here, just paintings. Big ones, little ones, framed in gold and white and black, they hung on walls so white they were shiny.

Eileen stepped into the room and listened to the slap of her tennis shoes against the floor. There were flowers here, too, in huge vases on tables. The air smelled sweet as she wandered the room, drawn from one picture to the next.

Just like in the Harry Potter books, some of these paintings actually moved. Trees waved in invisible winds, people strolled down those silver sidewalks, oceans rushed to snow-white beaches. But Eileen passed them all by as she was drawn to one painting in particular.

One where a solitary woman fell through an endless blue sky.

Chapter Seven

&

"What do you mean, the warriors won the battle?" Maggie stared up at Finn and noticed that he was looking a lot less relaxed than he had a minute ago. "What battle?"

"I assumed you knew, Majesty—Maggie," he corrected quickly. "The Dullahan were fomenting an uprising. Culhane led the warriors in to quell it. I assumed it was with your approval since he is your Chieftain."

"Is he?" Maggie had to wonder. Culhane had been missing in action for days now. The last she'd seen of him was in that oh-so-erotic dream a couple of nights ago. He hadn't popped in to annoy or seduce her. Hadn't stopped by to remind her of her "duties." Now she was discovering that he was in Otherworld, making decisions without even bothering to tell her about them?

Whose side was he really on?

Mab's last words to her came rattling back again and Maggie shivered. Wasn't Culhane the one who was always reminding her she was Queen? Why hadn't he told her anything? Why hadn't he come to her with talk of an "uprising"?

"I didn't know anything about this," she muttered.

Finn looked like he would rather be anywhere but there. Typical male, he was clearly worried that he'd gotten another male in trouble. Human or Fae, all men stuck together.

"I'm sure he meant to mention it."

"Mention? *Mention* a revolution?" Maggie turned around, stalked off a few paces, then came right back again. "Why wouldn't he tell me? Aren't I the damn Queen?"

"Of course, Majesty." Finn briefly bowed his head again.

"Doesn't feel like it to me," she snapped, then scrubbed her hands up and down her upper arms. "He should have told me what was happening."

"Mayhap he felt he couldn't wait," Finn suggested, his voice soft and low.

"Maybe," she mused, then shot a look up at him. "And maybe he didn't want to come to me. Maybe he prefers making the decisions all by himself."

Finn nearly winced. "If I may ... you haven't been in Otherworld often, Maggie, and some things cannot wait. If those in charge do not take action when necessary, it opens the gate for more troubles."

"So this is my fault." It wasn't a question, because she knew Finn would never say that. But Maggie knew it was what he was thinking. And maybe, she even agreed. Partially. Even if Culhane weren't up to something sneaky—making decisions without telling her about them—if she had been putting in the time in Otherworld, he would have had a tougher time taking over.

But she'd been so hesitant about accepting the crown and the role of Queen. There was a lot to consider. How could she make decisions affecting thousands of, for lack of a better word, *people*? What made her so special? What gave her the right to be Queen? Just because she'd managed to survive a fight with the other Queen and toss her royal ass out a window? *That* made her a destined leader?

If that was all it took, every school-ground bully in the world would be a minor dictator. Wasn't a queen supposed to be knowledgeable? Wise? Wouldn't a true queen have sat her ass on the throne, whether she wanted to or not? Would she be so selfish, she'd cling to a life that had already changed so much, it wasn't the life she'd known before, anyway?

"Isn't the most important thing that the uprising was successfully put down?" Finn asked in a quiet, reasonable tone that made Maggie want to shriek.

She didn't want to be reasonable. She wanted to kick something. Most specifically, *Culhane*. She wanted him right in front of her, explaining what he'd done and why. She wanted him to freaking understand that it wasn't fair to expect her to turn into some legendary queen overnight without any doubts or fears.

"I suppose so," she agreed, glad at least that a possible rebellion had been put down, because if it hadn't, these ... Dullahan would most likely have come after her. And they probably wouldn't have settled for tossing her out a window. They would have wanted a more permanent end to her less than spectacular "reign."

"Maggie, you must ascend the throne. Otherworld needs a queen to lead them. We need you."

She laughed shortly and felt a bubble of hysteria rising in her chest that she fought valiantly to squelch. "Otherworld needs me? How is that possible, Finn? I don't even know who I am anymore."

She sure wasn't plain old Maggie Donovan these days. Not with the superhuman strength and the weird floating thing she did when she wasn't concentrating. She was slowly becoming a full-Fae. Soon, she wouldn't be human anymore. Then what? Who would she be?

Would she still be Maggie Donovan, struggling artist and glass painter extraordinaire? Would she still want the same things, love the same things? Would she even *remember* being human?

Not to mention, this queen thing—it wasn't as if she'd been *elected* to the position. She'd sort of gotten the job by default. What if she was no good at it? What if she gave up her life in the real world, then failed in the Otherworld?

And wow. Wasn't that the most positive train of thought in the world?

"You are Queen Maggie," Finn said, his voice low and steady and filled with confidence. "It is who you were always meant to be."

Was he right? Was Culhane? Was she fighting something that had been destined, as Culhane had told her?

She held up one hand to stave off whatever else Finn might be about to come up with. She didn't need comforting. She didn't know what she needed. Commiseration? No, she was too busy throwing herself a pity party to need outside help. At that thought, Maggie frowned and realized that she'd been feeling sorry for herself since this whole thing started and it had gotten her exactly nowhere. When had she turned into a big wiener?

Since when did Maggie Donovan run and hide from anything?

Lifting her chin, she told herself she wasn't a coward. She was the kind of woman who stood up and faced her mistakes. Worked through the flu. Took care of business no matter *whom* she had to work for. And damn it, if she could survive the world's crabbiest pixie without resorting to homicide, she could take on Otherworld.

She was the Queen, elected or not. If some of the Fae didn't like her, well they'd get used to her. She was done hiding. She was done being worried. She was ready, willing and able to take on the job Culhane had been saying for weeks she'd been destined for.

The moment she accepted her destiny, her nervousness disappeared and a sense of . . . okay, not peace, but maybe *calm* came over her. Funny. She'd been trying so hard to avoid all of this to protect herself, when just going with the flow would have made her feel so much better.

"I wish I could read minds," Finn said, a bemused

smile on his face. "Because judging by your expression, your thoughts right now would be very interesting."

Maggie grinned. "Damn straight. You know what, Finn? I've had an epiphany."

"Is that right?"

"Oh yeah. I can do this."

He smiled. "You can."

"Culhane wants a queen; he's got one."

"Well done."

"If Mab gets out, I'll take care of her."

"No doubt."

Maggie paused, gave him a hard look and asked, "But she won't. Get out, I mean. Right?"

"Not without assistance," Finn assured her.

Well, that wasn't exactly the staunch reassurance she'd hoped for.

"Crap."

Finn smiled, took her elbow and started walking. "Come with me, Your Majesty."

Maggie didn't even flinch at the word. Progress.

"I want to show you something that will make you feel more at ease."

"A vodka tonic?" she asked, suddenly a little less assured than she'd been minutes ago.

Finn laughed and led her down the long hall.

*

Eileen leaned in closer to the small framed painting hanging just at eye level. At first, she couldn't figure out what it was. All of the other paintings in the gigantic room were of people. Or places. Some of them looked completely amazing, too. She was still pretty jazzed about actually *seeing* paintings move. And they looked way cooler than they did in the Harry Potter movies.

But this one was different.

This painting was of the sky. Just a really pretty blue sky with a few white clouds and one person, right in the middle. A woman with long, golden hair flying out around her, was falling and falling through that empty sky. Her mouth was open as if she were screaming, but Eileen couldn't hear anything.

"Well yeah," she whispered to herself, "if all these paintings talked, too, it would get seriously loud in here. But who're you supposed to be?" she asked the eternally falling woman. "And how come you're over here all by yourself?"

Chewing at her bottom lip, Eileen looked around, but she was the only person in the room, except for the ones in the paintings. And she wondered. Could she touch the painted sky? Could she touch the falling woman? Would it feel flat like human paintings, or would her hand go right through the painting like magic?

She gave one last glance over her shoulder and fought down the feeling of guilt pulling at her. It wasn't like she was going to ruin the picture or anything. She was just going to touch it. No biggie. Right?

She took a breath, held it and slowly, carefully, edged her right hand toward the tantalizing canvas in front of her.

Her eyes went wide. Her mouth dropped open. Her hand slid into that cerulean sky and an instant later, the falling woman landed in the center of Eileen's palm.

"Ohmigod!" She stared at the tiny woman with the long, gold hair as she stood up on Eileen's hand. The woman shook her hair until it rippled like sunlight on the surface of a lake; then, the woman looked directly into Eileen's eyes and gave her a slow smile.

"You have saved me, child," she said, her voice strong and rich, despite her size.

Eileen's insides felt as if someone had tossed her into a freezer. Suddenly she knew exactly who the woman was. And why she'd been falling. Swallowing hard, she said, "You're . . . Mab."

"I am the once and future Queen of the Fae, and for your service, you will be rewarded."

Before Eileen could say anything, the tiny image of Mab shifted and disappeared from the painting.

"Oh, crap."

&

The palace guards made themselves scarce when Culhane was there. Not surprising, he thought, since female Fae didn't have much use for the males, anyway. Plus, a warrior was a direct threat to most females. They didn't like that there was an entire clan of powerful males—the warriors wielded more power than the guards were comfortable with.

Things were changing, though. More slowly than he'd like, but put that down to his stubborn Queen. At the thought of Maggie Donovan, his body tightened and a hard, dull ache spread through him. The woman was making him mad with want. And not just for the ease he longed to find in her body, but for the changes she would bring to Otherworld.

"Perhaps it's time to try something else," he whispered to himself as he stalked along the wide, empty hallway of crystal walls. Within those walls, pulsing swaths of color shimmered and swirled whenever someone passed. Those colors were the only signs of life here, he thought. Every room stood empty, forlorn, a great palace with no one to shelter. Mab had long kept only her own guard in this massive castle because she had seen plots and revolution in the eyes of her subjects. She had trusted no one at the end and no one was exactly who had been there to help her when she had lost everything.

Now life in this palace would change. The female guards would soon understand that their eternal lives, as they had known them, were over—as soon as Maggie was on the throne and Culhane was ruling Otherworld at her side. All he had to do was *get* her here.

He'd tried patience, though the gods knew it was not a virtue he had been overly blessed with. He'd tried seduction. He'd even tried bribing her with the promise of treasure and a life of ease. But she'd stood steadfast against them all, determined to hold on to a life that was no longer hers.

So perhaps he would do what he should have done in the beginning. Snatch Maggie from her world, and hold her here, in the palace, until his body had convinced hers that she wanted nothing more than to stay.

His injuries from the battle with the Dullahan already healed, Culhane prepared himself for a battle of another kind. In this one, there would be no physical injuries. This battle would be one of the mind. His will against Maggie's.

"She's a strong woman, my Queen," he said to himself as he walked into the throne room. Here, the walls sparkled in the sunlight, catching the rays of the dual suns and splintering them through their crystal panels until prismed colors danced around the room. The dazzling display of light and color would have blinded a mere mortal. Only those with Fae blood could truly see and withstand the beauty in Otherworld without sliding into madness.

And it was for this, his Maggie Donovan had been born.

He stalked to the intricately carved, silver-sculpted throne, stepped up onto the dais and ran one hand across its cool, heavily jeweled surface. Rubies, sapphires, emeralds and diamonds winked from their settings on the Queen's chair. The throne meant for Maggie.

She'd sat here only a few times and hadn't looked at all at ease. But she had it in her to be a great queen and he would see to it personally that she both accepted and celebrated who and what she was.

He folded his arms across the top of the throne and spoke to the empty room as if facing his Queen herself. "Your place is here, Maggie. With *me*. It's time you learned that."

୧

"You'll see," Finn assured Maggie again as they walked down the wide hall. "Mab is contained. She will not escape so easily. She had no friends, only subjects. No one is eager to see her returned to the throne."

Maggie liked the sound of that, but asked anyway, "No one? What about the rogue Fae?"

"Well," he admitted regretfully, "they are, of course, not to be trusted. But as they're trapped on Casia in their own prison, they are in no position to offer assistance to Mab."

Casia. The frozen island where Culhane had stopped a budding revolution. God. There was so much she had to learn.

"Hope you're right," Maggie said.

"Ah," Finn answered with a wink, "I am a wizard. You can trust me. But even were I proved wrong, Maggie, you would have Culhane standing at your side. The warrior would do anything for you. He will keep you safe."

Would he? she wondered. Or had he given up on making her Queen and decided to pull off a coup of his own? Maybe he'd rather be a king in his own right than be the warrior of a reluctant queen. Was she really all that important in Culhane's little world?

Maybe all he'd wanted was help getting free of Mab. It was possible he hadn't wanted *her* for Queen as much as he'd wanted a new ruler. Anyone would have done as long as it wasn't Mab.

Well, that was a depressing thought.

"Are you thinking about the Dullahan, then?" Finn asked.

"No. How could I? I don't even know what they are."

She frowned, looked up at the tall wizard walking beside her and said, "I'm thinking about Culhane. And wondering if he really is *my* warrior."

"Ah, Maggie . . ."

"You said yourself he went into battle without even telling me."

"It is his duty to protect Otherworld."

"Yes, but *how* is the question," she muttered, then followed Finn into a room she'd never been in before. Enormous, she thought, not at all surprised, since this whole place seemed to have been built on a scale for giants. But the difference in this room pulled at Maggie as nothing she'd ever seen before had.

Paintings. Hundreds—thousands of them—dotting the walls in varying shapes and sizes, and she grinned when some of the subjects in those paintings moved. "This is amazing. Eileen's got to see this. She won't believe it. Really, Finn, this is—"

A slight sound caught her ear and Maggie looked off to the left. "Eileen? What're you doing in here?"

The girl whirled around guiltily, clasped her hands behind her back, winced and hunched her shoulders as she looked at Maggie. "Um, nothing?"

"What's going on?" Maggie had been down this road before with her niece and she knew that when Eileen wouldn't meet her eyes or answer a straight question, something was most definitely up. Besides, she was really trying to project the whole I'm-too-innocent-to-do-anything-bad look. "Spill. What happened?"

"Happened?"

"Eileen . . ."

"Oh, trollshit."

Maggie looked at Finn. Finn was staring at a painting. Eileen was staring at Finn. And *nobody* was looking at Maggie. Apprehension coiled into a tight knot in the pit of her stomach. This could *not* be good.

"What?"

"I didn't mean to," Eileen said.

"Mean to what?" Maggie asked.

"I'm sure it was an accident," Finn said softly, still wearing a worried expression, and that more than anything else made those brand-new knots in Maggie's stomach start writhing as if they were snakes in a pit.

"I didn't know it was real," Eileen whispered.

"What was real?"

"I should have locked the door," Finn said.

"If *somebody* doesn't tell me what's happening . . ." Maggie let the vague threat hang in the air until finally, Finn looked at her.

"That painting"—he stabbed one finger at the frame now holding a painting of an empty sky—"was Mab's prison. She's gone."

"Gone?"

"I only touched the painting, Aunt Maggie," Eileen said, her voice going whiny and thin. "I didn't know she'd land on my hand."

"Oh God."

"She shifted and sort of . . . disappeared," Eileen finished.

Maggie needed to sit down. But there weren't any chairs. So she locked her knees, looked at the wizard and for the first time since all of this had started, pulled rank and demanded in her most queenly voice, "Explain. I thought Mab lost her powers to me. How'd she get out?"

"Shifting isn't really a 'power,'" Finn admitted. "It is simply a part of being Fae. Once her fall was halted, Mab simply . . . left."

"Fabulous," Maggie muttered.

Finn pushed one hand through his thick, blond hair and said, "This has never happened before, my Queen. And the truth is, Mab could be anywhere. But wherever she is, she is no doubt plotting her revenge on you. You are in grave danger."

"I'm *really* sorry, Aunt Maggie." Tears shone in Eileen's eyes, and Maggie reached out to draw her in for a hug.

"It's okay, sweetie." Not like she'd done anything on purpose. Still, Maggie looked up at the wizard and noted the flicker of worry in his normally placid blue eyes. "Finn, would you see that Eileen gets home? I need to see Culhane."

The palace echoed with the sounds of her footsteps as Maggie raced down one corridor into the next. "Culhane!"

She didn't even stop when one of her female guards flew through an open window and stopped directly in her path. "Majesty," the tall woman said, "do you require assistance?"

"I require Culhane," Maggie said quickly, and stepped past the woman. She probably should have told Finn to send Culhane to her back in the real world. But at her house, there would have been too many distractions. Bezel. Jasic. Eileen. Nora. Quinn. Maybe Claire. Nope, she needed some one-on-one time with Culhane and the only place she stood a shot of getting it was here. In the palace. Where she could simply *order* people to leave them alone.

Maggie kept moving, looking into rooms as she ran down the hallway, not sure exactly where she was headed—and it occurred to her that there were probably a thousand or so rooms in the damn palace. It could take her *years* to find the man.

Frustrated, she shouted, "Culhane!"

"He's in the throne room," the female now behind her said softly.

Maggie stopped, looked over her shoulder and narrowed her eyes at the familiar woman. "Ailish?" The Fae she'd spoken to at the DMV.

"Yes, Majesty." She smiled, obviously pleased that Maggie remembered her. Well, she was hard to forget. "Have you come to tell the warrior of your decision to allow the females into the Warriors' Conclave?"

Hell. She'd forgotten all about that in her rush to find Culhane and tell him about Mab. Being Queen wasn't getting any easier. "I will tell him, yes. But first I have to talk to him about something else."

"Mab." Ailish frowned.

Maggie blew out a breath. "Word spreads fast."

"Bad news does, my Queen."

"Well," Maggie said thoughtfully, "at least you think it's bad news." She really didn't need her own palace guard turning on her and helping Mab retake the palace.

"We do. You have our support in the coming fight."

"Good to know," Maggie said, turning away again. "Now, which way is the throne room?"

"End of the hall to the left."

She was running before Ailish stopped speaking. Need pushed at her, fear chased her and at the moment, the only thing that would help, was seeing the fierce, unyielding features of her very own warrior.

Because Maggie needed to know if he really was *her* warrior.

"Free." One word and the taste of it was magnificent.

Mab took a deep breath of the icy air of Casia and smiled as if it were the sweet, floral-scented air wafting through the windows of her palace. This harsh, cold, biting wind slicing into her skin, dragging at her hair, was like fine wine, because it represented all she needed.

Opportunity.

Here in this prison she'd created millennia ago, she would find the help she required for ridding herself of Maggie Donovan and the warrior who had helped the human onto the throne. The throne that was rightfully Mab's.

A smile as cold as the ice beneath her feet touched Mab's face and she focused her gaze on the village lying at the foot of the mountain. Yes, there was danger here. Some of the rogue Fae she'd imprisoned so long ago would hardly welcome her with open arms. "There will be a few who are willing to look past old grudges to acquire what I now know to be most precious. Their freedom."

When she had been caught, out of time and space, falling through eternity, Mab had known only frustration and something she'd never experienced before. Fear. Fear that she would always be thus. That there would be no end to her fall. That the great and powerful Mab would become nothing more than legend as she spent perpetuity caught in a frame on a wall in Sanctuary.

"But the gods have smiled on me. Thanks to the mixed-blood human child." The niece of Mab's usurper. "One day, I will thank her properly. Perhaps by allowing her to serve me once I kill her aunt and regain my power."

That thought bothered her, only because of the difficulty in killing an immortal; then she dismissed her concern as she realized one very important thing: The new Queen wasn't fully Fae yet. Her powers were slowly overtaking her, but she was still part human. Easier to kill. There was still time. Kill Maggie Donovan and Mab's power would return. And with her power she would retake the throne and spend the next good portion of infinity punishing those who had schemed against her.

With that shining promise firmly in mind, she shifted, going to the village to begin to gather her forces.

Chapter Eight

Culhane grabbed Maggie as she raced into the throne room. He wrapped his arms around her and for one brief, tantalizing moment, buried his face in the curve of her neck. For one spectacular second, she allowed herself to relax in his arms and savor the feel of his solid strength surrounding her.

She felt his breath on her skin, the hard, broad expanse of his chest pressed to hers and the still-harder portion of his body pressing lower against hers. She held on to him, and just for that brief space of time, forgot that she was angry at him for going to war without even mentioning it to her. For not coming to see her in days. Even for deserting her dreams and leaving her body aching—though that last one wasn't really his fault, she reminded herself.

Everything else was, though, and so she let go of him and stepped away from his embrace.

"That's not what I came here for," she said, ignoring the shrieking inside her mind. The tiny voices calling out, *Are you crazy? He's right in front of you! Go get him! We want some Fae sex, okay?* Stupid mind. "Culhane, there's something I have to tell you and then we need to figure out what to do about it."

"I already know." He scowled at her, braced his long legs in a wide stance and folded his arms over his chest. "You've come to tell me about Mab."

"You know? How do you know? It just happened like thirty seconds ago, for God's sake!" She goggled at him, eyes wide, mouth open. "How the hell does word spread so fast?"

He shrugged. "There was a momentary hesitation in the flow of time. We all felt it. It was Mab, reentering this dimension. It could have been nothing else."

Fabulous. There was a Fae Spidey-sense network she knew nothing about. So fine. He knew about Mab's escape and Maggie's imminent danger. Yet he was still here. In the palace. Why hadn't he come to her? Why wasn't he in Maggie's house in the real world searching for her right this minute? Was he just planning on cooling his heels at the palace and letting Maggie sink or swim on her own?

"Were you planning on coming to me about it?"

"I didn't have to," he pointed out all too reasonably. "You came to me."

"Not the question," she told him. Temper began to spike inside her as she walked a slow, tight circle around the great Fenian Warrior. Now that she was here, with him, she felt better about Mab and worse about Culhane. If everyone knew Mab was out, the chances of her springing a surprise attack were pretty slim. But her very own protective warrior hadn't bothered to budge himself enough to leave Otherworld on her behalf. "You're here. Why aren't you at my house looking to protect me?"

He shook his head and his long, silky hair lifted from his shoulders. "You are *here*, Maggie."

"Yeah, okay." She could give him that much at least. "But you didn't know I'd come here. You should have been looking for me. To warn me. To I don't know . . . give a crap?"

Culhane turned in a circle, following her movements, keeping his gaze fixed with hers. "I already 'give a crap,' as you put it. I have for a long time. Do you forget that I have watched over you your whole life? That I am the one who sought to train you? To protect you? And for my efforts, I receive your disdain."

"Disdain?" She pulled her head back and stared at him in surprise. "Why would you think that?"

He laughed shortly, fisted his hands at his hips and gave her a slow, thorough glance up and down her body before fixing his gaze on hers. "What would you have me think? You don't trust me to teach you. You avoid your duties here in Otherworld. You avoid *me*."

"You're part of Otherworld," Maggie said, feeling some truth in his words, whether she wanted to admit it or not. "So the avoiding just . . . happened."

Maybe he was right about all of it, but who could really blame her? She had known, almost from the first moment when he'd popped into her kitchen and she'd knocked him out with a jug of milk, that he was a man a woman wouldn't be able to flirt with and then step away from. That the moment she surrendered to her feelings for him, she would be lost. She wouldn't be able to withstand what he could make her feel. Want. And once she gave in to her need for him, she would have to accept not only the warrior's presence in her life, but the duties and responsibilities waiting for her here. In Otherworld.

Talk about terrifying.

"And it wasn't you specifically I was trying to steer clear of. I just wasn't ready for all of this—" She waved her hands high, encompassing the throne room, the crystal palace and Otherworld beyond the open windows. "It's a big deal, you know. Not something you take on lightly. I've got a family and a house—"

"And a people expecting you to lead," he added, interrupting her rant neatly.

"I know that." Guilt, fresh and pure, rose up inside her. She'd turned her back on what this world offered because she hadn't been able to let go of her own world.

And in turning away from Otherworld, she'd kept Culhane at a distance. For her own peace of mind, she'd tried to ignore her feelings for him, but that wasn't working anymore. She thought about him all the damn time. She dreamed of him. She wanted him more than she'd ever wanted anything, so when was she going to just admit the truth?

She stopped, her back to the windows, her gaze fixed on the warrior in front of her. Through these last few weeks, Culhane had been her strength. He had defended her against enemies, stood with her against a raging, crazy-ass queen and protected her from demons. He had tried to show her that she was ready for her future, and all she'd been able to do was hide from it. She'd buried herself in her own world because the familiarity of it was a balm in some truly weird times.

But hiding wasn't a damn answer, she reminded herself. It was just another problem.

And speaking of problems, there was one question she needed answered before she said anything else. "Do we know where Mab is?"

"I have an idea, yes."

"Where?"

"Casia," he said, his gaze still locked with hers.

She knew that name. She'd heard about it only a short while ago, from Finn. "You mean where you had the battle with the dolphins you didn't tell me about."

"Dol—" His mouth quirked slightly as he nodded. "Dullahan, you mean."

"Whatever. You didn't tell me, Culhane. You went out with the warriors and didn't even bother to run it past your Queen."

"My Queen hasn't seen fit to rule yet," he told her, and when she would have stepped back, he moved toward her, closing the distance separating them, and Maggie could almost feel frustration ebbing from him in a thick wave.

"And these Dulla-things were so dangerous, you couldn't wait to talk to me *first*?"

"No."

He looked like a statue of an avenging angel. He didn't move. His features were tight and stiff and unrepentant. If she was waiting for him to apologize for doing what he thought necessary, Maggie knew she'd be waiting forever. "Fine. Just what the hell are they?"

"Rogue Fae." He sneered. "The darkest kind."

Maggie took a shallow breath and felt a chill as Culhane went on.

"They were quiet enough under Mab's reign because as mad as she was, they'd no wish to challenge her," he told her.

"There's a *but* coming, Culhane," she said, taking a breath to brace herself. "So just spit it out and get it over with."

"*But*, they don't fear a half-Fae Queen who spends so little time on the throne."

Guilt. That nasty, ugly, impossible-to-ignore feeling rose up in her chest again and fisted tight around her lungs. She took a shallow breath and forced herself to ask, "What would have happened if they had gone into my world?"

"Destruction."

One word, but said with such a deep bitterness, Maggie felt the absoluteness in his tone. She knew then without a doubt that Culhane had done the right thing. It was her own fault that her warriors made decisions without coming to her. Her own fault that she didn't feel as if she had a place in this castle or in this world. She'd neglected a duty she hadn't wanted to assume and she was just now beginning to realize how dangerous that decision had been.

"Allowing their rebellion to escalate was risking the greatest dangers," he said quietly. "My Queen wasn't here when the uprising began. We couldn't wait."

"I'm here now," she said, lifting her chin and facing him with as much pride as a former wiener-dog could muster. She was through hiding. She was finished pretending that this world wasn't as much hers as the human world.

Maggie might be a reluctant queen, but she *was* Queen, and it was high time she accepted it. She'd take her place on the throne and dare Mab to pry her off it. She'd listen to her warriors and make the best decisions she could. She'd stand up for the female warriors and make sure the male Fae weren't treated like second-class citizens anymore. She'd be the damn George Washington of Otherworld if she had to be and by damn, she was going to have Culhane. Over her. Under her.

However she could get him.

Right now.

"I am the Queen, Culhane," she said thoughtfully, drawing her words out, making sure he listened not only to what she was saying, but to the feeling behind the words as well. "*Your* Queen. I'm ready to do what I have to do. To learn what I need to learn. But I'm going to need *you*."

She walked toward him and saw the flash of something dark and dangerous in his eyes. A jolt of heat shot through her like a lightning bolt, leaving sizzling and burning sensations in its wake. Her knees shook and her insides went warm and gooey. She knew what she wanted now.

Culhane might have his faults, but he'd been there when she needed him. And would be there again. She knew it. And she was willing to take the risk of caring for him.

"So," he said warily, "you will listen to me? As your adviser?"

"I will," she told him, coming even closer. God. She could feel the heat of his body snaking out for her. Everything in her trembled. "But you'll have to listen to me, too, Culhane," she warned, wanting to make sure he understood going in that she expected a full partnership here. "No more secret wars. From now on, you tell me what's going on, even if I won't like it—no, *especially* if I won't like it."

One corner of his mouth tipped up. "I will."

"And," Maggie added as heat pooled in her middle and drifted lower, deeper, "we're going to have to do something about this palace, too. If I'm going to be spending lots of time here, I want a few comfortable things, you know?"

He reached out quickly, and pulled her close; she gasped as the hard, solid length of him pressed into her abdomen. Maggie's eyes slid half shut and she took in a slow, deep breath even as she wiggled closer to him, wanting, needing what only he could provide for her.

He dropped one hand to the curve of her behind, stroking her until she wanted to purr. Maggie's breasts ached for his touch, her nipples were hard and sensitive and she wanted to rub her body against his just to ease that ache.

"Comfortable things?" he whispered, dipping his head to nibble at her throat.

"Right. Yes." She sighed and shifted into his touch. "Um. You know. Soft chairs. Maybe a"—she sucked in air—"bed."

"Your wish," he murmured, and waved one hand idly in the air; then, still keeping her pressed tightly to him, he turned her slightly to show her what he'd done.

"Oh . . . my . . . goodness."

The bed was massive.

Four heavy posts, one at each corner, the bed itself was big enough to sleep six people. Several down mattresses were stacked atop one another, making it high enough that she'd need a ladder to climb aboard. There were a dozen or more pillows stacked against the intricately carved headboard and luxurious quilts in all the colors of the rainbow spilled from the bed to lie across the sparkling white floor.

"Do you approve?" he whispered, this time nibbling at her earlobe.

"I . . . um . . . well . . . it looks, yes . . ."

"Good. I have waited long enough to taste you, Maggie Donovan, Queen of the Fae. This night, I will explore your body and learn its every secret." He waved his hand again and the wide double doors behind them slammed closed and locked.

Maggie sucked in another breath and tossed a glance at the open windows, through which a starry sky stretched out toward eternity. "What about . . ."

"The window arches are warded. No one gets into the Queen's throne room uninvited."

Good to know. "But anyone flying by, and I can't believe I'm saying 'flying by,' could look in and—"

"No. The wards protect those within from being seen. We are alone, Maggie. You and I."

"We are, aren't we?" She looked up at him again and licked her bottom lip.

"Will you run?" he asked, studying her, waiting to see acceptance in her eyes. "Will you change your mind now? Turn aside from what burns between us? Or will you accept this new life? And me?"

Maggie reached up, wrapped her arms around his neck and stared into his pale green eyes as emotions, so varied and rich she couldn't identify them all, flashed across their surfaces. His mouth was tight, his body hard and he held perfectly still as he waited for her to make her final decision.

Still watching his eyes, Maggie slid her fingers through his hair and said, "I just accepted it, Culhane. This life. And you." Then, tired of talking, of reasoning, of thinking, she put an end to the conversation the surest way she knew how.

She kissed him. Slanting her mouth over his, Maggie

poured everything she was into the act. Her lips parted, her tongue slid into his mouth and instantly, her entire body lit up like a giant Christmas tree. She sparkled; she shone, inside and out. She felt the magic pooling between them and gave herself up to it completely.

Culhane groaned in response, tightened his arms around her middle and held her so she could hardly breathe. But then, she thought wildly, who needed air? His tongue delved into her mouth, dueling with hers in an ancient dance of want and need. His grip on her relaxed only enough to allow him to stroke his hands up and down her spine, along her sides, to her breasts.

He cupped them both, sliding his hands between their bodies and even through the fabric of her T-shirt and the pink lace bra she'd donned that morning (thank God she'd worn pretty underwear). She felt the power in his touch, the dazzling sensations that spread from his skin to hers. The heat welling between them until it was nearly an inferno.

Then he shifted his grip on her again, sliding his hands up, along her throat to cup her face, thread his fingers through her hair and hold her head steady for his tender assault. His kiss deepened further, his hunger grew and fed her own. Maggie felt the desperation in his touch and shared it.

This is what she'd needed for so long. From the moment she'd met him. Maybe even since before that. She felt as though she'd been waiting for this night for an eternity. Through countless lives. Through endless days and innumerable nights. All of her dreams, her desires, had led her here. To him.

"Culhane," she said brokenly as he tore his mouth from hers to slide his tongue along the curve of her throat. She tipped her head to one side, allowing him access, allowing him anything he wanted so long as he never stopped touching her. "I need you. I need you to touch me."

"I will and I am," he promised, his hot breath dusting her skin.

He held her firmly and she felt her molecules dissolve, dissipate, blend with his, become part of him, indistinct from the basic atoms that made up the mighty Culhane. And then in an instant, they were separate beings again and lying on the wide bed he'd created just for her. Just for this night.

The soft mattresses beneath them enfolded their bodies in a warm embrace. The silk of the coverlets was a cool kiss on her heated skin and all Maggie could think was that she wished she were naked.

Her clothes were gone an instant later. "Whoa!"

Culhane grinned at her, snapped his fingers and his clothing, too, was nothing more than a memory. His broad, tanned, muscular chest was sculpted and beautiful. His abdomen was flat and ridged with muscle and his . . .

"Wow." Maggie's eyes widened. She wasn't an inexperienced virgin or anything, but she'd never seen a man built like Culhane.

The hard, solid length of his erection was enormous and just a little worrisome.

"Culhane . . . you know I want you, but . . ."

"We are matched, Maggie," he assured her, taking her hand and guiding it down so that her fingers could encircle him. He pulled in a sharp, short breath and hissed it out at the glory of having her hand on him; then he stared into her eyes and said, "We are meant to be together. Our bodies are interlocking pieces destined to fit tightly and bind us together."

She ran her fingers over the silken steel of him and knew that she believed him. At that moment, she knew that she'd been born just for this. To be the one woman in the world who was the perfect fit for Culhane.

"Show me," she whispered, and slid her hands up his abdomen and across that beautiful chest of his. She loved the way he jolted at her touch and how his silvery green eyes darkened with hunger. His heartbeat pounded frantically beneath her hands and she knew he felt everything she was. Knew this moment was as monumental for him as it was for her.

He dipped his head and took first one of her nipples and then the other into his mouth. His silky hair spilling across her skin felt like the softest caress. She arched off the bed, moving into him, offering herself up to his ministrations. His tongue and teeth toyed with her sensitive skin and she groaned out his name as she held him to her.

Maggie lifted her head from the bed and watched as he suckled her. Culhane, the fierce and proud warrior, took her as tenderly as any woman could wish, yet at the same time, he caused a burning deep inside her.

He'd told her once that Fae sex for a human was so overwhelming, women had been known to faint from the experience. But Maggie wouldn't faint. She didn't want to miss a minute of it.

"You are everything I'd hoped," he said softly, his mouth still adoring her, tasting her. "And so much more ..."

He swept one hand down the length of her body and cupped her heat in his palm. Maggie jolted in his grasp, lifting her hips, trying to move into his touch, to fill the aching emptiness inside her.

Culhane smiled and lifted his head to watch her eyes as he pushed first one finger, then two into her depths. She hissed in a breath and tipped her head back into the blankets beneath her.

A warm breeze sighed through the room, carrying the scents of the garden below and the distant sea. Maggie moaned as he rubbed his thumb across the most sensitive part of her and he smiled as he watched her rush toward the peak of pleasure.

She trembled, she shook, she moaned and then cried

out when he took his hand from her before she could find release.

"Bastard," she whispered, tossing her head from side to side even as she grabbed at his shoulders, his hair. Her hips lifted and rocked, her legs opened wider as she silently demanded that which he had promised her. "Culhane, be inside me. Don't wait. I need you. Now."

"As I need you, Maggie. As I have needed you through millennia."

She opened her eyes and stared up at him as he moved to position himself between her thighs. Her dark blue gaze shone with the same need that held him in its tight grasp. He felt the heat building between them and knew that once he was within her, the fire would consume them both. And he hungered for it. A true mating. A merging of souls and bodies and minds and hearts.

"Once joined with you, we will never be truly separate again," he told her, lifting her legs, spreading them, looking his fill of her most honeyed flesh. He trailed the tip of one finger across her swollen folds and she jerked at his touch, her body so ready for release, the slightest touch would push her over the edge into oblivion. But for that, he wanted to be within her. To stroke her from the inside, to feel the tremors and quakes as her body splintered. To know that it was he and only he who would be joined with her in such a way.

"I understand." She shivered and lifted her hips in welcome.

"With this mating, I claim you." He said the words, even knowing she wouldn't understand their depth. He'd said the words only once before but had never meant them so deeply. Never needed to say them so much.

"Culhane . . ." She reached for him, but he caught her hands in one of his and held her wrists together.

"You are mine, Maggie Donovan," he told her as he slid his cock into her heat. Inch by glorious inch, he claimed her as he had known all along he would. "As I am yours. This is destiny, Maggie. *Our* destiny."

So tight, he thought, loving the slide of her heat against him. No more than halfway inside her, he paused and called on all of his strength of will to hold perfectly still and allow her body to become used to his presence. He was beyond need. Beyond desire. Maggie was his air. His life. She was all.

"Culhane!" She arched and moved into him. "Don't stop."

"We must go slowly," he told her, unwilling to hurt her now, when they were just beginning.

"No," she told him, looking into his eyes. "I need you now, Culhane. Fast and hard. I need to feel you need me. Next time, we can go slow."

Next time. She had already accepted there would be a next time. And a next. And one after that. The ragged edges of his self-control, his legendary patience snapped completely. He released her wrists, lifted her legs higher and drove himself into her, over and over again. Hard, demanding, and as he had wanted to from the beginning, with *possession.* She was his. And only his.

He would never let her go.

The inferno engulfed them as he'd known it would. Her eyes sparkled with the shine of a thousand suns and when she cried out his name and her body shuddered and shook around his, Culhane gave himself up to the inevitable and emptied himself inside her.

&

"I'm not going to Otherworld," Nora said for the twentieth time in the last fifteen minutes.

"You have no choice now," Quinn told her. "You heard Eileen and Finn. Mab has escaped."

"I didn't mean to," Eileen put in.

"We know that, baby," Nora said softly. She knew her daughter was suffering pangs of guilt and worry and no doubt, a heavy dose of fear. Nora was right there with her. But it *had* been an accident and at least now, they could all stop waiting for the other shoe to drop. Mab had escaped as they'd all feared she would one day and now they would just have to find a way to deal with it. But she wasn't about to go along with Quinn's idea to run to the Warriors' Conclave.

Quinn kept talking. "Mab is in Otherworld now, no doubt plotting Maggie's destruction. Think you she wouldn't use you or Eileen to make that happen?"

Nora quailed a little at the thought, but a moment later, she stiffened her spine, swallowed her fear and looked her Fae lover directly in the eye. "If Mab's in Otherworld, doesn't it make more sense for us to stay here?"

Quinn Terhune was a warrior. For centuries he'd fought the battles of the Fae. He was stalwart, proud and fearless. Yet, when faced with this one, stubborn, part-Fae woman, he was helpless. Irritation spiked through him. He knew very well that the safest place for his woman was at his home in the Warriors' Conclave.

No one, not even Mab herself, could breach those walls. His mate, his coming child and the child of his heart, Eileen, would be safe there.

He didn't want to force his will on a woman, but by the gods, he would if given no other choice. Even if that meant facing Nora's fury. Better she be alive to rage than dead and gone from him forever.

"If it starts looking bad," Nora said in an effort to placate him, "we'll talk about it again. But for now, we're not going anywhere."

"You are the most confounding female I have ever known," Quinn told her.

She grinned at him. "What a sweet thing to say."

Bezel made kissing noises from his perch at the kitchen table.

"Be silent, pixie," Quinn warned.

"Don't pick on Bezel," Nora said, measuring out a cup of white sugar. "And now that we're finished talking about Mab, I want to talk about our son again."

"For the love of Fae children, Nora," he whispered, "I beg you no."

She ignored that plea. "I still say you should have told me what you were doing when you were doing it," Nora said, and cracked two eggs into a bowl.

Afternoon sunlight slid through the kitchen windows and lay across the pedestal table where Eileen sat doing her homework. Bezel was nearby, talking to the dog; Quinn was stalking around the perimeter of Maggie's kitchen like an ancient Viking looking for someone to behead.

"It's not something males talk about," he argued.

Nora huffed out a breath and looked across the room at her lover. He'd come into her life in a rush, swept her off her feet and had made her love him more than she would have thought possible. But that didn't give him the right to plot out her child's life before that child had even drawn his first breath!

Before she could say any of that, though, Eileen spoke up. "Did you know that thirty-three percent of domestic violence begins with a simple argument?"

"There is no violence here, child," Quinn reassured her.

"Not yet," Bezel tossed in, "but it looks promising."

"Quiet, pixie! No one asked your counsel."

"I am," Nora said, waving a wooden spoon at Quinn as if it were a broadsword. "What do you think, Bezel? Do you think it's right for *him* to decide *my* little boy is going to become a warrior?"

"I think you should keep making those cookies," Bezel said, then hopped onto a chair beside Eileen. "My wife, Fontana, makes cookies with Terezia berries." He sighed. "Fontana's quite the cook. I miss those cookies."

"Terezia berries?" Eileen asked.

"Think raspberries but better," Bezel said, then stabbed a finger at her math homework. "That one's wrong."

"No, it's not," Eileen argued. "The answer's in the back of the book and I checked."

"The book's wrong," Bezel told her with a shrug. "Pixies know math."

"Pixies are a plague on the Fae," Quinn muttered.

"Don't you pick on Bezel because you're mad at me," Nora told him.

Quinn took a deep breath and Nora watched his chest swell to enormous proportions. And though she was still furious with him, she couldn't help the instinctive sigh of appreciation that slid from her lips. The man was really completely gorgeous. And normally very supportive.

"Woman, you must see that our child is already destined for great things," Quinn said, trying to be placating, which only irritated Nora further.

Grumbling under her breath, she went back to stirring the cookie dough. She'd had a craving for chocolate chip cookies and her oven was broken, so she'd come to the main house, since Maggie was off in Otherworld. This kitchen, the one she and her sister had grown up in, was comforting in a way the guesthouse just wasn't. This kitchen held memories, echoes of her family, her grandparents and the kids she and Maggie used to be. Watching Eileen doing homework at that table was comforting, too, and right about now, she could use a little comfort.

Everything was changing so quickly. Eileen was growing up, Nora was pregnant and Maggie was a queen. They had a pixie living in their tree and a grandFae who slipped in and out of their lives like a wisp of smoke and demons trotting through their hometown trying to kill them. Nora needed to hold on to a little normal. But even that thought made her smile, since for years she'd dismissed normalcy as boring. Funny, now that the everyday and ordinary was so far removed from their lives, it looked pretty good to her. Practically like a vacation.

"Mom?"

"Do your homework, honey," she said, and stirred the brown sugar and egg mixture until it was creamy. This she could cling to. Homework. Homemade cookies.

"I am, but—"

"Nora . . ."

"Quinn, I'm pregnant and crabby and you really don't want to push me right now."

"I'm only trying to say that—"

"Seriously?" She reached out for the flour and realized it was moving away from her. No, it wasn't moving. *She* was. "What the heck?"

"You're floating again, Mom," Eileen said wistfully. "Why can't I float? I'm part-Fae and I should get to float."

"All we need. Floating kids," Bezel muttered.

Sheba, sleeping under the table, opened one eye, spotted Nora in midair and slunk under Bezel's chair for protection.

"Stars and comets," Nora muttered, grabbing for a cabinet and missing completely. "Somebody get me down."

Quinn was there an instant later. He dragged her back until her feet hit the floor and then he cupped her face between his palms and bent his head for a brief kiss. "There is much for us to discuss, I know. But our child has a destiny, Nora. One that you will share as your blood becomes more Fae."

His touch was warmth and life and love and always sent shivers through Nora's body. She loved him. She wanted to be with him. But she had to know that her child got to choose what he wanted to be. She wasn't going to fall into line just because things had always been a certain way.

"Why does he have to be a warrior?" Nora fisted one

hand in Quinn's shirt and held on to keep from floating again. "What if he wants to be a carpenter? Or a Fae plumber or something else?"

Bezel snorted.

"He will have a warrior's heart," Quinn told her, ignoring everyone else in the room. "His choice will be to become that which he already is."

She dropped her forehead to his chest and blew out a breath. "That's not a choice, Quinn."

Tipping her chin up with the tips of his fingers, he looked into her eyes. Nora read so many emotions in those cool, blue depths, she was staggered by them all.

Even knowing that, though, Nora had to stand her ground. She'd fought too hard to regain it. During her first marriage, her sense of self had been systematically eroded. Her ex had, with tiny digs and cutting remarks, whittled away at Nora's confidence until she'd been plagued with self-doubts. He had made choices for all of them, dismissing Nora's opinion as worthless. By the time her ex had taken off with their former babysitter, she'd doubted even her own sexuality.

She'd come home with her daughter and slowly gone about rebuilding her self-assurance. She'd opened her mind and her heart to dreams of the mystical and had been delighted to find that her grandmother's stories of being part-Fae were all true.

She was raising a beautiful, loving daughter. She had a great sister and a good life.

Then Quinn had appeared out of nowhere and fulfilled wishes she hadn't even realized she was harboring. She'd felt empowered again. Strong again. She knew she was loved and had blossomed under his devotion. She knew she was a better person, a better mother, because he had come into her life. But still she had to stand up to him because not to do so was to risk losing everything she'd gained.

"Our son must have a choice," she said.

"We are Fae. We are who we are destined to be," Quinn argued.

Bezel snorted again. "Warriors."

"Little troll," Quinn countered, shooting him a hard look, "where would your kind be without the warriors who defend you?"

"Yeah, yeah . . ."

Shaking his head, Quinn turned back to Nora. "It is an honor to serve the Queen and all of the Fae. To stand with brothers in arms and defend all that is most precious to you."

She saw his pride in who he was and his desire to have a son who would follow in his footsteps. "But to decide his fate before he's born . . ."

"It is the way of things. The way of Otherworld and the life you are coming into."

She swallowed back a knot of nerves. Was there always a downside? Would becoming Fae mean losing her sense of self-determination? Could she survive having her choices stripped from her again? "What if I don't want it to be that way?"

"You humans. All alike. I want that. I don't want that." Bezel shook his head. "Sometimes a thing just *is*."

"Bezel, you pestilential pixie," Quinn ordered, "take Eileen to your tree house."

"Why do I have to leave?" Eileen demanded.

"Why should I?" Bezel asked.

"No, they don't leave," Nora told him.

Quinn muttered something unintelligible just under his breath and Bezel wheezed out a laugh.

"Fine. We do this here and now." Quinn looked into Nora's eyes. "Even now, you fight to stay on your own feet. You float, Nora. Soon you will be flying. You're becoming Fae, love. Your body, your blood, your very soul are changing and there is no way to stop that."

So, Nora thought, the choices she'd made already—to become involved with Quinn, to love him—had ensured that her future choices had disappeared. "Will I lose all that I am?"

Quinn smiled gently and smoothed his fingertips along her cheek. "Foolish woman. All that you are will remain and become even more so. Do you love me?"

Nora sighed. That was one thing she was absolutely sure of. "Yes."

He cupped her cheek, his fingers spearing up and into her hair. "We are one, Nora. As it was meant. When Culhane first sent me to you, to watch you because of your closeness to Maggie, I knew the moment I saw you that nothing in my life would be the same. Ever. You are the heart of me. And I will do all I can to ease your passage into your new life."

"I think I'm gonna hurl," Bezel said.

Nora ignored him. "But? I heard a *but* there."

"But you must *choose* to make it so. You must be open to it as you have been from the beginning." He smiled. "Take what is offered and see it for what it is."

She *had* chosen to become involved with Quinn. Even when she found out who and what he was, she had chosen to continue along this path. So she wasn't really losing anything, was she? She was already living her choices.

"What about Eileen?" Nora asked, with a glance at the table where her daughter watched her. "She's not fully Fae. What about my daughter?"

"*Our* daughter," he told her, and turned to smile at the girl beaming at him. "Eileen will be with us and if the time comes when she chooses to become fully Fae, your sister, the Queen, can make it so."

"Really?" Eileen piped up, eager and excited.

"Aw jeez . . ."

"Bezel!" Nora frowned at him, then looked back at Quinn. "*Eileen* chooses."

"Aye," he agreed. "She chooses for herself."

"Woo-hoo!" Eileen crowed, and hugged Bezel until the pixie sputtered indignantly.

Nora sighed and laid her head against Quinn's broad chest. Smiling, she said, "She'll choose to become Fae. She's already chosen."

"Our children will be well," Quinn assured her.

"You promise?"

"I vow it."

Nora closed her eyes and let his strength surround her. She'd trust in her warrior. Believe her own heart. And live with the choices she'd already made.

Chapter Nine

*M*aggie lay sprawled across Culhane's chest and didn't want to move. Ever. Here was good. She was comfy. Her body was still practically glowing and she felt more relaxed than she had in her whole life. Every cell in her body was replete. And what a good word that was.

Culhane had been absolutely right when he'd warned her what seemed like a lifetime ago that sex with a Faery would rock her world. Well, he hadn't used those words, but that was the basic meaning and, boy howdy, had he known what he was talking about.

With his hands on her, his body inside hers, she'd forgotten everything. The Mab threat. The worries over her sister. The duties of her new queenhood. Her suspicions over her grandFae. Absolutely every single thought that wasn't a celebration of what he was doing to her had just disintegrated.

Of course, now that the festivities were, if not over, at least at halftime, those thoughts came flooding back. But she mentally fought them down. She didn't want to think yet. She wanted to keep feeling. And if that made her selfish, then she'd just have to live with it.

"Are you sleeping?" he asked quietly.

"Are you kidding?" She turned her head to look at him and smiled. "Give me five or ten minutes to let feeling come back into my legs and we can go again."

He laughed, and it was a loud, rich sound that seemed to echo off the high ceilings and crystal walls surrounding them. "Maggie Donovan, you are a rare woman indeed."

"Thanks," she said. "You're not so bad yourself."

"I'm pleased you think so."

"Oh," she said with a sigh, "I really do. We should have done that weeks ago."

He slid one hand along her spine, down to the curve of her behind, and Maggie moaned softly in response.

"Everything in its time, my Queen." His deep, nearly musical voice rumbled out around her. He continued to stroke her skin with long, slow caresses designed to rekindle the fires inside.

And it was working.

She took a breath and thought about what he'd said.

"Queen," Maggie repeated, pushing herself up on his chest to look down into his pale green eyes. She gave him a wry smile. "*Queen Maggie*. Doesn't sound very regal, does it?"

"It sounds just as it should. As it was meant to be."

"You really believe that," she whispered, her gaze locked with his. "That I was destined to rule here."

"I do." He took her shoulders in his hands, reared up from the bed and deftly flipped her over onto her back. Now he loomed over her, his dark hair like a black silk curtain on either side of his face as he looked down at her. "You are the destiny of Otherworld. You are *my* destiny."

Her heart did a funny little flip-flop action as something ancient and powerful stirred inside her. Looking up at him, she felt, for the first time, that maybe he was right. Maybe this was destiny playing out. Bringing her to exactly where she was supposed to be at exactly the right time.

Maggie felt as though she could do anything as long as she had him beside her. He was strong and fearless and yes, okay, arrogant and pushy, too. But beyond all that, Culhane made her feel as if anything were possible. He made her feel alive. Important. *Needed.*

She reached up with one hand and stroked his hair back from his face, allowing her fingers to linger on his jaw, then trace the curve of his lips. When she thought about what that mouth had already done to her, what it could do in the days and weeks and hell, *eternities* in the future, her whole body trembled in anticipation.

"I never thought about destiny until I met you," she said quietly, almost surprised as the words slipped out.

He gave her a half smile and drew her fingers into his mouth. She breathed in fast, shallow gulps as his teeth nibbled at the pads of her fingers. When he released them, he said only, "Your destiny was linked to mine. I felt it when I first saw the prophecy. I *knew* it when I first saw you."

Maggie laughed shortly. "Ah. When I was twelve and drowning, you mean? When you pulled me out of the ocean before I could up and die on you? That's when you knew?"

"Yes," he said, suddenly solemn. His gaze moved over her features as surely as a caress would have. "You fought to live. Even when you were a child, your strength pulled at me. You showed me then that you were a warrior in your heart. And I knew you would one day be mine."

"Wow." She swallowed hard and reveled in the rush of emotion crowding her chest, filling her heart.

She probably shouldn't be feeling this good, Maggie told herself. What with everything going on at the moment. But she did. Everything was falling into place. She'd finally made a damn decision, accepted her role as Queen and even better, she'd had the Fae orgasm she'd been promising herself for weeks.

Now all she had to do was survive Mab's escape, clean up a pesky civil war among the Fae, buy a Christmas tree for the house and have more Faery orgasms. Not necessarily in that order.

He shifted over her and she felt his erection, hard and eager again, brush against her inner thigh. Her inner muscles clenched and she blew out a breath.

"Culhane ..." Something occurred to her and she stopped, tipped her head to one side on the pillow and asked, "Do you even have a first name?"

He frowned. "Of course I have a first name. Doesn't everyone?"

She'd always thought so, but in all the time they'd spent together, Maggie had never heard him called anything other than Culhane. "So what is it?"

"Unimportant," he assured her, and dropped one hand to rub his thumb across one of her nipples.

"That's cheating." She sucked in a gulp of air, grabbed his hand and stilled it, despite the celebration going on down in her hoo-hah. Her hormones were already putting on their party hats for a second go-round and God knew, she hated to disappoint them, but ... "Good distraction. Now, what's your name?"

"I am Culhane." He shrugged. "It has always been enough."

"Uh-huh." Wildly curious now, mostly because he was actually refusing to answer her, Maggie sat up straight, tossed her hair back from her face and folded her arms beneath her boobs. "Come on, let's have it. Is it embarrassing or something? Howard? Dwayne?"

"There are other things we could be doing," he muttered.

Oh yes, and she really wanted to. But first things first. "Come on now, tell the Queen. Please, God, your name's not Lance. I knew a Lance once. A complete dweeb."

He sighed. "It is not Lance."

"Horace?"

"No."

"Stanley?" Maggie was grinning now, enjoying watching Culhane squirm uncomfortably. Had she finally found a chink in the warrior's armor? He was always so arrogant. So sure of himself. Yet ask him his name and he turned all sulky and crabby. Yep, she was enjoying herself.

"No. There are no Fae named Stanley." Clearly irritated, Culhane pushed off the bed, waved one hand in the air and instantly, he was dressed in his usual clothes. Brown pants, green shirt, brown leather boots and a knee-length brown coat. Even his long, thick hair was neatly gathered at his neck. The image of a man completely at home with himself. Confident.

He looked, let's face it, spectacular.

Maggie wanted him all over again. Her entire body quivered at the thought. But, she guessed, playtime was over. His features were implacable, his stance that of a hard, ruthless man ready to fight at a moment's notice. Not a trace of tenderness could be found in his eyes. They were cool and steely as if he'd already separated himself from what had gone on before. Only moments ago, he'd been the kind of lover most women could only dream about. Now he was the warrior she knew him to be.

"Okay, you win this round," she conceded. "I suppose we have bigger problems to deal with at the moment than your name—"

He inclined his head.

"But that doesn't mean I'm forgetting about it," she warned. "I will find out."

"No," he said, with the barest hint of a smile. "You won't."

"You're a hard man, Culhane," Maggie told him as she scooted off the bed and faced him. She didn't miss the quick flick of his gaze as he took her in and she relished the flash of heat that look engendered. Still, if he was already dressed, party time was over for the moment. "So. Can you do me?"

His mouth quirked. "I believe I just have."

"Not what I meant. Nobody likes a funny warrior." Yet her mouth curved in amusement anyway. "Clothes. I meant can you dress me as quickly as you did you?"

He lifted his hand again and just like that, Maggie was wearing her favorite style of jeans, a dark blue sweater and a new pair of fabulous black boots.

"Excellent," she said, and bounced experimentally on her toes. "They're even comfortable. You're a lot handier than the mall, Culhane."

He smiled. "I live to serve, my Queen."

"Cool." She grinned. "Now, I think we should get back to my house and let everyone know about Mab."

He shook his head firmly. "That is not wise. I will go and get your family. Bring them to the palace for safekeeping."

Maggie laughed. "You can't be serious. This is Mab's old home. She knows her way around here way better than I do. Nora and Eileen wouldn't be safe in the palace. They're better off in the mortal world."

He smiled at her.

"What?"

"That's the first time you haven't called the mortal world *your* world."

"Huh." She blinked, thought about that for a second or two and was surprised to realize he was right. For weeks now, Otherworld had been his, the mortal world, hers. She wasn't sure when the shift had taken place, but it seemed that even her subconscious was recognizing the truth. She really had made her decision. This was home now. This world. This palace.

Him.

"You're right."

"I am pleased."

"Happy to help," she said, then added quickly, "I'm not giving up the mortal world entirely though, okay? I want to keep my house there and spend time there as well. This will be home base, but that world still has a part of me, too."

"I understand."

"You know," Maggie told him softly, "I think you really do. Which just makes this whole thing much easier."

She gave a quick look around the throne room. The bed was gone, thanks no doubt to more of Culhane's magic. But it would be back if they needed it—not that she needed a bed in the throne room. But some chairs, maybe a few of her paintings on the walls, a couch or two and some brightly colored rugs. And a fireplace in here and in her bedroom.

"Hey," she said, "do I even *have* a bedroom here?"

"Several," he said, smiling at her again as if he were really enjoying her getting into the whole queen thing. Well, good. He could enjoy. She'd be nervous.

"Good. Okay." She nodded to herself. "We'll get around to redecorating later. Maybe Claire can help. Not Nora, though. She'd hang wind chimes and macramé pot holders all over the place."

She was really going to do this, Maggie thought. Be a queen. Live in a palace. As those thoughts rolled through her mind, she waited for an internal shriek of panic to erupt. But it didn't. A good sign? Or was she just too crazy to realize the enormity of what she was doing?

From outside the palace came the sounds of music. Pipes, fiddles, drums. It was a lively tune, bright, upbeat, optimistic. Maggie was glad for it and took it as a good sign. She would soon be facing plenty of problems and she liked hearing something that sounded so stubbornly cheerful.

"This is going to work," she murmured, more to herself than Culhane. She could do this. She would do this. Her grandfather had always told her that the key to getting anything done was to just do it. Stop standing around. Jump in with both feet and get it done.

If you screwed it all up, you could always fix it.

"We should speak to the warriors before we go to your sister," Culhane was saying. "They may have further word of Mab."

"No." Maggie looked right at him and silently dared him to argue with her. If she was going to be Queen, then she should practice putting her foot down occasionally. Could you take queen lessons, she wondered, then dismissed the notion. The only queen she was vaguely aware of was Elizabeth, and what could a woman who carried an empty purse teach her?

"We'll go to my house first. I need to warn Nora now. Get her and Eileen to leave the guesthouse and move into my place. If we're all in one spot, we'll be safer."

"But you're staying here," he reminded her.

"Soon," she told him, and saw a flicker of doubt in his eyes. Well, she couldn't help that. He'd find out soon enough that she meant what she'd said. The palace would be home for her, but at the moment, other things had priority. "For right now, I need to be with my family."

"Maggie . . ."

"Just draw the portal, okay? We'll see Nora, then the warriors. . . ."

He did as she asked, though she could tell he was irritated. Ooh. News flash.

A golden circle opened up in front of her. Familiar scents of home blew in from the center of that circle and Maggie moved toward it; then she remembered something, stopped and said over her shoulder, "We also need to talk about the female guards. I want them to be warriors, too."

"You *what*?"

"I spoke to Ailish about this. Flying warriors. *Big* advantage. Huge." She stepped through the portal, still talking, and so didn't hear Culhane's shout of outrage until they were standing in her kitchen.

"Ooh, cookies." Maggie walked straight for the cooling rack on the counter. She hadn't even realized just how famished she was. Great sex really could make you hungry. Good thing she had that superfast Fae metabolism thing going for her now, because the way she was feeling, she could inhale the whole kitchen.

"Hello to you, too," Nora said as she tucked another full cookie sheet into the oven.

"Hi, Nora. Good cookies." Maggie took a big bite and smiled. "I'm glad you're here." She chewed, then swallowed and reached for another still-warm cookie. "We need to talk about something."

"Aunt Maggie, hi," Eileen said. "Finn told Mom and Quinn about how I accidentally let Mab out of her painting."

"I can't believe they had her in a painting where anyone could have touched her," Nora said with a shake of her head. "You'd think a wizard would have been smarter."

"Good point," Maggie told her, grateful that Finn had already broken the news. Looked like Nora was taking it all right. Of course, when Maggie's sister was nervous or worried, or for that matter happy or excited, she liked to bake. Kept her mind off things and kept her busy. Which worked well for Maggie, because in times of stress or joy, Maggie liked to eat.

"Oh," Eileen said with excitement, "also, Mom says I can be a Fae if I want to. And Quinn says you know how to make me one, so I'm like completely ready to—"

"No, you're not." Nora gave her "the look." Maggie was pretty sure they taught that move to new mothers right after giving birth.

"Anyway"—Maggie shifted a look at Quinn, who stood close to Nora—"I need to talk to you, too."

"No," Culhane told her as he stepped through the portal right behind her, "*we* need to talk."

"Trouble in Torea," Bezel muttered.

"Huh?" Eileen whispered.

"Think heaven but better," the pixie told her.

"Fine, but I want to talk about becoming a Fae. Mom said I could and—"

Maggie ignored Eileen's complaint along with everyone else, turned around to look at Culhane and saw that he was practically vibrating with banked fury. It was written all over his features. His pale eyes were flashing and his jaw was tight as he gritted his teeth.

Damn. What could have gone so wrong in one short portal jaunt?

"What's wrong with you?"

He glared at her as if she were crazy. "You want the female guard to join the warriors?"

"*Impossible!*" Quinn bellowed.

"What a great idea," Nora said, and dropped more cookie dough onto an aluminum sheet.

"According to my research, female Fae are just as mean in a fight as men, and they can fly," Eileen reminded them all. "I mean, remember how tough Mab was?" She frowned. "Um, let's not talk about Mab."

"Knock it off, kid," Bezel muttered, his gaze flicking from Maggie to Culhane and back again. "This is one fight we don't want a part of. Trust me on this."

Quinn crossed his arms over his enormous chest, scowled at Maggie and declared, "The females cannot be warriors."

"Why the hell not?" Nora demanded, then caught herself, glanced at Eileen and said, "Heck. I meant, heck."

"It is not possible." Quinn ground out the words.

Then Nora turned on Quinn even while Maggie faced off with Culhane.

Culhane stared in disbelief at the woman who only an hour ago had cradled his body inside hers. They'd connected on a level he'd never before reached with a woman. Their minds, souls and hearts had touched.

Bonded. *How* could she possibly think he would go along with this foolish plan?

"You do not know what you're asking," he said as calmly and patiently as he could manage.

"Not asking," Maggie told him. She was responding to his ferocity by letting her own temper rise. "Telling. I've already decided this, Culhane. I talked to Ailish and she and the other females are ready and eager to fight. You can use them, so hey, makes sense all the way around."

"You cannot do this."

"Just back up a step or two, Mr. Warrior. I'm the Queen here. Remember?"

"Good point, Mags!" Nora cheered for her sister, and glared at her warrior.

Fine, Culhane admitted silently. He'd handled that badly. He shouldn't have corrected her in front of her family and Quinn—not to mention, Bezel. When his Queen was in error, Culhane should calmly and quietly take her aside and show her the correct way of things. It is how he had always planned on her reign progressing. This was just going to take some time. After all, the greatest hurdle had been met. She had decided to accept her duty. Move to the palace. Rule Otherworld.

Now all they needed was for her to learn *how* to rule. So he tried again. More calmly this time. Though it was difficult.

"My Queen, I meant no disrespect, of course—"

"You're insane, too! You can't think to allow this, Culhane! The warriors will not stand for it!" Quinn shouted, and Culhane spared him one long, fulminating look.

"You're a genderist," Nora accused, a horrified look on her face.

"A what?"

"You're discriminating against the women because of their gender. Okay, there's probably a better word for it, but you know what I mean."

"Love," Quinn said, "I am not angry with you. . . ."

"Lame," Bezel muttered.

"Maggie," Culhane continued in a voice loud enough to drown out everyone else's so that he might regain her attention, "surely you see that to bring females into the Warrior clan could not possibly work."

"Nope," she said, grabbing up another cookie and taking a bite. "Don't see that at all."

Culhane took a slow, deep breath and *willed* himself to calm. She was doing this on purpose. There were too many people in this room; that was all. She felt backed into a corner because he had handled her badly. All he had to do was take her aside, explain the way of things and then she would do the right thing and agree with him.

"Chill out, Culhane," Maggie told him, then asked Nora, "Do we have any milk?"

"Just bought some," her sister said, still shooting daggers at Quinn.

"Chill out?" Culhane demanded. "What is that?"

"It means calm down, oh-high-and-mighty Fenian Warrior," Bezel told him.

"I *am* perfectly calm!" His shout rattled the windowpanes.

"Yeah, I'm getting that," Maggie told him as she moved around the table, headed for the fridge.

"Here's a glass," Nora said, handing one over.

"Thanks."

"We are not here to eat cookies, Maggie," Quinn announced.

"That's what *I'm* here for," Maggie told him abruptly, then narrowed her eyes. "And that's *Queen Maggie* to you, buddy."

Bezel laughed and scrubbed his long-fingered hands together. "Hoot! Listen to Her Majesty!"

"Quiet, pixie," Culhane ordered.

"Quit picking on him because you're mad at me,"

Maggie told him as she poured milk into her glass and took a long drink.

"You're a bully, Culhane," Nora threw in, then added just for good measure, "And so are you, Quinn Terhune."

"Me?" The Viking was appalled.

"Fifty-three percent of family squabbles end with a visit from the police," Eileen pronounced to no one in particular.

"Jeeez, kid, put a sock in it, will ya?" Since he didn't have a sock handy, Bezel shoved a cookie in Eileen's mouth and dropped one to the dog as well, to stop her whimpering.

Maggie whistled, a shrill, short blast of sound that had everyone in the room shutting up instantly. "I didn't mean to start World War Three here or something. I just talked to Ailish, the secondary commander of the guards. She said the girls were ready to fight and I said good idea. Told her I'd talk it over with my Chieftain"—she shot a disappointed look at Culhane—"and that I would make sure the females got their chance to fight."

"You should not have done that, Maggie. There are rules. Traditions."

"And I've already broken dozens of 'em, okay?" She picked up her milk glass, took a drink, then set it down again. "I get that I'm not your ordinary Fae Queen. And you have to understand that, too. I'm not going to be doing everything the way it's always been done, because I don't freaking *know* how it's always been done."

"I will tell you," Culhane said through gritted teeth.

"Fine. I'm willing to listen. But I'm also not going to be jumping every time you tell me to. You wanted me to be the Queen, Culhane. Well," she said with a sigh, "I am. And I'm going to do it my way."

"This road will lead to madness," Quinn mumbled.

Maggie frowned and said, "Look, all I'm saying is, it

makes sense that the female guards fight if they want to. They're trained warriors."

Quinn snorted.

"If you do this thing," Culhane warned, ignoring his friend because he was still trying to remain calm and coolheaded, "it will only cause more trouble. The warriors will not accept the female guard. And this is *not* why I fought so hard to help you become Queen."

Maggie tipped her head to one side, studied him for a long moment or two, then walked toward him. Suspicion glittered in her blue eyes, along with a hint of danger that should have warned any sane male in her vicinity to take a walk. Culhane, though, was made of sterner stuff than most males. He stood his ground.

"Just why did you fight to put me on the throne, Culhane?" she asked thoughtfully. "So I could be a good little warrior puppet? Was that the idea all along? Were you planning on jerking my strings and telling me which way to move, what to say, what to think?"

"Of course not." Not in those particular terms, at any rate.

She looked at him as if she didn't believe him and that stung more than he would have cared to admit.

"It doesn't really matter why, I guess," Maggie said. "Because if that was the plan, it's not going to work. I'm my own woman—Fae—Queen. You might not like everything I do, but you're not going to stop me from doing it. And I say the female guards are going to fight with the warriors."

"Insulting," Quinn muttered, then hissed out a breath as Nora punched him in the stomach.

Culhane was still striving for reasonable, though his temper was near the boiling point. How had this day suddenly turned asunder? Only an hour or so ago, he had been filled with hope for his world and his brave new Queen. How had he lost control of this situation? And more importantly, how could he get it back?

"Better to give the males the power of flight," he pointed out in a cool, rational, she'll-have-to-listen-to-me-now tone. "Then we have flying warriors without the trouble of females trying to fit in where they have no place. Males are the better fighters, remember."

"Maybe *you* should remember whom you're talking to, Culhane," Maggie said softly.

"Uh-oh," Bezel murmured.

Culhane's gaze was fixed on Maggie as she closed in on him. Gone was the tender, yet fiery lover he'd held so briefly in his arms. Here stood a queen in all her furious glory. And though she infuriated him, he couldn't help the swell of admiration he felt for her, either. She lifted her chin, squared her shoulders and glared at him hard enough to turn him to stone.

"I'm female, remember?" she asked. "And in the last few weeks, I've fought demons, rogue Fae and even a damn crazy queen. Not to mention, *you*."

"Yes," he agreed, then added, "Although—"

"Not finished yet," she told him, cutting him off before he could even end his sentence. "It's time you warriors get a grip. You guys are *not* the only ball game in town, you know."

"Ball game?" Quinn muttered.

Maggie didn't even glance at him. Her gaze remained fixed on Culhane's. "Otherworld needs *all* of its warriors fighting together now. No more of this stupid bickering about who fights better than who or who has better powers or whatever."

"You don't understand," Culhane said tightly as his carefully banked fury began to slip its leash. "You're new to this, Maggie."

"I may be new to Otherworld, but to this sexist crap?" She shook her head. "Old news, Culhane."

He grabbed her shoulders, pulled her in close and ignored the room full of people watching them both intently. He stared into her eyes and said, "You're new to ruling, Maggie. You've said yourself you have no idea how to be Queen. You have stalled and avoided your responsibilities for as long as you could and even now, there's a part of you that quails at the thought of taking your rightful place."

"*My* rightful place," she said, not arguing his point, just reminding him that like it or not, she *was* the Queen.

Irritation clouded his judgment. That was the only reason he could find later for what he said next.

"You are still more human than Fae. You are not immortal yet. Your powers are still growing. You are hesitant when you need to be strong. You need me to make these important decisions for you."

A second ticked past. Then two. Then three. Finally, Maggie asked, "Was this all nothing but a game to you, Culhane?"

"What?"

"You used me to fight Mab. Now you want to use me to make your changes to Otherworld. What's the plan? I'm Queen, but you're in charge?"

"It is not like that, Maggie." He had never used her. He'd thought only to train her. To help her. To set her on the throne so that he might . . . He groaned inwardly. So that he might rule in her stead.

"Do you even give a single damn about me?"

Too late now, Culhane saw the trap he'd stepped into so completely. All he could do now was try to ease himself free. "How can you ask that after—"

She shook her head and spoke up fast to cut him off. "You want to use me, Culhane. All I ever was to you was a tool."

"You're wrong." He wouldn't beg or plead. Wouldn't bloody well ask for forgiveness for doing the right thing for both his world and the mortal dimension. "You're wrong about everything."

She stopped, pushed both hands through her hair and

choked out a half laugh. "God. How stupid am I? You never wanted me to be Queen. You expected me to just let you be *King*."

He drew himself up to his full, imposing height and stared down at her. Those blue eyes he knew so well were clouded with suspicion and hurt and anger. He suspected those same emotions could be seen in his own eyes. Even if most of what she'd said had been true, he had never once thought of her as a puppet. Just some mindless body to sit on a throne. He'd wanted to rule *with* her. To show her what Otherworld could be.

And now, that chance was gone because she didn't trust him. That fact stung more than any other. Hadn't he been by her side through all of this? Hadn't he defended her? Protected her? Looked out for her when she had known nothing about the new life she was facing? Did he really deserve her contempt?

No.

"I am Culhane. A Fenian warrior," he said softly, though with such strength, his voice ricocheted off the walls and hummed in the room like a force of nature. "I am unaccustomed to being mistrusted. My honor—my word—is all-important to me and has been through the eons of my life. You are my Queen, Maggie Donovan, and your protection is my duty. But I will not defend *myself* to a woman who should know me better than this."

Then he gave her a half bow and shifted out of the room, out of her world. Quinn was just a heartbeat behind him.

Maggie was rocked to her soul.

Nora was crying.

Eileen looked confused.

When the back door flew open a moment later, Claire MacDonald rushed inside, eyes wild, hair flying. "Mab's escaped!" she shouted.

"Some psychic," Bezel snorted, and ate a cookie.

Chapter Ten

e

"*Female* warriors?" McCulloch repeated with a grimace, as if even the words themselves were distasteful. "It cannot be."

"So we tried to tell the Queen," Quinn muttered in disgust.

Muldoon poured a glass of nectar, downed it in one gulp and shook his head. "Surely this will be the end of the Warrior clan."

" 'Tis lunacy," Riley swore.

"Or perhaps not," O'Hara put in quietly.

Instantly, the others in the room turned on him, their voices combining to create a dull roar of outrage.

Culhane was only half listening to the debate that had been raging now for hours. He'd gathered his most trusted five the moment he'd returned to the Warriors' Conclave to tell them about Maggie's unreasonable demand.

Maggie.

His heart clenched in his chest and a ball of ice settled low in his belly. She'd been in his grasp there in her kitchen and yet farther from him than she had ever been. As if their time together in the throne room had never happened, she'd distanced herself from him completely. He'd seen it himself. The frost in her eyes, the disdain in her voice and the disappointed anger written all over her features. He would remember it always.

And know that he had been at the root of it all.

Yet a part of him rebelled against any regrets cloud-ing his thoughts. He had done only what he had always done. His best for Otherworld and his people. He would not apologize for simply being who and what he was.

Gods knew he had never meant to harm her in any way. Maggie would realize that eventually and come to see that she needed him. Needed his advice. His counsel. *Him.*

"Culhane, you must stop this insanity."

He looked at Muldoon, a fiery man with thick red hair, blazing green eyes and hands the size of platters. A giant of a man, he made the other warriors, including Culhane, look nearly small in comparison. At this mo-ment, Muldoon looked ready to explode.

"Is *this* what we waited for? For a queen who cares not for the tradition of the Warrior clans? Does she dis-miss us without even knowing us? She is not even fully Fae yet!"

A fierce wave of protectiveness rose up in Culhane as he stood to his full height and glared at Muldoon until the warrior's gaze flinched away.

"Maggie is Queen," Culhane said with deliberate em-phasis, his gaze moving from one warrior to the next to ensure that *all* of them understood how he felt about the situation. He didn't agree with Maggie about this, and he would certainly try to change her mind. But until that happened, he would defend her decisions. He would fight for her right to rule. He had waited centuries for her to ascend to the throne. He would not turn his back on her before she had been Queen even a month. "If she decrees the females as warriors," he continued, "it will be done."

"Ending the Warrior clans for good and all," Mc-Culloch muttered again, in spite of the glare Culhane sent him.

"Ach," O'Hara groaned, pushed to his feet and

snatched the bottle of nectar from Muldoon. "Such whining I haven't heard in this Conclave in years. Are you so afraid of females fighting alongside you? Do you fear they'll be a hindrance? Or is it that you fear they might prove themselves finer warriors?"

McCulloch stepped up to his friend, grabbed a fistful of O'Hara's shirt and yanked the warrior right off his feet. He lifted him until O'Hara's feet left the floor. "I fear no woman and there's not a female alive can out-fight me."

O'Hara laughed, punched his friend in the face and shifted out of Mac's grasp. When he rematerialized, he was still grinning like a fool as he watched Mac rub his aching jaw.

O'Hara moved to the sideboard, grabbed a glass and poured himself a healthy draught of nectar. "Then why do you moan and groan and complain like a troll in the rain? You've nothing to fear and mayhap we have all to gain."

More mutters of disgust and still more complaints rose up in the room and Culhane ignored them all. O'Hara wasn't threatened by the change. Most likely it was because O'Hara had probably had half of the female guards on their backs at one time or another. He, more than any of them, had seen firsthand the frustration simmering in the guard. He knew they were good fighters and didn't fear having them join the warriors.

There was that word again.

Fear.

Culhane mentally sneered at the thought. His warriors knew no fear. The very notion of it was insulting. Demeaning to the proud Fae he'd served with for centuries. This wasn't about fear. This was about the fact that for eons, the male Fae of Otherworld had been no better than servants to their women. All but the Warrior clan. Here, in the Conclave, the male Fae were respected and needed. Here, there were no women muddying things.

And now, the female guards wanted to be included in the only truly independent environment a male Fae could claim?

No, Culhane told himself. This would not go well. There were too many centuries of bad blood spilled to be forgotten because a new and foolish queen hoped to turn everyone into a happy team working together. The gods alone knew what she was thinking. Didn't she understand what this would do to his men? To all Fae males?

Those who did not serve as warriors looked to this clan as a source of pride. Here, they could say, the women did not rule. In the Conclave, it was a male's world. Bitterness rose in his throat and nearly choked him. He hadn't foreseen anything like this. The prophecies had said nothing about the future Queen turning Otherworld on its head. Had not mentioned that she would make Culhane want to beat his head upon a rock out of sheer frustration.

And had he known, he asked himself, would he have done anything different? Would he, even now, wish for Mab to be on the throne again rather than Maggie?

Ah. Such a question. And the answer was, no. He would rather Maggie with all of her unfounded notions be on the throne, because clearly, she was a female who appreciated equality. Though she was going about it in the wrong way. Giving the female Fae *more* power and stripping it from the men was not what he had had in mind.

"Enough," he shouted, silencing his own thoughts as well as the other warriors. His men turned to him, their personal arguments forgotten in the face of his authority. "We can do nothing about Maggie's plan at this time. Instead, we should concentrate on Mab. Send squads of warriors out. Groups of three. Search Otherworld until she's found and then report back to me. We five will meet at the palace tonight."

"Why the palace?" Mac asked.

"We'll search that place top to bottom," Culhane told him. "There may be clues to where Mab might go for help."

"Makes sense," Muldoon said.

"If we find her in our search, what then?" Quinn asked.

"*When* we find her," Culhane corrected, "we do nothing. We observe. See what she's stirring up. We won't be able to stop her unless we know exactly what she's doing."

"Aye." One by one, the warriors nodded and shifted out of the Conclave.

Culhane shook his head, thinking about what would have happened if the females had been given orders. Would they have shifted immediately into action? Or would they have stayed, demanding explanations and reasons and wanting to talk about all manner of things rather than simply accept a direct command and obey?

Gods, a warrior could go mad trying to figure out a woman. But as for his men, they would do their duty. As they had always done, he told himself. As *he* had always done.

Once they'd found Mab, Culhane could show Maggie that his warriors didn't need the females to fight alongside them. She would see that the males had protected all Fae for longer than most could remember and they didn't need any help.

Maggie was Queen. But he was Culhane, a mighty Fenian warrior. Nothing was going to change that.

e

"You haven't found out anything?" Maggie faced Bezel and fought back her frustration.

"Nada," Bezel said, grumbling. "There's something going on with that grandFae of yours. I just haven't caught him yet."

"Great." So she didn't know any more than she had before. "Seriously, could my life get more screwed up?"

"Probably," Bezel mused, rocking back and forth on his huge feet.

"Thanks for that." She shook her head, grabbed a couple of wineglasses out of the cupboard and looked at him again. "Just keep watching, okay? I want to believe Jasic's on the up-and-up, but . . ."

"He ain't," Bezel warned, his silvery eyebrows beetling on his forehead like live caterpillars.

"Then find something," she said, turning her back on the pixie to join Claire in the living room.

*

"Are you even trying?" Two hours later, Maggie took a gulp of her wine and gave Claire a dirty look. The two women were seated on the floor in Maggie's living room, a bottle of wine between them and a snoring Sheba stretched out across their feet.

It was nearly ten, and outside the living room windows, the night was dark but for the glow of the Christmas lights strung under the eaves. Up and down Maggie's street, the lights and reindeer and laughing Santas had been going up all week. Normalcy was all around her, yet somehow, it didn't quite come close enough to her to make a real difference in her life, Maggie thought.

Heck, she'd even used her still-growing Fae abilities to help her with the lights this year. Floating/flying? Much easier than dragging a rickety ladder around behind her. Of course, she'd had to hang the lights at night, so her neighbors didn't notice her doing the floaty thing.

Nora, Eileen, Claire and Maggie had spent most of the evening dragging out Christmas decorations from the attic. While Bezel kibitzed from a corner, the women had buried their fears of Mab under layers of holiday spirit. A snowman Nora had made in a ceramics class three years ago sat on a silver tray surrounded by shiny, red glass bulbs. Red and white silk poinsettias burst out of every vase they owned and Eileen's painting of a Christmas tree hung in a proud spot over the faux fireplace.

Maggie had floated up to the ceiling, stringing artificial pine boughs around the living room, and a wreath she'd had for years hung where the front door had been until her grandfather had paneled over it. There were cinnamon candles burning, scenting the air, Christmas music playing softly in the background and a half-empty bottle of Chardonnay on the table.

Nora and Eileen had gone to bed an hour ago, exhausted from the decorating—not to mention all the high drama and anxiety. Bezel was eating his way through more of Nora's cookies in the kitchen and Maggie and Claire were slowly, deliberately, working up a heck of a wine buzz.

"Of course I'm trying, you silly cow," Claire said with a short laugh that ended on a hiccup. "Visions come when they come. It's not like turning on a bleeding TV, you know."

"Bezel was right. Some psychic you are," Maggie muttered.

"You know," Claire mused, completely ignoring the dig, "if that dog didn't snore when she slept, a body would swear she was dead."

"She's exhausted," Maggie said in defense of the lazy golden retriever. "Like me."

It had been a full day, she thought, what with freeing Mab, having sex with Culhane, only to discover that he'd been using her all along, and then watching him shift right out of her life. Not to mention all of the decorating and the drain of keeping a determinedly cheerful attitude so she wouldn't upset anyone.

God. She wanted to curl up under the table with the dog.

"Yeah," Claire said, "because all those naps she takes must wear her out."

"Hello?" Maggie poured more wine. "Sheba's sleep schedule's not the most important thing right now. You're not even *trying* to have a damn vision."

Claire shook her head and sipped at her wine. "You know, when I first told you about being psychic and well, a witch, I was worried that you'd shut me out." Her Scots accent was a purr of sound on the words that tumbled from her. "Most everyone I've ever known has pushed away once they learned the truth about me."

Claire MacDonald had been Maggie's best friend for ten years. But it wasn't until a few weeks ago that Claire had confessed her little secret. Since then, the two women had become even closer. Since they were both dealing with the supernatural, it almost made them seem normal. To each other, at least.

"Ah," Maggie told her with a smile, "but I'm not everyone."

"That's the God's truth, I'll say." Claire laughed. "Most folks want to shuffle me out the door as fast as they can, while you, my very different friend, *order* me to have visions."

"Well, what the hell good are they if you can't drum one up when you need it?"

"A question I've often asked myself," Claire admitted.

"It's just . . ." Maggie blew out a breath, shifted slightly because her right foot had gone numb under Sheba and then said, "Everything's a mess all of a sudden. Mab's out. Nora's terrified, even though she won't say it. . . ."

"Yes," Claire said with a smile. "I noticed the two cakes, the muffins and the cookies in the kitchen. Though I thought there were more cookies a while ago."

"There were," Maggie told her, and laid one hand across her stomach. She'd had cookies for dinner. Not a good idea. "We'll probably all get diabetes in the next few days, the way Nora's baking. Especially now that she and Eileen are staying here because we have to watch out for Mab the Marauder trying to kill us in our sleep or something."

"Ah no," Claire said, lifting her wineglass in a salute to herself. "You're forgetting I warded the house tonight. The strength of the spell I put on this place will keep out anything with a mind to cause harm."

It had been pretty impressive, Maggie thought, watching Claire work. While Nora, Eileen and Maggie had been decorating like crazed elves with a deadline, Claire the Friendly Witch had been casting a spell around the house and grounds. She'd been pretty damn impressive, too. With the candles, burning sage and the fiery crystals humming with trapped energy, Claire had almost looked like an ancient wizard with the secrets of the ages shining in her eyes.

Maggie had actually *felt* the pulse of power when the spell had been completed, so yes, she did feel safer in the house.

"And I appreciate it," she said. "But we could have used Quinn and Culhane, too, and they're so pissed at me, they'll probably stay away just when we need them the most."

"You've got me, don't ya?" Bezel shouted from the kitchen, insult clear in his raspy voice.

"And how do we rid ourselves of you, you little troll?" Claire shouted back.

"Witches," he answered. "Always being snotty,"

"Go home, Bezel," Maggie called out.

"I would if Fontana would let me," he insisted, shifting into the living room to glare down at them.

Since he was standing and they were sitting, Bezel was actually taller than someone for a change. Maggie looked up at him. "I didn't mean go home to Otherworld. I meant go home to your tree."

He scrubbed one hand across his wispy silver beard

and looked away. "Uh, thought I'd just stay in the house for a few days. Just in case."

Maggie smiled up at the ugly little pixie in his green velvet suit. He talked mean and acted all the time as if he'd rather be anywhere but around them. Yet here he was, willing to stay inside the house—which he called a "human box"—rather than his tree house. Because, she knew, he was worried about them. Though Maggie also knew he'd never admit to that.

"Aww . . . that's so thoughtful," Claire murmured with a smile. "You'll be here so we can throw you to Mab just to save ourselves."

"You know," he said scowling, "if my wife, Fontana, knew how crazy you people really are, she'd let me come home."

"Tell her," Claire murmured, taking a sip of her wine. "I beg you."

Maggie smiled. Claire and Bezel had been at each other's throats since the moment they'd met. And Maggie was convinced they actually enjoyed trading insults.

Bezel's silver eyebrows drew together and his icy blue eyes narrowed into slits. "Witches, always got something to say."

"Hobgoblins, never go away."

"Why don't you two just make out and get rid of this sexual tension?" Maggie laughed at their horrified expressions and all at once she felt better. Things could have been worse.

Yes, the Fae Warrior she was fairly certain she was in love with had been using her as a pawn and then had disappeared as soon as she'd called him on it. And yes, there was a rabid former queen on her ass. Oh, and Christmas was like three weeks away and she had no tree, no presents and no more painting jobs until the after-Christmas sales.

But in spite of it all, she had her family. Nora. Eileen.

A grandFae she wasn't too sure about. And she also had Claire and Bezel. Friends.

"Uh, Maggie?"

She looked up at the pixie. "What?"

He pointed one long, knobby finger. "The witch don't look so good."

She slowly swiveled her head to look at Claire and the small hairs at the back of her neck went straight up.

Claire's eyes were completely white. Her head was tipped back, her long hair tumbling down past her shoulders. Her mouth dropped open and the wineglass she held fell from nerveless fingers. From under the table, Sheba issued a loud, insistent whine.

"What do we do?" Bezel asked.

"Beats the hell out of me," Maggie told him, fear rising up inside to squeeze her throat shut. She set her own glass on the table, picked up Claire's and then moved to lean over her friend. "Claire. Claire, can you hear me?"

No response. Fear danced up and down Maggie's spine.

"Maybe," Bezel whispered, "you shouldn't, you know, spook her, when she's all spooked out."

"I've seen her have a vision before and she didn't do this," Maggie told him, her whisper almost lost beneath Nat King Cole's rendition of "Chestnuts Roasting on an Open Fire."

Bezel moved closer and called out to Claire. Maggie glanced up at him and read her own worries reflected in his eyes. What was she supposed to do?

Claire was completely immobile. Sheba crawled out from under the table and, still whining, crawled on her belly into the kitchen.

"Have you ever seen anything like this?" Maggie asked.

'No," Bezel said. "And it's givin' me the trots."

Claire suddenly gasped, lurched up from her sitting position and sent Bezel a hard look. "That was disgusting."

He grinned, clearly relieved. "So were the white eyes, witchy."

"What the hell happened, Claire?" Maggie focused only on her friend. There were beads of perspiration on her forehead and upper lip. Her breath was coming fast and shallow and her hands, as she reached for Maggie's wineglass, were shaking.

"Holy Troll in Torea," Bezel said and whistled long and low. "Witchy, you look like *Ifreann*."

"Feel like it, too, little man." Claire's voice sounded raw and just as trembly as her hands looked.

"What happened?" Maggie demanded. "Was it a vision? What did you see?"

"Mab." Claire looked first at Bezel, then locked her gaze with Maggie's. "I saw Mab. She's not alone, Mags. And she's planning to steal Eileen."

⟡

Mab sat at a table, facing three of the Sluagh. Tremors of a feeling that might have been fear rattled around in the pit of her stomach like several small balls colliding. She'd never known real fear before, so she couldn't be sure of the sensation. But staring into the eyes of the Sluagh was enough to give even the mightiest ruler a qualm or two.

Especially in such a place. It was a tavern, she supposed. Though the rogue Fae had no access to true nectar, they had obviously devised other types of alcohol. Shouts and screams filled the air along with rough laughter and a few moans and groans from the dark corners of the poorly lit building.

Raucous music was a cacophony of sound layering over the stench and noise and Mab, who was more accustomed to the trill of pipes and the sighs of harps, realized more clearly than ever that she was out of her element. She didn't belong on Casia. Didn't have a place among these rowdy, dangerous Fae. She belonged in her crystal palace. On the bejeweled throne that had been her seat of power for centuries.

But getting that world back meant she had to come here.

As Queen, she never would have been seen speaking to such as the Sluagh, but times change and desperate measures must be taken. She shook her long, golden hair back from her face and forced a smile for the leader of the three.

The Sluagh were the most powerful of the rogue Fae in Casia. They were tall, and like most of the Fae, beautiful, with long, black hair, pale skin and black, glittering eyes. But their beauty was a trap. Before their imprisonment, they would draw innocent mortals to them, seduce them and steal their souls, leaving the mortal to die painfully with no hope of moving on to the next dimension.

It was rumored the Sluagh were actually fallen angels, beings who had tired of taking orders in the mortal heaven and were cast out for their disobedience. Able to travel through the dimensions, they had found the Fae realm and decided to stay. But they hadn't followed the rules there, either. Millennia ago, they were imprisoned here on Casia for their crimes against humanity. But then, at that time, the reigning Fae Queen was doing all she could to ensure that Fae and mortals lived in harmony.

Mab couldn't have cared less about harmony. The Fae were clearly the superior race and if the humans became too much trouble, they should be ended.

"Why do you bother us?" the beautiful man demanded.

Mab smiled at him and received no response in return. Her beauty would buy her nothing from these Fae. The Sluagh ruled this prison island through fear and intimidation and had been known to behead immortal beings for the smallest slight—even for pronouncing their name wrong.

Mab was very careful to say it right.

"Will the *Sloo-ah* help me or not?" she asked, keeping her gaze fixed on the merciless black eyes of the Fae in the middle of the group.

"Why should we?" he asked, a dismissive gleam in his eyes. Sweeping out his arms, he continued. "We have all we need here. In this place we rule. In this place, you are nothing. Less than. A queen no more, you are merely another beggar, demanding notice."

Fury spilled through Mab's body as she forced herself to sit quietly, regally, opposite those she wouldn't have deigned to speak to only weeks ago. And once this was over, she would never speak with them again. In fact, she assured herself silently, the Sluagh could be done away with once she'd gotten from them exactly what she needed. She smiled at the thought and the curve of her mouth was as bone-chilling as the wind battering at the walls of this tavern crowded with rogue Fae.

"You've been locked into this icy prison for so long, you've forgotten what it was that put your kind here," she said, her voice dropping to a whisper that was quickly swallowed by the surrounding noise.

In this dirty hovel, the imprisoned Fae gathered to drink, to talk, to scheme of what they might do if ever they were freed. She'd once pitied them, she thought wryly. Now, she'd been reduced to becoming one of them.

Mab leaned closer, ignoring the two females who sat on either side of the leader of the Sluagh. Staring directly into his black, empty eyes, she taunted, "Do you not remember the taste of innocence? The cool glide of an untouched soul sliding through your body?"

His features tightened and Mab saw she had his attention.

"You once gave up paradise because you refused to obey," she said softly. "Do you now willingly stay in a prison because you have the illusion of power?"

"It is no illusion, Mab," he said, leaning toward her as well. "Here in this place, the Sluagh rule and you are an uninvited guest. Do not forget that."

"Of course." She gave him a majestic nod and hid her smile. "But in this place, there are no innocent souls for you to feast on. Your hunger must be great." She tipped her head to one side, her long, golden hair swinging free of her body to hang like a bright curtain, a slash of light in the darkness of the room. "I can give you souls. I can give you a free path into the world of man where you might gorge yourselves until you're finally sated—and then beyond."

A flare of interest lit up the darkness in his eyes and Mab knew she had won her first battle. With the Sluagh, she could begin her return to power. And once she had regained her throne, the immortals who had dared to stand against her would see how quickly eternity could come to an end.

Chapter Eleven

$\mathcal{E}$

$\mathcal{M}$aggie left Bezel and Claire at the house to stand guard over Nora and Eileen.

It didn't matter any longer that she was furious with Culhane. She needed the warrior's help and she knew, deep in her heart, that no matter their private battles, he would do all he could to keep her family safe.

She drew the portal herself, focusing solely on Culhane. Maggie had had no idea where in Otherworld the warrior might be, so rather than concentrate on a destination, she made Culhane himself her focal point. When the portal had opened and the warm, floral air had poured from its center, Bezel had assured her that she'd done it correctly; then she stepped through the golden circle of light and found herself in the throne room at the palace.

Stunned, she looked across the room to see Culhane, leaning on the jewel-studded throne, holding court with five of his warriors. "What's going on?"

Instantly, the men went silent and turned as one to look at her. None of them, including Culhane, looked happy to see her. Which was okay by Maggie, since she wasn't real overjoyed at the moment herself.

"I repeat," she said, walking toward them, the heels of her boots clacking on the marble floor, echoing out around her like gunshots, "what's going on?"

"Go." Culhane said one word and before Maggie

could object, the five other warriors shifted space and were gone.

She'd come to him for help and found him holding court? Was he really trying to take over—planning a coup or something? What the hell? Was he as hungry for power as Mab? Was he building his own power base to undermine her?

God, how had she slipped into this whole intrigue thing? And why did she have to have so many doubts about Culhane now, when she needed him most? He stared at her from across the room and even with the distance between them, Maggie felt the power of those pale green eyes slamming into her.

A few hours ago, she'd been in his arms, feeling things she'd never imagined possible. Now she looked at him and knew that she loved him. She only wished she could be sure she trusted him.

Despite the mistrust simmering inside her, she was drawn to him and knew she always would be. She felt a connection with him that was more alluring than anything she'd ever known. How could she be in love with a man she wasn't sure of? A man whose loyalties were still in question? How had this happened? And how could she keep her feelings from him? He was already overbearing and arrogant.

If he knew she loved him, wouldn't that knowledge simply give him even more power over her?

Burying her feelings deep, she asked quietly, "What're you doing, Culhane?"

He stepped out from behind the throne, crossed his arms over his chest and braced his feet wide apart, as if preparing for battle. Which, she supposed, he was.

"My men and I are searching for Mab."

"From the throne?"

His jaw went tight. "You insult me. I've stolen nothing from you, Maggie. I am only trying to defend you. Defend Otherworld from the threat Mab represents."

"I insult you?" Maggie laughed as she walked toward him. Yes, she loved him, but that didn't mean that she wouldn't stand up to him every chance she got. When she got to the dais, she stepped up on it, moved even closer and tapped him in the chest with the tip of her index finger. "*You're* the one who's meeting with his pals secretly."

"My warriors."

"*My* warriors," she corrected, pushing one hand through her hair, to get it out of her eyes so she could give him a hard glare. "Isn't that what you told me? The warriors were mine to command? That as Queen, I'm the one who calls the shots?"

"I am taking *nothing* from you!" His shout rang throughout the room, reverberating off the crystal walls. One hand dropped to the sculpted back of the throne and squeezed until his knuckles turned white. "You insult us both if you believe I am with you only to use you."

"I want to believe that," she told him, staring up into the eyes that had mesmerized her from the first.

"Then do so." He reached for her and his hands on her upper arms were strong and sure and the heat from his body poured into hers like a salve.

Whether she completely believed in him or not, she had to trust him with this. Had to have faith that he would be the warrior hero she needed so desperately at the moment.

"Okay, Culhane. We'll call a truce, because I really need you right now."

"What is it?" Instantly, he was on alert.

She told him about Claire's vision. About the wards they'd put up around her house and that she needed help in keeping Eileen safe.

"Even Mab would not hurt a child," he whispered.

"Hope you're right," she said, "but I don't want to bet on Mab having a good side."

"No, we cannot take that risk," he agreed, pulling her close, wrapping his arms around her, nestling her head against his chest, so that she heard the steady, reassuring beat of his heart beneath her ear. "And we won't. Eileen will be safe, this I promise. We'll hide her at the Conclave. No one can get in there unless invited by a warrior."

"What if Mab's got some fans among your clan?"

He smiled and stroked her back. "She does not. We will protect Eileen. You have my word."

"Thank you."

"You do not need to thank me for protecting what is important to you." He pulled her back so that she could look up at him. "My life, my honor, are yours to command. I will stand between you and danger, Maggie. Always."

"Oh, wow . . ." Maggie was a goner and she knew it.

What woman wouldn't have been? Everything inside her heated, going silky and soft.

"Wait here. I will go to Quinn and send him to your house."

He shifted, leaving her alone in the quiet, her nerves hammering, body simmering. Culhane was back an instant later, though, and when she looked at him, he said simply, "It is done. Quinn will remain with Nora and Eileen until we bring them to the Conclave."

"I want to thank you again," she said with a smile.

His luscious mouth curved at one corner. "If you must . . ."

Then he kissed her, his mouth taking hers with a fever of need and desperation that jangled every nerve in Maggie's body. Wrapped in the heat of him, she forgot everything but what he could make her feel. And she gave herself up to the wonder of it.

She hadn't come here expecting this. But she wouldn't turn from it, either. His hands were everywhere, touching, exploring. Maggie squirmed against him and itched to get out of her clothes, feel skin on skin, heat on heat.

She hungered. She needed. He was the missing part of her and only by joining with him could she feel complete again.

How had he become so important to her so quickly? How had she ever lived without the feel of him against her hands?

She scraped her palms up and under his shirt, defining every sculpted muscle on his back. He hissed in a breath and deepened the kiss, tongue plunging deep, to tangle with hers in a needy dance of desire.

Blood sizzling, heart thumping, Maggie leaned into him, offering more, taking more. She wanted all of him and couldn't seem to get close enough.

"Now," he murmured, tearing his mouth from hers.

"Now? Huh? What?" Shaken, stunned, she wobbled unsteadily as he smiled down at her.

"I must have you now," he said, and snapped his fingers. Instantly, their clothes were gone and Maggie could look her fill of his truly amazing body.

"Good, this is good," she whispered, and moved toward him.

But he picked her up, swinging her into his arms, then turned swiftly to deposit her on the intricately carved silver throne.

"Hey!" She bolted up quickly, expecting the metal beneath her to be cold against her naked skin. But it was warm, as if the jewels and the silver itself were heated from within. "*Hey . . .*"

"This is how I have ached to see my Fae Queen," he said, his gaze moving over her in approval.

"Naked?"

"And hungry for me." Going to one knee before her, he gently lifted her legs and hung them over the arms of the throne.

"Culhane . . ." Maggie swallowed hard and shifted uneasily, not exactly comfy with being so exposed.

"Let me worship my Queen," he said, and bent his

head to her center. His mouth covered her and Maggie instantly forgot about where she was and how she was sitting. Nothing mattered except that he continue doing exactly what he was doing.

His lips and tongue worked her innermost flesh, lapping, tasting, delving deep, driving her higher and higher. Breathless, she looked down at his dark head bent to her body in supplication and felt the most amazing sensations. Warmth skittered through her chest, where it surrounded her heart and suffused her soul. Maggie threaded her fingers through his hair and held his head to her, loving the feel of his mouth on her body.

Again and again, he licked, tasted, swirling the tip of his tongue over the heated bud of her desire. She flinched on the throne, her body jerking helplessly as he claimed her in the most intimate manner possible.

As his mouth moved over her, he slid first one finger, then two, into her depths, stroking her both inside and out, and Maggie's mind began to shatter. There was nothing in the world beyond this room. Beyond this man. This Fae Warrior.

Her legs quivered as he pushed her higher still, demanding her release, demanding she surrender her ecstasy to him. Maggie's heart fluttered in her chest. She gasped for air, watched him as he took her and she whispered, "I can't take much more, Culhane. . . ."

He stopped. Lifted his head. Looked at her. "You will take all, my Queen."

And when he lowered his mouth to her again, he kept his eyes locked on her as she screamed his name and splintered into a billion jagged shards.

Before her body had even stopped rippling with release, he swept her up into his arms, sat on the throne himself and lowered her onto his shaft. Maggie groaned as he filled her. Her body stretched to accommodate him and she swiveled her hips against him to take him even deeper within.

His hands at her hips, she rode him, gaze locked with his, until his body erupted into hers, emptying all that he was into her body. Maggie held him close, heard him shout her name loudly enough to shatter glass and knew that whatever else lay between them, Culhane was hers. As he'd always been meant to be. She held him to her and deliberately banished the niggling doubts hiding in the recesses of her mind.

She tangled her fingers in his hair, loving the slide of that thick black silk against her skin. Maggie sighed and let her brain float into that lazy, half-alert world where everything was shiny and pretty, and as she did, she realized she'd felt this way before.

Not the sexually replete thing, because Culhane was really the best lover ever. But the cherished, special sense of wonder that she was feeling at the moment was somehow . . . familiar.

A memory slid through her mind, images rising up from her past, and Maggie sighed as she remembered. . . .

Her friend Amy had been a beautiful bride and Maggie didn't even mind the hideous bridesmaid dress she'd been forced to wear. What she did mind was not having a date for the wedding.

She felt like a paper sack in a luggage store. Out of place and unwanted.

Until he came.

With his long black hair and secretive smile, he swept Maggie into a dance and held her as if she were made of the finest crystal. He looked into her eyes and she stared up into swirls of green and silver that simply took her breath away.

"Who are you?" she asked.

"Only a man," he said, but that was a lie. She knew it. Felt it. She also felt as if she should know him.

"No, really. Who are you?"

"It only matters who you are, Maggie," he told her, moving around the dance floor so smoothly it was as if

they were floating. "You are too beautiful to be alone. To feel sadness."

"How do—" Was he a mind reader? He thought she was beautiful?

He smiled at her. "You are more beautiful than I could have imagined. And your heart and soul are even more so. One day, you will see this as clearly as do I."

"One day," she said as the room around them spun into a colorful blur. The magic of this man made her feel as if the two of them were alone in the hall.

"You will see, Maggie. Believe this. Believe in yourself." He steered her effortlessly into a secluded corner and the sound of the music was all that followed them.

There in the shadows he touched her face with tender fingers and she felt the heat of that caress zip through her system like a sudden fever. Maggie held her breath and waited, sure that she had somehow stumbled into a surreal moment that she didn't want to end.

"I must leave you," he whispered.

"Not yet," she told him.

He smiled. "Soon, Maggie, I will return and all will be revealed."

Then he was gone and an instant later, the memory of him had dissolved like sugar in water.

Until now. Until this very moment, when yet another memory of Culhane's connection to her had surfaced. He'd reawakened memories for her before, but this was spontaneous. Brought on by her growing Fae blood? Did it matter?

What was she supposed to think? He'd visited her throughout her life and never once had he hurt her. He'd saved her life when she was a child, and when she was a young woman, he'd come to her rescue on a crowded dance floor. He'd made her feel special. Like a princess.

Or a queen.

Her heart turned over and she fought to decide whether that memory made her trust him more—or whether it was just one more instance of Culhane manipulating her.

Then he shifted atop her, holding her closer, and Maggie let her eyes slide shut, losing herself in the sensation of being wrapped in his strong arms. This wasn't the time for thinking.

For now, Culhane was all she wanted.

Chapter Twelve

♪

"You'll keep us safe; I know you will," Nora said.

"You don't make it easy." Quinn's arms tightened around the love of his life while he wondered just how he had lived so long without her. And how he could face eternity if something happened to her.

He'd come here directly from the palace. Needing to see Nora. Needing to assure himself that all was well with her. Quinn felt that only *he* could properly protect her and he would be by her side, he vowed, until all was safe again. Here in the quiet of Maggie's home, in a bedroom where his woman slept, Quinn held on to all that was precious to him and vowed to defend her and her daughter at all costs.

In centuries of life, Quinn had never known true passion until this tiny, half-Fae had appeared in his path. One night with her would be worth eternities alone. But he no longer wanted to live a solitary warrior's life. He wanted more. And he wouldn't settle for less than forever. He would have Nora. And he would have his son. And the daughter of his heart.

He must ensure nothing happened to any of them. Soon, Nora would be fully Fae. The child she carried filled her body with the power of the Faery and it would, eventually, overcome her mortal blood, making it harder for Mab to track her. To find her. But Eileen, sleeping down the hall, dreaming her innocent dreams, was only part-Fae.

The child had come to mean much to him over the last weeks.

"You're too quiet," Nora said finally. "You're thinking about something that I'm not going to like, aren't you?"

"I'm deciding how best to protect you and Eileen and no, you will not like it. But I will do what I must, Nora. You will not fight me on this."

"If you try to kidnap me again, Quinn Terhune," she said, less relaxed and more worried now, "I'll make you so miserable, you'll want to *pay* Mab to kill me."

Irritation and frustration grew apace inside him. "Why do you wish to tie my hands, when I only strive to protect you and Eileen and our child? It is my *right* to see to your safety. My duty. My privilege."

She gave him a sad smile that touched Quinn's heart but did nothing to melt the thread of steely resolve inside him.

"I know you mean that in the best possible way. But I had a husband once who ordered me around and told me what to do and in general treated me like a five-year-old with a bad sense of direction." A solitary tear slid down her cheek and she wiped it away with one impatient sweep of her hand. "I won't let that happen again. I'm my own person. I'm in charge of me and my daughter and the baby I'm carrying. You're not my husband—"

He scowled at her. "I'm your mate."

"Not the same thing."

"It is to the Fae."

"Not to me. I'm not married unless there's a priest and some cake and champagne. Besides, I'm only part-Fae and you're getting me off the subject here," Nora complained. She sent a quick look around the cozy spare bedroom. "I grew up here, Quinn. And when my marriage failed, I came back. Here is where I rebuilt my life, my confidence, my belief in myself. This is my home, Quinn. Nobody's chasing me off. Not even that crazed ex-Queen of yours."

Disgusted, he blew out a breath and frowned. "You are much like your sister."

In spite of his furious expression, Nora smiled. "The Donovan women are made of stern stuff, Quinn. It took me a while to remember that once. I won't forget it again."

"But Mab—"

"I'll be careful," she promised, reaching up to cup his cheek with her palm. "I'm independent, not stupid. And you'll be here to watch over Eileen and me, right?"

"With my life," he vowed, holding her hand to his face, turning his lips into the palm to place a gentle kiss there.

"Then we'll be good." She moved into his arms, laid her head on his chest and stared at the closed door that led to the hallway and the room where her daughter was sleeping. "Yes, I'm scared, Quinn. But I have to teach Eileen that a strong woman makes her own choices."

"Your courage terrifies me," he murmured.

She smiled. "Yeah well, I hope I'm doing the right thing. But you know," she whispered, "Madame Star says that my moons are aligned perfectly. What could go wrong?"

He didn't want to consider all that could possibly go wrong.

A couple of long moments passed before she said, "You're quiet again. Are you worried?" She squirmed closer to Quinn, crawling onto his lap, nestling her head just beneath his chin. She fought to be brave, but he had heard the tremor in her voice as she tried to disguise her fear.

"I am *concerned* for Eileen," he told her. Quinn looked down into her dark blue eyes and willed her to see his absolute confidence in his ability to protect her. "Mab knows her. Has seen her. Spoken to her. Eileen set her free of her prison—"

"It was an accident."

"Of course it was, though that changes nothing. There's a connection now between our girl and Mab. The treacherous bitch will use it as well. She'll do whatever it is she thinks she must to win back her throne and kill Maggie." He cupped Nora's face between his big palms, saw fear flash in her eyes and regretted the fact that he must give her more worry. But he couldn't see how to avoid it. "She will use Eileen. She could steal her from us. Hide her where we'd never find her. Take her to Casia—"

"Oh God. The prison island?" Nora blinked at him, shook her head and said, "No. I won't let Mab have my daughter."

"The danger is there, but no, lass, we won't let Mab get *our* daughter." Quinn tightened his arms around her. "I should take Eileen to the Conclave. There are places in the warrior fortress that Mab could never find."

"I can't let her go without me," Nora said.

"She won't."

Nora tipped her head back to look up at him. "So we can't go yet. I won't leave Maggie here alone. She's my sister, Quinn."

"She's not alone. She has Claire and Bezel, and gods know Mac is always near the witch. And most importantly, Maggie has Culhane."

"That's all true," she said, and snuggled against him. "It's also true that she's my family and I'm not leaving without her. Besides, with all of us here, in the main house, we're easier to protect."

"Or destroy."

"You won't let that happen," she said, and the surety in her voice filled him with pride that battled the qualms of disquiet in his blood. She gave him her confidence, trusted him with the safety of her child. And he would do whatever he must to prove worthy of that trust.

&

"You had sex."

"Huh?"

Bright and early the next morning, Claire and Maggie were wandering through a Christmas tree lot. It was so early, in fact, that there was a layer of fog drifting in off the ocean that the morning sun hadn't yet dissipated. The air was cold and damp and wisps of steam lifted off the surfaces of the lattes they'd stopped for on the way to the lot.

The heavy scent of pine wrapped itself around them and the straw beneath their feet crunched as they walked. They were alone in the man-made forest, since it was too early for most people to be shopping for trees. Which had been the plan. Maggie wanted a damn tree and since she knew it wasn't completely safe to wander too far from their warded house, she figured it would be best if she bought her tree before most of the world was awake.

It had seemed like a good idea at the time. Now though, her eyes were barely open and she had to gulp at her latte for the jolt of caffeine her system sorely needed.

From above, Christmas carols trilled from speakers and out on the street, headlights cut through the swath of fog as early-morning commuters hit Pacific Coast Highway.

Maggie sighed and took another sip of her latte. "We should have gotten doughnuts, too," she whispered.

"Forget the doughnuts." Claire fixed her with a demanding look. "You didn't answer me before. You had sex. Didn't you?"

"What? Am I wearing a sign?" Maggie looked at the front of her navy blue peacoat. "Is there a giant red *S* for sex stitched into my jacket?"

"Might as well be," Claire told her with a huff. "Your eyes are shining, there's a bloody smug, satisfied smile on your face and you're altogether in too good a mood for this early in the morning."

"Well, if it isn't Sherlock MacDonald," Maggie said, smiling. "Or would that be Claire Holmes?"

"Hah! As if it takes a detective to see the stamp of good sex on a body's face."

"Good sex takes place a little lower." Maggie grinned.

"Ah, fine. Rub it in." Claire shook her head, sipped at her latte and shrugged deeper into her bright red coat. "Some of us are up all night worrying about protection spells while others of us are out—" She broke off. "Just what exactly *were* you doing?"

Maggie sighed heavily. After that time on the throne, Culhane had taken her to the Queen's bedroom, high in the palace, and there he'd shown her so many inventive Faery maneuvers that . . . wow. The memories of what he'd done to her, what they'd done together, made Maggie so warm, she could have tossed off her coat and danced naked down the street. A smile curved her mouth. "Mmmm . . ."

"Ah God," Claire mused with an envious moan. "You're killing me."

"Not yet," a deep voice intruded. "But that *is* the plan."

"Crap!" Maggie spun around and instinctively went into a deep crouch, just as Bezel and Culhane had taught her. She looked up into the face of one of the Christmas tree lot workers. He was about thirty, with a scraggly beard. He wore dirty jeans with a blue and green flannel shirt and work boots that looked older than he was; then she stared directly into his eyes and saw a telltale flicker of red. Definitely demon.

"Hey, thanks for coming to me," he said. "We tried to get into your place last night, but it's been warded."

"Yeah, I know."

"So you do have a witch in the mix." He fixed his gaze on Claire. "You?"

"Leave her out of this," Maggie warned him, not daring to let a demon get fixated on Claire. She might be a witch, but that didn't mean she knew how to fight demons. Maggie stayed low and muttered, "Move away, Claire."

"Yeah, Claire," he echoed in a cooing voice. "Step away. Wouldn't want you to get hurt before you and me have a chance to get *acquainted*. I'll be right with ya. Soon as I get rid of this bitch."

Maggie tossed her hot latte into his face, then swept out one leg, caught him behind his knee and he toppled over. "This bitch is so out of your league."

He hissed as the burning liquid hit his skin, but he rolled to his feet and popped right back up again. So did Maggie. She circled him, keeping her gaze fixed on her opponent. She couldn't afford to worry about Claire. If she split her focus, she'd only endanger her best friend.

As she had by even bringing her along. God, she was an idiot, Maggie told herself. She never should have taken Claire with her. Should have brought Quinn along. Should have called for Culhane. Hell. Even Bezel would have been welcome about now.

The demon dove at her, clipped Maggie's jaw with a tight fist and just for an instant, she saw stars. But she shook off the feeling fast and slammed the heel of her hand into the demon's nose. A fountain of blood sprayed from him and Maggie danced back, keeping clear of the mess.

"That's gonna cost you, bitch." He wiped his nose with the back of his hand and laughed. "You really think you can stand up to what's coming? Mab's gathering an army that's gonna make your tame warriors look like a herd of poodles."

Culhane? Quinn? McCulloch?

Those three? *Poodles?*

She smiled. "Talk all you want, demon boy. But between me and my poodles, you guys are toast."

Off to one side, Claire was murmuring softly, her hands waving like graceful white flags before her. She stared straight ahead as if unaware of the fight going on in front of her. Suddenly though, the air electrified and Maggie felt a charge of energy erupt just below the surface of her skin.

"You need a witch to fight me?" He sneered the insult.

"Nope," Maggie told him, and flew at him. Actually *flew*.

She'd been getting better in that area for days, practicing in the backyard at night when no neighbor would be likely to see her. All it took was concentrating the floaty thing into actual movement and voilà. *Flying*.

His eyes went wide, his mouth dropped open and when Maggie hit him dead square in the chest and knocked him over onto his back, he just lay there like a landed trout. She straddled him, pinning his arms beneath her knees.

He bucked and writhed, trying to twist free, but Maggie wasn't about to let him loose; then she drew on her power, gathered it into a single force inside her and blew a steady stream of sparkling, gold Faery dust right into his eyes.

He let out one hideous, earsplitting shriek of pain; then he poofed. Just exploded into dust and Maggie dropped to the straw-covered dirt.

Heart pounding, mouth dry, Maggie sat there for a long minute, simply trying to catch her breath. Fear eased off, relief crowded in and she let her head fall back so she could stare up at a gray, cloud-covered sky. When a rustle of sound caught her attention, she looked up into the face of the tree lot worker's friend. He appeared to be younger, more clean shaven and yep, flames were flickering in those eyes, too.

Before she could make a move, though, the guy held up both hands and took a scuttling step or two backward, half hiding behind a Scotch pine just for good measure.

"Hey," he said, "chill, Your Majesty. Hank was all crazed to be Mr. Queen Killer, not me, 'kay? I'm just doin' my thing here, spreadin' holiday cheer, 'kay? I told Hank to back off when you showed up. You know, it's all live and let live, I say. I got no problems with you, 'kay? All I'm doin' is trying to sell some trees and make a buck. You good with that?"

Maggie's ears were still ringing and the knees of her jeans were soaking wet, not to mention probably torn, and she didn't care *what* Hollywood was wearing; holey jeans just looked tacky and now she needed a new pair, which meant more shopping. And the demon was still staring at her, waiting for an answer.

"Huh?" she asked, shaking her head.

He talked slower. "No. Kill. Me. 'Kay?"

"Twenty bucks off any Christmas tree," Maggie countered.

He groaned. "Dude. You're killin' me here."

"No, I'm not," she told him as she pushed up off her knees and brushed her hands together, getting rid of the clinging demon dust. "That's the point."

He watched that dust blow away in the wind and then nodded. "Twenty bucks off. Right there with ya. Deal. 'Kay?"

" 'Kay."

He faded back into the trees then, and Claire walked up to join Maggie. "You lead an interesting life."

"A little too interesting sometimes," Maggie told her, and winced when she looked at her torn jeans; then she glanced at her friend. "I shouldn't have brought you with me, Claire. I'm sorry."

"Oh, please." Claire waved one hand in dismissal, then handed Maggie her latte. "Not like I've never seen a demon before."

That was the good side of having a friend completely at home with the world of the supernatural and weird.

"True," Maggie said, taking a sip before handing the latte back. "And you *are* a witch."

"See?" Claire hooked her arm through Maggie's. "All's well that ends with dead demons and bargain Christmas trees."

"Good point."

"You know, your fighting skills have really improved. Not to mention the whole flying thing."

"Thanks." Maggie stopped to look at a particular tree. At least six feet tall, it was wide and fresh and completely beautiful and with her demon discount, she could totally afford it. Perfect. Smiling, she said, "How about this one?"

"Looks gorgeous," Claire agreed, reaching out to check the freshness.

"So what was that spell you did?"

"Oh." She shrugged, leaned in and took a sniff of the tree. Smiling, she said, "That was just a centering incantation, to help you focus."

Maggie grinned. "Good idea."

"We witches do what we can," Claire told her. "Now, are we going to get this tree so we can go home and get warm?"

"That's a plan." Maggie turned and shouted, "Demon boy, we found one!"

"While we wait," Claire prodded, "why don't you tell me more about Faery sex?"

Maggie smiled, stuffed her hands in her coat pockets and said, "Why don't you just jump McCulloch and find out for yourself?"

"Mac?" Claire pulled her head back, stared at Maggie and tried to look appalled. "That arrogant, pushy, argumentative, know-it-all warrior beast? Are you insane?"

"A hottie, isn't he?"

Claire huffed out a breath. "Aye, if you like men who are so big they blot out the bloody sky. If you've no care about a man thinking you're his bleeding property because you've given him a smile or two and one time he kissed you until you were swaying in the dusk like a man who'd spent too long over a bottle of good, single malt scotch. Or if you—"

Maggie grinned. "I notice your Scots accent gets a little thicker when you talk about Mac. Have you noticed that?"

"I've not and neither have you," Claire snapped, then stopped, listened to herself and muttered a curse. "You're entirely too know-it-all yourself sometimes, Maggie."

"Queen. Remember?"

"Aye, I do at that," Claire murmured. "So just tell me this. The Fae sex. Is it really worth putting up with those warriors?"

Maggie's smile widened even further. "Aye, my friend. Give that one a big *aye*."

&

"You call that fighting?" Bezel snorted, shook his head and brushed dirt from the front of his green velvet suit. "My wife, Fontana, could clean your clock, *Majesty*."

Right about then, Maggie thought, her lazy dog, Sheba, could have cleaned her clock. She was exhausted. Sex with Culhane could wear a girl out. Then there was the fight that morning with the Christmas tree demon. Then there was decorating the tree, which still wasn't finished because Nora kept rearranging everything. Then Bezel and Claire had wanted to plan battle strategies. Now, several hours later, Maggie was stretched out in the backyard, wheezing for air.

Why was it, she wondered, that the pixie and the witch could fight with each other, then team up against *her*? Quinn just had to get his two cents in, too, and then

Eileen was hovering nearby as if she sensed things were getting stickier. And all in all, the little Donovan house was starting to feel like a cramped hotel.

But she was grateful for the company. The less she was alone right now, the safer she felt.

"You gonna lie there all day like a Scythian slug or you gonna get up and fight some more?"

Scythian *slug*? Okay, there was one creature she was in no hurry to run into.

"Twenty-seven percent of women in their thirties die of unexpected heart attacks after excessive activity," Eileen pointed out from her perch on Bezel's tree house.

"Where do you get that stuff?" Bezel shot the girl an irritated frown. "Never mind. Don't want to know." He looked back at Maggie. "Pay no attention to the kid. You're not a pitiful human anymore. You're a pitiful Fae. Better stamina. Not as good as a pixie's, but what is?"

"You know," Maggie said from flat on her back in the dirt and grass, "I'm the Queen now. I shouldn't have to be doing all this jumping and spinning and stabbing." She lifted her head and pinned her little torturer with a hard glare. "Don't I have minions for this?"

He laughed, that raspy, sandpaper-on-steel sound. "Minions? Right. Let me just bend over, Your Queenliness, and you can kiss my pixie ass."

"You're to train her, you miserable pile of trollshit," a deep voice thundered from the back porch. "You've no call to be insulting the Queen."

Bezel's eyes rolled up in his head. He gave McCulloch the same amount of respect he did Culhane and Quinn. Which was none.

Maggie closed her eyes briefly and tried to ignore the muttered sounds of Mac and Claire bickering. Again. If Claire would just take Maggie's advice and jump the warrior's bones already, things would quiet down around there.

Romance, it seemed, was blossoming. In the middle

of yet another threat from Mab, there were hearts and flowers all over the damn place. Nora and Quinn. Mac and Claire. Maggie and Culhane—maybe.

Yes, they'd had great sex. And she hoped to do it again, really soon. But that wasn't romance. And she was in love with him, but that didn't mean he loved her, because if he did, he sure wasn't bothering to tell her, and even if he did, she wasn't sure she could believe him anyway and ... Oh God. She was starting to ramble just like Eileen. Maggie needed a vacation.

She dropped her head back to the ground and stared up at the cloud-swept sky. "She's coming, isn't she?"

"Mab?" Bezel walked closer, his wide, bare feet scuffing on the lawn that needed mowing. "Yeah, she is."

A wind blew in off the nearby ocean and gave Maggie a chill. At least, she hoped the wind was the cause and not some damn foreboding or other.

"I'm going to need help to beat her this time," Maggie told him. "Last time, I pretty much caught her by surprise."

"Hell, you took her. That's all that counts."

Maggie squinted at him. With the sun behind him, Bezel's hair looked as if it were on fire and his ugly little face was in shadow. "Yeah, I did. This time, though ..."

"This time," Bezel told her, "I brought you an edge."

"Huh?"

"Will someone open this gate?" A deep voice shouted from the other side of the backyard fence.

Nora went to open it and Maggie sat up, ready to defend if she had to. But she needn't have bothered. Quinn shifted from wherever he had been and appeared directly in front of Nora. He opened the gate and barely managed to hide a sneer as Jasic stepped through.

Maggie's grandFae stopped dead in the yard, looked around and then fixed her with a hard stare. "Why have you tried to keep me out?"

"What?"

"You've a spell around the house. I was having so hard a time trying to break through it, I gave up and was forced to knock on your door like a common pixie."

"Hey!" Bezel shouted.

"And why are you lying in the dirt, Maggie?" Jasic smoothed the lapels of his dark blue jacket. "You're a queen now. You've appearances to maintain."

"You couldn't get through the wards?" Claire asked from the back porch.

"I could have. It was just a bit ... difficult," Jasic explained; then his gaze narrowed on her. "Did you raise the spell?"

"She did," Mac spoke up, stepping in front of Claire as if ready to defend her.

But Claire stepped out from behind him to speak for herself. "I did, yes. A protection spell against potential enemies."

"Ah." Jasic nodded and a moment later, beamed an appreciative smile at them all. "A wise decision, no doubt."

"Anyway," Bezel said, drawing Maggie's attention back to him, "as I was saying, I brought you something that will help you fight Mab."

"An army? A bazooka?" Maggie asked hopefully. "An army *with* bazookas?"

He sneered at her, his ugly little face sliding into familiar wrinkle patterns. "As if that would help. No. This is better." He reached into the front of his jacket and pulled out a sword.

"A *sword*?" Maggie asked, brushing her hands off and glaring at the pixie. "This is your big help? A sword?"

"An iron sword," Bezel said, gazing lovingly at the dark gray blade that seemed to absorb the watery, winter sunlight.

"Fool pixie!" Jasic's panicked shout rang out, and he walked a wide berth around Bezel and Maggie as he hurried toward the back porch. "Are you trying to kill her?"

"Kill me?"

"Don't you know it's iron, you little troll?" Jasic called out.

"I do, and who asked for your opinion?" Bezel shouted back at him. Looking at Maggie, he added, "This was Culhane's idea and it's a damn good one."

"Culhane?" That got her attention. Maggie eagerly looked around the yard as if half expecting to see the warrior step out from behind a tree. But of course, he didn't. "When did you see him?"

"This morning." Bezel nodded to McCulloch, looked back at Maggie and said, "He popped in, left this with me and went off again."

Well, didn't she feel special? After what they'd done ... what *he'd* done to her last night, he couldn't even say hello? He didn't want to see her? Stop in for a quickie? No, he just visits the pixie, drops off a sword and goes back to Otherworld. Well, Maggie thought, guess that told her just how much she mattered.

"Fool pixie!" Jasic shouted. "Iron is poison to our kind and well you know it!"

"Poison?"

"It really is, Aunt Maggie." Eileen leaned out from her seat in the tree house. "According to my research, the Fae can't touch iron without getting really sick. Of course, it can't really kill them, because they're, you know, immortal, unless you cut off their heads, but they can really *wish* they were dead, you know?"

"Jeez," Bezel said, shooting the girl a withering stare. "Who's the teacher here?"

"You? A teacher?" Jasic sneered from safety, just below the porch where McCulloch and Claire stood speaking in hushed tones. "What could you possibly teach my granddaughter that would be worth learning? She's a *queen*."

Maggie tuned Jasic out. He probably meant well, but the truth was, Bezel had taught her a lot. He'd trained her in using her newly found powers. Helped her focus to straighten out her flying and had even coached her in hand-to-hand combat. Plus, he was now her secret agent. Double-0-Bezel. Not bad for a pixie only three feet tall and two thousand years old.

"So, if it's poison, why do you have it?" she asked.

Bezel's pale blue eyes locked on hers. "It was Culhane's idea. He wants you to carry it. Learn to wield it. Says you can use it when you face Mab again. Get in a couple of swipes and the ex-bitch-Queen-of-the-universe will be slowed down. Get sick. Might be enough to give you the edge." He paused, looked at the long, lethal-looking blade again and mused, "You're still part human, so it's not going to affect you like it does us. So use it to get close to Mab. Get really close and lop off her head. Take her out permanently."

"Cut off her head?" Maggie's stomach pitched. Sure, she'd dusted some demons, killed a couple rogue Fae. But could she really cut off someone's head? Even Mab's?

"Don't get queasy on me now, kid." His eyes narrowed, his silver eyebrows drawing together, forming a V on his forehead. "It's brass-ring time, you know? When Mab comes after you this time, she's not gonna be pussyfootin' around. She's coming to kill you. So you'd better be ready to kill her right back."

"Right." Maggie stood up, took the sword from Bezel and hefted it, getting used to the feel of it in her hand. The sterling-silver hilt fit her palm as if it had been made for her. The blade was long, curved and wicked looking.

Maggie's gaze locked on its razor edge and let the hard, unshakeable truth settle inside her. Another fight was coming. And this one was likely to make her last scuffle with Mab look like a picnic in comparison. So she'd better do just what her pixie had said. Get ready.

"Okay," she murmured, shifting a hard look at Bezel. "Show me how to use this thing."

~

"Eileen!"

A whisper of a voice calling her name had Eileen turning around to look into the darkened interior of Bezel's tree house. She'd been inside it lots of times and she knew that the house only looked tiny on the outside.

Inside, it was huge, with fireplaces and comfy furniture and staircases to a second story that no way would anyone see from the outside. Bezel had built it with magic when his wife, Fontana, told him if he liked spending so much time with humans, he could just stay here—which Eileen totally hoped he would. Stay, that is. Because he was fun and didn't treat her like a little kid, which everyone else in the whole world did, no matter that she was practically a teenager.

"Eileen!"

The whisper came again and she chewed at her bottom lip. Who could be in there? Everyone but Culhane was in the yard. Maybe it was Mab, she thought with a stab of fear so sharp she sucked in a gulp of air and it got caught in her lungs. No, not Mab, she assured herself. Claire's spell kept out anyone who meant harm, so it couldn't be the former queen.

Eileen's brain was moving so fast, all of these thoughts took only a second or two. Quickly, she shifted another look at the ground below the tree house.

Aunt Maggie was swinging the sword, looking pretty cool. Mac and Claire were still talking on the porch, Jasic standing unnoticed beneath them, and Eileen's mom was headed for the kitchen, probably going to make more cookies. Quinn was watching Bezel and Maggie, and Sheba was asleep under the tree.

So who . . .

"Eileen, it's me."

Fear fell away as she smiled and excited bubbles filled up her tummy. Turning around completely now, she peered into the darkness, trying to see. "How did you get here?"

"Come inside," the voice urged. "I'll show you."

With one last look at her family, Eileen grinned, and eagerly crawled through the open door of the tree house and into the shadows.

Chapter Thirteen

&

*J*asic moved closer to the back porch, where Claire and the warrior McCulloch were having a heated discussion.

"If you take Eileen to the Conclave," Claire was saying, "she'll be too easy to find."

"Do you not think we've considered that?" Mac countered. "Culhane has it all worked out. Eileen will be safe in our care and it's an insult for you to suggest otherwise."

"You hardheaded Faery, I'm not saying that at all."

Jasic chuckled to himself at the outrage in the witch's voice, then listened more carefully as she continued.

"I only think you should consider somewhere else to hide the girl. And Maggie agrees with me. Don't you think Mab will figure out to look at the Warriors' home?"

Jasic sidled a bit closer as their voices hushed into strained whispers.

"Mab cannot enter the Conclave. No one can enter the Conclave uninvited. But we've no intention of keeping her precisely there, anyway."

"Then where? *Precisely*."

There was a long pause as if Mac were trying to decide whether or not to tell her. Finally, he spoke again. "There's a small alcove, at the edge of the training field. If you didn't know it was there, you wouldn't even *see*

the blasted thing. The chamber is used for official ceremonies. Mab couldn't know of it and so won't find Eileen. Tomorrow we tuck her away there and she's safe as
can be."

"Jasic?" Nora had spotted him on her way to the
kitchen. He jumped, surprised at her call, and as soon as
he did, Mac and Claire turned to glare at him.

"How long have you been there, Fae?" Mac demanded.

Jasic straightened to his full height and tugged at his
lapels with the tips of his fingers. "Long enough to know
that you shouldn't be spilling secrets. Lucky for you, I'm
family. Imagine what might have happened if an enemy
had happened to overhear your conversation."

"An enemy wouldn't be here. The wards," Mac reminded him.

"Aye, well, that's true then. No harm done." Jasic
smiled, gave Claire a courtly half bow, then turned back
to Nora. Taking her arm, he steered her into the kitchen.
"Now, my darling girl, would you be brewing me some
of your fine tea again? What was it we had just yesterday? Orange Zinger?"

Inside the kitchen, Nora filled the teakettle and set it
on the stove to heat.

"Jasic," she asked, turning to face him at the kitchen
table, "why were you really eavesdropping?"

"Why, to be sure all is being done to protect my family, of course." He gave her a sorrowful look. "I am the
head of the family, Nora. It's my duty to look out for all
of you."

Nora nodded and moved to take down two teacups.
While her back was turned, Jasic reached for a brownie,
bit into it and smiled to himself in satisfaction.

ε

A couple hours later, the house was quiet for a change.
Sheba was, of course, asleep under the kitchen table.

Bezel was out in his tree house. Eileen was on the computer in her room doing more Fae research. Claire was talking long-distance to her mother in Scotland and who the hell knew where Nora and Quinn were. Though wherever they were, Maggie was pretty sure she knew what they were doing.

Lucky bastards.

She scowled as she carried her coffee out of the kitchen and into the dimly lit living room. This was all Culhane's fault. He'd taught her about Faery sex, made her want it—and him—and then poof. He was gone. Off in Otherworld doing who knew what instead of being here with her.

So, with no hope of sex, because she absolutely *refused* to go to Culhane, she was going to wait him out and make him come to her. And since no one was bugging her to fight or train or make royal decisions, she had decided to do something for herself.

Maggie was headed for her bedroom and the easel she'd tucked under the window. She hadn't had a chance to paint in days and since Nora had moved back into the main house, she'd lost her "artist studio" room. But that was fine. She could work in her cluttered bedroom. And right now, losing herself in the magic of putting paint to canvas sounded like a vacation in Fae heaven.

The scent of pine welcomed her into the living room and her gaze went straight to the multicolored strings of lights on the tree. She smiled. Nora always wanted too many lights, but now that the work was done, Maggie had to admit, it looked gorgeous.

"I've never understood the human need to drag foliage into their homes."

Maggie jumped, slapped one hand to her chest and steadied her mug full of coffee. Her gaze shot to the man comfortably seated on the couch, with his feet kicked up and crossed atop the coffee table. "Jasic. I didn't know you were still here."

"Ah, a sad state of affairs to be sure," he said, patting the couch beside him in a silent invitation for her to join him. "The grandFae, already forgotten by his loved ones."

Loved ones? Well, they were family, at any rate. And Bezel hadn't found any dirt on him yet—at least he hadn't reported anything back to her. Maybe it was time Maggie took a minute to simply talk to the grandfather she'd never known. Nora and Eileen liked him, she knew. He'd charmed them both, which Maggie couldn't really fault him for. Why wouldn't he want his family to care for him? So maybe, she thought, bidding a silent good-bye to the painting she'd been about to indulge in, it was high time she tried to get to know him herself.

After all, he seemed to spend a lot of his time here lately. Whenever she turned around he was there, smiling.

Maybe that was the problem, she thought. People who smiled constantly made her nervous.

It was more normal to have a bad day once in a while. To be crabby. Grumpy. Fight the urge to shriek in frustration and yank at your own hair. Or maybe that was just her.

Maggie sat down in a nearby chair, passing up the chance to sit on the couch beside him, thanks very much, anyway. She curled her legs up under her and took a good long look at the man—Fae—who had begun their family line.

He was gorgeous, no two ways about it. And she supposed he did have plenty of charm as well. So looking back, it was easy to see how her grandmother, at the tender age of seventeen, had been swept off her feet and seduced by him.

She had been hardly more than a kid. On a family vacation to Ireland. He had been a centuries-old Faery looking for an easy mark. No way had Gran had the experience to deal with someone like him. It couldn't have been too difficult for him to smooth talk a young human girl into going to Otherworld with him.

Some of what Maggie felt must have been written on her face, because when he spoke again, he asked a pointed question.

"You don't like me much, do you?"

Instantly, Maggie felt guilty. Why, she wasn't sure, but it seemed impolite at the least to make your ambiguous feelings toward someone so easy to read.

"I didn't say that, Jasic," she told him. "I don't even know you."

"A wise queen," he mused. "Reserve judgment until all the facts are in?"

She lifted her mug in a silent toast. "Something like that."

"You've a suspicious mind, Maggie," he said, wagging a finger at her as if admonishing a child.

"No, just a curious one," she said, pausing for a sip of coffee. "For example, a curious mind wonders why a grandfather who's known about his family for *years* waits until one of his grandchildren is the new Queen to drop in and say howdy."

He laughed a little and the sound was musical, if a bit off-key. "I would never say 'howdy,' " he told her, giving her a brilliant smile aimed to disarm and reassure.

"No, I suppose not." He was too elegant for that. Too ... emotionally distant. At that moment, she wondered if he had ever really been touched by anything deeply enough to shatter the shallow facade he showed to everyone.

Nora and Eileen both had embraced this newest member of their family and Maggie really wished she could, too. But the niggling little doubts tugging at the corners of her mind prevented it. What would Gran have to say about him now? she wondered.

It was eerie how he seemed to know just what she was thinking.

"Your grandmother knew exactly what she was getting into, you know," he said, his voice soft and smooth. He lifted his wineglass and stared at the Christmas tree lights through the veil of the straw-colored wine. "I made her no promises. I simply offered to take her to Otherworld for a holiday." He sighed in fond memory. "She was more than eager to go, I assure you."

"Uh-huh." Why wouldn't she have been, Maggie thought. Jasic must have looked like a rock star to Gran. Tall, gorgeous, worldly and exciting. Someone so far from her ordinary world that she'd been unable to resist.

Which, Maggie was willing to bet, Jasic had counted on.

"Your grandmother was a lovely girl," he was saying. "A delight, as I recall. We spent some delicious times together in Otherworld. She was a boon companion, as we used to say."

"Uh-huh," Maggie said as irritation began to rise inside her. "Until the holiday was over. Let's not forget you deserted Gran and ran like a bunny the minute you found out she was pregnant."

He touched one finger to his forehead as if tipping a hat he wasn't wearing; then he smiled benevolently. "You're more than welcome."

Her irritation mounted. Okay, clearly she wasn't going to be charmed into welcoming her grandFae into her life. He was conceited, and not in a sexy way, like Culhane. Arrogant and not because he'd earned the right, like the warriors. And just a little on the snide side, which was supremely annoying all on its own. He behaved as though Maggie owed him a favor for seducing and abandoning her grandmother.

At the moment, he was watching her expectantly, as if waiting for applause.

"I should thank you?" she asked, just a little dumbfounded. "For what?"

He clucked his tongue in disapproval. "For what you are. What you will be. For the world that is opening to you and serving itself up on a jeweled platter." His mouth tightened and his eyes didn't look quite as congenial as they had a few minutes ago. "It's thanks to me, Maggie my love, that you are now Queen of the Fae. All-powerful, poised to rule for eons in an eternally youthful body. Great power. Immortality. Wealth beyond anything your poor human imagination might be willing to construct. And all because I dallied with your grandmother, giving you, my descendants, the blessings of Faery blood."

The twinkling Christmas lights, the scent of pine and the hush of the house did nothing to soothe Maggie's rapidly fraying temper. That he could sit there and act as though everything that had happened to her in the last few weeks had been some kind of gift, like an unlimited credit card to Macy's, absolutely amazed her.

Maggie's fingers tightened around the handle of her coffee mug until she was surprised she hadn't snapped it clean off. She wouldn't have even needed her new Fae strength to achieve it, either. Just good old human indignation. But a cautious voice in her mind warned her not to show him just how much she didn't like him.

She still didn't know much about Jasic. For all she knew, he could be a Mafia Faery or something, with connections to the very beings who really wanted her dead. So she forced an innocent expression on her features, deliberately loosened her grip on the mug and told herself to take a sip of coffee. The hot, black brew slid down her throat and sent a welcome warmth rushing through her body.

"You call all of this a blessing?" she asked. "Having my life turned upside down? Worried about enemies coming after my family? Fighting for my life every other minute?"

Despite her own instincts clamoring at her to watch

her step, Maggie's indignation was rising at a fever pitch.

He waved one elegant hand as if dismissing her complaints. "Minor inconveniences in the grand scheme of things, I'm sure you'll agree."

"Why would I?"

"How can you not?" He leaned forward, bracing his forearms on his thighs as he met Maggie's gaze and held it. "This hovel you call home is no longer where you belong. Your place is in the crystal palace in Otherworld." Briefly, his eyes went soft and shiny. "You will be Queen—no longer bound to this world and the limitations of your species."

She was pretty sure she'd just been insulted.

"And more importantly," he continued, leaning back now into the couch cushions, taking another sip of his wine, "you will be in a position to grant me my heart's desires."

Here we go, Maggie thought. Finally down to what he really wanted. She should have guessed long before this that good ol' grandFae had had darn good reasons for reconnecting with a human twig on his family tree.

"What is it that you want, Jasic?"

His gaze speared into hers. Hard, unrelenting. Unyielding. Those brilliant blue eyes glittered like broken glass. "Status," he said flatly. "Status among the Fae. I want what's rightfully mine."

"Of course you do," she murmured, encouraging him now to spill it all. She wanted to know exactly where she stood with this guy.

He stood abruptly, pushing himself to his feet, setting the wineglass on the table and moving toward the Christmas tree. Reflections of the colored lights seemed to sparkle on him, giving him the look of a man standing in the shadows of a stained-glass window.

When he turned his head to look at her, his features were once more affable, his eyes benign.

But Maggie wasn't fooled.

"Did you know," he said, "that as a young Fae, I once trained with the warriors?"

"No." And frankly, she couldn't see it. He was pretty, but he was soft. Not like Culhane and the others with their natural strength.

"It didn't last, of course," he mused, more to himself than to her. "Warriors are mostly born into the clan, but there are a few who earn their way in. In the end, I decided not to continue with that plan."

"What stopped you?"

"The training was brutal." He shrugged. "Not to my taste."

Translation, she told herself, it was too hard. He'd been expected to work for something and that hadn't sat well with Jasic. Maggie was getting a true picture here. A selfish male, her grandFae wanted the good things in life and he didn't want to work for them. He wanted to be special. To be admired, but didn't have a clue how to go about earning that admiration.

He spoke again and Maggie stopped her wayward thoughts and paid attention.

"You do know that of the males in Otherworld, only the Warrior clan has any true position?"

"Yes." Hadn't Culhane explained all of that to her when he'd first come to her? Hadn't he said that his plan was for her to make things equal in Otherworld? So that the male Fae could expect the same kinds of rights and privileges that the females enjoyed?

"Then you will understand that after centuries of living as less than what I should have been, I find my patience is at an end." Once again, his eyes hardened. "I want my due, Maggie. Is that really so much to ask from my Queen? My blood?"

*Hours later, she was sitting alone in her bedroom, curled up on the window seat, staring through the glass at the sleeping world beyond. Up and down her narrow street, colorful, twinkling lights shattered the night.

Fog was creeping into the city, sliding off the ocean like thick ribbons of gray silk coming off a spool to wind itself around buildings and trees. The holiday lights shone as tiny beacons in the darkness and not for the first time, Culhane thought how Otherworld might shine in the reflected glory of those small, brightly colored lights.

But his gaze fixed on the woman who had, over time, become the very center of his thoughts. She had been destined and he'd watched and waited for her. She was Queen and held the future of Otherworld in her small, talented hands. She was his sovereign, deserving of his protection and service. But she was more.

She was the heart of him. Maggie had slipped inside him, taken him over, meat and bone. She filled him in places he hadn't known were empty before meeting her. And he must bring her news that would only cause her more worry. Make her look at him and wonder.

"Maggie." Her name sighed from his lips.

She didn't even turn her head, but she smiled, a slight curve of her mouth that pulled at him. "I knew you were here," she said. "What does that say about me? I wonder. Am I getting attuned to you? Or to the Fae magic?"

"A little of both, I think."

"Where've you been, Culhane?" She lifted one hand and idly traced a single fingertip down the length of the glass.

He moved closer, his steps silent as he walked across the rug-covered wood floor. One day, he would come to her and there would be nothing between them but fire and heat. But that was not this day. "There was trouble."

"Of course there was," she said. Finally then, she turned her face up to his and Culhane's heart clenched in his chest. As her Fae blood blossomed inside her, overtaking her humanity, she became even more beautiful. Her skin was pale, with just a few freckles sprinkled like gold dust on cream. Her eyes were dark and, as he'd suspected, worried, and her shoulder-length dark red hair was pulled back from her face. She wore a long-sleeved shirt and blue jeans and her bare toes were painted a lusty red.

She meant everything to him and it annoyed him that she couldn't see it. That she still held on to her mistrust. Hadn't he proven himself to her yet? He had defended her even when she suggested turning the female guards into warriors. What must he do to convince her of his worth?

"So what happened?" she asked.

He sat down beside her and she drew her feet back, as if loath to touch him. Deliberately, he reached out, took her hand in his and said, "There was a . . . skirmish. The Bog Sprites performed a raid on the very spot where we would have been hiding Eileen in the next day or so."

"What?" Her fingers tensed in his grip.

"Somehow, they knew," he said solemnly, and could read in her eyes that she understood just what this meant. "Someone had to have informed the Bog Sprites of our plan. There is no other possibility."

She pulled her hand free of his and bounded to her feet. Walking off a few paces, she suddenly turned to face him again. "Was it Mab?"

"No." He stood up, too, facing her in the pale wash of moonlight that painted her room in hushed tones of silver. "It could not have been Mab. The former queen didn't even know of the alcove's existence. No one outside the Warrior clan does," he explained quietly. "It's a sacred chamber. Used only for our most hallowed ceremonies. That is why we felt the child would be safe there."

"But not now," she whispered.

"No." Culhane walked to her and even when she backed up, he followed, maintaining a closeness between them that he needed. "The Bog Sprites were defeated and sent back to Ireland, but the alcove is no longer a safe hiding place for Eileen."

"Fabulous," Maggie muttered, and scrubbed her hands up and down her arms as if fighting a bone-chilling cold.

Culhane reached for her, pulled her in close and wrapped his arms around her. After one long, indecisive moment, Maggie surrendered to his embrace, circling his waist with her arms, laying her head upon his chest.

"So Otherworld's out," she said softly. "We can't take Eileen there if she won't be safe."

Though it infuriated him to admit it, Culhane was forced to agree. "No. Until we find out who turned this information over, we cannot trust Eileen's safety to any but those in this house."

"So home sweet home becomes a prison. Great."

"We can still take her directly to the Conclave," he offered. "Eileen wouldn't be *hidden*, but she would be protected."

Maggie shook her head, then leaned back and looked up at him. "Not yet. Let's wait on that, okay? I want you and the warriors to look around. See what you can find out about Mab, what she's doing, whom she's talking to. Who might have found out about the alcove and spilled the beans."

"Agreed," Culhane said.

"And," she added, "I know you think I've forgotten about this, but I want you to start getting used to the idea of the females as warriors."

His features froze over. "That is not so easily done."

"I know it won't be easy, but I still think it's a good idea."

"And my plan?" he countered. "To give the males the gift of flight? Are you considering that as well?"

"I am," Maggie said thoughtfully. "I even have a vague idea of how to work it."

"That is good news," he said, smiling now. If the warriors could fly, they would be more than a match for any enemy. And he would eventually be able to convince Maggie that they didn't really need the female guard. "The males of Otherworld will be pleased. They will all follow you willingly, Maggie."

"So the males will love me and the women will undoubtedly be pissed when they're not the only ones flying," she said quietly. "Well, I always thought that politics probably sucked. Turns out, it does."

"Change is never easy, Maggie. Still, I think you are going to be a great queen, if my opinion matters to you."

She looked up at him, blue eyes linking with green. "It does, Culhane. A lot. But . . ."

"But?"

"There's one more thing I need you to do," she said quietly. "I want you to look into Jasic."

"Your grandFae. Has he done something to alarm you?"

"Not really," she said with a shrug. "It's just a feeling. I've got Bezel watching him, but I'd like you to watch him, too."

"It will be done." He cupped her face in the palm of his hand and savored the feel of her skin against his. This is what he hungered for. The touch of her. The scent of her. He was incomplete without her by his side.

"Maggie . . ."

"Don't," she said, lifting one hand to place her fingers against his lips. "Don't say anything, okay? I don't want to talk. Heck, I don't even want to think. Not now. Not until morning, at least."

She lifted her chin to look up at him and her blue eyes were wide, but steady. No tears welled there. No fear shone out at him. This was a woman made to stand beside a warrior. There had never been another like her. And for him, there never would be.

Then she moved against him, wiggling her hips until his cock burned with the need to be buried inside her. He saw in her eyes that she felt his hunger and shared it. That, he told himself, would have to be enough for now.

"No more talk," he whispered, and lowered his head to take her mouth with his.

*

"Consider it an early Christmas vacation," Nora told her daughter over the breakfast table.

"But I don't want to miss school," Eileen answered, using the tines of her fork to push the last of her French toast around on her plate.

"You must be the only kid in the country who would say that," Maggie said.

Morning sunlight filtered in through the yellow and white curtains across the kitchen window. The scent of fresh coffee and maple syrup hung in the air as the three Donovan women sat at the table arguing.

Well, Eileen was arguing. Maggie and Nora were totally on the same page. Maggie had been awake all night—first, because of Culhane and then later, because of what Culhane had had to say. As soon as Nora woke up and headed downstairs, Maggie had followed her and brought her up to speed. Just remembering their conversation made Maggie anxious all over again.

"Now we have a spy?"

"I don't know," Maggie admitted. "Culhane says someone told the Bog Sprites about the hiding place we were going to use for Eileen. Otherwise, they never would have known about it. The question is, who?"

"Maybe . . ." Nora stopped, shook her head and whispered to herself, "No. No way he'd do that."

"He who?"

"*Jasic,*" Nora said finally. "*I caught him eavesdropping on Claire and Mac when they were talking about taking Eileen to the alcove. But Maggie, he's our grand-Fae. Why would he want to hurt Eileen? It doesn't make sense.*"

"*None of this does,*" Maggie told her.

"Mom," Eileen wailed, dragging the one syllable word into at least ten, and successfully dragging Maggie up and out of her thoughts. "I have to go today. I can't stay home."

"I'll call in. Get your assignments for you," Nora said brightly, picking up her coffee mug for a quick gulp. "That way you won't get behind."

"That's not it," Eileen countered. "I want to see ... my friends."

"You mean Devon," Maggie corrected, then glanced at Nora with an I-told-you-so expression stamped on her face. Her older sister looked horrified at the prospect of dealing with not only a crazy ex-queen, demons, a Fae pregnancy, a possibly treacherous grandfather and a pushy boyfriend, but also *teen love*.

And who could blame her?

"You're too young to be thinking about boys," Nora said with a sort of "Please, God" tone to her voice.

Good luck there, Maggie thought wryly, picking up her own coffee mug with as much tenderness as a mother for her newborn. She was exhausted, on edge and, okay, scared. Someone was after Eileen and if she didn't figure out who ... Nope. Not going there, Maggie told herself. What she needed was sleep. No one should be expected to hold their own against a too-smart-for-her-own-good kid on zero sleep.

"You both keep saying that." Eileen glared at her mother, then at her aunt, spreading the venom around completely. "But I'm *not* a kid. I'm almost a teenager and that's practically grown-up."

"You are so not grown-up," Nora said hotly.

"Eileen," Maggie said, speaking up fast, before Nora could say something that would start World War III, "it's not that we don't trust you . . ."

"We don't trust *him*," Nora finished for her.

"You don't even know him," Eileen told them both. "Devon is totally nice and sweet and he actually *cares* what I think."

"I'm sure he's terrific," Nora said, though her tone clearly said otherwise.

"Sweetie," Maggie spoke up, knowing it was dangerous but going for it anyway, "we don't trust *any* boy around you, okay?"

Eileen sighed heavily, emphasis on the drama. "No, it's not okay. I'm not an idiot, you know. I *do* know a nice guy from a total jerk."

"They can fool you," Maggie muttered, and earned a dark scowl from her beloved niece.

"Did you know that twenty-seven percent of teenagers who are treated like prisoners revolt and end up on the streets?"

"You're making that one up," Maggie told her.

"I am not." She sniffed. "Devon would believe me."

"Okay, you know what? Enough about the great and fabulous Devon," Nora told her, using the "mom voice" that always got results. "I'm still in charge of your life and I say you're not going to school again until we're sure there aren't any demons or crazed Fae after you, so just get used to it."

"I'm a *prisoner*, then?" Eileen's tone took on the outraged pitch that only a teenage—almost—girl could manage.

"Bingo," Maggie told her, gulping more coffee desperately. "Welcome to cell block D for Donovan."

Eileen pushed her chair back so fast, its legs shrieked against the wood floor. "Fine. Then I'll just go to my room. Where you can lock me in and starve me."

So said the person who had just polished off three

pieces of French toast and four slices of bacon, Maggie thought wryly.

"Do I still have phone privileges? Or am I in solitary confinement?"

"Of course you can use the phone, but your friends are in school, sweetie." Nora was trying for placating now, but Maggie could have told her it was way too late. The *Good Ship Friendly* had already sailed.

"Fine," Eileen said again, squaring her shoulders and lifting her chin. "Is it all right with my prison guards if I go out and talk to Bezel? Do you trust *him*?"

"Not really," Maggie said with a shrug.

"Of course," Nora told her, frowning at her sister.

Eileen headed for the back door, opened it, then paused and looked back at her mother and aunt. "I'm so not speaking to either one of you ever again."

When the door slammed, Maggie winced and Nora laid her head down on the table.

"Why did I have kids again?" Nora asked no one in particular.

"Spoken by the completely pregnant Fae-mom-to-be," Maggie said, gulping her coffee; then she reached out, patted Nora's head and got up to brew another pot. This was looking to be a very heavily caffeinated morning.

Chapter Fourteen

&

$\mathcal{I}$t was just luck that Maggie happened to glance out the kitchen window a half hour later. Nora was busy upstairs, Claire had gone off to her studio to paint—since she actually made a living at being an artist—and Quinn was off doing warrior stuff. Somewhere.

So Maggie was alone and looking out the blasted window, when a blond boy who looked about sixteen stepped through a portal into the backyard. Maggie almost dropped her coffee; then she *did* drop it when Eileen ran to him and, holding the boy's hand, stepped back through that portal and disappeared.

"What the—"

Maggie hit the back door at a dead run. She didn't even stop to shout for Nora. She just raced into the yard and called up to Bezel in his tree house. "Get down here, you sad excuse for a pixie bodyguard!"

Bezel shifted into place instantly and stood before her in the most god-awful clothing she'd ever seen. It was actually a nightshirt. One of those old-fashioned things men used to sleep in back when they clearly didn't give a damn what they looked like.

Bezel's was bright red and white plaid and hung down to fall across his big feet. It was buttoned up to the neck, thank heaven—she wasn't up for a peek at pixie chests— and the whole outfit was completed by the stupid sleep hat he was wearing pulled down over his pointy ears. It was the same material as his nightshirt and had a silly red ball at its triangled end.

"You're kidding," she said. "Hell, no wonder Fontana threw you out."

Insulted, he waved one hand in the air and was instantly wearing his usual green velvet suit. Sad to say, it was quite the improvement. "Fontana *made* me that nightshirt, just so you know. She thinks I look sexy."

Maggie shook her head and held up both hands in a desperate plea for no more information. "Don't want to know. Not why I called you."

"Why in *Ifreann* did you call me then? I was sleeping and you know, it ain't easy sleeping around here, what with all the people you got popping in and out and—"

"Eileen's gone," she said, interrupting the flow of words.

"Gone?" He looked worried. "Where?"

"That's the point. I don't know," Maggie told him, and walked to where she'd seen the portal open. "A blond kid showed up a couple of seconds ago and when he drew another portal, she left with him. She left with a *boy*. Nora will have a cow."

He snorted.

"And you were supposed to be watching her."

"Damn kids," Bezel mumbled, "always causing trouble." He shook his head until his hair lifted and flew out wildly. "Told Fontana that after the thirteenth one was born."

"Thirteen kids?" Why had she never known that before? Why did she know it now?

"Twenty-two, total," he said, not really paying much attention to what she was saying, anyway. His eyebrows wriggled like caterpillars doing a belly dance. "Course, if I ever get back home, we might make more."

"Oh, God . . ."

"Yeah, it was here," Bezel muttered, hands stretched out in front of him as he "felt" the air.

"Well, I *know* that," Maggie pointed out. "I told you, remember?"

A cold wind blew into the yard and Maggie shivered. She threw a quick look back at the house and was grateful she didn't see Nora coming out to investigate. Her sister just didn't need the extra worry right now. Much better if Maggie found Eileen and got her home before letting Nora know anything about this situation.

"Yeah, you told me, but you can't do this, can you?" Bezel smiled and his face fell into a series of thousands of wrinkles with the pleased expression; then he sketched a portal in the air and as the gold light shimmered and a soft, warm wind sailed from its center, he looked up at Maggie and grinned even wider. "This is where he took her."

"Which is *where* exactly?" Maggie stared into the portal and could only make out the vaguest shapes and colors. Blues, greens and a pearly white that seemed to shimmer.

"The beach."

Her jaw dropped as she stared into the portal. "The *beach*?"

"Yeah. They're at one of the lakes in Inia."

"Inia?"

Bezel scowled and that expression looked much more at home on his ugly face. "Think Minnesota but warmer. Lots of lakes. Lots of sand. Lots of nothing else."

"Great," Maggie whispered. "Okay, I'm going to get her. You keep Nora busy."

"I'll get her to make me some more cookies," he said thoughtfully.

"Yeah. You're a giver." Maggie took one last look around her yard and stepped through the portal.

The Sluagh were a formidable foe. And they were almost as unnerving as allies.

Mab shuddered to see herself here, in Casia, with the outcasts she herself had sentenced to this dismal place. Small wonder she hadn't found many friends since her arrival.

But then, she wasn't looking for friends. She wanted fighters. Those beings who were willing to risk all for a chance at freedom. And she was willing to make whatever deals necessary to ensure that she regained her throne and disposed of those who currently rejoiced in her fall.

"The Dullahan will ride with us. As will the Pooka."

Mab whirled around and faced the Sluagh who stood in her open doorway. It was the male. Corran. His dark eyes were void of light. No smile creased his beautiful face. But it didn't matter. Not to Mab. Nothing mattered but that he would do all he had promised.

"Will your brothers join us as well?" she asked.

Corran moved into the room, silently prowling the perimeter. Each step was muffled. There was no rustle of his dark coat. No whisper of movement from the leather pants he wore. He was . . . and yet he wasn't. It was as if she were alone in the room, but for the cold that was as bitter as the icy storm raging outside her room.

Her room. How far she had sunk, Mab thought with a dismal glance at her surroundings. Four walls, naked wood and a bed that looked less than inviting. That she would have become subject to such as this. She shook her head, disgusted at this turn of events. All because of a half-Fae and Culhane, the traitorous bastard.

She'd lost everything.

Yet she lived. And while she lived, Mab knew that she would fight to reclaim the past. What was rightfully hers.

"You risk great danger in bringing together so many of the rogue Fae." Corran's voice was as still as a breath. No inflection. No hint of emotion.

Were the Sluagh capable of emotion? As Fallen Angels, had they been stripped of pride, envy, the need for revenge? If so, could they even understand those emotions in others?

Mab gathered herself, perched on the edge of her bed and with a deliberately casual movement, crossed her legs. "I risk much to gain much."

Corran swiveled his head to look at her. "There are those in Casia who would sooner see you dead as back on the throne."

She knew that all too well. Mab hadn't drawn an easy breath since entering this horrible place. But there were prices to be paid and she was willing to meet them. If that meant working alongside the Pooka and the Dullahan, gods help her, that's what she would do.

"There are always impediments to goals. That's what makes them worth striving for." She threaded her fingers together atop her knees, more to stop her hands from shaking than anything else. Tipping her head to one side, she allowed her fall of golden hair to slide off her shoulders in a silken move designed to seduce.

Corran remained unmoved.

"The only goal my people have is to walk among the humans again," he said, and for the first time displayed an emotion. Longing. "It has been far too long since we feasted and we grow tired of the constant hunger."

Their need for souls, the essence of innocence, was what would drive them, Mab knew. But it was only humanity they endangered and she cared little for that miserable species. Let the Sluagh feast and when they were finished, Mab would rule *both* dimensions, Fae and human; then she would move on, eventually laying claim to all the worlds.

But she kept her thoughts to herself and said only, "I know."

He walked toward her, his steps as silent as before. "You may be the path to freedom. It is the only reason we did not kill you the moment you entered this place."

She swallowed hard and made a silent promise to herself that all who had had a part in her downfall, forcing her to deal with such as this, would pay with their immortal lives. "I know that, too."

"Yet you trust me?"

Mab smiled up at him. "No, I'm not so foolish as that, Corran."

"A wise queen." He cupped her chin in the palm of his hand and ice crystals formed inside her.

He waited, watching her, and she knew that he was aware of what his touch was doing to her. The aching cold. The bitter frost settling over her bones.

"Yes," he said softly. "Very wise. See that you remain so."

He left her then and Mab closed her eyes with a sigh of relief. The cold within her was hideous and only slowly began to ebb.

She knew that if he had touched her for much longer, she would have frozen completely.

An ice statue of a former queen.

She wrapped her arms around her shivering body and stared out the window as sleet tapped at the glass with eager fingers. Those responsible for this humiliation would pay.

&

"Your mother is going to *kill* you," Maggie said for what had to be the twentieth time in the last five minutes.

"You don't have to tell her," Eileen pleaded, her gaze sliding from her aunt to the blond boy standing tall and straight beside her.

"Oh, yes I do." Maggie's gaze slid from the two guilt-stricken teenagers in front of her to their surroundings. Bezel had said lakes.

What he hadn't told her was, the lake waters were

aquamarine, so clear and beautiful a color, Maggie was sure she would never be able to capture it in a painting. The shoreline was pristine white sand, dotted with what must have been the Faery equivalent of palm trees, long pale green fronds rustling in the warm, tropical breeze. White clouds fluffed their way across a cobalt sky and some really big birds wheeled in the air high above them.

Inia was a place Maggie would like to visit—sometime when she wasn't, you know, fighting for her life or wearing a crown or chasing down a runaway teenager.

"It is my responsibility," the boy said, his voice a deep rumble of sound that had Eileen looking up at him with stars in her eyes. "I will confess to your sister, my Queen. And make all things right again."

"Devon, is it?" Maggie asked.

He nodded.

"Trust me when I tell you that confession is not going to make all things right."

He frowned and shifted position, his booted feet sliding on the sand. "We did nothing wrong."

Oh God, Maggie really hoped he was telling the truth about that. When she'd seen Eileen disappear with a gorgeous Faery, all she'd been able to think was *History repeating itself.* Years ago, Gran had slipped away with Jasic and come home pregnant. Nora was now pregnant by Quinn. And Maggie had her own Fae lover to deal with.

Eileen was just *way* too young to be doing . . . *anything* with a Faery. Even if he was completely cute.

Eileen was watching Devon and Devon was watching Maggie.

He stood about five foot eight, had shoulder-length blond hair and blue eyes that were almost the color of the lake stretching out behind them. He was wearing brown leather pants, a cream-colored, long-sleeved shirt and knee-high black boots. He was pretty much the stuff young girls' dreams were made of.

He held himself tall and proud, with just a touch of arrogance that most teenage boys didn't acquire until at least eighteen and there was a look in his eye that Maggie had become accustomed to seeing in Culhane's.

With that thought firmly in mind, she asked, "Just how old are you, Devon?"

"Aunt Maggie!"

She ignored the outraged hiss from her niece and waited for an answer. Devon looked about sixteen, which was way too old to be hanging around a twelve-year-old. But Maggie had the sinking sensation that he was much older than she thought.

"It is all right, Eileen," he said, with a reassuring nod. "The Queen has the right to demand any information she desires from her warriors."

"You're a *warrior*?"

"Isn't that cool?" Eileen sighed.

He bowed at the waist, his blond hair falling forward. "A warrior in training, my Queen."

"Okay, stop with the queen stuff for right now." Maggie waited until he straightened up and looked her in the eye. "You're in training. At the Conclave."

"Aye," he said, and damn if he didn't sound like Culhane. Same arrogant, proud tone.

Were they born like that? Or was that attitude drilled into them during training? And did they start training as teenagers? Maggie didn't think so.

"Let's hear it, Devon," she said, folding her arms across her chest. "How old?"

"I will be four hundred in six months," he told her.

Eileen sighed.

Maggie groaned. And she'd thought sixteen was too old for her niece. Good God. This was . . . well, it just wasn't going to happen. Four hundred sounded old, but she knew Culhane had been around for thousands of years. So probably in the Fae world, Devon actually *was* a teenager. Good God. And human mothers thought *they* had it bad. Fae children had as long an adolescence as a golden retriever!

"Isn't he something . . . ," Eileen said wistfully.

"Yeah," Maggie agreed. "He is *something*." Eileen was about to turn into a puddle of goo, so Maggie reached out, grabbed the girl's forearm and dragged her away from Devon's side to stand next to her. She didn't miss the fact that the two kids were still staring at each other with big, wide, googly eyes.

Stifling another groan, Maggie spoke up and waited until Devon was looking directly at her again to give him a good glare. "Okay, Devon, here's the deal. No more sneaking around with Eileen. No more dropping by my house uninvited. No more drawing portals and whisking her off for minivacations."

He looked mutinous.

Eileen sounded horrified when she moaned, "Aunt Maggie, *please* . . ."

"And here's what happens if you don't listen up," Maggie said, wanting to make her threat very, very clear. "I catch you hanging around Eileen again, you're out of the Conclave. Understand? You'll be expelled. Or fired. Or . . . whatever the hell it is I'd have to do."

His face actually paled.

Good. Her threat had hit home.

"So," she asked, obviously unnecessarily, "we're clear?"

"Yes, Majesty."

"I am *never* speaking to you again," Eileen hissed.

"You said that already this morning," Maggie told her, then glanced at Devon. "Draw a portal to my backyard, kiddo. And make it fast."

He gave Eileen one last, soulful look before he did as he was told and an instant later, Maggie and Eileen were back at the Donovan house. Her niece took off in a mad huff for the back door. Maggie watched her go and spoke to Bezel. "So, how old's your youngest?"

"Still just a kid. Six hundred next spring."

Shaking her head, Maggie sighed. "Does he make you crazy?"

"Hey," Bezel said, "teenagers'll kill you."

&

The trouble with rain was, Maggie thought early the next morning, if it came too soon after painting a window . . . if the decorations hadn't had time to age and dry in the sun . . . your beautifully crafted holiday paintings tended to wash away.

And when one of Maggie's best customers called at the crack of dawn to wail about losing half of her snow scene, Maggie had to gather up her paints and go in for a fix-it job.

Betty's Beauties was a small hair salon on the edge of town, and Betty Bartosh, owner and head stylist, loved to decorate her windows for every holiday ever known. Valentine's Day, St. Patrick's Day, hell, Maggie had even once painted an oak on her glass for Arbor Day. So it was just good business to drive over to Betty's place and touch up the paint washed away by last night's storm.

The fact that Maggie was practically sleep-painting really didn't figure into things. She'd been doing this for so long, she actually could have painted in her sleep. Which was a good thing, since she really wasn't getting much sleep these days.

Two nights before, she'd been busy with Culhane. Last night, she'd spent most of her time refereeing the battle between Nora and her daughter. Nora hadn't been happy to hear about Devon, boy warrior. And Eileen hadn't been any happier to have her crush, crushed, so to speak. So the argument had raged for hours, with Quinn beating a hasty retreat and even Bezel and Claire hiding out.

Nobody could battle like a Donovan woman when she was pissed.

Still, the upshot was, Eileen was grounded, Nora was torn by guilt because she was breaking her daughter's heart to protect her and Maggie . . . Maggie only wanted at least six straight hours of sleep.

But that wasn't going to happen anytime soon.

Betty was busy, what with every woman in town wanting her hair done before Christmas, so there was no one out front talking to Maggie as she did her work. Just the way she liked it. She replaced the snowy hill and the solitary sledder. She redid the snowman's face, painting in a new carrot nose since the old one had shrunk to the size of one of those mutant baby carrots—and even snowmen knew it was all about size.

It felt good, she thought, to be doing something normal. Something from her everyday routine. Here, she wasn't some fated queen or the scourge of demons everywhere. She was simply Maggie Donovan, glass painter.

The red ribbons on the door wreath were done and Maggie was finally finishing up refreshing the holly berries when she heard the voice behind her.

"I've been looking for you."

"Damn it," Maggie muttered. Her stomach turned into a sinking pit and her chin hit her chest. "I knew I was jinxing myself even as I thought about how nice it was to do normal things."

"Who are you calling abnormal?"

Maggie focused on the reflection in the glass of the rogue Fae standing behind her. His human glamour made him appear to be about forty and balding. He was wearing a suit and tie and looked every inch the corporate-ladder type. If not for the silver flickering in his eyes, Maggie would have guessed he was a lawyer. Or maybe even an accountant.

Red eyes would have meant demon.

Silvery eyes meant Fae. Clearly a rogue Fae, though. One who was all too eager to kill Maggie.

She didn't turn around to face him, since once she did that, game on. As tired as she was, Maggie knew she'd be at a disadvantage in a fight. But it wasn't as if she had much of a choice here, either.

"Do we really have to do this? Couldn't we just call each other names and leave it at that?"

The Fae in a lawyer suit checked his wristwatch, then shook his head. "Nope. Got an appointment in half an hour. Best to just do it now so I can make my meeting."

Maggie dropped her paintbrush into the jar of tempera she was holding and looked through the window into Betty's salon. Thankfully, no one was watching her.

"They can't see us," he told her impatiently. "Do you think I want witnesses? I live here, too, you know. I erected a glamour. It's just you and me."

"Fine," she said, stepping off the ladder. "Just let me put this paint down."

"Could you wash your hands, too?"

She glanced at him and he was wrinkling his nose at her.

"You're covered in that stuff and I don't want to get paint on my suit when we fight, okay? That meeting I have?"

"Right." Maggie shook her head, set down the jar of tempera and while she did, she plucked up the iron-based knife she'd taken to carrying with her. The sword Bezel had given her was great, but a little too unwieldy to carry around every day.

When she straightened up, she was holding it out, fisted in her paint-streaked right hand. With any luck, she'd slice him good and get paint on his precious suit all at the same time.

"That won't help," he said, his eyes narrowing on her.

"We'll see." She swept the blade out in a wide arc and as he jumped back, she crouched, then flew at him, taking his legs out from under him.

They went down together, hitting the pavement with a jarring thud that felt as though it rattled every one of Maggie's bones. The asphalt tore at the already-frayed knee of her jeans and ripped right through the fabric.

But she couldn't spare much time worrying about torn jeans and scraped knees. The Fae was up and over her in an instant and before she could think much about it, he slammed his fist into her jaw.

She actually *saw* stars. Again.

He grinned and Maggie stabbed him with the knife. Instantly, he recoiled, looked down at his pristine white shirt and hissed as blood seeped into the fabric. "Now look what you've done! I can't go to my meeting looking like this!"

Fury filled his features, but a moment later, a look of stunned surprise flashed across his eyes. He stumbled back and had to fight for his balance. "You ... bitch ... *iron*?"

"So iron does help, after all," Maggie said, scrambling to her feet as her opponent glared at her.

"A lucky shot," he told her, already recovering his balance, shaking off whatever sickness the iron blade had introduced into his system.

"Then come on and get me," she taunted, keeping in a crouch as Bezel had taught her, circling him as she'd seen Culhane do during a fight. Her gaze was locked on his. She knew that she'd see his plans in his eyes before he made a move, so she focused everything she had on reading that decision.

So when he charged her again, she was ready. She moved down and up, slicing at him again with the knife, dragging the blade sharply across his chest, while at the same time punching with her left hand. She caught his chin, saw his eyes roll back and really blessed all the superstrength she'd gotten as part of this whole queen thing.

The Fae in a suit was moving with stilted steps now,

shaking his head as if to clear his vision, bending over double occasionally as if in pain and Maggie was glad to see it. Not that she actually liked hurting people—Fae—whatever. But if it came down to a choice—them or her—she picked *her*.

Then he moved suddenly and swatted the knife from her hand. It clattered as it slid across the asphalt, but Maggie barely had time to acknowledge it. The Fae's huge hand was at her throat and she was gasping, choking for air. She felt her heartbeat thundering. Her feet left the ground as he continued to squeeze.

"You stupid bitch," he snarled, silvered eyes locking on to hers. "Did you really think you could take us all? Defeat Mab? You're pathetic. You can't win this."

Maggie fought desperately for air. She kicked at him and missed. She threw desperate lightning bolts from the tips of her fingers, but they seemed to bounce off the guy as if he'd been Scotchguarded. Her vision was graying at the edges and Maggie was scratching futilely at the hand that held her in such a tight, unrelenting grip.

"You lose, Your *Majesty*."

She looked down into his eyes and saw him laughing, celebrating. And she knew he was right. It was all finished. Her destiny was going to end right here in a Fae glamour on Pacific Coast Highway.

Game over. She hadn't even lived long enough to grow into all her Fae powers. She'd never reach her full potential. Now she had no chance to move to Otherworld and rule. No fights with Mab. No more sex with Culhane.

No more anything.

Her lungs were bursting, clamoring for air that wouldn't come. The world was going completely gray and even the Fae who held her so closely was looking blurry.

And then everything changed.

Culhane appeared out of nowhere.

He didn't speak. Didn't threaten. He simply swung a sword in a wide arc and decapitated the Fae trying to kill Maggie.

Instantly, she dropped to the ground, grabbed at her throat and hissed in glorious, wonderful, smog-filled, ocean-scented air. Shaking, still terrified, she glanced at the fallen Fae, then looked away just as quickly. Not in time, of course, to prevent her mind from indelibly carving the image of a headless Fae sprawled out on a city street. She knew she'd be seeing that image in her nightmares for years.

But the point was, she'd be alive to *have* nightmares.

Then Culhane was there. Kneeling beside her in the street, his pale green eyes locked on her face, his hands cupping her cheeks. Worry glittered in his gorgeous eyes as he kissed her forehead, her eyes, her nose and finally, all too briefly, her mouth. "Are you all right?"

She nodded, her throat still too sore to speak.

He glanced at what was left of his enemy, then shifted his gaze back to hers. "He was a follower of Mab. A known supporter."

"Great." She croaked out a single word and winced at the effort.

Culhane took her hands and pulled her to her feet. Keeping her face turned to his so she wouldn't have to look at her enemy again, he said, "We have word that she is gathering her strength. Building an army of rogue Fae in Casia. Soon, she will come to challenge you."

Maggie nodded, and leaned into him.

"You're not alone, Maggie. There is no reason for you to ever have to face any of them on your own again. It is time to move to Otherworld. Take your rightful place in the palace. Let all Fae see that the Queen is in residence." He cradled her head to his chest and she listened to the rapid-fire beat of his heart. "It is time," he whispered.

She knew he was right. It *was* time. Time she gave up

her ties to the world where she didn't belong anymore. Time to move her family and her friends to a palace that could be safeguarded more thoroughly than her little beach house ever could be.

Time to be what destiny had already named her.

More bad was coming. But then, she'd known that all along. She wrapped her arms around Culhane's waist and clung to him so tightly he'd have to peel her off later.

She was shaken. Scared. And royally pissed off.

Maggie was done being the nice Queen. It was time to kick some serious Fae ass.

And she was just the Donovan to do it.

Chapter Fifteen

ε

$\mathcal{M}$aggie was never going to make it living in a castle that was entirely white.

She was a girl who loved color. Texture. She enjoyed the tactile experience of putting paint to canvas. She relished being surrounded by jewel tones, by soft greens and pale yellows. She liked flannels and silks and those nubby bedspreads that used to be so popular.

In a crystal palace with white marble floors and the occasional pulse of faded color, Maggie felt . . . uneasy. Uncomfortable. She wanted warmth and coziness.

And she wasn't going to find it here.

"Stupid," she mumbled, doing a half turn in her new bedroom. Here she was worrying about white walls and floor when she had half of the Fae population out for her blood. But then again, if she didn't feel at home here, how could she fight to remain?

"Can't do it," she muttered.

Culhane's head snapped up, his gaze locked on hers. "So you will not stay after all?"

"Oh, I'm staying." She fisted her hands at her hips and turned in a slow circle, taking in the Queen's chamber.

Her new bedroom was as big as her entire house back in her old life. Wide windows, opening out onto gardens that were so rich and beautiful, they were a painting in themselves. Sparkling marble floors and crystal walls shone like mirrors, reflecting her own image back a thousand times.

Mab might have enjoyed that, but for Maggie . . . she looked at herself and saw five extra pounds, hair that needed a trim and the beginnings of panic shining in her eyes. Nope. Didn't need more mirrors.

There was a closet, empty of all but the space she might need to hang her pitifully small wardrobe. A bathroom that could have been right at home in the Taj Mahal and a formal sitting area beside a fireplace—again white marble—big enough for her to stand up straight in.

It was gorgeous, palatial and so not her.

"I can't live like this," she murmured.

Culhane looked stunned. "You do not like it?"

"Oh." She turned quickly to face him. "It's gorgeous. Like a museum or a castle you pay ten bucks to tour. It's just not . . . *me.*"

He smiled, a slow curve of his mouth that was comforting as well as sensual. "Ah. I think I understand. Perhaps something more like this."

He waved one hand and Maggie's breath caught as she watched the room transform, molecules scattering, rearranging themselves in the blink of an eye. Her own paintings, now in luxurious frames, were hanging on walls painted a soft blue. Dark blue, overstuffed chairs now sat in front of the roaring fire, with a small table drawn up between them.

Pillows, all kinds and colors, were stacked on the window seat, making it look as though a rainbow had spilled into the room and settled in for a long stay. The bed, which she'd already had Culhane change out since no way had she been willing to sleep in Mab's old bed . . . ew, was now a massive four-poster.

The very one he'd conjured for their first night together down in the throne room. It looked invitingly plush, with its thick quilts and throws piled atop the mattresses and the mountain of pillows stacked against the headboard. At either side of the bed, lamps burned with soft yellow glows from atop the twin tables that appeared magically. The book Maggie had been reading at home lay on one of the tables also, just waiting for her to pick it up again.

Maggie grinned as rugs in shades of blues and greens dotted the floor that now looked like oak planks the color of warm honey. Beside one of the windows, her easel and painting supplies blinked into existence and her chair popped in next, all ready for her to pick up her brushes and do what she did best.

She laughed, delighted. "It's wonderful."

Maggie gave Culhane a grateful smile and shook her head in amazement. "It actually feels like my place now."

"It is your place, Maggie. You are Fae," he said. "Magic is your birthright. You may do what you will to the palace. You are Queen. You must make of it whatever you see fit."

"You're a dangerous man, Culhane."

"Not to you," he countered.

"Oh, especially to me," she told him. She knew he'd never meant more to her than he did right this minute. He had, with a wave of his hand, made this new world seem possible. Made her feel as if she might actually belong here.

"Oh. My. God." Nora wandered into Maggie's room. "Did you see my room? It's bigger than my whole house and I think I had a sexual experience when I saw the bathroom and—" She broke off, took in Maggie's sumptuous bedroom and said, "This is. Wow. I mean. Wow."

"I know." Maggie smiled at Culhane and walked toward her sister. "So you're okay with moving to the palace? I know I didn't give you much of a choice about this, but I really think we're all safer here."

"Yeah, you said all that." Nora shook her head and

looked at her sister. "Don't worry about me, Mags. The important thing is, we keep Eileen safe."

"We will." Maggie glanced at Culhane for confirmation and the warrior gave her one quick nod.

"But you said before that you were worried about us staying in the palace. Because Mab used to live here and she'd know it so well."

She had believed that, until it had become all too clear that Castle Bay, California, was not the safe haven she'd hoped it would be. There were too many Fae wandering around her hometown. Too many demons making tries for her and her family. So the only thing left to do was to move to Otherworld. Pick up her destiny with both hands and hold on for everything she was worth.

Maggie was going to do whatever she had to do to keep her family safe. Period. Besides, she had a little idea, which, if it worked, was going to up their safety quotient by a lot.

"Trust me, Nora. We're going to keep Eileen safe. And, we've got something Mab didn't have and probably doesn't know about. Claire."

"Claire?"

e

"This is amazing, Aunt Maggie," Eileen said, trying to look at everything at once as they walked through the palace.

Thanks to Culhane, Maggie had made quite a few more changes to the crystal castle. The walls were now different hues, from pale blue to green, to yellow. Instead of empty, cavernous spaces, rooms were inviting now, with comfy furniture, and paintings on the walls. Fires blazed in every hearth and even the Fae who worked there seemed pleased by the changes.

There was a warmth to the place that it had probably never known before. Plus, this way it didn't give Maggie the creeps.

She didn't know if she'd ever get used to the way the palace staff were forever bowing to her, but that was a worry for another day.

"So," she said, with a glance at her niece, "you're speaking to me again?"

Eileen scowled, remembering that whole situation with Devon. "Well, you are the Queen and everything. . . ."

"Gee, thanks. Feel the love." The two of them entered the main dining hall and Maggie looked at her gathered "family"—Nora and Quinn, of course, Culhane, Bezel, Mac and Claire. Along the wall, a brand-new doggie bed held a snoring Sheba. And naturally, Jasic had insisted on joining them.

Since Maggie hadn't been able to find out anything specific about her grandFae just yet, she'd figured it was a good idea to keep him close enough to watch. But he'd settled into palace life more easily than any of them. It had only been one full day and already, she'd heard that he was keeping the palace staff hopping with his demands. That wasn't going to fly for long, she promised herself.

Once Maggie and Eileen were seated, dinner was served. Conversations rose and fell around the table as they ate and Maggie tried to listen to everyone at once.

"The baby's moving around a lot," Nora whispered to Quinn.

"My son is strong," he answered.

"I don't see why Devon can't come to the palace," Eileen said to anyone who was listening.

"Female warriors are not a good idea." McCulloch was lecturing Claire.

"Afraid of a little competition?" Claire countered, making Mac sputter in outrage.

Maggie hid a smile, then listened to Bezel boast. "Gotta get Fontana over here to see me. That crimson tree out back is gonna be perfect for my new house."

"The pudding is warm," Jasic complained, tugging at the sleeve of one of the serving Fae as he passed.

Maggie frowned at Jasic, made a mental note to have a chat with Grandpa Faery and looked at Culhane. Now that dinner was mostly over, she asked, "What do you think? Do we tell them now?"

He smiled and nodded.

"Excellent," Maggie said, "that's what I thought. Okay, everybody, listen up."

Instantly, a hush fell over the table and the male Fae servants began to back out of the room.

She waved them back in. "No, you guys stay here, too. This is going to involve everyone who lives in the castle."

The males looked dumbfounded that not only had their Queen noticed their existence, but had spoken to them directly and included them in whatever it was she was going to say. Maggie sighed.

Culhane had been right about one thing. The males of Otherworld had been treated way too crappy for way too long. She had the distinct impression that good ol' Mab had never once considered her male subjects' wants or needs.

Well, Maggie was coming at this from a whole different viewpoint. She was from a world where until the last hundred years or so, *women* had been getting the shaft. Sure, now everyone said that equality had arrived, but women were still overlooked for jobs, paid less for doing the same thing men did *and* they managed to give birth to more men determined to keep them at bug level.

So she was just a touch more understanding about the whole even-steven rule. And she was going to take care of that, fast.

First things first, though. She waited until everyone was looking at her and then she said, "I know you thought we were here just until we settled this thing with Mab. But . . . we're here in Otherworld to stay, people."

Everybody spoke at once.

"What about school?" Eileen demanded.

"What about our house?" Nora asked.

"Holy *Ifreann,* it's about time," Bezel shouted.

"What about my painting?" Claire wondered aloud.

"Ahhh . . . ," Jasic sighed with pleasure.

Maggie frowned at him, but let it go for the moment. Instead, she looked at her sister first. "Nor, you know this is where we belong now. Not just me, *you.*"

Nora inhaled sharply and held that breath trapped behind lips clamped tightly together.

"Come on," Maggie chided. "You float all the time. You're pregnant with a Fae and you breathe Faery dust almost constantly these days. Somebody's going to notice if we stay in the human world."

"But it's home," Nora said, with a guilty look at Quinn. "Sorry, honey. Otherworld is nice and everything, but it's not home to me."

"It will be," he assured her.

"It has to be," Maggie said quietly, reaching out to take her sister's hand. "Look, I know none of us asked for this. But the truth is, we're not human anymore, Nora."

Bezel snorted.

Maggie sent him a glare, then continued talking to her sister. "Not completely human, anyway. Everything's changed and it's time we accepted it. You're turning into a full-Fae and so am I."

"When do I get to?" Eileen demanded.

Maggie sighed. "The point is, we're in Otherworld for good."

"I'm not Fae, Maggie," Claire put in, and Maggie looked at her friend.

"No, you're not. But Claire, you're my best friend. The Fae know that. You wouldn't be safe in the human world alone."

She looked as if she might argue for a second or two; then she simply slumped back into her chair. Claire didn't seem to notice that Mac was grinning like a big dork.

"And we just abandon our house? Our things?" Nora demanded, shifting the conversation back to her.

"You can bring them all with you," Quinn told her.

"It's not the same thing," she said, with another look of apology for him before turning her gaze on Maggie again. "We just walk away from the house Grandpa built practically all by himself?"

Culhane spoke up. "Time runs differently here, remember that. You can be months in Otherworld while a single night has passed in the mortal world. You can return whenever you like."

"Or bring the blasted house here plank by plank," Jasic muttered, and motioned for a server to pour him more nectar.

"Huh." Maggie looked at Jasic for a long minute and realized he was right. They could bring the house here. Set it up in the backyard of the palace if they wanted to. With a little Faery magic, they could make it so the neighbors didn't even remember the Donovan house having once been there.

Then she shook her head, and added the question of the house to her mental list of things to look into as soon as she had time. For now . . .

"So anyway, you should all know that Claire's going to be doing a warding spell on the palace tomorrow."

"It is already warded," Quinn pointed out. "No enemies of the Queen may enter."

"Yeah, but that was Mab's warding," Maggie told him, and picked up a slice of what looked like a pear. She bit into it, smiled and said, "We need some new ones. With a different kind of punch. Spells Mab won't be expecting and won't be able to get around."

"You can do this?" McCulloch asked.

"I can," Claire told him, smiling at Maggie.

"Besides," Maggie added, "it's not just *my* enemies we have to worry about. Eileen's in danger. So is everyone who even knows me." She groaned internally at that. She'd somehow become like Typhoid Mary or something. She was just the center of some big black tornado that sucked in everyone she cared about.

To protect them, she was going to have to seal them up inside a Faery palace. Oh yeah. This was going to be fun.

"It's not your fault, Maggie," Nora said, trying to smile through her fears.

Wasn't it? Maggie wasn't so sure. This had all started because she'd killed a demon and inhaled the Fae dust it was carrying. If she hadn't gone to her ex-boyfriend's place that day, none of this might have happened. Or, another voice in her mind pointed out, Culhane was right and this had all been destined from the beginning of her life. This was where she would have ended up no matter what.

The trouble with destinies, she thought, was that they were continually being rewritten. She had no guarantee that she was going to survive all of this. Nothing was written in stone about how *long* her reign was supposed to be.

So she had to do the best she could with the information she had at the time. And suddenly, she had a lot more sympathy for presidents and kings and queens. They were probably all stumbling around in the darkness, hoping to make the right decisions.

"Anyway," Maggie told everyone seated at the table while she plastered on a happy face and a bright smile so brittle it felt as though it might crack her face, "that's the story for the short term. New spells. New home. New way of life. Everybody excited?"

That question was met with glowers, complaints and hushed mutters filled with worry.

"Yeah," she muttered, reaching for her wineglass, "right there with you all."

Hours later, Culhane held Maggie close and buried his face in the curve of her neck. Her scent filled him, wrapped itself around him and held him in a grip as gentle as it was tenacious. Behind the locked doors of the Queen's chamber, the two of them came together on the luxurious bed as soft breezes drifted through the open windows to slide across their skin and the scent of flowers filled the air.

"You were magnificent, Maggie," he whispered, hands skimming along her naked body, loving how she arched into his touch. "You are the Queen I always knew you would be."

She blew out a breath, sighed a little, then rolled over to lie on top of him. Flesh to flesh, heat to heat, she rubbed her body along his and Culhane hissed in air through gritted teeth. His cock swelled, his body ached to join with hers.

"It's not your Queen who needs you at the moment, Culhane," she said, going up on her knees to straddle him. She reached down, curled her fingers around his thick shaft and smiled at him. "It's just me. Maggie Donovan."

"You are she and she is you," Culhane told her with a groan as she rubbed and stroked him until he felt as though he might explode. "The Queen and Maggie are interlocked now. One does not exist without the other."

She frowned and in the soft lamplight, she looked more beautiful to him than she ever had before. Golden light spilled over her, making her skin appear luminous. Her blue eyes shone and glittered with an inner pride.

She had finally accepted her duty. Her destiny. She had come to the palace and already was turning everything in Otherworld on its head. This would not be an easy transition, but he knew she had been born for this.

And he had been born to be at her side.

For so long, he'd expected merely to serve as her consort. To rule Otherworld through her. But he knew now, there would be nothing at all without her. That he would be empty without her. She had become the best part of him.

Shaking her thick dark red hair back from her face, she looked down at him and whispered, "In this room, Culhane, we're not Queen and Warrior, okay? Here, we're just *us*. Here, what we have together is all that matters."

"You are right, Maggie," he told her, watching her breathlessly as she rose up on her knees. "Here, we are two lovers caught in our own storm."

"Now that," she sighed as she slowly, inch by tantalizing inch, lowered herself onto him, "sounds wonderful."

Culhane groaned, arched up, pushing his body into hers, forcing her to take him faster, harder than she'd planned. He watched her face as he filled her. Watched her tip her head back in pleasure as his body claimed hers completely.

She moaned and swiveled her hips atop him, grinding her center against him, twisting and writhing, making them both fight for air, fight for release.

Her breasts swayed with her movements and he lifted his hands to cup them, his thumb and forefingers tweaking and pulling at the hardened nipples until she gasped and offered herself more fully into his touch.

She was all. Everything. Whether she wanted to believe it or not, even in this room, she was a queen. *His* Queen.

His hands dropped to her hips and he guided her as she moved on him, rocking her body in a timeless rhythm. Releasing his body only to reclaim it again a moment later. The smooth slide of his body into hers tore at him, rending his heart, his soul.

He felt her inner muscles bunch and tighten, fisting around him, squeezing him as she rode the first thundering wave of her climax. She called out his name and he tightened his hold on her hips, holding her down, pinning her to his body as she quivered and shook with the force of their joining.

Groaning, Culhane pumped up and into her until the same wash of sensation took him over and he surrendered to the pleasure of emptying himself inside her heat.

Moments later, Maggie curled into him and Culhane held her close. Outside the room, night ruled Otherworld and the lights of the city stained the starlit sky with a wash of brightness. She was now officially a part of his world and Culhane felt the rightness in that. Otherworld would, undoubtedly, be better for her presence, but he knew that she herself was the world he would willingly die for.

Culhane stared up at the ceiling, felt Maggie's breath on his chest and knew that something profound had happened to him. He felt something for her that he had never known before. Something he hadn't counted on or prepared for. She touched him in places that had long been empty and cold. She made him want to be more. Do more.

His eyes widened and his heartbeat suddenly galloped in his chest. He *loved* her.

Culhane examined that knowledge for a long moment. In all his long years of life, he had never been more surprised. Yes, he had known from the beginning that she would be his. But he had always assumed that she would love him and he would allow it. *This*, his love for her, had not been a part of his strategy. Loving Maggie would only complicate things. Would make his plans for Otherworld more difficult to bring about. Yet, how could he not love her? And how could he not tell her?

No, he told himself, now was not the time for such confessions. Things were still too unsettled. She had been in her palace all of one day. It wasn't time yet for new revelations.

But he could say something else.

Sliding one hand up and down her spine, he waited for her to look up into his eyes; then he smiled and whispered, "Now that we are married, I think we should make children together, Maggie."

She went absolutely still.

Several seconds ticked past.

Finally, she said, "What?"

"Children," he repeated, confused by her reaction, but willing to explain his reasoning so that she might see the logic in it. "To ensure your bloodline continues on the Fae throne. Even though the Fae are immortal, there may come a day when you wish to step down. It is necessary to have one of our children ready to succeed you."

Abruptly, Maggie sat up and scooted away from him. He felt the loss of her warmth far too deeply for his own comfort.

"We should have *children*? Now that we're *married*?" she repeated. "When did that happen? When did we say, 'I do'? Hell, when did you *propose*?"

Culhane frowned at her and shifted position, to recline against the heavily carved headboard. He shoved a pillow behind his head. "Propose?"

"You know," she told him sharply. "When did you *ask* me to marry you?"

Bewildered, he only looked at her. "Why would I do that?"

"What?" She shook her head as if she weren't hearing him clearly. *"Why?"*

"Maggie," he said with a patient sigh, not really understanding her cause for alarm, "when we had sex for the first time, I told you then. I said, *With this mating, I claim you.*"

She frowned, pushed one hand through her hair and thought about that for a second. "Okay, yeah. I remember hearing you say that, but . . ."

He shrugged. "We are joined."

"Joined. That meant you married me?"

"Of course." Culhane frowned slightly, shook his head and said, "Why else would I have claimed you?"

"For the *sex*?" she countered.

"Sex is separate from the joining. They are not at all alike."

"Well, I didn't know that, did I?"

He sat up, reached for her and was irritated anew when she pulled free of his grasp. "It does not matter if you knew or not. The deed is done."

"Well, undo it."

"I cannot," he told her calmly. "And would not, even if I could."

"I'm the Queen. I'll undo it."

He smiled. "Even the Queen cannot dissolve a joining until a child has come from it."

"Are you serious?" Maggie couldn't believe this. How could she be married? Then something else occurred to her. "What exactly is a Fae marriage? Are we bound together now? Inseparable or something?"

"No." He shook his head. "We are connected deeply, but it is a joining much like a human marriage, though for the Fae, a marriage happens only when a child is desired."

"I don't desire one." Not right now, anyway, she told herself.

"But I do."

"This is ridiculous," she muttered, scrambling off the bed, stumbling as her foot caught in one of the draping quilts. She grabbed it up, wrapped it around her naked body and clutched it as a warrior would a shield. "I am *not* married and I am *not* getting pregnant."

He smiled. "Your passion burns so brightly, you will keep me warm for centuries," he mused. "And you will fight with me, I know. But you are married and you should have a child."

She couldn't believe this. She was *married*?

It couldn't possibly count, could it? Not if you didn't

know you were being married. Not if you weren't *asked*. There'd been no ceremony. No party. No *cake*. Just a sneaky Fae Warrior slipping something past her. Bastard. He'd used Faery sex and his big . . . *self*, to knock her off kilter a little. He'd made her crazy with want and need and then married her when she wasn't looking! Talk about a sneaky bastard.

"You're nuts, Culhane," she accused, stabbing one finger at him. He slapped negligently at the blue flame that struck his chest. "And just wait a damn minute here. I thought the male Fae didn't have any rights in Otherworld. How do you get to marry me without even telling me?"

He sighed and leaned both forearms on his upraised knees. "The Warrior clan has rights other males do not. We have the right to marry whomever we choose in order to create children who will one day take their place in the Conclave."

"And the woman has no say in it at all?" She backed up a step or two.

"None." He shrugged wide, muscular shoulders. "But they have never complained. All female Fae wish to be with a warrior. We are strong, powerful . . ."

"Humble?"

"What is humble?"

"Big surprise," Maggie muttered, then spoke up louder. "So these women are just married to some guy for freaking *ever*, with no say in it at all?"

"It is not forever, Maggie." He chuckled, letting one long leg slide out in front of him lazily. "The marriage remains until the child has come of age—for a warrior, that is around one hundred years old—then the bond is dissolved and we are free to move on."

Maggie felt like thunking the heel of her hand against her head. He didn't even realize what he was saying, did he? *Joining* had so little meaning in Otherworld. What about white weddings? Pretty dresses? Being together through thick and thin?

Cake?

"You move on?"

"To be with others, if we so choose." He smiled at her. "We cannot marry forever, Maggie. We are immortal."

She took a step toward the bed, half tempted to hit him with something, but she didn't trust herself that close to him. The sexual energy he put out was damn near overwhelming. She couldn't risk being pulled back in, so she stopped dead.

"That's not marriage, you jerk! Marriage is forever. Till you're old and gray and fat and then you die!"

He laughed again and damn it, the sound was sexy as hell. "We are Fae. We do not get old and fat. Though I would no doubt look good with gray hair. Shall I use a glamour to show you?"

"No." Maggie spun away from him, stumbled with her quilt toga wrapped around her and walked to the windows overlooking the palace gardens. She couldn't believe this was happening.

Then she thought about her sister and realized that Nora was probably married, too, and she was willing to bet that Quinn had never told her, either. Small consolation that *both* Donovan women had been had.

Another thought popped into her brain and Maggie really wished she'd stop thinking already. Her head was killing her and nothing was getting better. She looked over her shoulder at the smug male still ensconced in her bed. "So, how many marriages have dissolved for you?"

He frowned. "One."

Even though she'd been half expecting it, she felt her stomach sink. "You've been married. And you didn't think you should tell me about that?"

"It is over," he said, shrugging again. She could really come to hate that movement.

Might be over for him, but for her it was brand-new. "What was her name?"

"Who?"

"Your *wife*," she said tightly, clinging desperately to the last-remaining threads of her temper.

"Ah." Culhane thought about that for a moment. "Leah? Lynnia?"

"You don't *remember*?" Maggie reached up, grabbed a handful of her own hair and yanked at it. Much more time around him and she would be bald. She just knew it. "How do you forget your wife's name?"

The scowl on his face deepened. Clearly, he didn't appreciate being questioned. Well, too damn bad, she thought.

"It was long ago. The marriage was dissolved several hundred years ago. I have not seen her since."

"And your child?"

"A boy." He smiled proudly. "He is in training at the Conclave."

"Do you remember *his* name?"

"Devon."

Maggie groaned. "Of *course* it is."

This little circle of doom just kept spreading. No wonder Devon had had the same attitude as Culhane. He was the man's son. And no wonder he was as devastatingly attractive as Culhane. He came by it naturally.

"You do know," she told him flatly, "that your son has been sneaking around with Eileen."

His eyebrows winged up. Nope, he hadn't known. "Sneaking?"

"As in, not allowed, but doing it anyway?"

"My son is honorable," Culhane argued. "He would not harm the girl in any way."

"He shouldn't be hanging around her at all," Maggie countered.

"He probably senses she is the one meant for him."

"She's *twelve!*" Maggie was shouting now and it wasn't making her feel any better.

"And you were eleven when I first knew," Culhane

reminded her coolly. "I did nothing to harm you then. Devon will not harm Eileen now."

"He whisked her off to a beach in Inia! All by themselves. That's just asking for trouble, Culhane," Maggie told him.

He frowned. "I will speak to him."

"Good."

He made it all sound so reasonable. That was his gift. Her curse. He spoke and the longer she listened, the more sense he seemed to make. Which made no sense at all when you stopped to think about it.

This was really all *his* fault.

Culhane.

He'd brought Bezel to train her. He'd fought at her side. He'd married her without bothering to tell her. Brought her to Otherworld. Made sure she accepted her role as Queen.

A giant freaking lightbulb went off in her mind and Maggie felt as though she had another epiphany headed her way. Slowly, she turned around to face him again.

"I see what this is, you know. I finally get it. My eyes are wide open and you are so not fooling me."

He sighed patiently as if he were a man pushed to his limits. Poor baby.

"What are you rambling about, Maggie?"

"You. Your plans. Your schemes." She moved away from the window and a bit closer to the bed.

Oh God. Maggie's heart was thumping in a wild beat and her stomach was churning. She couldn't believe this. She'd just been starting to trust him completely. Just been thinking that he was the one stable point in her brand-new world.

Now she knew she couldn't trust him at all. Now she remembered completely all of the little things. How he would meet with his warriors in the throne room. How he made decisions about going into battle without telling her about it first. How he had been maneuvering her into stepping into her destiny because *he'd* needed *her*.

"You used me to beat Mab. Used me to get to the power of the throne. Now you've *married* me, without even bothering to ask me and you want to make babies to ensure you'll always have that tidy little inroad to the throne." She threw one hand high and held on to her makeshift toga with the other. "That way, even when you 'dissolve' our marriage, you'll still have our child to tie you to the palace."

All amusement fled from his features. His face went hard and cold and his eyes were pale green fire. "This is what you think of me?"

He sprang from the bed and was at her side in an instant. His hands came down on her shoulders, his fingers digging into her skin. He forced her to look up at him, meet his eyes. When she did, Maggie had a moment's pause. She'd never seen him look so fierce. So "otherworldly," to make a pun she didn't intend.

His body bristled with pent-up fury as he stared down into her eyes. But Maggie's own anger was more than a match for him. She yanked herself free of his grip and planted both hands on his chest and shoved. He hardly moved.

"I give you the honor of joining with you and you accuse me of using you for deceitful purposes?"

"You *were* deceitful!"

He blew out a breath, waved one hand in the air and was instantly dressed in leather pants, a long-sleeved shirt and knee-high boots. His long, black hair hung free about his shoulders and his green eyes still burned with intensity.

"I am an honorable Fae. I joined with you because I want you. I . . . care for you."

She snorted an inelegant laugh. "Try not to stumble on the hard words."

"You are unreasonable."

"And you're a jerk."

"I will not stand here and be insulted like a common pixie."

"Hah!" Maggie shot back. "Don't you insult Bezel! *He* doesn't lie to me!"

"I did not *lie!*" Culhane's shout crashed through the room with the crack of thunder.

Maggie lifted her chin, glared at the lover who'd lied to her, used her and worst of all, had made her love him. "Get out, Culhane. I don't like you much right now."

"Oh, I will go, Maggie," he said quietly, and grabbed her again, pulling her tight against him. "But not before I leave you with one more thing to remember me by."

He kissed her.

Hard and long and deep. He kissed her until she forgot how to breathe and didn't care. He kissed her until every cell in her body was screaming for more.

Then he shifted.

And was gone.

Chapter Sixteen
&

"I have done nothing wrong, Father." Devon stood tall and proud before Culhane, his chin held high, his shoulders squared.

"You should not be *sneaking*," Culhane said, using Maggie's word deliberately, "into the human world. You should not be seeing the Queen's niece in secret."

He was still angry after his earlier confrontation with Maggie, and he feared his anger was finding an easy target in his son.

For just an instant, Devon frowned; then his expression once again represented a stoic warrior in training. "I do not 'sneak,' Father. I am a warrior. Son of the Chieftain. I go to the mortal world to see her because Eileen is mine."

Culhane sighed. It was as he had thought. His son was laying claim to Eileen Donovan much as Culhane had with Maggie. Though he knew his Queen and Eileen's mother would not be pleased by this news, his son was honorable and would never harm the girl. And yet, he felt he had to say, "She is but a child, Devon. Unused to our ways. Too young for the claiming."

Devon looked horrified and his stiff posture slipped a bit. "Father, I would not. I wish only to be with her. To protect her as is my right."

Culhane understood that feeling all too well. Hadn't

he himself been keeping watch over Maggie all her life? Yet, he could also understand Maggie's concerns. It was a thin line he was now forced to maneuver. Standing up, Culhane walked toward his son, laid one hand on his shoulder and asked, "How did you come to find her?"

Sheepishly, Devon admitted, "I followed you into the mortal world one day. You went to see our Queen at her home. I, too, wanted to see the future Queen. Then I saw Eileen there." He smiled and shrugged. "I knew her for mine instantly."

As had Culhane at first sight of Maggie. Some things were fated and could not be avoided. His son would one day lay claim to Eileen Donovan, he knew. But that day was far in the future.

"You took her to Inia, did you not?"

"I did," Devon admitted, lifting his chin even higher. "Only to show Eileen the beauty of Otherworld. Our Queen found us there. She was not pleased."

"I can imagine," Culhane muttered, knowing that Maggie's fury would have been a sight to see.

"You must not go to Eileen again," Culhane told him.

"Father—"

Culhane knew all the arguments he would face if he gave his son a chance to speak. So he didn't let him. "This is as your Queen and your Chieftain wish it. You will stay away from Eileen Donovan. Do you understand?"

Devon's eyes looked tortured and his mouth twisted as if he were biting back words of argument. But centuries of training in the Conclave stood him in good stead. He nodded once. "I understand, Chieftain."

Culhane sighed again. He understood why his son was furious. Being kept from the one woman destiny has chosen for you was a painful thing. But there was nothing to be done about it. Until Maggie and her family had fully accepted the Fae way of life, they would not understand Devon's need to be with Eileen.

"Good," Culhane told his son, and gave him an approving smile. "Return to your rooms and rest. I will see you at training tomorrow."

"As you wish it." Devon nodded again; then he shifted out of the room.

⌇

The next morning, Culhane swung the heavy sword in his hand like a Fae possessed. He couldn't seem to burn off the fury riding inside him no matter how long and hard he trained.

Quinn was his target, as he had been the last few hours. His fellow warrior was just as indefatigable as he, and the clash and clang of their swords coming together rang out like a cacophony of violence. The other warriors around them on the Conclave's training field gave them a wide berth, as if they were all tuned to the Chieftain's state of mind and had no wish to get too close to him at the moment.

A wise choice, Culhane thought, again swinging his sword in a wide arc toward Quinn. His arms vibrated all the way up to his shoulders with the power of that blow and even Quinn staggered backward. The warrior lifted his blade, though, and parried the next blow, dodging to one side and coming up behind Culhane.

But Culhane was too tense, too tightly strung to be slow that morning. He whipped around, sweeping the sword out and following it with a hard punch to Quinn's jaw from his left fist. Pain jolted up through his hand and it felt good. Tangible.

The twin suns shone down from a cloudless blue sky. A soft wind streamed across the battleground and from the surrounding trees came the catcalling and cheers from their always-present pixie audience.

All was as it should be. Except, Culhane thought, for the rage bubbling just beneath his skin. His mind raced as his body slipped into the training it was so familiar with. Once more, he was thinking about the row he and

Maggie had had the night before. The one where angry words had flown and he and his Queen had circled round and round and none of it had amounted to anything beyond another fruitless battle. *Why* was the woman so determined to be as un-Fae as possible?

She'd accepted her role as the destined Queen, he told himself. Uprooted her family to Otherworld. Vowed to make her stand and defend both those closest to her heart and the Fae world she hardly knew.

Yet she still managed to cling to her human values, to thoughts of happily ever after, of two people linked together through all time.

He grunted and brought the blade down again. "Through time. She has no idea of the reality of time. Let her be immortal. See the centuries fly past and then I will listen to her thoughts on the passage of time."

"Cease!" Quinn shouted, and Culhane instantly halted his charge. When two or three of the closest warriors turned to look at Quinn, surprised, he jerked his head at them. Silently telling them to walk away. Give him privacy to speak to the Chieftain who was so far out of control that morning.

Culhane didn't even notice the others. He stabbed the point of his sword into the dirt and folded both hands atop the hilt. Leaning on it, he steadied his breathing and stared off into the distance. But he wasn't seeing the trees, the cobalt sky, the pixies or the crystal spires of the city beyond. Instead, he saw, once again, the hurt and anger in Maggie's eyes as she shouted at him. As she'd thrown him out of her room. She'd dismissed *Culhane*.

By the gods, had he ever known such a humiliating moment? No. Not in an eternity of life.

The woman was tearing him in two. Driving him to a state of desperate frustration he'd never experienced before. She'd even shattered his focus. Until Maggie had entered his life, he'd been a Fae with vision. Able to look at a situation and see several different outcomes. Weigh the advantages of one strategy against another. He'd led his warriors with a steely determination and fought for his people with a near-legendary concentration.

He knew the course Otherworld should take and had set about arranging matters to suit that course. He'd found the destined Queen, shown her the world that could be hers and slowly eased her into accepting what *had* to be. Now she was on the throne and his focus was gone. She'd shattered something elemental in him and Culhane didn't have a clue as to how to restore things to their proper order.

And things were only getting worse.

"Are you ready to speak now of what's pushing at you?"

Culhane turned his gaze to Quinn, his friend, fellow warrior, his brother. Gritting his teeth, Culhane shook his head no. There were some things a male didn't speak of. Not even to another male as close as Quinn was to him.

But his old friend didn't give up easily. "What did Maggie do?"

Culhane snorted. He should have known Quinn would insist on an answer. That he wouldn't walk away from this. They'd known each other far too long. Fought side by side in too many battles.

Surrendering to the inevitable, Culhane blew out a breath. "She tossed me out of her bedroom."

Quinn's eyebrows went high on his forehead. "There's a first time for everything, they say."

"Human sayings now, Quinn?" Culhane asked bitterly. "Is that what we've come to? Our race has been here since before man crawled up out of the muck." He paused, then waved one hand out as if to encompass all of Otherworld. When he spoke again, his anger fired every word. "We were an advanced civilization when they were learning to make fire. We live as gods, never age, never die. And now, because we have a once-human queen, we are to give that up? Become human like them? Accept human rules? Their way of life? Are we to be no more now than a cheap copy of humanity?"

Quinn's eyebrows went even higher. "No one has suggested this, Culhane. We are who we are. That cannot change."

"Can't it?" Culhane swept his gaze past his friend, scanning the training grounds that had been his home for as far back as he could remember. This was what he knew. This was his life. His calling. His destiny, as ruling was Maggie's. He could not change that even had he wished to.

"Even my own son has fallen under the spell of the Donovans," he muttered, thinking back to his talk with Devon that morning. He'd told the boy to stay away from Eileen and as his Chieftain, he expected to be obeyed. And yet, if Devon were anything like his father, he would be hard-pressed to obey that order.

"Devon? With Eileen?" Quinn frowned. "She is a child."

"Aye and so is he," Culhane argued hotly. "Do you forget that?"

"No," his friend said, still frowning, "but she is new to our ways and she is my daughter now, Culhane. I will protect her."

This infuriated him beyond all measure.

"I tire of hearing my son insulted. You think you must stand guard over your daughter because *my* son would bring her to harm?"

Quinn's scowl deepened. "No, but—"

Culhane waved a hand in disgust, silencing his warrior before he could anger him further. "This is more of the human way of thinking, Quinn. It poisons us just as slowly and surely as an iron knife wound would."

Quinn grumbled something unrepeatable and Culhane almost smiled. At least his friend still cursed in the old tongue.

"This problem with you and Maggie?" he asked. "It is more than your usual fight, then?"

Culhane pulled his sword free of the earth, swung it high and tipped his head back to study the brilliant sunlight glinting off the edge of the blade. "Aye. It is." Disgusted, he slid a sideways glance at his friend. "I told her we were married."

"Good."

"Not so very good, my friend," Culhane said on a sigh. "Our Queen was not pleased. In truth, she was furious and used the fact of our joining as a needle to poke and jab at me. Told me she didn't trust me."

Quinn huffed out a breath. "She is female. They think with their hearts, not their minds. That is why they will not make good warriors."

"Maybe," he allowed, not sure of anything anymore.

"It's trollshit and you know it, Culhane."

Though he appreciated the support, Culhane wasn't certain Quinn was right. Some of what Maggie had said still resonated all too clearly within him. He *had* used her to defeat Mab. *Had* planned to rule through her as soon as she was Queen. *Had* counted on her need of him to give him the leverage he required to set Otherworld on a course of equality for his fellow males.

So how could he be insulted when she threw those very accusations at his head? He wondered if what he was feeling was shame. He'd never known that emotion before, so how was he to tell? Did he regret what he had done, or was it only her discovery of his true intentions that was bothering him?

Now that she had discovered these truths, where did that leave him and Maggie?

She still needed him, but would she be less willing to accept his aid now? More cautious of coming to him with problems and questions?

He was worried he might have destroyed the very thing he'd sought to build.

Had he ruined whatever chance he and Maggie might have had together?

"You did what was right for Otherworld," Quinn intoned darkly.

Lowering the blade again, Culhane looked at his oldest friend. "Aye. I did. But now I find that Otherworld doesn't matter to me as much as one redheaded former human does."

Quinn sighed and nodded with great solemnity. "I understand completely."

"There's something else you should know."

Quinn waited for him to continue.

"I told her about Leah." His former wife's name had come back to him late the night before. He refused to feel badly about forgetting it, either. Leah had not been his love. She'd been tall and strong and the perfect mother for his son. That was all. And during the time they had been joined, she'd made his life a constant misery with her eternal complaints and demands. The moment their union had dissolved, Culhane had felt as though he'd been pardoned from his own personal Casia.

"That was so long ago, what could it matter?" Quinn countered, and Culhane took consolation in the fact that his friend knew his human lover no better than he himself did.

"I told her about Devon as well." He frowned to himself. "That is how I found out about him and Eileen."

"She should know about your son. He will be a fine warrior one day. And I am ... proud he has seen how pure of heart Eileen is."

Culhane smiled to hear his friend try to recover from his first reaction to the thought of Devon seeing Eileen. "Yes. He is a fine warrior." He didn't see Devon much. It was the way of the Warrior clan. Those in training lived separate lives, away from their older brothers and fathers, so that they might learn and grow in seclusion.

Training the younger fighters was all-important to the continued safety of Otherworld.

"Maggie will 'get over it,' as the humans say," Quinn said cautiously.

"I wonder," Culhane murmured, then looked at his friend again. "Maggie also knows that you and Nora are married as well."

Quinn laughed until his shoulders shook and the booming sound of his laughter rose up and seemed to echo off the high walls surrounding the training field. When he finally stopped to breathe, he shook his head and said, "That is no matter. Nora will be pleased to hear of it."

Culhane wasn't convinced of that. Privately, he thought that his friend was going to discover that he knew his human woman as little as it seemed Culhane knew his.

*

"Married?" Nora looked at Maggie, then laughed. "No, I'm not."

"Uh-huh."

It had been a long morning already and Maggie had been in no shape to face it.

Her eyes felt gritty from lack of sleep. She'd been up all night, staring out the windows at the world that she'd chosen to call home. She'd even briefly considered changing her mind. Running back to the world she knew, the house she loved, the life she understood.

But that hadn't lasted long.

Maggie figured any woman in her position would have thrown herself a little pity party. And she had thoroughly enjoyed hers. All that had been missing were the party hats. She had a good cry, kicked a few pieces of furniture, then planned sweet, savory revenge on Culhane, even though she knew she wouldn't go through with it.

What would have been the point? The big jerk didn't even think he'd done anything wrong. Nothing wrong. Marry her. Use her to rule Otherworld. Make a baby, then dissolve their marriage and eventually forget her name as he had his first wife's—all while still holding a key to the throne through their child.

And he was already a father and hadn't bothered to tell her that, either.

It was about then that she decided she wasn't giving up. Wasn't running away. She'd made her call. Moved her family and accepted her life in Otherworld. So now all she had to do was forget Culhane before he had the chance to forget her.

Shouldn't be too tough, she had assured herself. All it would take was a few hundred years. Surely by then, she'd stop remembering how he made her body burn. How he laughed in the night. How he looked at her and made her feel invincible. How he . . . Damn it.

"Maggie," Nora said with sympathy, "you're just tired."

"Oh, I really am." She'd come downstairs that morning to discover that there were literally *hordes* of Fae waiting for an audience with the Queen. And though she'd really wanted Culhane at her side to help explain everything, she'd ended up muddling through on her own.

She'd solved disputes, heard complaints and granted favors. When the crowd had finally dispersed, she'd met with Ailish of the female guard and assured her that she hadn't forgotten her promise to have them join the warriors.

And that had all been before lunch.

This queen business was a lot more involved than she'd counted on.

When starvation had finally sent her in search of food, she'd found Nora sitting alone in the dining hall.

It was an actual hall, too, not a room. The table alone

could have easily sat fifty people. The place was cavernous, though it was a lot less stark than it had been the
day before. The table was now light oak. The sideboard
running along one wall was made of the same wood and
the matching chairs were covered in bright swatches of
silk in all the colors of Maggie's painting palette. The
ceiling, at least two stories overhead, was painted much
like Sanctuary's ceilings, with an elaborate mural of
Otherworld and life in the palace.

Maggie told herself that now that she was getting better at flying, as soon as she had an extra minute—if
ever—she was going to fly on up there and examine the
painting more carefully.

But for now . . .

"Trust me on this, Nora," she said, draining the last of
the coffee in her cup and wishing for more, "you're as
married as I am."

Nora chuckled. "Quinn and I have actually talked
about this and he said something about this but I didn't
pay any attention. Maggie, I would know if I was married or not."

"Yeah," she mused, "you'd think so, wouldn't you?"

Nora smiled at the Fae server who brought two silver
urns to the table—one with coffee, one with a Fae
version of tea. And when he was gone again, Nora
poured herself a cup of that tea, leaned back in her chair
and gave Maggie a superior, I'm-the-older-sister-who-is-
much-smarter-than-you smile. "Honey, did you and Culhane have another fight?"

"Oh, you could say that." Maggie poured more coffee
and nibbled on something that tasted a lot like Bezel's
famous Tarkian pot roast. "If you consider the Second
World War a scuffle. Or I know, maybe the Revolution-
ary War was a spat. Yeah, that's about right."

"So, what did he do this time?" Nora asked, still smiling that older-sister-superiority smile.

"Oh, where do I start?" Maggie asked, sipping at her

coffee. "How about with ... you know the Fae boy who sneaked off with Eileen?"

"Yes ..."

"Culhane's son." Maggie nodded as Nora's jaw dropped.

"He has a son?"

"Oh yeah. Along with an ex-wife whose name escapes him at the moment."

"That bastard," Nora said, in complete supportive mode now. "And he just dropped this on you all at once?"

"He really did." Maggie nodded and drank more coffee. "Then he said we should make a baby."

"A *baby*?"

"Uh-huh," Maggie took yet another gulp of coffee and with a grateful sigh let the heat slide through her system. "Said as long as we're married, we might as well have a child to you know, secure my spot on the throne." She paused and gave Nora a wry smile. "It was all *very* romantic."

"Unbelievable!" Outraged, Nora demanded, "He wants to have a baby with you so he can keep one hand on the throne?"

"Just how I put it, thank you. And yes."

"And just when did this marriage take place?" Nora was hot now and getting hotter by the second. "Did you ask him that? Because I don't remember a church or a priest or buying a new dress and eating cake!"

"This is why we're sisters! That's exactly how I felt!" Maggie slapped one hand on the table and her coffee cup jumped in its saucer. "He didn't even *ask* me, Nora. Just said the magic words and made me a wife. Just boom. Like he was ordering Thai takeout. I'm telling you, I was so mad I could hardly see straight. He didn't get it, of course. Idiot. What kind of person just *marries* somebody without even mentioning it? That's what totally pisses me off. Well, that and all the 'Gee-

I-forgot-I-used-to-be-married-and-did-I-mention-I-have-a-son?'"

"And completely understandable," Nora said.

"No proposal. No ceremony. No priest, or white—er, beige—dress, no *cake*. I'm still pissed."

"Who could blame you?" Nora commiserated.

"So let me ask you something now."

"What?"

Maggie watched her sister and asked, "In all your time together, has Quinn ever said something like, 'With this mating I claim you'?"

Nora actually blushed, squirmed uncomfortably in her chair and answered, "A little personal, don't you think?"

"Please. So, has he?"

Nora smiled a little. "If you must know, yes. But how did you know?"

"Mazel tov," Maggie said, lifting her coffee cup in a toast. "You're as married as I am."

As Nora spewed her sip of tea and sputtered a list of curses that were both inventive and colorful, Maggie sat back in her chair and smiled to herself.

Turned out, misery really *does* love company.

❦

Mab felt the rush of new power filling her as she walked into the main room of the tavern and sent her gaze searching over the faces of those clustered there. She'd killed another rogue Fae just outside and the raw flood of Fae energy sizzled inside her. Heat from the fire and the closely packed bodies of the ostracized Fae made the temperature nearly unbearable.

But she forbore.

All was coming together now.

Soon, she would be back in her rightful place as Queen and the mortal world would be crushed beneath the invading hooves of the rogue Fae. There would never be another human trying to take from Mab what was hers alone.

She spotted Corran standing to one side of the multitude. A part of the crowd and yet separate. Even the other rogue Fae chose to distance themselves from him. And who could blame them?

The dark emptiness of his eyes worried even Mab, but she was willing to strike a deal with the darkest of her brethren.

She moved through the crowd, silently pleased as those in her way melted back, making way for her. As it should be. Even most of those she'd sentenced to this dismal prison still held enough innate fear of her to leave her alone.

The others? Those who sneered at her, or worse, cursed her to her face and threatened revenge at some future date? They would be dealt with when she was once again on the throne. She would burn this world of ice and everyone in it. She would turn it into ash and laugh at the spectacle.

Corran's gaze locked on her as she neared him and even from a distance, Mab felt a chill snake along her spine. But she refused to allow him to see her reaction to him. Instead, she straightened her shoulders, lifted her chin and gave him the small, regal smile she'd perfected centuries ago.

When no more than a foot or two of space separated them, he inclined his head ever so slightly. A smirk curved his delectable mouth. "My Queen."

Mab stifled the spurt of insult she felt at his words. He was taunting her, she knew. He had no real regard for her. But he was willing, as was she, to use whatever weapon lay at hand to help him take what it was he wanted.

All around them, raucous voices rose into a wild chorus of untamed gratification. Liquor flowed like water, clashing music tried to drown out the crowd and the harsh light threw nightmarish shadows on the walls. It was a hideous place and Mab resented every moment she was trapped there. But at least she knew she could speak in this crowd without being overheard.

She moved in next to Corran until they were standing side by side. Cold seeped from his body into hers and Mab fought the resulting tremors that rattled through her.

"I have news," she said, smiling through the cold and the misery. At least something was working well. Her spies had kept her informed of everything that was happening in the great city. At *her* palace.

"I am listening." He tipped his head and looked down at her. Those black eyes watched. Waited.

"The human queen," she said with a sneer, "has taken up residence in the castle."

He snorted and dismissed her plan without even hearing the entirety of it. "The magical wards around the palace will keep us out."

"But only the palace itself is warded, my friend." Mab smiled and the eager glint in her eyes must have caught his attention. He looked directly at her as she added, "There is a child. . . ."

&

Eileen told herself she wasn't breaking any rules.

After all, the palace *gardens* were still pretty much the palace, right? Sighing, she walked along a silver-bricked path that wound through acres of flowers and bushes and small fruit-bearing trees.

She looked around. No one was there, so she reached out, pulled what looked like a tiny, yellow apple from the closest tree and looked at it. Not so long ago, she'd looked up *Faery* on the computer and she remembered telling her aunt Maggie that if she went to Otherworld, she shouldn't eat anything. Because if she did, she would be trapped there for like a hundred years or something.

Of course, Bezel said that was a big lie, just like mostly everything else the human world thought they knew about the Fae. But still …

"Guess it doesn't matter if I eat it now, anyway," she told herself. "Since we live in Otherworld, it doesn't matter if I'm trapped or not."

She took a big bite and the flavor of the fruit exploded in her mouth. A mix of apple and pear and weirdly, almost a banana taste, the fruit was soft and juicy and totally good. Grinning to herself, she kept walking, munching on the fruit as she went.

Eileen thought she could get used to being here all the time. The palace was great and Quinn had used magic to make her room exactly the way she wanted it to be. Which was completely awesome. And there were so many Fae wandering around asking her all the time if she wanted anything or needed anything, she could get totally spoiled. Except that Mom and Aunt Maggie would probably still make her do things like make her bed and go to school—

She stopped. "Do they even *have* schools in Otherworld?"

Was it weird that she hoped so? She'd always liked school. She and her best friend, Amber, always had a great time in English class because the teacher was completely clueless and didn't pay any attention to what they were really reading, so Amber and Eileen read whatever they wanted to and—

"No more Amber," she whispered, looking around again at the lush garden, the twin suns shining overhead and the incredible crystal palace behind her. "Who am I supposed to talk to?"

A twist of sadness wrung at her insides and she felt … alone. Bezel was off visiting his friends, so she didn't even have him to hang out with. She hadn't had time to meet any Fae her age yet and the only one she *did* know, nobody would let her see.

"Which is completely unfair," she muttered, and wandered over to a bench tucked behind a low hedge bursting with violet flowers. There was a fountain with a waterfall flowing into a huge tub that had red fish swimming in it.

She wished she could see Devon. He never treated her like a kid. He would understand how mad she was at being told that she couldn't explore the new world her mom and Aunt Maggie had dropped her into. "But no, can't have Eileen making friends. Talking to boys. Don't want her to be normal or anything."

Disgusted, she walked on, nearing the edge of the palace gardens. Beyond them, the Fae city stretched out in front of her, crystal towers sparkling in the sunlight. Ancient trees with windows cut into their trunks stood like soldiers, lining the streets. And she knew that way beyond the city, there was an ocean kind of like the one at home. She wondered if there was a lighthouse. Or a pier. She wondered what people did here for fun. And wondered when she'd get to have some.

"Eileen!"

Her head whipped around at the sound of that hushed, but familiar voice. A smile broke out on her face as she scanned the surrounding flowers and bushes; then she laughed in delight when Devon stepped out from behind a tree and waved to her.

"How did you get in here?" she asked, already hurrying toward him. She hadn't seen him since the day he'd shifted into Bezel's tree house to surprise her.

He shrugged as if it had been no big deal, and Eileen's heart did a funny little spin and drop. He always made her feel strange. Her tummy would jump like there were thousands of butterflies inside and her throat got all tight like if she tried to talk, she'd sound like a frog or something.

But she was so glad to see him, she didn't even mind the weird factor.

When she was close enough, he spoke again. "It was not difficult. Only the palace itself is warded. The gardens are for all Fae. Well, not the rogues. They can't get in at all."

Eileen laughed again and it felt so good. Suddenly she wasn't alone. She did have *one* friend in this strange new world and she wasn't going to let her mom or Aunt Maggie stop her from talking to him.

"So cool. At least we know you're not a rogue."

He frowned briefly, then shrugged again. "I am a warrior. We are not rogue. We serve the Queen."

"I know," she said. "I was just kidding."

Devon smiled and Eileen's heart did that funny, squeezy thing again. "You make me smile. It's good that you've come to live here now, Eileen. That your aunt has accepted being our Queen."

"Yeah, I think so too. . . ."

"But you are not happy," he said, bending his head a bit to look into her eyes. "Tell me why this is."

"It's just, I don't know anyone and I don't really have any friends here yet. . . ."

"You have me," he said quietly. "I will protect you. Let no harm come to you."

"That's so sweet." Eileen sighed a little dreamily. He was *way* cuter than Jensen Ackles.

Devon straightened to his full height and squared his shoulders proudly. "My father says it is the privilege of all warriors to defend the Queen and her family."

"Your dad? Is he a warrior, too?"

"Yes. He is Chieftain. Culhane."

Surprised and excited, Eileen grinned. "Seriously? Culhane's your dad? I know him really well."

"I know," he said softly.

"You're lucky, you know," she said as they started walking along the silver path toward the city that lay in front of them. "I never see my dad."

She didn't really think of him much anymore, either.

She used to, back when she was a little kid. Eileen used to dream that he'd come and move back in with her and her mom and they'd be happy. But then as she got older, she remembered that they'd never really been a happy family to begin with. Her dad had always been mad about something and her mom had cried a lot back when they were together. So slowly, she'd just accepted things the way they were and really, she didn't miss having a dad so much most of the time.

Especially lately, since Bezel and Culhane were always around. And Quinn was really nice, too, and he was sort of like a dad since he was married to her mom and stuff—even though her mom didn't think so . . . but she didn't want to be sad right now, anyway. Or even to think complicated things. She just wanted to walk with Devon and have him tell her all about Otherworld.

Devon took her hand in his and Eileen's heart started beating so hard, she was sort of afraid he might hear it. But his hand was big and warm and it felt . . . special to be with him. Where no one could see them. Where no one could make her feel like a little girl.

"My father," he was saying, "is not around much, either. I live with the training warriors, so I do not get to see him very often. He is very important to our people."

"What about your mom?" she asked.

"She does not see me anymore," he said with another shrug, as if it didn't matter to him at all, but Eileen could tell it did.

"Bummer."

He looked at her and smiled a question. "What does that mean?"

"It means, that's too bad."

"Ah." He nodded and smiled again. "Yes. It is. But I am happy. You are here in Otherworld now and that makes me glad."

Oh my God. If only she could tell Amber about this!

"Me, too," Eileen said, then asked, "So, where are we going?"

"My father says I am to stay away from you. That the Queen would not be pleased to have me here."

Frowning, Eileen threw a glance over her shoulder to the palace, glittering in the light of twin suns. "They don't have to know."

"We will 'sneak'?"

"Sure."

He smiled. "Shall I take you to the city?"

She wanted to really bad, but ... Eileen turned and looked back at the castle. If anyone in there found out she'd sneaked out with Devon again, they'd lock her up until she was dead. But if she went back right now, she'd still be in trouble for leaving, she told herself. So, as long as she was already in trouble, she might as well really enjoy herself, right?

"Okay," she said, and was rewarded with another of his great smiles.

"There is much I want to show you," he said, walking faster now, as if eager to get where they were going.

Eileen laughed out loud because it just felt so good to be there. With him.

Then everything changed.

A creature, dressed all in black, with long, snaking arms and dark gray skin, shifted into place directly in front of them. One moment he wasn't there. The next, he was.

Devon jumped in front of Eileen to protect her, but the *thing* picked up the young warrior and threw him as if he weighed nothing at all. Devon's body slammed into the trunk of a tree and then dropped to the forest floor without a sound.

Terrified, Eileen tried to run.

Tried to scream.

But in the blink of an eye, the thing grabbed her, covering her mouth with a scaly hand. Eileen looked up at the castle and realized that no one there would even know she was missing.

Then the creature holding her shifted and they were gone.

Chapter Seventeen

&

"*D*on't tell me to be *calm!*" Nora shrieked when Quinn patted her shoulder. "That *bitch* has my baby!"

Maggie totally understood. Quinn was trying to be supportive, but it was wasted. Nora wasn't the fainting or swooning type. She wasn't going to melt into his big chest and cry oceans of tears. If she wasn't stopped, she was going to storm out of the palace, hunt Mab down personally and tear her—and anyone else standing between Nora and her daughter—limb from limb.

Still, at least Nora was now focused on killing Mab instead of Quinn, for marrying her without bothering to mention it.

The palace guards had already disbursed the crowd of Fae who'd lined up for an audience with the Queen, and Maggie was grateful. She couldn't think about anything but Eileen right now.

Where was she?

Was she hurt? Scared? Of course she was scared. God, looking at Devon's face was enough to make Maggie want to shriek right alongside Nora. Half of the young warrior's face was bruised and swollen and his eyes were filled with fear.

Culhane's son had shifted to the Warriors' Conclave as soon as he'd regained consciousness. Terrified, he'd reported to his father, who had then gathered his five top warriors and come to the palace to break the news to Maggie and Nora.

Mab had somehow known just how to get to Eileen. How? Did she have help here inside the palace? Was someone spying on them and reporting to the former queen? How else could she have guessed that Eileen might be off wandering in the gardens? How else would the Bog Sprites have known about the Warriors' alcove?

And why in the *hell* hadn't she had Claire ward the damn gardens as well as the palace? Idiot. Stupid. But no, she'd gone along with Fae tradition of the palace grounds being open to all Fae. She should have bucked all of them and done whatever she had to, to protect her family.

Now Eileen was paying for her mistakes.

And that just didn't fly with Maggie.

She glanced at Culhane's son, standing off to one side of the small crowd clustered together in the throne room. He looked just what he was. A scared kid. No matter that he was four hundred years old. Culhane and Bezel had been right about that. He was young and scared and despite his fear and his own injuries, like the purplish bump on his forehead, he'd gone for help immediately, so she loved him for that.

Nora was practically vibrating with rage and an eagerness to get moving. Quinn looked murderous. Muldoon, O'Hara and Riley had the cold, set features of men ready for battle. And McCulloch was standing beside Claire, aligning himself with her, whether she wanted his protection or not. Ailish and Audra, of the palace guard, were in the mix, too, and the warriors didn't look happy about it, but tough shit, Maggie thought firmly. She'd use whomever and whatever she had to get Eileen back. Bezel stomped his big feet in a circle around them all, muttering curses under his breath and Culhane . . .

Maggie slid a sideways glance at him. Her own personal hero/nemesis stood shoulder to shoulder with her, listening as suggestions, ideas and plans were tossed out and then dismissed. She was glad he was there. Yes, she was still royally pissed off at him, but she wasn't stupid.

She needed help. And she knew that if nothing else, she could count on Culhane to provide that help. Just having him there made her feel stronger. But for her own peace of mind, she'd keep him close while maintaining a safe personal distance between them. She needed him too much and didn't quite trust herself to keep from falling into his arms if he made even the slightest move in her direction.

According to him, they were married. According to her, he was a lover she couldn't completely trust. And that left them exactly nowhere.

"We go to Casia," Muldoon snapped.

"Foolhardy to crash in without knowing where the girl is," O'Hara pointed out.

"We could get into Casia," Ailish suggested with a glance at her commander. "Let them think we are unhappy with the new Queen. . . ."

"Risky," Audra said.

"Especially if Mab sees you herself. She knows her guard well and won't believe you," Mac told her.

"We must act," Riley said. "Let it be known this will not be tolerated."

"And we will," Quinn shouted. "But my daughter's safety comes first."

"If *somebody* doesn't find my baby fast, I'll do it myself," Nora threatened, and no one doubted her for an instant.

"The problem is"—Maggie tried for calm, despite the images of Eileen's face that kept rising in her mind—"we don't have a clue where to start looking."

"We might."

Everyone turned as one to look down at Bezel. The pixie was furious. His long, silvery hair was practically writhing with the anger churning inside that squat little body. His eyes were chunks of ice and his mouth was fixed in a sneer. Though he had the attention of everyone in the room, he looked only at Maggie.

"You're not gonna like it."

"You found something," Maggie whispered.

Bezel nodded.

"Who *cares* if she likes it," Nora told him. "Just say it."

He nodded briskly. "I think your grandFae might know something about this."

"You think or you know?"

Bezel scowled. "Pretty damn sure."

Jasic.

Maggie's insides frosted over and turned into a hard ball of ice. She should have thought of him right away. If she hadn't been so completely freaked over Eileen's disappearance, she would have. Ever since the day Jasic hadn't been able to shift into her backyard, she'd been seriously worried about her grandFae. Claire's spell had been very specific. Designed to keep out those who meant the Donovans harm.

It had been right there in front of her and she hadn't done anything about it beyond asking Culhane and Bezel to look into him. And with everything that had been going on, she and her warrior had pretty much forgotten all about Jasic in the bustle.

Good thing Bezel hadn't.

Stupid. No excuse for this, she told herself. She should have paid closer attention. Hounded Bezel and Culhane for more information. If she had, Eileen would be safe right now.

So where was Jasic? He should have heard Nora's screams. Should have come to investigate. Instead, he'd made himself scarce.

Coincidence? She didn't think so.

Maggie looked at Culhane. "Find him."

～

It didn't take long.

An hour later, Jasic was perched uneasily on the edge of a chair in the throne room, with a crowd of furious warriors surrounding him. He looked worried, which only made the knots in Maggie's stomach even tighter.

Sunlight speared through every window. One of those slices of golden light lay across Jasic and for the first time since she'd met him, Maggie thought he looked old.

"We found him in an alehouse," Muldoon said with a disgusted glance at Jasic.

"Did you do this?" Nora spoke softly, and anyone who didn't know her would assume she was calm and in control. Only Maggie recognized the danger in her tone when Nora approached the grandfather they'd recently found. "Did you steal my daughter?"

"No!"

He looked horrified by the very idea and if he wasn't telling the truth, Maggie could only think, *And the Oscar goes to . . .*

Nora wasn't convinced. She grabbed hold of Jasic's lapels and gave them a hard jerk as she pushed her face into his. "Do you know where she is, then? Who did you talk to about her? Who took her? Is she all right?"

"I don't know," he muttered, unwilling to meet her gaze, but having nowhere safe to look instead. The features of each person surrounding him were studies in barely controlled rage. He had to know he was way outnumbered.

"Talk, Fae," Culhane ordered, carefully prying Nora's hands off Jasic and turning her over into Quinn's care. "Talk now and hope for the sake of your immortal life that you have something useful to say."

Unfortunately for him, Jasic fought past his fear and tried for bluster. Insulted, he sniffed, and asked, "Why do you all assume I am somehow at fault?"

"Because I saw you, you slug-eating piece of trollshit," Bezel told him, scurrying up to Jasic as fast as his short legs would take him. He stabbed at the Fae with one long finger and said, "You think I've been doing nothing since we got back to Otherworld? I was watching you. The others, they were willing to give you a chance. And Culhane's been busy. But me? I got time. I never did trust you, and turns out I was right. I *saw* you, meeting with a Pooka outside the tavern last night."

"Pooka?" Ailish turned a questioning glance at Culhane. "They should not be able to leave Casia."

"I know," he said.

Maggie frowned. She'd been studying the Fae lately, so she knew the Pooka were shape-shifting creatures, able to change their appearance from that of old men to flying horses with cloven, razor-sharp hooves, somewhat like the Dullahan. If the Pooka were roaming free of Casia, then their troubles had just multiplied.

Culhane looked down at Bezel. "You should have come to me with this immediately."

Bezel snorted and shook his head. "*Ifreann* take me, I haven't trusted this son of a troll since he showed up. Maggie asked me to watch him, so I did. I've been waiting to get some whatcha callit? Evidence on him. How was I s'posed to know they'd go after Eileen?"

"It wasn't your fault, little man," Claire told him in a soft voice. "I should have seen this. Tried to focus my visions more."

"Witches don't know everything," Bezel told her in commiseration.

"Neither one of you was at fault." Maggie spoke up then, her gaze fixed on her grandfather.

"Yeah well . . ." Clearly still disgusted, Bezel looked up at Culhane. "The spell around Casia's wearing off, oh

Great and Mighty Fenian Warrior. Which means we're all in deep trollshit. I'm guessing Mab's found a way to gather some power."

"Ifreann," Quinn murmured.

"Exactly," Bezel snapped, clearly enjoying himself now as he turned his icy gaze back on Jasic. "So, how about you cut the crap and tell us where Eileen is."

"Do it." Culhane spoke up then, his deep voice resonating with barely restrained venom. Laying one hand on Bezel's shoulder, he nodded at the little man and when the pixie moved aside, Culhane took his place. "You have one chance, Jasic. Speak and tell us what you know or you will be spending the rest of your eternity in one of the iron cells beneath this palace."

Maggie would have interrupted, reminding him that *she* was the Queen here, but he was doing a damn fine job of intimidation and she really didn't want to break his concentration. Besides, it didn't matter who found Eileen. All that mattered was finding her.

Jasic looked from one to the other of them, futilely searching for compassion. Understanding. *Reason.* Finally though, he gave it up and slumped his shoulders.

"I meant no harm to the child," he muttered.

Nora inhaled sharply and clutched at Quinn's big hand for support.

Jasic looked at Maggie, then to Nora. "Why would I bring harm to the child? She is of my blood. As you are."

"Don't remind me of that right now," Nora said tightly.

He winced. "I only meant to strike a deal with Mab. To use what knowledge I had about you and the palace. To *ingratiate* myself with Mab, in case Maggie didn't finish this war in victory."

"Why?" Maggie demanded as she stepped up alongside Culhane and stared down at her grandfather. "Couldn't you figure out how dangerous she is? Why would you do that?"

"To have *this*," he snapped, waving both arms out, indicating the palace and the luxurious life he'd so recently become a part of. "To have the life I have always coveted. To be safe. To know that I could stay here, whichever one of you won your coming battle."

Bezel cursed and rushed Jasic. Muldoon grabbed hold of Bezel's green velvet suit and held him in place where the pixie kicked and thrashed, trying to attack the Fae who'd endangered Eileen to save his own ass.

Maggie knew just how her little friend felt. And maybe later, she'd indulge both of their desires for some heavy-duty physical revenge. But for now, she needed Jasic to get Eileen.

She swallowed her disgust for the Fae as she looked at him through cold, hard eyes. "Do you know where they're keeping her?"

Lifting his miserable gaze to hers, he shook his head. He looked pitiful, old and alone. But damned if she could bring herself to feel sorry for him.

"No," he said. "I only know they took her to Casia."

"Oh my God—" Nora's voice broke off as she finally gave in to her fears, turned her face into Quinn's chest and allowed him to hold her.

"*Where* in Casia?" Culhane demanded.

"I told you I don't know!" Jasic shoved both hands through his hair, then folded them tightly together in his lap. "If I knew, I would tell you. I don't want Eileen hurt any more than you do. I simply don't *know*. They don't trust me enough to tell me."

"Wonder why!" Bezel shouted.

"Enough," Culhane snapped, giving the pixie a glare. He understood Bezel's outrage. It was beyond Culhane's comprehension that any male could protect himself at the cost of his family. But that Jasic would allow a child to safeguard his own future was unthinkable.

Culhane felt helpless and he didn't like it. He felt trapped and wanted to strain against the invisible bonds holding him in place. In truth, Culhane wanted to do exactly what his friend the pixie was doing. Shout and curse and vent his rage on the closest target.

But that wouldn't help Eileen. Wouldn't help Maggie. And right now, those two things were all that mattered. He glanced at his Queen and in her eyes he saw fear. Not for herself, but for the child they all loved. And he admired her more than ever. Even frightened, she was every inch a battle-ready sovereign.

Culhane hated that there was a distance between them. Especially now, when they should be holding on to each other, feeding each other's strength.

Their problems would not be solved now, however. Now was the time for action. His warriors awaited commands. His own son stood to one side, waiting for Culhane to make this right. He would let none of them down. But he also wouldn't repeat the mistake of acting without consulting his Queen.

He glanced at Maggie, and waited for her to meet his gaze before he whispered, "Do we move or do we investigate further, my Queen?"

She chewed at her bottom lip and cast one disgusted glance at her grandFae, sitting dejected in his chair. Her gaze slipped to Nora then and an aching love shone in her eyes before she looked back at Culhane. "We can't fight Mab until we know Eileen's safe."

"Agreed." On this at least, they concurred. Eileen's safety was paramount and there was no way they could attack Casia or try to put Mab's fomenting rebellion down until they were sure Eileen wouldn't be a casualty of a former queen's twisted ambitions. Mab had fallen far. There had been a time when no Fae would ever threaten a child. Now, it seemed, they couldn't trust that the former queen wouldn't do whatever was necessary to gain her revenge.

"So," Maggie asked him quietly, "what do you think?"

Honored that she would ask his opinion, trust him on this if not personally, he said, "We must know where they are keeping Eileen. I will go to Casia myself and find her."

"I will accompany you," Quinn told him.

Before Culhane could agree, Bezel spoke up. "That's just stupid and you all know it. Warriors have to be here, getting ready to face that crazy bitch queen." He looked up at Maggie, took a breath and blew it out. "I'll go."

The pixie twisted loose of Muldoon's grip, brushed at his suit and lifted his whiskered chin so that he could stare at both Maggie and Culhane. "Pixies can come and go most anywhere. The Fae—you guys or the rogues—don't pay much attention to us."

True enough, Culhane thought, remembering the centuries of enmity between the races of Pixie and Fae. He and Bezel had long ago formed an unlikely friendship, but their relationship was the exception, not the rule. Mostly, the pixies were given a wide berth. Known as pranksters and troublemakers, most of the Fae deliberately ignored the pixies' existence.

Which could work in their favor. But this plan wasn't without risk.

"If they discover why you're there . . ." Culhane's warning faded off. Since they all knew what would happen to Bezel if he was caught, there was no point in saying it aloud.

The tiny termagant would either be imprisoned or beheaded. Probably the latter.

"Yeah, yeah," Bezel said sourly. "I know. Don't get your leathers in a bunch. Nobody catches me unless I let 'em." With that, he threw an angry glare at Muldoon, the warrior who only moments ago had had a death grip on his fine suit.

Culhane smiled to himself at the courage coiled inside such an unlikely package. But then, he'd long ago learned that Bezel, with all of his complaints and insults, was a male to be trusted. And he knew Maggie had learned the same lesson.

"You have the heart of a warrior, my little friend," Culhane said softly.

Bezel snorted. "No time to be insulting me, Fenian."

Maggie went down on one knee so she could look the pixie in the eye. "You're sure about this?"

The pixie frowned again, but nodded. "I'll find her. Not that I care about the kid or anything, you understand. It's just that I'm sorta used to having her around, you know? And I'll be cursed in *Ifreann* before I let Mab get her."

Maggie smiled knowingly at Bezel. "Yeah, I know."

Culhane hid a smile. The pixie would die before he would admit to loving a part-Fae child. But he cared for Eileen as much as the rest of them. Clearly, Maggie was aware of the truth as well. But even more, Culhane knew that Bezel would do all in his considerable power to see the young girl safe again.

"Well, don't go getting all gooey on me or anything," Bezel warned gruffly, and wiped the back of his hand under his long, hooked nose. "I'll find her. Be back tomorrow at the latest. Then we can figure out what we're gonna do."

He shifted instantly and the small crowd in the palace fell into an uneasy silence.

*

Eileen curled up in a corner of the dark, dirty room and tried to make herself as small as she could. Outside these walls, she heard laughter and music and a lot of shouting. Every once in a while, a loud crash sounded out like something heavy breaking. And every time that happened, the wall behind her back trembled in response, as if the whole place were going to come falling down.

Her stomach was turning and tears kept filling up her eyes, making everything look blurry. Since she had been grabbed in the garden, she'd been in this place. Nobody had come to talk to her since the ugly kidnapper locked her in.

She was pretty happy about that. In fact, she was kind of hoping they'd all forget about her.

But the chances of that were pretty slim. "Probably only about two or three percent," she whispered to herself.

Something crashed into the locked door across the room. Eileen jumped, the wall behind her shuddered and she tucked her face into her knees and wrapped her arms around her legs.

"Mom. Aunt Maggie. Somebody come find me, please, come find me." Rocking, whispering to herself, she thought about everyone at the palace. Besides her mom and Aunt Maggie, there were Quinn and Culhane and Bezel, too. They'd all be looking for her, wouldn't they? But what if they didn't know she was gone yet? What if Devon was hurt really bad and hadn't been able to go for help? After he hit that tree, he'd been so still.

Worry had her chewing at her thumbnail and watching the locked door through slitted eyes. Devon was okay; she knew he was. He was a warrior, so he was strong and stuff. So he probably went right to Culhane and they were all looking for her now. Of course they were.

One candle burned in the room and the tiny flame danced and jigged in the darkness. Crazy shadows spun on the walls and Eileen tried really hard not to cry.

Her mom wouldn't cry. Aunt Maggie wouldn't, either. Mom always told her, *Donovans don't get scared. They get mad.*

Eileen would rather be mad than scared, anyway. Why'd that guy take her? *Where* did he take her? There was only one window in the room and it was so high up, she couldn't see anything out of it but a small piece of dark sky with stars. Why was she in this place? Why couldn't she go home?

Why didn't anybody come?

She heard a key turning in the lock and held her breath and watched as the door slowly swung open. Instantly, the noise from the other room was twice as loud. People shouting and cussing and laughing and singing. There was another crash and some strange music played loudly over everything.

Eileen jolted, squirmed farther into the corner where she was already trying to disappear; then a woman stepped into the room and closed the door behind her.

"Mab." Eileen whispered the ex-Queen's name on a pent-up breath.

"That's right, my little part-Fae." Mab strolled toward her, with tiny steps, as if she were afraid to get dirty by walking on that nasty floor. She frowned at the tiny room, shook her head and clucked her tongue. "One candle?" She huffed out a breath. "The Sluagh are not the most congenial hosts, are they?"

Eileen didn't know what the Sluagh were and really didn't want to know, either. All she wanted was to go home. "Why am I here?"

Mab tossed her golden hair back over her shoulders, went down into a crouch and gave Eileen a sunny, bright smile. Her silvery eyes were sparkling in the single light of the candle. "To help me, of course," she said.

"How can I help you?"

"Oh, don't you worry about that, little one," Mab told her, standing up again and walking to the one small window, high on the far wall. Slowly, she rose into the air, peered outside, then looked down at Eileen.

"You once did me a favor," she said. "Do you recall?"

"Yes," Eileen answered, and stiffened her shoulders. Mab looked a little scary, hovering up there in the air and looking down at her. Mab's face was white as snow and her eyes looked weird, constantly changing color, from silver to blue and back again.

Then Eileen remembered her mom and her aunt Maggie, and fought to be mad, not scared. It worked. A little. "I remember. I let you out of the painting. And you said you owed me a boon. Mom says that means favor."

"It does indeed," Mab said with a nod as she slowly lowered herself to the floor again. "Aren't you the clever little half-breed."

"So is this the favor?" Eileen asked. "Locking me up in this room? It smells bad and it's cold and dark and—"

"Hush child!" Mab frowned and tapped her chin with one finger. "Locking you away was necessary. It was not the boon I owe. But I do intend to pay. I always pay my debts."

Eileen stood and flattened herself against the wall. "So, are you gonna let me go?"

Mab laughed and the sound was so pretty, like music and sunlight, that Eileen almost forgot that Mab was the bad guy. She remembered quickly enough when Mab reached out a hand, took Eileen's chin in her fingers and studied her for a long second or two.

Finally, she said softly, "The Sluagh want you, you know. You're a tasty treat to them. One such as you they have not sampled for many centuries." Mab smiled. "You shine with innocence, child, and your human soul calls to them."

Eileen's knees started shaking and she didn't know if she could keep from crying much longer.

"But I won't let them have you." She frowned and threw a dirty look at the closed and locked door before turning her gaze back to Eileen. "You're a child and as such are under my protection. You will come to no harm here. Besides, I have other plans for you. So now I gift you with the boon I owe. You will be made fully Fae. Your soul will no longer be streaked with the taint of humanity and so you will no longer interest the Sluagh."

Mab's fingers on her chin tightened. Eileen tried to

look away from her swirly eyes, but couldn't quite manage it.

"Then child," Mab continued, "you will live an eternity as a servant in my palace. You will never know freedom again and for all of your immortal life, you will remember that it was your own blood who sentenced you to this. Your mother's sister thought to steal what was mine."

"Aunt Maggie's gonna find me," Eileen said, "and then you'll be sorry."

Mab laughed, bent low and stared into Eileen's eyes. "That will not happen. The upstart queen will soon be gone and things will return to being as they were meant."

Eileen twisted in Mab's grip, but though she looked fragile and delicate, the Fae was really strong.

"But"—Eileen swallowed hard—"you don't have any powers anymore. You can't make me Fae."

Mab smiled again and this time, the curve of her mouth looked mean. "I have acquired much of what I lost, young one. Trust me when I tell you I have all the power I will need to change you and then dispose of your . . . family."

"No!" Eileen tried to jerk free, but Mab held the girl still, pursed her lips and blew a slow, steady stream of golden Faery dust into Eileen's eyes.

Chapter Eighteen

"The good news is, the kid's fine."

"Oh, thank God." Nora shuddered and let out a long sigh of relief.

Bezel grabbed a glass of Diet Coke, courtesy of Maggie's pulling in everything from her old house. He took a drink, set the glass down and looked at each of them in turn before finally staring at Maggie.

The pixie's hair was dirty, his green velvet suit torn at the shoulder and he was sporting a heck of a black eye. But he was grinning.

"Told ya a pixie could get in anywhere."

"Yes," she said, letting him enjoy his moment of triumph. "You were right. Yay you. Now, details."

"First," Bezel said with a sneer, "where's good ol' grandFae?"

Culhane answered that. "He is in one of the cells below the palace. There he stays until this is finished."

Maggie wasn't proud of locking up her own grandfather. But the choice had been simple. Him, the male who had betrayed them all and made it possible for Eileen to be kidnapped—or *them*. It was not a hard decision.

Jasic had shrieked and pleaded like a little girl before the warriors had tossed his ass into that cell. But she'd been beyond listening to him. When this was all over, she'd have to figure out a more-permanent solution to the problem of Jasic, but there were more-important things to concentrate on at the moment.

"Good." Bezel nodded. "Okay then. Eileen's in a small room off the back of the tavern at the edge of the Dark Woods."

"The *woods*?" Nora echoed that word with horror. "My baby's in the *woods*?"

Bezel looked at her, but instead of being as snarky and snotty as he was usually, his voice sounded almost . . . kind. "She's not in the woods. She's in this room. I caught a look at her when they took food into her."

"Thank God. And they're feeding her. That's good. Is she okay? Is she hurt? Scared?" Nora stopped, then looked at Quinn. "Of course she's scared. God, she's all alone."

"We will get her back."

"She didn't look scared to me," Bezel said with a tight smile. "Kid looked pissed. Heard her yelling at the troll taking her food in and he came running out fast."

Nora grinned, despite the tears shimmering in her eyes. "That's my girl."

"Oh, there's one more thing," Bezel told them all, pausing for dramatic effect. "Not only was Eileen pissed, she was floating."

"Floating?" Maggie repeated, stunned.

"Yep." Bezel burped, pounded his chest, then said, "Looks like somebody turned our girl into a full-Fae."

"What?" Nora shouted. "Who would do that?"

"Only one person I can think of," Bezel muttered. "Looks like Mab got some of her powers back. Word on Casia is that she's killed a few of the rogue Fae and stolen their powers. Every power she steals makes her stronger. And since she was Fae to start with, those powers are growing fast."

"But why would she make Eileen Fae?" Maggie wondered aloud.

"Before we kill Mab," Quinn said tightly, "we will ask her."

"Okay." Nora was talking, but more to herself than anyone else. "Eileen's a full-Fae now. That makes her immortal. That's safer, right? Of course it is."

Quinn frowned and dropped one arm around her shoulders.

She ignored the offer of comfort and focused her gaze on Maggie. "How do we get Eileen back?"

"Won't be easy." Bezel looked at Culhane and Maggie. "Mab's been working. She's got herself a little army. A few Pooka, a couple of Dullahan and some Sluagh."

Quinn hissed.

That reaction couldn't be good, Maggie thought. "Who are they?"

"Later," Culhane told her, with a warning glance at Nora.

Okay, Maggie understood. He didn't want to explain everything with Eileen's mom sitting there, already on the edge of hysteria. But once they were alone, she was going to want to know it all, Maggie vowed silently.

"Anyway," Bezel said loudly enough to gain her attention again, "the rogue Fae Mab's got on her side are so unreliable, they're just as likely to turn on her as to follow her. I figure if the battle starts going badly for her, they'll desert her to save their own skin."

"So how do we get Eileen back?" Nora's demand had them all turning to look at Maggie.

But no pressure, she thought. They had to fight Mab, true. But they also had to get Eileen to safety first. They couldn't risk Mab using the girl to cover her own ass.

As she studied the group of people gathered around one end of the great dining table, a sort of with-any-luck-at-all-maybe-possible kind of plan began to take shape in her mind. But before she could set it in motion, she had to do one more thing.

"We're going to need everyone in this fight," she told Culhane, making sure her voice was loud enough that everyone heard.

"The warriors are ready, my Queen," he said.

"Not just the warriors." She slid a glance at Ailish and Audra. "The female guard will fight with you. Flying warriors are a very good thing."

The two guards looked electrified by the prospect, despite the groans from Quinn and McCulloch. Culhane, on the other hand, nodded. "It makes sense," he said. "They are trained fighters and we must win this battle."

Surprised, Maggie smiled at him, appreciating the fact that he hadn't given her a load of grief on this one. Of course, that thought was followed immediately by the big question of *why* was he being so nice about this? Was he trying to keep her off balance? Or was he actually being sincere? And how could she possibly know for sure either way?

"What about me?" Nora demanded. "I want to help. She's *my* daughter."

"I know, Nor," Maggie said, looking at her sister. "But you're pregnant, so you're not in this."

Her sister's eyes flashed fury at her, but Maggie wasn't impressed. She'd lived with Donovan tempers her whole life and she could give as good as she got.

"You can't stop me." Nora glared at her.

"I can't, but he can," Maggie said, with a nod at Quinn. "Make sure she's safe."

"I would have anyway, my Queen."

"You can't do this to me!"

"Nora, we're gonna get her back," Maggie told her sister, her voice hard and cold. "But we can't do it if we're worried about you."

Nora looked as if she might fight that statement, but a moment or two passed and she slumped in her chair and nodded.

"Good. Also," she said, turning her gaze to her best friend, "I need to go to Sanctuary. Claire, you come with me."

"I will go as well," Culhane told her.

"No," Maggie said quickly. "I need you here, getting the warriors and the female guard ready."

He looked as if he wanted to argue, but again he backed off and Maggie wondered anew what was going on with her Fae Warrior. Why was he being so damn accommodating? And God, she wished she could trust him completely.

"It will be done," he told her, "but McCulloch goes with you. As escort."

"Fine."

"Um," Claire spoke up, raising her hand as if she were a second grader wanting the teacher's attention. "Excuse me ... but how come you need me at Sanctuary?"

Maggie smiled. "Because, my favorite witch in the world, *you're* going to do a spell for me."

*

Culhane went with Maggie to the Queen's chamber. He wanted a word with her before they all left for their separate missions.

Maggie marched into her bedroom, took a few long steps, then stopped, turned around and faced him. "Okay, tell me what you weren't telling me downstairs. Who are the Sluagh?"

He told her and watched her face mirror the fear that was rattling through her.

"Fallen angels who drain human souls?" She moved to the bed, sat down on the edge of it and shook her head. "Good plan not telling Nora that."

"Eileen is safe from them now, if what Bezel says is true. They do not devour Fae souls." He walked toward her and took a seat beside her on the bed. Thoughtfully now, he said, "Perhaps that is why Mab changed her."

"Yeah," Maggie said snidely, "because Mab is such a giver. She's so caring and nice, of course she'd want to protect the kid she *stole*."

Culhane frowned. "All I am saying is that Mab has never allowed a child to be killed. In centuries of her rule, that is one law she never allowed broken." He looked down at Maggie. "Mab must have known that she could not control the Sluagh and after hundreds of years in Casia, the soul eaters would have been drawn to Eileen's innocence. By changing her, she protected the girl from them."

"Great," Maggie said without emotion, jumping up from the bed to pace. "We can give her a big thank-you later. You know, just before we kick her ass."

"She will be defeated, Maggie. This time permanently," he promised, swearing a silent oath that the former queen would never be allowed to bother Maggie again.

"She has to be. I have to get Eileen to safety."

"I will lead a raid into Casia," Culhane told her, standing up to walk to her side. "We will get her out before the battle."

Maggie shook her head. "No."

"You do not trust me."

"With Eileen?" she said quietly. "Of course I do. But Culhane, you'd never be able to get close enough to Mab to pull it off and you know it. Besides, I have someone else in mind. Someone unexpected."

Reaching out, Culhane grabbed Maggie, pulled her close and felt her stiffen, then slowly yield to his embrace. He didn't want this distance between them. Especially not now, when they were preparing for a battle that might be the end of them all.

Holding her tightly to him, he muttered, "Trust in me, Maggie."

"I already told you I trust you with Eileen."

"That is not what I meant and you know that, I think."

Yes, she knew it. Maggie told herself to step back and away from his embrace, but she didn't. Just for a moment or two, she wanted what he could offer. The strong safety of his arms. The solid strength of his body pressed to hers.

Outside the palace walls, night was crouched, drenched in stars, the pale moon shining down on a world where nothing made sense to her. Where the one person she wanted to trust the most was the one she absolutely couldn't afford to. Where little girls were stolen from their homes to use as bargaining chips. Where pixies showed the courage of lions. Where everything rested on *her* decisions.

God, she wanted to be able to turn to Culhane and know without a doubt that he was with her in this. She wanted the closeness that Nora and Quinn shared. The absolute knowledge that the man she loved would never betray her.

"I order you to trust me," he muttered in a thick, emotion-clogged voice.

She laughed shortly, as his words came so swiftly after her own jumbled thoughts and the sound was muffled against his chest. "You can't demand trust, Culhane."

"It would be much easier if I could," he said.

Well, he was a male used to issuing commands and seeing them followed. She supposed she couldn't blame him for that. Maggie sighed, pulled her head back and looked up at him. His features were tight and grim and he seemed almost uncomfortable. Not a look she'd ever seen before on the mighty Culhane.

Frowning, she asked, "Why don't you just tell me why I *should* trust you."

He let her go then and she missed the feel of his arms around her. But she watched him as Culhane took two or three long steps away from her, scrubbed one hand across the back of his neck, then turned and came right back. His jaw worked as if he were silently saying words and then biting them back before they could slip out. But finally, he simply blurted, "Because I *love* you."

Okay, that she hadn't expected.

She blinked up at him and oh God, Maggie really wanted to believe him. She yearned with everything in her to take those words and hold them close. But how could she? He'd lied to her. Used her. How could she be sure he now wasn't simply using as leverage those three words she so longed to hear?

Heck, her own *grandfather* had sold her out!

"You do not believe me."

Amazing that he could look both hurt and insulted all at once. Even more amazing, Maggie felt badly for putting those emotions on his face. But then she reminded herself of everything he'd done and said over the last few weeks. Suspicion and doubt clamored together inside her and she couldn't shake the feelings. Didn't know if she should try. If she believed, if she let herself have faith in him and then she found out none of it had been real, it would kill her.

"I really want to, Culhane. But how can I?" she asked, her voice little more than a whisper.

"Because I say it!" Culhane glared at her, clearly affronted, with banked rage practically shimmering around him in the air. "I have never before given those words to any female. I have never *felt* those words before you."

"Culhane—"

He grabbed her upper arms and held her tight. "Do you think it is easy for a warrior to humble himself before his woman? My kind do not speak of love so easily, Maggie. To humans, it is merely a word. Used casually and without thought. To the Fae, it is a treasure. To know *real* love is something rare. Eternity is ours, Maggie, and I will give you mine willingly. All I ask is your faith."

Maggie looked up into those pale green eyes of his and actually felt him trying to convince her. To know, instinctively, that he meant everything he was telling her. And she so wanted to. Wanted to reach out and grab what he was offering her. It was only her stupid, stubborn suspicions that held her in check.

"I can't do it, Culhane," she finally said before her emotions could win out over logic. "I can't let myself believe you. Not now, anyway. Not yet."

Abruptly, he let her go and obviously disgusted, took a step back from her. His features clouded up, his eyes went dark and smoky and his delectable mouth twisted into a sneer. "Must I *die* for you then, to prove my loyalty?"

Now he was just being mean. And male. She hadn't given him what he wanted. She hadn't curled up into a soft, purring kitten and thanked him properly for the gift of himself that he was making. Maggie's temper spiked just as high as his must be. If he loved her, really loved her, surely he could see that *now* wasn't the best time for all of this?

Looking at him, the proud, arrogant warrior, Maggie gave in to her own anger to protect her heart and snapped, "That would be a start."

"So be it." Culhane's eyes went cold and dark; then he shifted and she was alone.

❦

There was one thing Maggie was sure of: She needed to make her next move fast. They were going to need all the help they could get to save Eileen and get rid of Mab for good.

So no more wishy-washy stuff. No more wondering if she was doing the right thing or how the Fae might react to her decisions. They didn't like it? Too damn bad. They could move on to a different dimension.

Because Maggie was about to shake up Otherworld like it had never been shaken before.

"This," Claire said in a shocked gasp, "is completely

amazing. I had no idea. I know you said that it was big, but this isn't big. This is . . . *big*."

Maggie had known Claire would be impressed with Sanctuary. Looking at the place now, through her best friend's stunned eyes, Maggie saw it all again as if for the first time. The white marble walls and floors with streaks of silver snaking through the stone, lending warmth to what should have been cold. Miles of bookshelves, stuffed with hundreds of thousands of books. Elegant tables boasting tall crystal vases filled with flowers no human had ever seen before. Wide windows, all of them open, allowing warm, sweet-scented breezes to waft through Sanctuary. A place out of time and space. A place where all Fae were welcome and safe. Since power was stripped from everyone the moment they entered and not returned until they left the same way they arrived, all in this place were equal.

Well, except for Finn, the scholar/wizard who ran the place.

Claire wandered the marble halls, her head turning from side to side as she tried to take it all in. In fact, she looked pretty much like Eileen had, on her first morning in the palace.

And that one small thought of her young niece brought a chill to Maggie's spine and reinforced her determination to do what she'd come here to do.

"This is incredible," Claire murmured in a soft hush most people reserved for libraries and hospitals.

Maggie smiled in spite of the turmoil still roiling around inside her. Spending time with Claire was way better than being on her own at the moment. And being here, in Sanctuary, meant to Maggie that she was at the very least going to be doing something proactive.

"I do not understand why all powers are stripped when we enter," McCulloch grumbled in a voice just loud enough for Finn to overhear.

Maggie threw a glance at the long shelves lining the

wall and looked briefly at the whirling tornado of gold dust spinning weirdly behind a crystal screen. Her power. Strange, but for so long, she'd felt odd, carrying around that whirlwind of strength and energy. Now, she realized, she felt somehow . . . wrong without it.

Beside her own power, a smaller cyclone of Fae power spun. McCulloch's. Mac had accompanied Maggie and Claire to Sanctuary since a warrior guard was necessary at all times. Culhane was making himself scarce, mobilizing the warriors. Quinn was busy trying to hold Nora together, so it was left to Mac to be their escort.

"It is the only way *all* are safe in Sanctuary," Finn told him patiently, as if he'd had to explain that very rule over and over again to whichever warrior happened to be there.

Maggie got it, though. It was why she'd chosen this place for her last fight with Mab. She'd known that the far more powerful Queen would lose her Fae powers the moment she entered Sanctuary. It was the only place Maggie had felt as though she'd had even half a chance at beating Mab.

It had worked, of course. Maggie had won, Mab had gone out a window and they all should be living happily ever after. But, real-life Faery tales had nothing in common with the myths she'd grown up listening to.

Instead, the proverbial shit Maggie found herself in now was every bit as deep as it had been back then. Maybe even deeper, since now she didn't even have the illusion of Culhane to comfort her.

Whatever. No time to worry about her love life or lack of same. Now was the time to pull it together and get Eileen back safely.

"We need your help," Maggie said to Finn as the tall, blond Fae stared down at her. "We're looking for a spell."

He frowned and ignored the others, focusing solely on Maggie. "What kind of spell?"

Mac spoke up quickly before Maggie could. "The gift of flight for the males, Finn. We need to find the spell Mab used to strip us of the gift so that Claire can reverse it."

Finn actually looked shocked.

Maggie nearly laughed. She hadn't thought surprising the wizard was even possible. But then, the males of Otherworld hadn't exactly been treated well over the last couple of millennia.

"Is this true?" Finn asked.

"Yes." Maggie looked him square in the eye. "We need to do this and we don't have a lot of time. So can you help us or not?"

"I can." He didn't ask any further questions, just turned on his heel and hurried off down the long, wide hallway, clearly expecting them to follow. Which they did.

Their footsteps echoed off the high ceilings and smooth walls and sounded like the rapid clatter of heartbeats. Which, Maggie thought, made sense, since her own heart was pounding hard in tandem with her steps. They had to hurry. They had to find the spell. Make it work. Then find Eileen and deal with Mab.

After that, she told herself, we'll relax and take the rest of the day off.

~

Culhane rallied the Warriors.

The males he'd led for more than two hundred years sprang into action at his command, and he could only wish that his Queen had done the same. She was as stubborn as she was beautiful. As prideful as she was strong. And he loved her for it, despite the fact that she made him want to rage in frustration.

Still. His fury at Maggie notwithstanding, he had no intention of dying to prove his loyalty to her. He would help her win this battle. Save her family. Save Otherworld from a mad queen; then he would kidnap Maggie, take her to Inia and keep her naked and filled with him until she saw the truth. Until she accepted that he, Culhane, had been born to love her. Until she admitted that she loved him as he did her.

Then they would return to the palace and she would be the greatest Fae Queen of all time. And he would proudly serve at her side.

Grimly, Culhane smiled and started issuing the orders that would prepare his warriors for the coming battle.

 ✦

The spell was finally located in one of the oldest tomes in Sanctuary. The book was leather bound and encased with gold. The language was indecipherable until Finn waved his hands across the thick, creamy pages and the letters rearranged themselves into English.

"Impressive," Claire murmured, then quickly read the list of supplies. What wasn't on hand, Maggie had sent Finn to find and in less than an hour, they'd been ready.

"You can do this, right?"

"Oh, and now's a fine time to ask, thanks," Claire told Maggie wryly.

"Uh-huh, you can, right?"

"Aye, I can." Claire smiled, shrugged and said, "Just another reason it pays to have a witch around."

Maggie grinned. "Just what I've always thought."

"What do we do?" Mac asked, watching Claire as if he were both eager for her to begin and worried for her safety.

Claire looked at him. "Stand back and hold your breath."

He did.

She laughed. "I didn't mean that *literally*, you big goof."

Mac blew out his breath and sent a disgusted look toward Maggie as her laughter joined Claire's.

Finn ignored them all and looked at the witch. "Is there anything else you need?"

"No. Just a little space." Claire centered herself, closed her eyes and began to chant beneath her breath in Latin. The ancient language sounded melodious, rising and falling with a steady precision, almost like music.

Maggie watched her best friend and though she knew she didn't have to, she found herself holding her breath just as Mac had. Seconds ticked past and the silence in the room was broken only by Claire's soft chant. Over and over and over again, the Latin words rushed from her friend's mouth in a steady stream that seemed to fill the room with power.

Lights sparkled around Claire's still form. She knelt on the marble floor in a circle of herbs and crystals and she seemed to glow from within as power coiled and built deep within her.

Later, Maggie wasn't sure just how much time passed while Claire's invocation continued unceasingly. All she knew for sure was that finally, Claire's head fell back, the crystals surrounding her lit up like tiny neon lights and Claire's long black hair twisted in a wind that touched no one else in the room.

Tension mounted.

Mac shifted from foot to foot.

Finn never took his eyes off Claire.

Maggie held on to her hat, so to speak, and waited for whatever was coming next. And still she was surprised.

Claire lifted both hands toward the ceiling, opened her eyes and shouted, *"Incipio!"*

A thunderclap of sound rattled through Sanctuary and every hair on the back of Maggie's neck stood straight up. She flinched at the deafening noise and had to shake her head when Claire spoke to her. "What?"

"Sorry about the noise," her friend said, standing and stepping carefully out of the circle. She looked from Maggie to the males watching her. "The spell's done."

"What was that you shouted at the end?" Maggie asked.

Claire shrugged. "Latin for 'commence' or 'begin' or . . . basically, I was saying, 'Get this show on the road already.'"

"Ah." Maggie looked at the guys, too. "So, did it work?"

Mac tried to fly, then apparently remembered that he had no power in Sanctuary. Glancing at Finn, he said, "You'll have to test it."

Finn nodded, closed his eyes for focus and then slowly levitated. A few feet off the floor, he seemed to realize what was happening and he opened his eyes and grinned; then he flew to the ceiling, touched the murals painted there and zoomed back down to the floor.

Still smiling like crazy, he gave Claire a half bow. "My thanks, daughter of the MacDonald. And to you, my Queen, for rectifying a wrong done to the males of Otherworld far too long ago."

"You're welcome," Maggie said, and Claire smiled.

"I was glad to help," Claire added.

"And so you have!" Mac grabbed Claire, pulled her in for a hard, quick kiss, then gave her a brilliant smile. "Thanks to you, lass, the Warriors won't *need* the female guard. And it's long past time for Fae females to—how do the humans say it?—*Take a backseat for a change*?"

Claire went absolutely rigid with anger. Her features went cold and tight and her eyes were blazing with fury. "You . . . Neanderthal!"

"Aw, crap," Maggie muttered.

Mac and Finn gave each other confused stares before Mac finally looked at Claire again. "I don't understand. Why're you angry?"

Claire kicked him. Hard. "You don't see, do you? You unbelievably stupid male! I was trying to undo an injustice!"

"As you have!" Mac shouted.

"Uh . . . ," Maggie tried to interrupt, but they ignored her.

"No, you big idiot. I haven't. All I've done is make it possible for you to get revenge on women who had nothing to do with taking away your powers in the first place!" She fumed silently for a moment, clearly trying to gather her patience, and just as clearly, she failed. "I feel as though I've undermined my own gender!"

"Claire," Maggie said quietly just as her friend turned on her.

"Get me out of here, Maggie. I want to be back at the palace."

"Done," Finn said, and an instant later, Claire was gone.

Which left Maggie alone with two males who didn't have a clue why Claire had been so angry. She was happy to explain.

She looked from Mac to Finn and back again, because she knew she had to make this point firmly to the warriors, most of all.

"I'm gonna say this just once and you make sure you tell all the boys back at the Conclave *exactly* what I tell you."

Mac nodded.

"All of this infighting with the men and women, it's over."

"But—" Mac tried to interrupt.

"No." Maggie shut him up by holding her hand up for silence. Sometimes it really was good to be Queen. "It's done. The Warriors and the female guard will fight together, or I promise you, I will disband the Warriors and start over with the females."

He looked horrified at the prospect.

Good.

"It's time for you guys to get over yourselves," Maggie told him, walking closely enough that Mac was forced to look directly into her eyes and read her determination for himself. "You're not the only game in town. The women are capable of fighting, too, remember. But if we all fight *together*, we're stronger than we are separately. So bag the attitude and tell the other guys, it's fight together or don't fight at all. Understand?"

He gritted his teeth; then he nodded.

Maggie gave him a fierce smile. "Good. Now let's get this party started."

Chapter Nineteen

ɛ

*B*y the next afternoon, the warriors were all flying and training with the female guards. Maggie was itching to go free Eileen herself. Immediately. But the two she'd sent to do the rescue were already moving on Casia. And once Eileen was safe, the battle with Mab would get started.

While Maggie watched her warriors at the training field, she tried to keep from looking at Culhane.

But how could she?

He was the fiercest, the strongest, the most amazing man she'd ever known and she loved him desperately.

He must have felt her gaze on him, because he turned in midair to look at her. From a distance, his expression was unreadable, but she felt the power of his stare right down to her bones.

So, she thought, still angry.

Well, couldn't really blame him. But in spite of his fury, he was uniting two fighting forces into a team that Maggie sincerely hoped was unbeatable.

Now all she needed was for the rest of her plan to work.

ɛ

Eileen held on to the wall to keep from floating to the ceiling. She'd been telling Aunt Maggie for weeks that she wanted to be all Fae, but she hadn't really understood before how hard having powers was going to be. It took a lot of concentration just to stand still.

Of course, it was hard to concentrate when you were so scared, your throat kept closing up. She'd been in that tiny room for like *forever*. Why hadn't they found her yet? Why weren't they coming for her?

Maybe they were looking and just *couldn't* find her.

"Oh, wow . . ." Her stomach twisted into tiny little knots and she swallowed back the urge to cry. She hadn't cried since that first night. She'd been tough and strong, and now she'd had enough and she really wanted to go home.

Floating again.

This time, though, Eileen didn't fight it. She allowed herself to rise slowly to the window so she could look outside at least. It was really dark out there. And with the woods so close and the trees so tall, she almost couldn't see the stars.

"Where are you guys?" she whispered.

An explosion of sound rocked the tavern and the night sky lit up like a million lamps were all turned on at once. Eileen squeezed her eyes shut and covered her ears. On the other side of the locked door, she heard people shouting, screaming, and then more explosions happened and the walls of her room shuddered and shook like they were about to fall down.

What if the building was on fire? What if no one let her out? What if—

The door to her room swung open and slammed into the wall behind it with a crack of noise that was covered up beneath all of the booming outside. Eileen spun around in midair, terrified of who might be coming. But an instant later, she shouted, "Bezel!"

The pixie hurried into the room, and Devon was right behind him, a huge grin on his face. She'd never been so happy to see anybody before in her whole life.

"Get down here, kid," Bezel ordered. "We gotta get outta here."

"I can't," Eileen said, floating helplessly and so happy she could hardly see straight. They'd found her. They'd come for her.

Bezel shot a look at the boy. "Well, go on. Get her down!"

Devon flew to her and Eileen shrieked, "You can fly!"

"I can and I can show you how, too!"

"Not *now*!" Bezel commanded as the young warrior dragged Eileen to the floor. Once she was on her own two feet again, she dropped to her knees and threw her arms around the pixie.

"You came. You came for me. Thank you, Bezel."

"Course we came," he muttered gruffly, giving her an awkward pat on the back. "And we got about a hundred pixies running around in the forest like trolls with the trots."

"Really?" Okay, Eileen thought, she just might cry again.

Bezel gave her one last pat and let her go. "Yep, my cousins are blowing things up and making things crazy so we can get you out. Which is why you should shut up now and keep low. Maggie sent us to get you while she and the others fight Mab."

"They're fighting now?"

"About to and you gotta be safe before it starts." He led the way, one small pixie in a torn, dirty, green velvet suit.

And none of Eileen's imaginary heroes had ever looked as brave.

e

The battle was horrific.

Maggie had thought she was prepared, but there was no way she could have been. The Warriors and the female guard were working together, which was good. They were flying in and out of the tumult, raining destruction down on the rogue Fae who'd chosen to bet their lives and freedom on Mab's promises.

Many of their enemies had broken ranks and run at the first sight of flying warriors. Their terror and sense of self-preservation had won out over their greed, which cut down on the numbers substantially.

But there were still the Dullahan, terrifying creatures, to deal with, not to mention the shape-shifting Pooka and the Sluagh, those gorgeous soul-eaters riding the shifters into battle. And there was Mab.

The sounds of war were overwhelming. She had a whole new respect for the military in her home world. They faced the threat of such battles every day. And voluntarily put themselves in harm's way all the time.

And the shouting—the shrieks of fear and the screams of pain—was terrifying. The scent of blood and sweat hung heavy in the air and Maggie fought to breathe it all in, anyway. She swung her iron sword like an avenging angel, cleaving her way through the Fae that stood between her and the former queen at the center of the melee.

Again and again, Maggie's iron sword clashed with the sterling-silver blades of the rogues and she saw them react in panic to the dull gleam of her own weapon. They knew it was iron. Knew they could be poisoned, taking centuries to recover, and so they ducked when they should have fought and she was making actual headway.

She was grateful. Through the din of battle, a wild, stray thought scuttled through her mind. She was an artist, not a warrior queen. She hadn't been built for this. Her arms ached, her shoulders screamed in quiet agony and her heart thundered in her chest like a runaway horse. She was so far out of her element, it wasn't funny. How in the heck had destiny ever decided to choose *her* for this gig?

Fear and fury clogged her throat. There was no time to think. No time to worry. She had to trust that Bezel and Devon had succeeded in getting Eileen away safely. She had to trust that her Warriors and guard would stand together, forgetting their former enmity as they faced a common foe.

And she had to trust Culhane.

Strange, but all of her worries now meant nothing. When it really mattered, when everything was on the line and she was fighting for her life—of *course* she trusted Culhane.

He was near her throughout the battle and she was aware of him on a soul-deep level that didn't even require *seeing* him. She felt him. Felt their connection and it steadied her even in the middle of this horror.

Maggie ducked, parried a blow and came back up screaming at the Sluagh attacking her. She swung her sword blade to slice into her enemy and was both sickened and gratified at the sensation.

"Maggie!" Culhane shouted her name.

She whirled around and watched him fly at her, skimming over her head to impale an attacker she hadn't noticed; then Culhane landed in front of her, planting his own body between hers and danger, and Maggie knew without a doubt just how important he was to her.

When this was over, when they were back safely in the palace, she was going to tell him that she loved him and that she *did* trust him. Did believe he loved her. And then she was going to hold on to him and not let go for at least a hundred years.

"How touching!" Mab's voice carried over the clashing battle raging around them and Maggie turned to face her.

Cold raced through her veins as she looked at the female who had brought them all to this because of her own thirst for power. Fury pumped anew as Maggie remembered that this bitch had changed Eileen into a full-

Fae, taking all choice from her. And rage settled into a seething brew in the pit of her stomach with the recollection of all the pain Mab had caused.

Was causing.

"Flying warriors," Mab said over the tumult. "A nice trick."

"I don't need tricks, bitch," Maggie told her, and enjoyed the flare of insult in Mab's eyes.

"Just your own private bodyguard?" Mab's gaze slid to Culhane. "I told you once he couldn't be trusted."

Yes, she had. And Mab's words had fed Maggie's own doubts and fears until she'd turned from Culhane when every instinct she possessed had screamed at her to cling to him. Maggie smiled. She'd trusted Culhane all along, really. It was only her own fears that made her doubt him. Her hesitation at accepting her new life. Her worry over the destiny that had claimed her. When she doubted herself, she doubted what she felt and she felt the most, for him.

God, she was an idiot.

Looking at Mab, Maggie said, "Let it go, Mab. You can't come between Culhane and me. You've already lost and I think you know it."

Astonished, the other woman said, "You believe in Culhane? You are a fool."

"Nope. I'm the Queen. You're the fool."

Mab screeched, throwing her head back to howl at the sky in frustration. Maggie could almost sympathize.

"I don't need Culhane to take you, either," Maggie said, and really hoped that was true.

"Prove it." Mab swung her sword and the blood-drenched weapon hummed as it whipped through the air.

Maggie lifted her own blade, countered Mab's thrust and swung one of her own.

Vaguely, she was aware that Culhane had stepped to one side, allowing her to fight her own battles despite the fact that he no doubt wanted to jump in and take care of it for her. And Maggie felt a swell of courage rise in her, born of his belief in her abilities.

Again and again, her blade crashed against Mab's. The power of those blows sang up Maggie's arms and into her shoulders. Their swords collided over and over as the battle around them was slowly won by Maggie's forces.

The two women were oblivious to anything but their own private war, though. The rest of Otherworld could have slipped into another dimension entirely and they wouldn't have noticed. All that existed was the two of them. This fight. This clash of two wills.

The sounds of the battle died away. Maggie thought of nothing but Mab. All she could focus on was the feeling that this was it. The moment of truth. The powers, the strength, inside her were fierce, but would it be enough to defeat the bitch Queen of this dimension? Was she fast enough, strong enough to end this here and now? And did she really have it in her to cut off the woman's *head*?

Mab charged, forcing Maggie back, step by step, parry by parry. She couldn't look away from Mab. Couldn't see where she was walking, because to take her eyes off her opponent would mean her own death.

So she didn't see the fallen Fae behind her. Didn't know that she would fall, until she hit the ground with a thump hard enough to knock the breath from her lungs. Didn't know this was the end until she looked up into Mab's fierce face and saw triumph written in her silvery stare.

Then Maggie closed her eyes. She really hadn't expected to lose. And in an instant, images of her life flashed in front of her in a sorry sort of slide show that had a well of self-pity rising up inside her. It was over and no way did she want to actually *watch* Mab's sword come slicing down into her own chest.

She braced herself and waited for the pain.

Instead, a heavy weight dropped across her. A moment later, she heard Mab scream.

And then there was silence.

Maggie opened her eyes again, saw Culhane's body draped over hers and saw Mab's sword, jutting up from his back.

"Oh God!" Panic erupted as Maggie screamed and shoved at Culhane's body to get him off her. He'd saved her by sacrificing himself? What the hell had he been thinking? Why would he do that?

Love, her brain whispered.

He did it for *love*.

Then she heard his voice in her mind. *Must I die for you then, to prove my loyalty?* She cringed and felt tears well in her eyes as she remembered her response as well. . . . *That would be a good start.*

"No, it wouldn't! Damn you, Culhane, no!" Maggie scrambled out from under him, rolled him onto his side and looked around wildly for help. Any kind of help. What she saw was Mab's lifeless body—missing its head—lying nearby, with Quinn standing beside it and warriors and guards racing toward her.

And she didn't care.

All she cared about at that moment was that her warrior was lying so still, his glorious eyes closed, a damn sword sticking out of his back. She yanked it free, tossed it to one side, rolled him over and stared down into his face.

Around her, she was just barely conscious of a crowd gathering. She couldn't look at any of them. The guards or the warriors. She couldn't tear her gaze away from Culhane. She was too focused on keeping him alive and well. Yes, they were immortal, she thought wildly, but that didn't mean they couldn't be incapacitated, wounded so mortally it might take generations to recover.

"Don't you check out on me, you bastard," she

shouted, grabbing hold of his shirt and shaking him with what was left of her strength. "Open your eyes, Culhane! Open them. You're not dead; you're immortal! Damn it, somebody make him open his eyes!"

"Maggie . . . ," Quinn's voice, as if from far away. Sad. Quiet.

She didn't want sad. She wanted pissed. Or helpful. Screw sad.

"Damn you, Culhane," she shouted again, on her knees now, pushing her face into his. "Wake up!" She slapped him. Once. Twice. Then she caught his face between her palms and kissed him hard and long and deep.

Now she knew. She knew just how much he meant to her. He loved her? She believed him. He wanted to make babies? She was ready.

When the kiss ended, she lowered her voice and hissed into his ear, "I do believe, Culhane. I believe in Faeries. I believe in everything you've ever told me. I believe in destiny and you're *mine*. I believe you love me. I believe we're freaking married. And I *believe* that if you die, I will kill you myself."

He opened his eyes then, looked up at her and smiled. "You really are crazy, aren't you?"

Relief poured through her, quickly followed by a flood of gratitude. Maggie laughed like a loon. "I must be, because I'm married to an arrogant know-it-all and I'm going to have babies who will have a pixie godfather and learn how to fly and—"

Culhane grinned, reared up and kissed her until Maggie was gasping for air.

"Are you really all right?" she asked.

"I will be." He winced a little. "The blade was not iron, so I will heal quickly."

"Then why the hell were you playing dead?"

"The sound of my love's gentle voice was soothing me to sleep." He gave her a wry smile.

"Very funny. I should be so pissed," Maggie said, then smiled through her tears. "But honestly, I'm too glad you're alive."

"For which I am grateful, my Queen," he said, then pushed himself unsteadily to his feet, wincing with pain, but clearly willing to withstand it. When she reached out to help him, he shook his head.

Then he turned, scanning the faces of the males and females surrounding them. Battle-weary, bloodstained and filthy, they all smiled back at him. Quinn nodded, plucked Culhane's sword from the ground and handed it to him.

Holding the tip of the blade high, Culhane glanced at their victorious troops, then shifted his gaze to Maggie. Smiling, he shouted, "Together we have accomplished what we could not have done separately. We have won the day. We have found new unity."

Cheers broke out, a shouting chorus of triumph.

But Culhane wasn't finished. Grinning widely, he called out, "To our Queen!"

And as one, the Fae Warriors, male and female, echoed his shout, slammed the tips of their swords into the bloody earth and went down on one knee in front of Maggie.

Epilogue

A week later, Maggie slipped into the palace living room and hoped her escape from the dining hall had gone unnoticed. Fighting Mab was one thing. Listening to Nora's never-ending wedding plans was something else.

Her sister was bound and determined to have a "real" wedding. And since her pregnancy was so far along that Nora was spewing Fae dust regularly, like Old Faithful erupting, the wedding would be there, at the castle. If they all survived Nora's incessant strategic meetings.

"Peace," Maggie whispered, and walked across the room filled with cozy furniture, burning pine-scented candles and a roaring fire in the hearth. She glanced at the giant Christmas tree in the corner, blazing with real Faery lights, and the dozens of gaily wrapped packages lying beneath it.

Their first Christmas in the palace and so far it looked like a winner. In fact, she thought they just might start a new tradition for the Fae. She'd already heard that indoor trees were becoming quite the rage in the city.

And all over Otherworld, the males were beginning to come into their own. Sure there were a few problems, but mostly, things were looking good. Although Bezel was insisting that pixie rights should be the very next thing Maggie looked into.

She'd put it on her list. But all in all, life was good.

Mab was defeated and she wasn't coming back. Jasic was still spending quality time in his cell ... until he earned his way back into the family, though Maggie was thinking she might spring him for a few hours on Christmas Day. Bezel had made up with Fontana and was now boasting a cherry red velvet suit. Devon was spending as much time at the palace as he was at warrior training and Eileen hardly floated at all anymore.

Claire and Mac were still at each other's throats, which explained why Claire had gone back to the human world for a vacation before Christmas. And as for Maggie and Culhane ...

She grinned to herself, reached out and jingled a bell ornament just to hear the chime. Real wedding or not, warriors really did make the best husbands. Of course, Maggie had already told him he could forget all about the dissolving-the-marriage thing. He was in this for eternity, so he might as well get used to it.

She was happy. Really happy for the first time in her whole life. She could hardly wait for her birthday, the day after Christmas. Culhane was taking her to Inia and had promised to keep her naked and—

"There is trouble," Quinn announced as he and Culhane stalked into the living room.

"Oh, for Pete's sake," Maggie complained, knowing that she'd jinxed herself again. "I was relaxed for what? Like ten seconds?"

Culhane came to her, wrapped his arms around her and kissed the side of her neck. "It is nothing, Maggie. Nora has turned our fearless friend into a quivering pixie. Quinn is an old woman."

At that insult, the other warrior blew up like a puffer fish. "This is not about Nora." He glanced around the room. "She is not here, is she?"

"No," Maggie told him, smiling. The big brave warrior had drawn his personal line at choosing flowers for Nora's bouquet.

"Ah." He sighed, then scowled, remembering his mission. "Maggie, the warriors are threatening to riot because the female guards are insisting on moving into the Conclave."

"Seriously? That's the big problem? Dorm troubles? Hello? You guys do magic, remember? Add another building for them," Maggie said, and smiled, tipping her head to one side so Culhane could kiss the spot he'd missed.

He grinned and complied.

"That's not all," Quinn said, clearly disgusted with both of them. "There is talk that one of the sacred relics of Fae has been discovered in Ireland. If this is true, the rogue Fae will be after it."

"Oh, for—" Maggie broke off and glared at Quinn. "Can I have one damn weekend? Can I just enjoy Christmas and my birthday? Eat too many cookies? Have some Chardonnay? Lots and lots of Chardonnay? Open presents? Can I just relax for a few days? Is that really too much to ask?"

Culhane grinned wider. "It is not, my Queen. Why don't I see if I can help you with your relaxation?"

"Oooh," Maggie said with a sigh, turning her back on Quinn to look up into the pale green eyes she loved so much. "Now that sounds like a good idea."

"There is trouble!" McCulloch shifted into the palace living room, eyes fierce.

"What?" Maggie and Culhane shouted the word together.

"I went to the human world to see Claire," Mac said, gaze fixed on his Chieftain and his Queen. "I wished to bring the witch back to Otherworld. But her house had been ransacked. Claire is gone."

About the Author

Maureen Child is the award-winning author of more than one hundred romance novels and often says she has the best job in the world. A six-time RITA nominee, Maureen lives with her family in Southern California.

ALSO AVAILABLE
from
Maureen Child

Bedeviled

Maggie Donovan isn't interested in overthrowing a Faerie queen. She barely had time to kill the demon that devoured her fiancé. Then she comes home to find a scrumptious hunk in her living room who informs her that saving the Otherworld just happens to be her destiny, and Maggie realizes she may not have a choice...

"[Maureen Child] will leave readers begging for more."
—*New York Times* bestselling author
Katie MacAlister

Available wherever books are sold or at
penguin.com

ALSO AVAILABLE
from
Maureen Child

More than Fiends

Cassidy Burke finds it hard to believe that she's next in a long line of demon dusters—Burke women paired with centuries-old cleaning solution to shine windows and spot demons. But Cassie's surprised by her sudden fighting instincts and fierce new strength—both of which she's going to need. For one thing, her teenage daughter thinks her dad is dead, but in truth he just never knew about her—and now he's moved back to town. And after many dateless years, men are finally lining up on Cassie's doorstep.
Sadly, most of them aren't human.

A Fiend in Need

It's only been a month since Cassie Burke unexpectedly became the hottest demon killer in town—and already there's a price on her head. Then a sizzling hunk of a faery shows up on her porch in need of protection. Cassie's happy to help because, after all, he is an expert love slave. Plus, he gets along great with her teenage daughter—a heroic feat in itself. After a few not-quite-chaste nights, Cassie knows why Queen Vanessa wants him back so badly—and why she's planning an all-out attack on her. Suddenly Cassie's wondering if she can fend off an entire city of demons—and if a little faery tail is even worth it...